She studied him ▮▮▮▮▮▮▮▮▮▮▮▮▮▮▮▮ "You sound like a gamb▮▮▮

"Oh, yes. Are y▮▮▮

"Only for high ▮▮▮▮▮▮▮▮▮▮▮▮▮▮ curving against her cre▮▮▮▮▮▮▮▮▮▮▮▮ ▮ess is worth the trouble."

"Or gives the same kick." He smiled slowly. "Would you like to step out onto the balcony with me? It's a little crowded in here."

Particularly for what he had in mind . . .

Erin eyed him in pure admiration. "Oh, you've got talent."

He grinned. "Well, yes. But that doesn't mean I'm not sincere."

A blond brow rose. "Are you trying to get me into bed, Champion?"

"Yes." Testing, he ran his fingertips over the curve of her bare shoulder. "How am I doing?"

Berkley Sensation books by Angela Knight

JANE'S WARLORD
MASTER OF THE NIGHT

MASTER
of the
NIGHT

ANGELA KNIGHT

B

BERKLEY SENSATION, NEW YORK

THE BERKLEY PUBLISHING GROUP
Published by the Penguin Group
Penguin Group (USA) Inc.
375 Hudson Street, New York, New York 10014, USA
Penguin Group (Canada), 10 Alcorn Avenue, Toronto, Ontario M4V 3B2, Canada
(a division of Pearson Penguin Canada Inc.)
Penguin Books Ltd., 80 Strand, London WC2R 0RL, England
Penguin Group Ireland, 25 St. Stephen's Green, Dublin 2, Ireland (a division of Penguin Books Ltd.)
Penguin Group (Australia), 250 Camberwell Road, Camberwell, Victoria 3124, Australia
(a division of Pearson Australia Group Pty. Ltd.)
Penguin Books India Pvt. Ltd., 11 Community Centre, Panchsheel Park, New Delhi—110 017, India
Penguin Group (NZ), Cnr. Airborne and Rosedale Roads, Albany, Auckland 1310, New Zealand
(a division of Pearson New Zealand Ltd.)
Penguin Books (South Africa) (Pty.) Ltd., 24 Sturdee Avenue, Rosebank, Johannesburg 2196, South
Africa

Penguin Books Ltd., Registered Offices: 80 Strand, London WC2R 0RL, England

This is a work of fiction. Names, characters, places, and incidents either are the product of the author's imagination or are used fictitiously, and any resemblance to actual persons, living or dead, business establishments, events, or locales is entirely coincidental.

MASTER OF THE NIGHT

A Berkley Sensation Book / published by arrangement with the author

PRINTING HISTORY
Berkley Sensation edition / October 2004

Copyright © 2004 by Angela Knight.
Cover art by Franco Accornero.
Cover design by George Long.
Interior text design by Julie Rogers.

ISBN: 0-425-19880-4

BERKLEY® SENSATION
Berkley Sensation Books are published by The Berkley Publishing Group,
a division of Penguin Group (USA) Inc.,
375 Hudson Street, New York, New York 10014.
BERKLEY SENSATION and the "B" design
are trademarks belonging to Penguin Group (USA) Inc.

PRINTED IN THE UNITED STATES OF AMERICA

10 9 8 7 6 5 4 3 2 1

THE TRUTH
IN THE LEGEND

Once upon a time, there was a boy named Arthur who drew a sword from a stone and became High King of Britain. Advised by the wizard Merlin, he formed a Round Table of heroic knights—Lancelot, Galahad, and all the others—whom he sent on a quest for the Holy Grail. The king and his gallant knights were beset, as heroes always are, by beautiful and treacherous women: Arthur's faithless wife, Guinevere, and the witches Morgana and Nimue.

You'll have heard the tale. How could you not? The bards have sung of it for sixteen hundred years.

But Arthur and Merlin and all the others are more than bards' songs. They are real, though little of the legend bears any resemblance to truth. And they live still, in a form your poets and historians could never have imagined.

For Merlin was no simple sorcerer. In truth, he was not hu-

man. He was not even of Earth. He and his love Nimue were beings of the Mageverse, the universe that is twin to ours, except that there, magic is as much a law of nature as gravity.

Merlin's starfaring people, the Fae, had seen how often intelligent races destroy themselves in infancy. Far too many, the Fae found, become extinct in the wars they fight or the ecological disasters they bring down on themselves.

The Fae loved life, and such extinctions struck them as a great waste. Yet they were wise, and they knew aid with a heavy hand could be as destructive as doing nothing at all.

Instead they thought to create guardians among each young race they encountered, champions who could guide and nurture their people into maturity. The Fae decided to give these guardians the ability to use the magic of the Mageverse and the knowledge to do so wisely. So they sent out teams of Teachers to find new races and create the champions who would protect them.

Thus Merlin and Nimue came to Earth, where they discovered two native peoples: The humans of Realspace Earth and the fairy Sidhe, an advanced race who occupied the Earth of the Mageverse. Merlin and Nimue decided the Sidhe were in need of no magical assistance, but humanity was more vulnerable.

So it was that the two set about testing men and women from every land. The bravest, most intelligent, and most skilled were allowed to drink from Merlin's Grail. Among them were Arthur and his knights, as well as Guinevere and her ladies, but there were many others, too.

The grail's magic changed the genetic structure of all who drank from it, granting immortality and power. The males who took that fateful sip became Magi, or vampires, while the females became Majae, or witches. The vampires could use the energy of the Mageverse only within their own bodies in feats of great strength or shapeshifting. The witches, however, could use that power in feats of magic.

In time, Merlin and Nimue left Earth for the next world in

need of their guidance. But that was not the end of Merlin's Gift.

For the children of the Magekind are born mortal, but with the potential to become vampires and witches themselves. These Latents transform only if one of the Magekind makes love to them in adulthood. Repeated exposure to the Maja or Magus's passion triggers Merlin's Gift within them, making them powerful and immortal. Then it becomes their duty to join the Great Mission, guiding and protecting humanity.

But always from behind a cloak of secrecy.

For Magekind well knows if humanity ever discovers their existence, fear and politics may motivate mortals to war against them, thus triggering the very catastrophe they were created to prevent. To avoid that danger, the Magekind live on Mageverse Earth in the mystical city of Avalon, forever hidden and unknown to those they protect.

Yet because it is sometimes necessary to work more openly with mortal governments, each nation is assigned a vampire Champion. It's the Champions' task to work in secret with certain trustworthy mortal leaders, while keeping their allies in ignorance of the Magekind. 'Tis no easy path to walk, and it takes a special man to walk it.

This is the story of one such Champion, and the Latent he came to love.

—Merlin's Grimoire

PROLOGUE

Charles Town, South Carolina
September 10, 1780

Candlelight from the massive chandelier overhead shimmered over satin, brocade, and the brilliant scarlet of British regimentals. Somebody played a violin with more vigor than skill, competing with the sound of dancing feet in the ballroom across the hall. Laughter rang out, a little too heartily from Loyalist planters, a little too smugly from the Redcoat conquerors who now occupied Charles Town.

Reece Champion sipped his wine and smiled down at the pretty Tory who was under the delusion he'd make a good husband. The square-cut décolletage of her brocade gown framed a pair of lovely breasts that would have claimed his full attention under different circumstances. As it was, though, Reece was far more interested in a conversation between two British lieutenants who stood nearby.

"By fall, Tarleton will have that Fox's tail," one of them said, his voice slurring slightly.

God, Reece loved a drunk. They made a spy's job so much easier.

He'd come to Charles Town three months ago, not long after the port had fallen to a six-week British siege. Since then, Reece had managed to establish himself as a rabid Loyalist bitter about abuses he'd suffered at the hands of his Patriot neighbors. It was a believable cover: In the Southern colonies, the campaign for independence had taken on all the viciousness of a civil war.

His pose had been convincing enough to win Reece acceptance among a few Tory hostesses eager to curry favor with the invaders. Most of the city was less enthusiastic about the occupation, so the British welcomed the distraction of whatever dinners and balls the Loyalists cared to host.

Reece made himself equally popular, largely by way of deep pockets and a feigned willingness to let the Redcoats fleece him over cards. Even as he smiled and lost, he collected a steady stream of useful intelligence he could pass on to his Patriot contacts.

And he wasn't the only one taking advantage of Redcoat gullibility. Reece had assembled a ring of Patriot agents who circulated among the British and Tory militia. Any information they collected, he sent to Patriot commanders like Francis Marion, whom the British had christened the Swamp Fox.

There was a certain irony to the whole thing, of course. Magekind vampires like Reece had served British interests for centuries, yet now they were helping England's rebellious colonies break that country's yoke.

It had not been a popular decision among the Magekind

High Council, at least not at first. Luckily, enough of the Majae had experienced enough visions to convince them the fledgling United States needed her independence.

So now Reece spent his evenings playing a lethal game of lies and eavesdropping. These two drunken lieutenants were just the sort of source he loved to plunder. But did the British really have a plan to capture Francis Marion, or was the officer just bragging in his cups?

To cover his interest, Reece leaned down to whisper something flattering to the little Tory, who simpered in response. Her pulse fluttered temptingly in her long, slender throat, and he felt his fangs twinge. *None of that,* he told himself sternly. *Keep your mind on the job.* Still, he was unable to resist a quick sniff of her deliciously tempting skin. She wasn't a Maja—or, for that matter, even a Latent—yet the rich femininity in her scent brought the Desire to quivering alert.

Until, as he breathed in, a sudden draft delivered a scent that definitely wasn't female. He lifted his head sharply. Another vampire? Here?

Reece looked up to see Thomas Westlake working through the crowd toward him. Westlake's gray wig was askew over wide, desperate eyes. And unless Reece was very much mistaken, there was blood on his friend's collar.

"Pardon me, sweet," Reece said to the Tory as he shot a regretful look at the two lieutenants. Judging from the expression on Westlake's face, something had gone very wrong, something he didn't dare ignore. He left the Tory pouting and started working his way through the crowd.

"What's the—?" Reece began, but didn't even get the question out of his mouth before Westlake's hand clamped down on his forearm with strength enough to make him wince.

"I need help," Tom hissed.

"Yes, I thought as much from the wild light in your eyes," Reece said dryly, catching his friend's shoulder and turning him smoothly toward the door. "Let's step outside, shall we?" This was not a conversation for mortal ears. Intercepting an interested glance from a Loyalist, Reece added more loudly, "What were you thinking, coming to Mrs. Mason's home in this condition? Shame, boy."

"Shorry." Westlake added an artistically drunken stagger to his step and allowed himself to be hustled outside.

"All right, Tom. What is it?" Reece demanded softly as soon as they were safely outside on the street. All around them the homes of wealthy merchants blazed with candlelight as people made the best of the British occupation. Wheels rumbled over the cobbles, and a dog barked frantically nearby, driven to a frenzy by the scent of vampire on the wind.

Westlake lost his drunken smile. "I've signed my own death warrant. And Lizzie's, too."

Reece stopped in his tracks, feeling the bottom drop out of his stomach. "God, Tom, tell me you didn't." When his friend looked away, miserable, he exploded. "Have you taken leave of your senses? What possessed you to do something so asinine?"

"Reece, I love her. It was the only way we could stay together. Besides, I thought . . . I thought we could use her. You know what a fine agent she is—"

"Keep your voice down!" Reece snarled as he grabbed Westlake's shoulder to manhandle him further from a passing Hessian. Dropping his own voice to a whisper no human could overhear, he said, "You know the Council expressly forbade you from Changing her. You know that! Why did you disobey?"

"God, I don't know! I just thought . . . after she came through the Change all right, I'd go before the Majae and argue how much we need her." Westlake's face twisted and his shoulders began to shake.

If anything, the chill in Reece's gut deepened. "Oh, God. She didn't make it."

His eyes squeezed shut, Westlake shook his head, unable to speak.

Reece swore. "And you left her alone! For God's sake, where is she?"

"At the house," Westlake said. "My servants are watching her."

"You'll be lucky if she hasn't killed them all!" Cursing all disobedient romantics straight to hell, he pushed his friend into the thick shadows of a nearby wall. "Come on," Reece growled. "We'd better get to her before she turns the house into a crater."

"Lizzie wouldn't do that!" Westlake objected.

"Normally, no, but if she's got Mageverse Fever, the situation is far from normal." After a quick glance around to check for observers, Reece leaped, caught the top of the fifteen-foot wall, and boosted himself over into the garden beyond it. Westlake hit the ground beside him an instant later, and the two men took off for the next street at a hard run. *Good thing there's no moon,* he thought as they shot around trees and over bushes at a speed no human could match. *We can move a little faster.*

Not that it mattered. Saving Lizzie had become impossible the moment Tom climaxed inside her for the third time.

Like Reece and Thomas, Lizzie was one of the descendants of the original Lords and Ladies of Camelot. As such, she carried Merlin's Gift in her blood, just waiting for some Magus to trigger it with his passion, bringing her to her full power and immortality.

Thomas would have been safe if he'd taken her only once or pulled out before climaxing. Or simply refrained from taking her that third, lethal time. But he hadn't. And he'd Changed her.

It wasn't as if he hadn't been warned. Back when Lizzie and Tom had first met, he'd asked permission of the Majae's Council, the body of witches who decided who could safely receive the Gift. The Council had examined Lizzie—and determined that her mind could not withstand the strain of gaining the almost godlike power that is a Maja's birthright.

But Thomas hadn't believed them. Reece had begged him to stay away from her, had reminded him that both he and

Lizzie faced the possibility of execution if they flouted the Council.

The stubborn bastard had done it anyway. And now . . .

They plunged together out of an alley across the street from Westlake's townhouse just in time to see the top story light up as though from a lightning strike—from inside the house. The boom made the ground shake.

Reece's heart sank. "Now that," he said, "is just not a good sign at all."

"No," Tom agreed grimly, "it's not."

Westlake's valet swung the door wide as they trotted up the walk. "Thank the good Lord you're back, Mr. Thomas." The tall, lean black man wore an expression of deep worry. "Miss Elizabeth has been raving since you left. The threats she's made . . ." Benjamin shook his graying head.

"We'll take care of it," Westlake told him shortly.

If they could. Lizzie was fully capable of carrying out any horror she cared to commit.

"What's gotten into her?" Benjamin asked with the boldness of a trusted servant as they strode past. "She's always been a lady down to the toes of her slippers, but the language she's used tonight would make a drunken wagoneer blush. You'd think she's possessed."

Reece heard his friend make a choked, agonized sound, but neither man replied.

There was really nothing to say.

As they strode across the foyer and up the narrow wooden stairs to the second floor, waves of magical force began ruffling over Reece's skin. He winced. The strength of the backwash told him the new Maja had a hell of a lot of power. Which was very bad news under the circumstances.

As if to confirm his fears, he heard a low female voice hissing something incomprehensible from the master bedroom at the end of the hall. As they approached, the words became all too clear. "Kill them," Elizabeth said. "I've got to kill them all. Wipe them off the face of the world before they get me.

They're after me. They—" A sharp crack rattled the house, another lightning strike. Something shattered.

The two men exchanged a grim look.

"Lizzie," Westlake called as he pasted a fixed, desperate smile on his face. "I'm back. And look who I brought to help us!" He opened the door cautiously.

Reece's heart lurched at the sight of the hunched figure crouching in a corner of the room. He'd last seen Elizabeth Thompson just the day before in his capacity as Charles Town spymaster. A valued member of his little ring, Lizzie had passed along intelligence she'd charmed from a British colonel.

It had been easy to see why the officer had said more than he should. Her big hazel eyes were enough to melt anyone's sense of discipline.

Now those eyes glittered wildly from a tangle of black hair, like something small and feral glaring from a thicket. "Oh, look—two big, strong vampires." Lizzie's mouth contorted into a twisted parody of her usual warm smile. The hunger in her gaze was chilling. "I wonder—would it give me twice the power if you both fuck me?"

Westlake made an involuntary sound, like a man grunting at a body blow. Reece hid his own shock. Though Lizzie had always been a charming flirt, she'd loved Tom more than life. The Change had twisted her savagely if she could make such a suggestion.

"Elizabeth—"

"Don't be cross with me, dear Thomas." She uncoiled from her crouch and started toward them, putting Reece uncomfortably in mind of a cat creeping up on a pair of fat pigeons. Between one step and the next, her white nightrail vanished, leaving her slim body naked and pale. "I only want a little more magical cock. You—" She broke step. Her head turned, as if she watched something small and fast fly around her. "The sparks are so pretty!" she said, her voice suddenly as bright as a child's. She pointed into the empty air. "Look—there and there and there. Like lightning bugs. Is it June?"

"Put your clothes back on, Lizzie!" Westlake managed, his voice choked and gruff with strangled grief. "Reece has come here to help, and you're embarrassing him."

Forgetting the Mageverse energies she alone could see, she resumed her seductive slink. "But I want to fuck." Before Reece could retreat, she stepped against him and twined both arms around his neck. "Don't you?" She smelled of old blood, sweat, and sex.

"No," Reece said firmly, taking her wrists in his hands as he put a more discreet distance between them. He was careful not to let his gaze drift downward. Under different circumstances, he might have appreciated the view, but as it was, he felt sick. "Come, Lizzie, dress yourself. This is serious business."

Very serious. Given their powers, the Majae would have sensed the disturbance in the Mageverse the moment Westlake Changed his Latent lover. The fact that an execution team hadn't arrived meant only that The Council was giving the couple a chance to plead their case.

Unfortunately, being vampires, Reece and Thomas couldn't open a Mageverse gateway to Avalon themselves; only a magic-wielding Maja could do that. And neither of them was stupid enough to step through any gate Lizzie created in her current state. God only knew where it would lead.

As he pushed Lizzie back a pace, Reece struggled to think of something to say when the Knights did arrive. He grimaced as he realized it was an exercise in futility. In trying to keep the woman he loved, Westlake had destroyed her—and put them all in danger from an insane Maja. The Knights would believe he'd earned his death.

As for Lizzie—she was simply too dangerous to be allowed to live.

"What's that?" She shrank back in fear. "Who's coming to kill us?"

Reece silently cursed. Touching him as she was, she'd picked up his thoughts.

"Knights." Hazel eyes rolled like a panicked mare's. "Armor and magical swords. Arthur and Lancelot and Galahad." Lizzie cringed, wrapping her arms protectively around herself as her voice spiraled into a wail. "They'll murder me! They'll kill me and my sweet Thomas!"

Westlake licked his lips, a sick sheen of sweat rising on his face. "Calm down, sweetheart. Nobody's going to hurt you."

"Liar!" Lizzie scuttled away from him, pulling at her own hair in agitation. "They're coming, coming with their magic swords." Her eyes narrowed as she suddenly straightened. "But I have magic, too. You gave it to me."

Light flared around her body with such intensity both vampires had to look away. When it faded, she was covered head to toe in armor that shone with an eerie green luminescence. "That's better," Lizzie said, pleased with herself. "Now I'm ready for them."

Her attention was focused on the sword she held in one hand. She waved it like a child with a new toy, watching the trail of sparks it left in the air.

Hell and damnation. Reece and Westlake retreated a wary pace. Vampires could heal virtually any injury except those inflicted by a magical blade. Mad as she was, Lizzie could kill them both.

The Maja drew a figure-eight pattern in the air with her new weapon, admiring the dancing sparks. "We're safe now, lover," she told Westlake. "Now I can get them first."

Not very damn likely. She might be a menace to Reece and Westlake, neither of whom was wearing armor, but the Knights had been fighting magical battles since Merlin walked the earth.

She was simply no match for them.

"Lizzie, don't," Westlake pleaded. "Sweetheart, you're only going to make them angry. And they'll be angry enough at me as it is." To Reece he added softly, "You'd better go. I shouldn't have pulled you into this to start with." He shook his head. "I panicked. I thought if anybody could save us, it would be you. But now . . ."

Reece felt his heart clutch. They'd been friends for years; Westlake had coached him through his first days as a vampire. To be unable to help when his friend needed it most was agonizing. "God, Tom—" He broke off helplessly, unable to think of anything comforting to say. This was not a situation in which comfort was possible.

His expression resigned, Westlake turned to Lizzie, who'd been distracted again by some new magical delusion. "Give me the sword, sweetheart," he said gently.

She started, her gaze focusing on him as she shrank back, clutching her weapon protectively. "No. I need it."

"Lizzie—" Thomas reached for the blade as Reece moved a little closer himself. Maybe while Westlake distracted her, he could . . .

"No!" She backed away a pace, bringing the weapon to bear on her lover's chest. "No. I see now, you're helping them. You want to kill me!"

"No! Lizzie, I—" Westlake took another step forward.

She swung.

Reece ducked under her arm and grabbed her, expecting Tom to leap clear. "Dammit, Lizzie, would you—"

A choked, wheezing sound interrupted him.

Lizzie's eyes flew wide. "Thomas!"

Reece snapped his head around. Westlake stood a pace behind him, looking blankly down at the blade embedded in his chest. She'd chopped into his side, the magical sword biting halfway into his rib cage. He looked up, his gaze meeting his lover's. "Sweetheart, I'm so sorry." His voice was faint, wheezing.

Reece released Lizzie and jumped to catch him as he toppled. "Jesus, Tom, why the hell didn't you dodge?"

Westlake looked up at him, eyes already glazing. "It didn't"—he stopped to gasp in a bubbling breath—"didn't seem worth the trouble."

"Tom!"

Westlake drew in a rattling breath as his gaze tracked past Reece to the woman he'd loved and destroyed. He made one last wrenching attempt at a smile the instant before his face went slack.

"Damn you, Tom," Reece whispered as the vampire's heart stuttered and stopped.

"You should have saved him." Lizzie's breath hitched. "You were supposed to save him."

Eyes burning with tears, Reece looked up to snarl at her. "And you weren't supposed to kill him, you bloody bi—" He broke off.

Energy shimmered and sparked around her fingers in a lethal corona. "No, it's *your* fault! *You were supposed to save him!*" She flung out both hands.

As her first strike seared the air, Reece snatched the sword free of Thomas's body and rolled clear, tumbling right to her feet as thunder echoed in his ears.

"Bastard!" she spat, dancing back a step. "Traitor! I'll kill you!" From the corner of one eye, Reece saw the energy blazing brighter around her hands as she gathered herself for another blast. "Die!"

Knowing her next strike would kill him, Reece thrust the sword blindly upward. The blade bit home with a sickening jolt he felt in his own gut.

Lizzie gasped. Her eyes met his over the sword he'd driven through her heart. For an instant, the madness lifted from her gaze, replaced by a pitiful kind of gratitude. Then she toppled backward, sliding free of the blade.

Reece stared wordlessly at the body of the woman who'd been his friend just hours before. His knees gave out from under him and dumped him to the floor.

He was still sitting there, surrounded by stillness and the smell of cooling blood, when yet another silent explosion lit the room. He didn't even bother to look around. He knew the Knights of the Round Table had arrived.

"Thomas West—" a voice began, only to break off. Somebody else swore, the words weary and profane.

Reece looked up. They'd sent the whole team for this—Arthur, Lancelot, Galahad, Gawain, all the others. All twelve armed in mystical armor, with Morgana Le Fay to provide whatever magic was needed.

The vampire who'd once been High King of Britain looked down at the crumpled bodies and shook his dark head. "Oh, Westlake," Arthur said softly, "you made a botch of this."

"He loved Lizzie." Reece's voice sounded hoarse and choked to his own ears. "And he knew you'd never let him stay with her unless he made her a Maja."

"Yes, well, if Westlake loved her so much, he should have walked away," Morgana said coldly, her elegant lip curling in disgust as she bent to examine the wound in Lizzie's chest. "We told him she wouldn't be able to withstand gaining a Maja's powers, but he had to go and Change her anyway. And look what happened. They ended up killing each other."

"For once, Morgana, you're wrong. She killed him, but he didn't kill her." Reece rose to his feet, feeling stiff and old. "I did." He started toward the door.

Arthur caught his arm before he could brush by. "You did what you had to do, lad. There was no saving her."

"I doubt that." He looked at Morgana, bitterness and grief making him reckless. "With your powers, you could have found a way to cure her."

The Maja sighed. "No, actually, we couldn't have. Oh, we could have restored her to sanity for a few minutes, but the energies of the Mageverse would have quickly overwhelmed her mind again. And once a Maja has access to her magic, the connection can't be severed." She shook her head, her long hair swinging around her lean, elegant face. "Their fates were sealed the moment Westlake came in her that last time."

Reece pulled free of Arthur's grasp. "I knew that before I walked in the door."

ONE

Avalon, Mageverse Earth
Present Day

Reece sprawled on one of the iron benches around the central square, watching the witches dance in the moonlight. Ageless, immortal, and beautiful, the Majae circled in an energetic eighteenth-century reel, jeweled hands glittering as they clapped and stamped.

The Desire stirred, hungry for a taste. He quieted it with a sip of donated blood from his goblet. It tasted of heat and magic, as different from mortal blood as aged bourbon is from tap water. Reece preferred to drink from a witch's throat, but in lieu of that, the goblet would do.

Swallowing another sizzling mouthful, he eyed the dancers, wondering if he'd be able to seduce one of them into going home with him for the night. It was a distinct possibility. Majae needed to give blood as desperately as vampires needed to drink it; otherwise they both suffered unpleasant health effects. He'd never been sure whether that erotic symbiosis was a very neat system or simply Merlin's wicked joke at their expense.

Perhaps a bit of both.

"You know," Lancelot du Lac said in his ear, "I don't remember that particular dance being so damned sexy."

"Probably because the dancers weren't wearing miniskirts and tight leather pants at the time," Reece retorted as his friend threw himself onto a nearby bench.

"God, I love progress." Lance sighed.

Reece grinned, noticing the way Lancelot's hungry gaze tracked his new bride, Grace, as she sang and spun her way through the dance. "How's married life, newlywed?"

"Anything but boring. You should give it a try."

He snorted. "What right-thinking Maja would have me? If I'm not on a mission for the High Council, I'm hunting spies or terrorists for the Americans."

"Hey, you were the one who agreed to be the Champion of the United States."

Arthur, himself Champion of Britain for the past sixteen hundred years, had asked him to work with the fledgling country's government as the Magekind's eyes, ears, and hands. Since then, Reece had fought Redcoats, Johnny Reb, Apaches, and Germans—twice—as well as communists and terrorists. He'd spied, lied, and killed, walking an uncomfortable tightrope between the needs of his country and the demands of Avalon. The two did not always coincide, particularly since he had to keep his allies in the CIA and the FBI in complete ignorance about the Magekind. As far as they were concerned, he was merely a lone vampire with a patriotic streak.

"Yeah, I agreed," Reece said. "Two hundred and twenty-eight years ago. A man's entitled to a little time off."

Lance laughed. They settled into a companionable silence,

watching the Majae dance as other vampires shouted ribald encouragement from the sidelines.

All around the square, the city of Avalon thrust into the Mageverse sky. Medieval castles, French chateaus, and thoroughly modern townhouses shouldered against one another, each designed to suit the individual whims of its magical owner. Towering Mageverse trees stood between them, draped in swags of fairy moss, surrounded by drifts of jasmine and roses.

Listening to the music, Reece let his head fall back. Something small and glowing shot past overhead, almost lost against the shimmer of the Mageverse. "Look," he said to Lance, "there goes a fairy."

His friend shot a jaundiced glance skyward. "Probably spying."

"Relations haven't improved with the Sidhe court, I gather."

"Not since the Majae's Council turned down King Llyr again," Grace said, dropping down beside her husband, delightfully sweat-dewed and panting. She was a lithely muscular woman, as blond as her husband was dark, an elegant match for his power. "I warned Morgana they're pissing him off for no good reason, but as usual, Grandma ignored me."

Reece lifted an interested brow as she wiped sweat from her forehead with the back of her wrist. "Is he still set on marrying a Maja?"

"Yeah, and if we had any sense, we'd let him. We need all the allies we can get, given the situation on Realspace Earth."

"What, with the terrorists?"

Grace stared at him. "No, the Death Cults. Didn't you get CNN in Iraq?"

"Oh, *those* cultists." Over the past year, dozens of cults had sprung up from D.C. to California. On the surface, none of them seemed related: Their rhetoric ranged from white supremacist to far-left ecco-looney, while their preferred weapons ran the gamut from poisoned cold medications to human sacrifice. Their only common denominator was the murders they committed and the panic they'd inspired in the public. "So we've decided they're nasty enough to warrant attention."

"Exactly," Lance said. "Seems one of the Majae has had a vision the cults really are using magic."

Reece stared. "The High Council thinks a Maja is involved?"

"No, and that's the really terrifying part," Grace said. "They swear the magical signature is not one of ours."

Oh, that wasn't good news. "Sidhe, then? Llyr?"

"I doubt he'd get involved in something like this," Lance said. "Though I wouldn't put it past that psychotic brother of his."

Reece grunted. "I'll see what I can find out from the Feds. I'm probably going to be stateside for several months anyway." Catching Grace's questioning look, he explained, "Hunting a mole."

"The CIA thinks they've got another double agent?" Lance asked, interested.

"No, it's the FBI. One of their counterintelligence guys asked me to look into it. Unless I get lucky, I'm going to spend months talking to bureaucrats to see who lies."

His acute vampire senses allowed Reece to hear a liar's heartbeat jump, or smell the faint trace of fear in sweat. Once he had a suspect, he could bring in a Maja for a little surreptitious mind reading. The Feds didn't know about the Majae, so Reece had to conduct the bulk of such investigations without magical assistance. It was annoying, but he had to ensure the Magekind's secret stayed secret.

"When are you heading to Washington?" Lance asked.

"Day after tomorrow. I've got to put in an appearance at Champion International first."

Grace propped her head on her husband's shoulder and smiled at Reece. "Have I mentioned how cool it is that you founded that company to provide for your descendants?" She cut her eyes at Lance. "Instead of just fathering bastards all over the place and letting them fend for themselves, like some people I could name."

"Hey," Lance protested. "He's only been around a couple of centuries. They're easier to keep track of when there's not so damn many of them."

"Which wouldn't be a problem if you'd use protection once in a while," Reece told him. "Hell, just pull out . . ."

"Now wait a minute. First off, I'm married, so I'm not doing that anymore anyway. . . ."

"Damn straight," Grace said, and nipped his ear in warning.

"Back off, you. I do the biting in this relationship." Laughing, he threw up an arm as she tried to get him again. "Second of all, if every Knight of the Round Table had pulled out every time he banged a girl, neither of you would be here to bitch at me about it."

"He's got a point," Reece reminded Grace.

"Except in my case, it was Morgana who did the bastard-spawning. Anyway, they could at least take an interest." She punched Lance lightly in the ribs and told him, "When I was a cop, I never found one of *Reece's* granddaughters living in squalor. *They're* all pulling down a hundred thou a year working for one of the biggest multinationals in the world."

"You want me to keep track of who Galahad's knocked up, too? Now, there would be a full-time job." Lance rolled his eyes. " 'Virgin knight' my ass. I don't know where the poets got *that* idea."

"They made it up." Reece grinned as he took a sip from his goblet, remembering the legend that painted Lancelot's son as the saint of the Round Table. "Just like the one about vampires being sterile, walking corpses."

Lance's eyes took on a wicked glint as he turned to Grace. "Speaking of not being sterile, has it occurred to you that Galahad is now your stepson? Which makes all his descendants your step-whatever. And then, of course, there's my sons and daughters and grandsons and great-great-et cetera." As her expression became steadily more hunted, he purred,

"We poor, limited vampires could never find them all, but with your goddesslike magical powers, you could. Given your keen sense of responsibility."

She looked so horrified, Reece shouted with laughter. "I think you just lost that one, sweetheart."

"No, he's right." Cool determination sparked in her eyes, and she rose to her feet. "At the very least, I can make sure none of them are starving."

"Hey, wait, where are you going?" Lance said to her retreating back as she strode away. "Grace, we had plans!"

Reece slapped him on the back and stood. The last dance was breaking up; it looked like a perfect opportunity to do some seducing. "Well, you'll have to excuse me. I want to get laid."

"Yeah, well," Lancelot said, staring glumly after his wife, "I'd say your chances just got better than mine."

Atlanta

Reece hesitated at the door to the crowded ballroom, the scent of gin, caviar, and packed humanity teasing his senses. The light from dozens of chandeliers blazed over designer gowns and black tuxedos, and the air was full of practiced laughter.

With his vampire hearing, it was easy to pick up the dozens of conversations going on around him. Eavesdropping being a spy's old habit, he listened with interest as the CEO of Champion Steel chatted up the pretty president of Champion Electronics. The woman laughed and turned the conversation to his branch's search for new superconductors.

During the past two centuries, the little shipping company Reece had started with his son, Caleb, had grown and diversified beyond all recognition.

Not unlike his bloodline.

Most of whom seemed to be at this party. Some were legitimate descendants through his son, but others had been fathered inadvertently by Reece himself when a condom had broken, or—before modern condoms were invented—he'd failed to pull out in time.

The Maja's Council frowned on birth control spells. They wanted the available pool of Latents as broad as possible, since the percentage they considered worthy to become Magekind was so small.

Like Grace, Reece had always found the Magekind's careless attitude toward their mortal offspring a bit appalling. Whenever he learned of one of his own children, he made sure they were provided for. The High Council did not allow the Magekind to marry mortals, so the best he could do was to offer them or their mothers jobs at Champion International. Some branches of his extended family had worked for the company for generations.

"Reece!"

He turned to see the CEO of Champion International shouldering through the crowd. Steve Champion clapped him on the back and gave him a handshake, grip firm and warm despite the age spots on the back of his hand. "Glad you could make it," the man said, his faded blue eyes lighting up in pleasure. "I know how busy you are."

"Wouldn't have missed it," Reece told him with genuine pleasure. "I don't see you enough these days."

Damn, time didn't just fly, it was jet propelled. Reece could remember when Steve had been the bright-eyed protégé he had tapped to run the family company forty-five years before. The boy must be pushing eighty now. Soon—all too soon—Reece would find himself attending yet another funeral.

Years ago, he'd tried to convince the Majae's Council to send some pretty Maja to Turn Steve, but they'd refused. Evidently, the boy was one of those who couldn't withstand the transition. Reece didn't argue, having learned his lesson on that score two centuries before.

Now he was going to have to bury yet another child he'd come to love.

To make matters worse, he'd have to choose the lad's successor. He dreaded that, too.

On paper, of course, Reece was no more than a junior VP who should have no say in such a vital decision, which was supposedly made by CI's Board of Directors. Usually Reece let the board and CEO run the company without interference, but this was different. The board would damn well approve his choice, even if he had to have a Maja magically convince the holdouts.

When it came to CI's future, Reece could be as ruthless as any other captain of industry.

"I suppose you're aware of this deal I'm trying to put together to acquire ComTec," Steve said now, dropping his voice. He was one of the few at CI who knew Reece was a vampire. Like the others, however, he was under a spell that prevented him from speaking about it to anyone else, a safety measure the Magekind High Council had insisted upon.

Reece nodded. "I've heard something about it."

"ComTec's CEO is here tonight. George Gavel." Steve hesitated delicately before his voice dropped even more. "I'd appreciate it if you'd have a word with him. See how serious he is about this deal."

Reece smiled slightly. "For you, Steve, anything."

An hour later he was listening to Gavel drone on about his golf swing when he scented a Latent that was definitely no descendant of his. Her enticing blend of musk and spice seemed to bypass his brain and wrap around his sex like long female fingers. As his body hardened in instant response, Reece glanced around the crowded ballroom for the source of the scent.

Blue eyes met his over the CEO's shoulder, amused and

faintly mocking. A delicate blond brow lifted. The Latent's carmine mouth quirked in a taunting half-smile.

Then she turned with a roll of a deliciously curved hip and sauntered away through the cocktail party crowd.

Reece's eyes narrowed, scarcely aware of Gavel's complaints about his new custom-made titanium driver. Her strapless gown was the same fuck-me crimson as her lipstick, in brilliant contrast to the cream of her slender shoulders. The dress clung to her tight, narrow waist and heart-shaped rump before ending at mid-thigh, displaying long, sleekly muscled legs. She wore her shimmering blond hair piled on top of her head like a crown, baring a tempting length of nape. He imagined pressing a kiss there.

He'd always been a neck man.

Then someone stepped in front of her, and she was gone.

"Excuse me," Reece murmured to the CEO as he started after her. "I see someone I need to have a word with." He could smooth any ruffled feathers later. Besides, he'd already discovered what Steve had wanted to know: Beneath Gavel's endless prattle lay fear and desperation. ComTec was sinking fast, and Champion International's offer was the only life raft in reach. Steve would soon add another holding to the family's impressive portfolio.

In the meantime, Reece planned to take care of more personal needs. If the Latent let him.

Absently he reached into his lapel and checked the foil packets he carried everywhere he went. Hungry for her as he was, Reece had no intention of entering a Latent without protection. Thomas and Lizzie had taught him the folly of that more than two centuries ago.

It wasn't a lesson he was ever likely to forget.

Pleased with her work, Erin Grayson scooped a champagne flute from the tray of a passing waiter and slid deeper into the chatting crowd. She'd circle back around and give Champion another good look later. Tonight's objective was simply to establish contact, and piquing his interest was a good place to start.

So far it was definitely piqued. When Champion had looked at her, instant heat had leaped in his eyes, as if somebody had ignited a mental Molotov cocktail.

Erin meditated on the surprising strength of his reaction and frowned slightly. She wasn't that damn good looking. Not that she was coyote material, of course, but she'd played the game long enough to know what male response to expect. Most men were appreciative, but Champion had stared with a searing primal heat she'd felt to the soles of her spike-heeled Pradas. The man packed quite a punch.

There was something just a little bit off about him, though, something that made her instincts hum. A sense of danger. But was it the danger of a handsome, sexy man—or the evil of somebody who'd bankroll a death cult?

A slight frown curving her mouth, Erin took another sip of her champagne.

Champion certainly looked the part of a wealthy corporate prince. His tailored Ralph Lauren tux showcased the kind of broad-shouldered build that spoke of frequent, time-consuming trips to a gym. His mink-brown hair had been cut by someone who'd probably charged him two hundred bucks, and those broad, long-fingered hands had recently been subjected to an expensive manicure.

He could probably afford to give Death's Sabbat the money to buy weapons-grade anthrax. But was he the kind of man who'd do it?

True, there was a visible edge to him that didn't fit the pampered persona. The line of that hawk nose wasn't quite true, as if broken by either a fist or a polo mallet. The businessman he appeared to be would have gotten that fixed years ago. God knew his family could afford it; the Champions had been wealthy when Vanderbilt was a social-climbing upstart.

Actually, his whole face was subtly, oddly battered, despite its rough-cut good looks. A thin scar angled along his upper lip, and a shorter one slashed across a chiseled cheekbone. The resulting effect suggested knife fights and bar brawls rather than old money and Harvard.

But it was Champion's jungle green eyes that really made Erin's instincts chime. The last man she'd met with a stare that feral had been a DEA agent who'd gone deep cover in a Columbian drug cartel a little too long.

None of which jibed with the dossier she'd spent the morning studying. Champion's childhood had been spent in private schools, with Christmas vacations in Aspen and summers in Greece. Between racking up indifferent grades at Harvard, he'd kicked around Europe and gotten his heart broken by some Parisian bimbo his family had flatly refused to let him marry.

Yet her gut told her the owner of those hard eyes wouldn't have let anybody dictate who he could or couldn't wed. Not even on pain of losing a multimillion dollar inheritance.

On the other hand, she found it just as hard to believe such a handsome, suave man would be willing to bankroll an anthrax attack on Atlanta. So was the Outfit's intelligence that far off, or had Erin's instincts gone that far south? Neither alternative appealed.

Frowning, she looked back in his direction, expecting to see Champion still talking to that boor from ComTec. Instead he was barely six feet away and closing fast, his pirate's mouth curved in a lazy half-smile. His gaze met hers with predatory heat.

Erin almost bobbled her champagne as her instincts buzzed like cicadas. No junior VP would have dared walk away from George Gavel, not with the kind of power the CEO wielded. Particularly not when Champion International was trying to buy Gavel's company. And certainly not just to chase a woman. Champion would have to be an idiot.

Unless he'd made her. Erin didn't think she'd ever seen him at one of the cult's Sabbats, but what if she was wrong?

Her heartbeat took on an adrenaline-rush rhythm as every instinct demanded she run. Instead she gave Champion her best seductive smile.

One thing Erin Grayson knew was how to play the game.

"Good evening," Reece said when he was again close enough to breathe in the Latent's delicious scent.

"Hello." He could hear her heartbeat pounding as she smiled that sensual smile at him. There was fear under the exotic musk of her perfume, an alarm that didn't quite mesh with her hooded come-get-me gaze. It made Reece wonder if she knew what he was. What she was.

What he could do to her.

Then again, maybe she was playing some other game altogether. Could be harmless, could be something that would get him killed. He didn't have enough information to be sure either way. Which meant he should probably cut his losses and walk.

And normally, Reece would have done just that, if it hadn't been so damn long since he'd tasted a Latent. Or a Maja, for that matter, since none of the witches last night had been interested in doing more than teasing him.

After all those months in Iraq, he was due for a night's respite. One night's sweet peace. It wasn't so much to ask after everything he'd given up.

"I hope I didn't lure you away from our host," the Latent said as he reached her. Her heartbeat slowed from its original startled slam, and she gave him a teasing smile. "Don't you like golf?"

"Other games interest me more," Reece said. Her carnal scent teased his senses and soothed his jangling instincts. He let his eyes drift to the impressive cleavage mounding in the heart-shaped frame of her bodice. "Particularly with the right partner."

"Partner?" She took a sip of her champagne and pursed her sensual mouth. "Or opponent?"

He toasted her with his own glass. "Partner, definitely. Partners share the same goals."

A spark of cynicism glinted in those clear blue eyes. "Nobody ever really has the same goals. The best you get is similarity. The focus is always different, no matter what it seems on the surface."

He studied her, intrigued. "Depends on the game, Ms. . . . ?"

"Erin," she supplied, extending a graceful hand. "Erin Grayson."

"Lovely," he murmured, reaching to take those long fingers in his. Her skin felt deliciously silken. His own seemed to heat in instant response. "Reece Champion."

She let her hand linger just a moment before she slowly reclaimed it, brushing his fingers with her own in the process. The Desire purred in hot response. "What's it like being a member of a family you can trace back for centuries?"

"Confining," Reece said, smiling easily. He'd fielded the question so many times, the answer had become rote.

Erin lifted one pale, perfect brow. "You don't find it romantic—all the lives that came before yours, all the struggle to build everything you enjoy?"

Not particularly, since he was the one who'd done the building. He wasn't about to tell her that, though. "It also comes with the responsibility not to screw it up for those who come after you."

"I suppose everything has a price." A waiter slipped through the crowd and paused beside them with a tray of canapés. Erin chose one and took a bite. Reece watched as her tongue swept a crumb from her lower lip with an agile pink flick. "The cost may not be evident, but it's always there."

"Sometimes that's part of the rush," he said, giving her a lazily suggestive smile. "How much can you get without paying more than you want?"

She studied him over the rim of her champagne glass. "You sound like a gambler, Mr. Champion."

"Oh, yes. Are you?"

"Only for high stakes." Her eyes shuttered in pleasure as she sipped, lashes curving against her creamy skin. "Nothing less is worth the trouble."

"Or gives the same kick." He smiled slowly. "Would you like to step out on the balcony with me? It's a little crowded in here." Particularly for what he had in mind.

Another waiter approached. Erin set her glass on his tray and took another. "Why not?"

Reece led the way through the double French doors. Instantly a flood of cool night air blew against his hot skin, carrying the high wavering wail of a siren and the rumble of traffic. Just beyond the balcony's railing, the lights of Atlanta glittered across the dark earth, as if the sky had cast its stars on the ground.

"Beautiful view," Erin murmured.

"Yes." A full moon rode overhead, painting her face with pale, soft light. He moved closer, savoring the anticipation, the sheer elegant purity of her features, the lush scent of her body. "What color are your eyes?"

She blinked at the question. "Blue."

"Yes, but what shade? I've been wondering." He dipped his head and scented her hair. His inhumanly acute hearing picked up the answering thump of her heart. Reece concealed a smile and went to work. "The blue keeps changing. Sometimes it's sapphire when the light is good, sometimes cerulean. Right now it's a deep, mysterious . . . cobalt, I think." He drew back to consider those long-lashed eyes. "Definitely cobalt."

Erin eyed him in pure admiration. "Oh, you've got talent."

He grinned. "Well, yes. But that doesn't mean I'm not sincere."

A blond brow rose. "Are you trying to get me into bed, Champion?"

"Yes." Testing, he ran his fingertips over the curve of her bare shoulder. "How am I doing?"

"Let me get back to you on that." Smiling wickedly, Erin turned away, slipping skillfully from beneath his hand. "Are you always this brazen?"

"Occupational hazard." He followed her as she moved to the balcony and leaned against the glass-and-chrome railing.

"Of being a VP at Champion International?"

That hadn't been the occupation he was thinking of, but he shrugged lightly. "Of being a second cousin in a very large, very talented family. The Champions may have raised nepotism to a high art, but you've still got to impress those who run the show."

"Ah," she said, on a note of revelation, and took a sip of her champagne. "The family gene pool is stocked with sharks."

"Not necessarily, but it does pay to be able to swim." Reece studied her, wondering suddenly how she'd gotten invited to this very exclusive party. He did hope she wasn't someone's wife. He wasn't sure his willpower was strong enough to resist the temptation. "So who do you swim with?"

That red mouth curled. "Fishing, Champion?"

"I like to know whom I'm trying to seduce."

"Meaning, can I leave with someone other than the one that brung me?" Erin asked, lengthening her vowels into an exaggerated Southern drawl. "What if I said I crashed the party?"

"Did you?"

"I'm not that brave." She shrugged and looked off across the glittering city. "Actually, I called in a favor from a certain ComTec exec."

"Why?"

Erin gave him a shimmering glance that swept from the toes of his Gucci loafers all the way up into his eyes. She smiled slowly. "Maybe I'm fishing."

He grinned, appreciating her wit. "For what?"

She grinned back. "Shark."

"Better be careful. You might get eaten."

"Only if I'm lucky."

"Mmmm. Strikes me the shark would be the one with the luck."

She shot him a teasing, sidelong look. "You're such a gentleman."

"But am I lucky?"

"I doubt luck has much to do with it."

"Luck has everything to do with everything."

"What, no faith in talent and preparation?"

Damn, he liked her. "No matter how talented and prepared you are, bad luck can torpedo you every time. But even the bumbling and lazy get lucky."

"The talented and prepared make their own luck."

He stepped incrementally closer until the lapels of his tux brushed the bodice of that maddening dress. "Is that my cue?"

Erin tilted her chin to look up at him. "I don't know. Is it?"

He lowered his head. "I think maybe it is."

"There you go," she said, just before he took her mouth. "Talented, prepared, *and* lucky."

He slid into the kiss slowly, savoring the moment, knowing what it would do to both of them. How the taste of her would hit him after his long fast.

The Latent's lips bloomed open under his, silk parting for that first, eager thrust of his tongue. She tasted even more like sex than an ordinary woman did. Richer, darker, searing his senses like a slug of straight Scotch after drinking white wine. Like tangled limbs and darkness and drumming hearts.

God, he was ravenous for her. It had been too damn long.

With a groan, he eased his tongue deeper. Erin met it with a wet velvet stroke of her own. He licked at her, caught her full lower lip gently between his teeth. Suckled.

The Latent leaned into him, her soft breasts pillowing his chest. He eased his arms around her and drew her closer, deeper into the kiss. The red silk of her dress felt slick under his hands, warm from her body. Erin shifted on her high heels, her silky legs whispering against the fabric of his trousers. Curling her slender arms around him, she spread her fingers across his back. Reece could sense her body slowly awakening, readying itself for him, unconsciously eager for the Gift. His own blood began to burn with need.

Dangerous, he thought. *She's so dangerous.*

Erin was the kind who would blow into the Gift like a detonating bomb if he took her too many times. He could almost taste the power stirring under her skin, even from so little contact. The Majae's Council would have his head on a pike if he turned her without permission. Assuming she didn't go mad and kill him herself.

But once . . . his clamoring body whispered. Once wouldn't trigger her Gift, particularly if he used protection. He could take her once without taking her too far.

And finally slake his grinding, maddening thirst for the first time in a year. The thirst for a Latent with Merlin's Gift running hot in her veins.

His cock swelled and heated even more behind his fly. In his mouth his fangs slid to full extension. He hoped she didn't notice.

The taste of Champion's mouth shouldn't have hit her so hard. It was, after all, a simple kiss, a touch of lip and tongue, barely qualifying as foreplay by any reasonable standard.

Oh, she'd expected a little sizzle. Reece knew his business, and so did she. Both of them were fully capable of spinning a kiss into something sweetly erotic, a sensual aperitif, a promise of more to come.

But then something happened. Something magic that sizzled in the taste of his mouth, in the way those powerful hands caught her against his straining erection.

As he dragged her closer, she felt every inch of that big body, hard and brawny under the elegant camouflage of his tux. His tongue played around hers, teasing her arousal to blazing life. Every time he moved against her, the lace of her bra tormented her hard, sensitized nipples. Deep between her thighs, she felt the first heated trickle of desire.

Some instinct sounded a dim alarm. Erin wasn't a dewy-eyed virgin. She'd played the game before, knew her way around a man's body. Knew the dance of lust so well the steps had lost their urgency.

This was more.

His scent and taste swamped her blood like a narcotic. Need rolled over her, drowned intellect in fire.

It wasn't simple desire, or even simple lust. It was more primal than that. As if he'd triggered some imperative buried in her cells, a drive to give herself up to him in some ancient erotic ritual.

Unprofessional, whispered the voice of sanity. For God's sake, she was investigating this man's possible involvement with Satanists.

True, she'd been ordered to establish a relationship with Champion, play on his well-known weakness for pretty women. But she wasn't supposed to actually tumble into bed with him.

She'd better get herself under control. Now. Fight the spell of those magical hands and drag herself out of his reach.

But then those broad, strong fingers cupped the curve of her breast through her bodice. His thumb flicked across her nipple.

Oh, God, Erin thought, even as her body purred, *Oh, yes.*

TWO

It had been more than a year since a man had touched Erin with such bold sensuality. Even David had been too much the professional, as aware as she'd been of the rules.

Until it had been too late.

But Reece Champion cared nothing for polite, professional distance, for political correctness. He wanted her. Period.

Temptation surged through Erin on a river of pounding blood. Why not? Yes, sex with him would be well beyond the call of duty, but what better way to win his trust? The Outfit wasn't the FBI, after all; its agents specialized in breaking the rules. And once she'd become his lover, Erin could gain the leverage to break this case wide open.

God knew she'd been coming up empty so far. She needed a break, and he could give it to her. One small opportunity could be the key to avenging David and finding out just what the hell had happened last year.

Champion's mouth brushed along the straining cords of her throat, bringing the rapid spin of her thoughts to an abrupt halt. The teasing sensation made her breath catch as he paused to nibble gently. She breathed a soft sound, somewhere between a sigh and a whimper.

The helplessness of that tiny noise jolted her, forced her to wonder if her judgment was entirely sound. She certainly had reason to doubt it; her head was spinning, and spots of light floated in front of her eyes.

Blinking, she realized the lights were stars. She'd tipped her head back as Champion pressed his lips to her banging pulse. His teeth nipped gently.

Erin felt her weakened knees give. He caught her against him, one hand wrapped around the curve of her bottom, the other still cupping her breast. Driven by pure instinct, she lifted one leg and curled it behind his, opening herself to him.

There are a hundred people in the next room, some fragment of self-preservation whispered. "Champion, we can't do this," Erin moaned.

"Not here," he agreed, his voice so rough and dark with anticipation, a ball of need began to heat between her thighs. "Where are you staying?"

"The Ambassador. On"—she broke off with a gasp as he raked his teeth across her pulse—"on Peachtree Street."

"Not a hotel. Not for this." He drew back. "I'll take you home with me."

Her mouth opened to say, "No, you won't," but then she met his hot animal gaze and found the words beyond her willpower.

Champion raised a strong hand and tucked a lock of hair back into her elegant French twist, then scanned her with a single, searing glance. "There." He smiled crookedly. "You're presentable."

She automatically glanced down his big body until her gaze snagged on his zipper. The bulge there made her eyes widen. "You're not."

He looked down, then up at her again through the feathered screen of his lashes. "Now look what you've done. You'll just have to walk in front of me."

A giggle escaped her. Horrified, she clamped her teeth together. She never giggled. It was so damn unprofessional.

But then, looking into those hot green eyes, it was easy to believe professionalism was overrated.

He took her elbow in one big hand and guided her toward the door. His grip was gentle as he escorted her into the brightly lit ballroom, yet something about it made her feel like a pirate's conquest being borne off into the night.

I shouldn't be doing this, she thought as she walked just ahead of him through the crowd. *I've got to tell him to stop. Now, before it goes too far.*

It shouldn't be this difficult to tell him no. Not for her. Over and over again, Erin had proven herself the master of her own emotions. Even with David, the man she'd loved.

Maybe that's why I'm finding it so tough now. For years her partner's cautious determination to play by the rules had kept them apart. Erin had gone along with him at first, but toward the end, she'd grown tired of it. She'd wanted David far more than she'd wanted to go by the book.

But David *was* the book.

In the end his precious rules hadn't saved them from the nightmare that had destroyed them both. Of course, giving in to their mutual passion probably wouldn't have saved them, either. One way or another, David would still be dead, and Erin's FBI career would still be in ruins. On the other hand, she might also have something more to remember than grief, regret, and cold, dead dreams.

She was sick of regret, of yearning uselessly for a passion she'd never tasted. She wanted to feel Reece's clever mouth on her bare skin, wanted to feel him drive to his full, hard length inside her. Wanted him so badly, she didn't give a damn about rules, risk, or even common sense.

For once, Erin Grayson was going to get what she wanted.

Poor little Latent.

Reece could sense Erin's losing battle with the demands of her body. She had no idea of the power of the erotic undertow they'd been caught in.

He did.

He supposed if he was any kind of gentleman at all, he would release her and walk away. He'd probably have done just that a year ago, before he'd spent months locked in a hell of hate and sand, among wary women who wouldn't even meet his eyes.

As it was, she wasn't the only one skidding out of control. Now Reece craved the release he'd find in her lush, hot femininity far too much to care about playing fair.

They'd both have to take their chances.

The waiter balanced his tray of canapés as an overweight guest made her selection. His gaze, however, was focused on Reece Champion and Erin Grayson as they slipped out through the ballroom's double doors.

"Targets are leaving," he murmured, just loud enough for his body mike to pick up the words.

The woman looked up, her plump fingers hesitating over a quiche. "What?"

He smiled at her. "Nothing, ma'am. Nothing at all."

Inside a catering truck in the ComTec parking lot, James Avery frowned as he watched the monitor for the elevator security camera. Erin was wrapped in Champion's arms again as they kissed with the same ravenous hunger the waiter's button camera had recorded when they'd stepped onto the balcony.

At his elbow Steven Parker snickered. "I thought you said she was a pro."

Avery frowned. "She is. I've known her ten years—hell, I trained her. She's intelligent, capable, and controlled, and she breaks the rules only when she has to. That's why I hired her for the Outfit to begin with, despite the mess with her partner. So what the devil is she doing now?"

The blond's lips curled into a thin smirk. "Looks to me like she's about to put her assets to good use."

Which certainly played into their plans. And yet . . . Avery drummed his long brown fingers on the monitor console. "This is totally out of character. Wonder if Champion's doing something to her?"

"If he's not, he certainly intends to." Parker's pale eyes were focused hungrily on the monitor. "At least, judging by the way his hand is sliding up her skirt."

Avery eyed the other agent in distaste. Parker might be the nominal head of this operation, but if he kept up the attitude, Avery was going to bitch to the FBI until they sent in somebody else.

Frowning, he switched his attention to the monitor. Grayson and Champion stepped hastily apart as the elevator neared the lobby. The camera angle didn't allow a view of her face, but Avery thought she staggered slightly.

But why? He knew good and damn well Erin wasn't tipsy. She'd had one glass of champagne and a sip or two of another. Not nearly enough to test the tolerance of a woman who'd drunk Avery himself under the table a memorable time or two.

Had Champion done something to her?

"We should have told her what she was getting into," Avery said aloud, voicing the thought that had been nagging at him since he'd learned the details of Parker's plan. "I don't like sending her in blind."

The agent snorted. "She'd have been terrified, and with Champion's senses, he'd have known it."

Avery glowered as he remembered watching a tech tape a body mike to Erin's flat belly just last week. They'd all known if the cultists of Death's Sabbat made her for a government agent, they'd kill her on the spot. Yet there'd been nothing in those clear blue eyes but ruthless determination.

Erin was completely dedicated to shutting down the cult she held responsible for her partner's death, and she was willing to do whatever it took to accomplish that aim. Her hunger for justice was so great, it left no room for fear or self-doubt. "Erin Grayson is no coward," he growled.

"She'd better not be." Parker leaned back in his seat and laced his hands behind his head. "But think about it. What if we'd asked you, 'How'd you like to be a vampire's dinner date?' What would you have said?"

"I'd have done my job," Avery said stiffly. "Just like Erin."

"And Champion would have known something was off. She wouldn't have gotten close enough to sniff his after-shave." Parker jerked his chin at the monitor showing the view from the lobby's security camera. The vampire was guiding her toward the revolving door with a hand resting on the small of her back. "He's sure letting her in close now."

Avery frowned, knowing the Fed was right.

That didn't mean he had to like it.

Erin watched in admiration as the valet drove Champion's car up to meet them at the curb. The black Ferrari convertible looked more like a jet fighter than a car, and its engine rumbled like a tiger's purr.

"I'm not compensating for anything, if that's what you're wondering." Champion grinned as he beat the valet to the passenger door and opened it for her.

She remembered the bulge he'd pressed against her belly. "The thought never even crossed my mind." He laughed as she sat down and eased her legs inside, careful of her short skirt.

A fire truck roared by, its shrill siren piercing the spell Champion had spun with his big body and raw silk voice. Erin took a calming breath of cool night air as he started around the car.

Pausing in front of the Ferrari's nose, he pulled a cell phone out of his pocket. "Pardon me," he said, raising his voice to be heard as he dialed with a thumb. "I have to give my housekeeper some instructions."

As he murmured into his cell, Erin frowned, not entirely comfortable with the idea of going to his house. For one thing, she hated giving up the home-court advantage.

Besides, her hotel would be safer. A place filled with so many people would make him think twice about any criminal intentions he might be harboring.

As Champion slid in next to her, she opened her mouth to tell him she'd changed her mind. Then he looked over at her, one corner of that pirate's mouth kicking up. Something in that half-smile sent adrenalin and heat surging through her.

It was the same reckless exhilaration she felt going undercover at one of the Sabbat's dark celebrations—half fear, half pleasure.

What the hell. She really couldn't afford to pull the plug anyway, not now that they were actually on the way to his house. Her objective, after all, was to get him into a relationship she could use to find out if he was financing the cult. Pissing him off by playing cock tease was not the way to do it.

As Champion pulled out of the parking lot, the wind made its first pass through her hair. Erin tilted her head back, letting the breeze cool her face.

No, she wouldn't back out. Getting close to Champion might give her the weapon she needed to blow the cult wide open. Which in turn would both restore the shine to her tarnished reputation and avenge David's death.

That was worth any risk.

* * *

"I'm going after them," Parker said, rising to his feet. "I'll take my car. This van would stand out like a hooker in church. Want to back me up?"

"Yeah, sure." Avery rose from his seat as the FBI agent slid open the truck's door. As the two men strode over to the nondescript blue sedan parked nearby, he frowned. "Shouldn't we mobilize the rest of the men?"

"No point." The agent shook his head. "We won't be taking him tonight. I do want to keep an eye on them, though."

Avery nodded and got in the passenger side. For once, Parker had said something he agreed with.

Champion's home was far more impressive than Erin would have expected, given his self-described status as a second cousin in his sprawling clan. As they drove through a wrought-iron security fence, she gazed around in admiration. The house looked more like an English manor than anything else, complete with a turret entry and redbrick walls. Towering windows accentuated the effect with cream brick borders that reminded her of a medieval castle. "Nice house," she drawled in dry understatement.

He threw her a flashing grin. "It's not mine. Belongs to the family."

Erin grinned at him. "You squatting, Champion?"

"Something like that." He whipped the Ferrari up the curving drive and parked it in front of the door. As he slid out of the car, she stayed put, suspecting he intended to open the car door for her.

She was right. He extended a hand to help her out. She took it and slid from the car. "Thank you."

Champion tucked her hand into the bend of his brawny arm. "Would you like a tour of the garden?"

"In the dark?"

He shrugged. "It looks best by moonlight."

"Why, Champion—if I didn't know better, I'd think you have a romantic streak." She let him guide her to the brick sidewalk that curved around behind the house.

"Of course."

"Of course?" She cocked her head at him. "Most men I know would rather be called a barbarian than a romantic."

Champion smiled slightly. "The most dangerous men are always romantics, Erin. A barbarian will kill for self-interest. A romantic will kill for a dream."

She opened her mouth only to close it again as she remembered the assorted cops she'd worked with over the years, in the FBI and out of it. "You know, you're right." Erin canted him a look as he led her around the well-lit walkway. "So are you saying you're dangerous?"

"What do you think?"

She eyed his pirate smile. "I think you just may be the most dangerous man I've ever met."

He didn't answer, but that smile took on a feral cast that made her heart kick in anticipation.

When Erin dragged her fascinated gaze away from his face, she saw the garden. "Now this," she said, stopping to admire it, "really is a garden made for moonlight."

White roses nodded in the night breeze, almost glowing in the light of the moon. Magnolias stood sentinel between the bushes, their spreading branches heavy with pale, waxy flowers. Creamy azaleas circled the bases of the great trees like drifts of snow, and lightning bugs flashed among them, putting Erin in mind of nocturnal fairies.

"I've got to ask," she said, gesturing around them as they strolled among the trees. "Why design a garden to be viewed at night?"

"I'm too busy to use it during the day." He smiled slightly.

They rounded a hedge to see a marble fountain in the shape of a wide, round bowl, backlit by stands of candles burning in tall, wrought-iron candlesticks. From the center of the fountain thrust a shape Erin first took for a stone obelisk. As they moved closer, she realized it was a sculpture of a woman's arm, extending upward from the water, holding a white marble sword. Streams of water rolled down the length of blade and arm, as if they had just thrust from beneath the water.

"The Lady of the Lake?"

He shrugged. "I've got a soft spot for Arthurian legend."

On the other side of the fountain, they found a white comforter spread out on the grass, light from the surrounding candles spilling in golden pools across its padded surface. A bottle of champagne cooled in a silver ice bucket beside it.

"I gather this is the reason for that call to your housekeeper," Erin said.

He turned to face her. "A woman like you deserves moonlight and the smell of beeswax and roses."

She cocked her head. "You going for romance or seduction?"

"A little of both." Champion caught her chin in his hand and tilted it up as he lowered his head. "I didn't want you in some impersonal hotel room. I wanted you here, like this."

The moment his lips took hers, she realized he'd held back at the party. Champion kissed her with a starved intensity, using lips and tongue and teeth as if drinking life out of her mouth. He tasted of champagne and heated masculinity in a seductive combination that made her nipples tingle. A beat later his hands were on her, stroking gently at first, here the tip of a breast through her bodice, there the curve of her hip. When she moaned in surrender, he grew rougher by delicious degrees, cupping, squeezing, claiming her. All the while, he feasted at her mouth, his tongue dancing around hers, his teeth tugging gently on her lips.

Erin tore free to gasp in a breath. Her zipper whispered as he tugged it downward, the sound loud in the moonlit stillness. She started to reach for him, but he'd already caught the hem of her dress in both hands. He drew the skirt up until she felt the kiss of a cool breeze on the heated flesh of her butt.

Then that same little gust teased her waist and breasts as he slowly bared them. She shuddered in need.

Finally Champion stepped back, her gown in his fist, his eyes drinking her in. She wore only a few bits of red lace and red spike-heeled Pradas, but he was still fully dressed in his elegant black tux. His green eyes looked pale and hungry in the moonlight as they explored every inch of her.

That look from any other man would have made Erin feel vulnerable and uncomfortable. But coming from Champion, it gave a sense of erotic power. She smiled, and suspected the expression had a taunting edge. "Like what you see?"

His mouth curled in that buccaneer smile. "Oh, yes."

She looked like one of Reece's more shameless midnight fantasies: miles of creamy leg sheathed in sheer stockings, a tiny triangle of a thong baring most of her lush hips, a red lace bra cupping the soft, full mounds of her breasts. The wind had pulled her hair from its neat French twist on the ride over, and long gold streamers curled around her shoulders. Her blue eyes shimmered at him, mysterious with that primal power women have. Her smiling mouth promised carnal pleasures.

Reece's cock ached. He wanted to snatch her against his body, sate himself in long greedy swallows and deep lunging thrusts. Instead he put a stranglehold on greed and gave her a practiced smile. He was not, he reminded himself, a barbarian. Even when he felt like one. He would make love to her slowly, giving her all the sweet pleasure she deserved for her unwitting gift of blood.

"You do realize you're overdressed." With a roll of her hips, Erin moved toward him, slow and sexy, putting an edge on hunger that was already more than keen enough.

Reece didn't dare move. He was too close to the edge of his control.

Smiling into his eyes, she reached up with long, slender

fingers and plucked at his bow tie. He looked down to watch, but his eyes were caught by the delicate quiver of her pale, full breasts. Her nipples peaked, tempting shadows behind the lace cups of her bra.

Erin slid his jacket off his shoulders. He had to relax his bunched muscles so she could pull it away. His dove-gray vest went next, slowly, after she'd plucked each pearl button free. Reece clenched his fists and let his head fall back, determined to savor the feeling of those long, clever fingers moving over his body through the barrier of his shirt. Such sweet torture.

He managed to cling to his self-control through the removal of his shirt. But then a hot female mouth closed suddenly around his left nipple, and the tether he had on his lust snapped with a mental *twang*.

He had Erin down on the comforter without quite knowing how he'd gotten her there.

Reece heard her hot purring laugh of approval as he dragged down the scarlet cups that kept him from her breasts. Her nipples jutted for him, hard and flushed rose. With a soft growl, he pounced, sucking the peak into his mouth.

Distantly he felt the sting of her crimson nails digging into his biceps, the sharp heel of one of her Pradas riding his backside. He didn't care, too swamped by the taste of her skin, the smell of her sexual cream, the pounding drum of her blood.

She was so damn ripe.

Erin gasped as Reece suckled the aching tip of one breast, his tongue rolling the little peak against the edge of his teeth, then drawing it hard into his mouth. A cataract of glittering sensation poured down her nerves with each silken pull. She writhed under him, but he held her effortlessly still in the brawny cage of his arms.

"God, Reece!" she groaned. He rumbled a hungry sound back at her, but didn't release his drugging hold on her breast.

One big hand moved up her body to claim her other breast, squeezing and stroking until she whimpered.

As if he'd been waiting for that soft signal, he wrapped his free hand in the fabric of her thong and ripped it away. She sucked in a breath, then released it in a strangled scream as his hand slid between her thighs.

Strong fingers probed her, slipping between her slick inner lips. Instinctively she grabbed the thick curve of his shoulders and held on tight. He delved into her slowly while he caressed and suckled, driving her into a fine erotic madness. She rolled her hips against his hand, tangling her fingers into his thick, curly hair and holding him close as he suckled her taut nipples.

Delicious as it was, though, it wasn't enough. She craved his thrusts, hungered to feel him drive into her. The pressure of that need built and built until she moaned, "God, Reece—now!"

He lifted his head and looked down at her, his eyes burning. "Not yet," he said hoarsely. "I want you hotter than this."

She gasped out a strangled laugh. "I'm not sure I'd survive being hotter than this!"

"Let's find out." He pushed up onto his hands and knees and moved down her body to settle between her thighs. Catching her behind her knees, he lifted her legs and spread her wide.

Licking her dry lips, Erin propped herself up on her elbows to watch as Champion parted her lips with two fingers. He tilted his head, studying her wet flesh. "You're so pretty here," he said softly. He inhaled, his eyes closing slowly. She saw him swallow. "It's been a very long time since I've had a woman like you."

She laughed uncomfortably, instinctively rejecting the idea. It had far too much power. "That's kind, Champion, but you've probably got women throwing themselves at you everywhere you go."

His eyes opened as he looked up at her over the length of her naked body, his gaze going fierce and narrow. She realized he didn't like having his word questioned. "Not like you."

Eyes fixed on hers, he lowered his head. Erin found herself holding her breath.

The first pass of his tongue brought her arching off the comforter with a gasp. Over it, she could hear his groan of pleasure. As if the taste had snapped some fragile hold he'd had on control, he began devouring her, tonguing her creaming flesh, suckling her clit until she writhed. Desperate to give him everything, she lifted her legs, catching them behind the knee and spreading them wide. He growled a rough sound of approval and reached up around her body to find her breasts. As he licked, he squeezed and rolled her hard nipples, spurring her pleasure into a plunging gallop.

The climax took her by surprise. She gasped at the first explosion of searing delight, but it kept right on pulsing, consuming her entire nervous system with fire. Mindless, frenzied, she let go of her legs and threaded her fingers through his silken hair, holding on for dear life.

Reece savored Erin's cry of pleasure as he lapped her cream like a greedy cat. The salty taste seemed to bypass his brain and wrap around his cock. The roots of his fangs throbbed.

When she finally went limp and stunned in the aftermath of orgasm, he rose to his knees and reached into his jacket, lying discarded by the quilt. He pulled out one of his condoms, tore the packet open with his teeth, and jerked the button of his fly open.

Freeing himself, he sheathed his aching erection with hands that shook. Magekind neither carried disease nor caught it, but he was damned if he'd expose her to his sperm. Though it never took less than three unprotected encounters to turn a Latent, it was always possible another vampire had left her Gift primed for somebody else's climax. And having the little Latent go Maja under him was one surprise he really didn't need.

She stirred, her eyes sliding reluctantly open. They widened deliciously at the sight of his condom-covered shaft jutting at her, hard and eager.

With a dark smile of anticipation, he mantled her soft, dazed body with his own.

THREE

Reece caught his breath in anticipation as he slid his cock through her lips, found her slick opening. Throttling the need to simply impale her in one hard thrust, he slowly slid inside, savoring the way her tight, wet flesh gripped his shaft.

She arched under him. "Champion!"

"God, you're slick. And snug. And . . ." He lost the rest of the sentence in the sheer glory of her. He lowered himself until her sleek, naked body was crushed against his. Her legs wound around his hips as he braced himself on his elbows and began to pump. Looking down into her eyes, he watched her pleasure build with every slow thrust.

This was going to be a long, long ride.

* * *

God, he was so damn big. Erin whimpered as Champion's thick shaft slid out of her in a long silken glide, only to pump inside again. She threaded her arms around him and held on tight, digging her nails into his satin skin. The muscles of his back felt like slabs of marble under her hands. She inhaled, breathing in his exotic scent, so different from any other man she'd ever known. There was a hint of musk beneath the tang of sweat, something that struck her as intensely erotic. Hungering for him, half crazed by the pleasure, she lifted her head and sought his mouth.

He kissed her back with a ravenous intensity, tongue thrusting deep even as he drove into her again and again, his hips slapping against hers. It struck her dimly that one of his corner teeth seemed longer than it should be, but she couldn't hold on to the thought in the face of the sensual storm he'd unleashed. She could feel another climax building like a storm on the horizon, the pressure deep and full inside her, growing with every lunging thrust.

So close. So . . .

She came again, screaming into his mouth. Maddened, he released her soft lips and buried his face in the curve of her jaw, lunging harder.

Her pulse banged against his lips, thundered in his ears. Goaded, he sank his fangs deep. She made a soft, startled sound, then screamed again as if the little pain had intensified the pleasure, spurring it higher.

Reece scarcely heard as her blood flooded his mouth with that hot blaze he associated with Latents, like a shot of straight whiskey rolling over his tongue. He swallowed, careful not to drink too much, too fast. He didn't want her to black out.

Still feeding, he rolled over with her until she was spread over his body, impaled on his thrusting cock, his fangs in her throat. He wrapped one fist in her hair and caught her soft butt in the other, holding her still as he took her, intent on spinning the pleasure out, making it last as long as he could.

He knew it would end too soon, and then he'd never see her again. He didn't dare.

Reece knew he could easily become addicted to Erin.

She lay sprawled and dazed across Champion's body as his cock shuttled in and out and he gave her what must be the world's biggest hickey. Somehow the slight, stinging pain made the pleasure that much greater. Her third orgasm of the night rolled over her in a lazy wave. Erin gasped. Champion arched and stiffened, driving to his full length, so deep she cried out yet again.

As she rose up through the glittering waves of pleasure, it occurred to her she was in trouble. And she really ought to care.

They'd parked around the corner.

"You sure this is safe?" Avery asked, shifting in the passenger seat. "What if he feeds on her?"

Parker's smile had an unpleasantly lewd edge. "He probably will, but it won't hurt her even if he does. According to every source we've got on him, he never drinks more than a cup or so from his partners. And none of them has shown any adverse effects."

"Yeah, but I still don't like the idea of just handing her over to him." Avery drummed his fingers on one knee, restless and disturbed. "I've worked with Grayson too long to be comfortable with just letting some undead thing make a meal out of her. She's suffered enough."

The agent snorted. "From what I've read about Champion, I doubt there's any suffering involved. Look, the man is a national hero. According to his dossier, he's spied in every war from the American Revolution to Iraq. He's not a monster."

"So why in the hell are we planning to abduct him? Do you seriously think he's going to want to work for the government after that?"

"If we can figure out a way to make more vampires, it won't matter." Parker's cold, pale eyes lit up with a fanatic's fervor. "We need more agents like Champion, Avery. You should see what he can do. There's a videotape of him punching through a steel door before taking out half a dozen men in thirty seconds, bare-handed. He's a phenomenal undercover agent. Sometimes it seems he can almost read minds, the way he can sense a lie or tell when people know more than they're saying. He speaks a dozen languages so fluently, he can pass for a native damn near anywhere he goes. He—"

"So why the hell are we planning to take our best agent out of service right when we need him most?"

Parker gave him a narrow look. "Because the President has decided the payoff is worth the risk."

"What if the President's wrong?" Avery shook his head. "I know you've heard about the chatter we've been picking up. With these cults killing people all over the country, do we really need to be playing chicken with an intelligence asset like Reece Champion?"

"Yes, because we need more agents like him, and this could get them for us. What if somebody gets lucky and kills him? We need another vampire. Once he's changed Erin, she can produce more for us."

Avery scrubbed a hand through his hair. Too much of this made no sense at all. "Wouldn't it be simpler just to ask him to recruit a few of his toothy friends?"

"He swears there aren't any."

"He's lying. If there's one, there's more."

"Probably, but we can't prove it."

"Walk people in front of a mirror," Avery said. "When you see somebody without a reflection, there's your boy."

"That's a myth. So are most of the other legends about vampires." Parker rubbed his thumb against his lower lip, his expression brooding. "He's got no problem with crosses, holy water, or garlic, either. He sleeps during the day, but I don't think he bursts into flame in sunlight. So . . ."

"But we think if he has sex with Erin, he could change her?"

Parker shrugged. "That's what he's implied. On December twenty-first of last year, to a Corporal Thomas Rysentat. Who reported the conversation to his superiors." As if reciting a report from memory, he quoted, "When I saw Agent Champion turn into a wolf and turn back again with his injuries healed, I told him I wanted to become a vampire. He said, 'You're not my type.' I said, 'So becoming a vampire is a sex thing?' and he said 'yes.' "

"So just on the basis of some kid's testimony, we're going to kidnap a vampire and force him to go to bed with my agent?" Avery grimaced. "Oh, she's going to just love this."

"I suspect the idea will grow on her." Parker smirked. "Champion's got a way with women."

"Assuming he cooperates."

"Oh, he'll cooperate. Once we get him locked up, he won't have a choice."

"Yeah, right." He snorted. "So why have I got this mental image of myself on CNN, saying, 'I'm sorry, Senator, I do not recall.' "

Parker shrugged. "One way or another, Avery, we've both got our orders." Suddenly he lifted his head, an arrested expression crossing his face. "And I think that's my cue."

"What's your cue?" Avery demanded as the FBI agent swung open the driver's door and got out. "Parker, what the hell are you doing?"

Reece cradled Erin in his arms, licking delicately at the small wounds he'd left in her throat. Now that he'd finished drinking from her, healing agents flooded his saliva, giving it a brassy taste. By morning, the marks of his fangs would have faded until she'd probably mistake them for mosquito bites.

He just needed to keep her away from mirrors in the meantime.

She moaned and stirred against him, a limp, warm weight in his arms. He'd taken no more than a cup from her, not enough for her to even notice. Still, he could sense she felt dazed and weak from the intensity of their passion.

So did he.

"Oh, God," Erin groaned softly against his chest. "You're lucky the word hasn't gotten around about you."

He stiffened. "Oh?"

She coiled her arms around him. "Yeah," she said sleepily. "Women would be raping you in the street."

Reece grinned and cuddled her, enjoying the way she lay over him like a sleepy kitten. "Glad you approve, milady."

"Approve? You could say that." She yawned. "You could also say Hurricane Hugo was a storm. It's true, but the term doesn't quite capture the full effect."

He laughed, thinking again how damn much he liked her. Her wit and intelligence were every bit as appealing as that lush little body.

It was a damn shame he'd never see her again.

Maybe he could mention her to the Majae's Council. She'd make a worthy addition to the ranks. And then he could . . .

Suddenly the wind shifted. Reece stiffened at the scent it carried before pushing Erin off him and onto the comforter. Naked, a snarl curling his lips, he sprang to his feet.

"Whoa, there, big guy." A man stepped from the shadows of a hedge. As Reece whirled on him and prepared to leap, he flipped open a badge case. "Steven Parker, FBI."

As Reece stopped short, a tall black man hurried up to join the blond, his expression harried. "Parker, what the hell are you doing?" The hissed whisper carried clearly to Reece's vampire ears.

Parker jerked a thumb at the other man. "Agent James Avery with the Office of Foreign Analysis."

The Outfit. Reece's frown deepened. He'd heard of it. A very small counter-terrorist agency loosely connected to the FBI, specializing in black ops.

But what the hell were they doing here?

Quickly he stooped to pick up his pants, aware that Erin had flipped the comforter over herself and was trying to dress under its concealment. He could almost feel the heat of her furious embarrassment from where he stood. "This isn't a good time, gentleman. What do you want?"

"Just trying to confirm a theory," Parker said, smiling easily as he strolled across the lawn toward them. "Even though you were wearing protection, I could feel the power stirring in Agent Grayson."

"Agent Grayson?" He repeated, and frowned as the second part of the agent's sentence sank in. "What power?"

"Parker!" the black agent hissed.

"Didn't she mention it?" The blond smiled pleasantly. "She's Outfit, too. And a Latent, unless I miss my guess. We thought she might be."

Reece stared at him in shock, his mind working frantically. Jesus, who'd told them about Latents? This was a major security breech. The High Council was going to have a mass stroke.

As he struggled to work through the implications, Erin scrambled to her feet, dressed again in her snug red gown. Fighting with her zipper, she snapped, "Avery, who the hell is this guy? What are you doing here?"

Parker smiled at her pleasantly, clapping a hand on the big man's shoulder as he reached into his lapel with one hand. "Actually, he's getting ready to die."

Before even Reece could react, the blond jerked out a knife and plunged it between his partner's ribs. Avery choked out a gasp, his eyes going wide. He toppled.

Erin's scream rang across the garden. "Avery!"

Reece didn't look back as he shot toward the two like an arrow from a bow, intent on taking Parker down. He'd crossed the twenty feet separating them and was reaching for the blond when the agent threw up both hands.

Reece glimpsed a violent flash of manifesting magic just before he slammed into an invisible wall. The impact drove the air from his lungs. Before he could suck in another breath, something closed around his body and snatched him off his feet.

"What the hell?" He struggled to free himself, but the spell held him suspended like an ant in honey. Instinctively he started to look around for the Maja who'd caught him.

And glimpsed Parker's hands. Hands surrounded by a familiar magical nimbus.

Impossible! Reece thought, shocked. *Men don't become Majae.*

Then he remembered his conversation with Lance and Grace earlier in the night: the Council's conviction that the Death Cultists were using magic without a Maja's involvement.

Oh, hell, Reece thought as the bottom dropped out of his stomach. *This isn't good.*

The grin on Parker's face was wide and white and not entirely sane. "God, what a buzz. I get a power spike from any killing, but nothing gives quite the same charge as murdering somebody who trusts you. I feel like I could light up Atlanta."

"Geirolf!" Erin spat furiously. "It's you, isn't it, you son of a bitch?"

Reece twisted around in the spell until he was able to catch a glimpse of her from the corner of one eye. She hovered three feet off the ground, caught in the same kind of mystical power field that had trapped him.

Her expression was contorted with rage as she sneered, "So you've given up the demon scam in favor of passing yourself off as FBI?"

Parker laughed. "Actually, I'm not Geirolf. Though I'm flattered you'd think I was. And he's not a demon." His eyes glinted. "He's a god."

"You're also not FBI," Reece growled. "What the hell are you?"

"Oh, to the contrary, I'm definitely FBI," Parker said, strolling closer. "In fact, I work for Mike Richards."

Reece's counterintelligence contact. The light dawned. "You're the mole."

"And you would have made me the minute you laid eyes on me in Mike's office," Parker agreed cheerfully. He looked at Erin. "Almost as fast as they made *you* when you joined Death's Sabbat. The disguise was good, baby, but you can't fool a god."

"Geirolf's not a god," Erin gritted, her voice rough with exertion as she fought to escape the spell. "He's a con artist with a collection of hallucinogens."

Parker sneered. "You think a hallucination's holding you three feet off the ground? Idiot. It's *magic*. Mageverse physics manifesting itself in our universe—with a little starter fuel provided by your dead friend's life force." He stepped closer to her, looking up into her face. "And you still don't believe me. Then again, you didn't even recognize a vampire when he had his dick in your twat and his fangs in your throat." He gave her a contemptuous smile. "So much for that keen, investigative intellect."

Erin's heart pounded in long, jarring beats. It was happening again. Just like the night David died. Things that could not possibly be were happening again, and another man was dead.

All the shrinks had sworn she'd been under the influence of some kind of hallucinogen, but this felt no more like a delusion than that night had.

But it must be. Because if it wasn't . . .

Erin sneered at Parker, even as her instincts shrieked all this was horribly, impossibly real. "So now you want me to believe Reece Champion is a vampire. Yeah, right. Do you seriously think you can sucker me with this bullshit?" Her mouth was dry as sand. "If you're going to kill me, get it over with and quit insulting my intelligence." She almost wished he would. Better to die than discover it had all been real.

Better to die than learn a demon really had killed the man she loved.

"We have no intention of killing you, sweetheart." Parker's grin took on a chilling cast. "At least, not until Count 007 over there has had his fun. But I think I'll let my master explain it to you."

He took a step back and closed his eyes. Again, the mysterious nimbus appeared around his hands, snapping and fizzling like a Fourth of July sparkler.

Even frustrated, furious, and terrified, Erin felt a niggle of curiosity. How was he *doing* that?

As she watched, the FBI mole lifted both hands, rising onto his toes as he threw his head back, his face contorting with effort.

"I wonder what it is about working magic that gives them all that melodramatic streak?" Champion muttered. "I've never met a Maja yet that could resist striking a pose."

What the hell's a Maja? Erin thought.

Before she could ask, a rolling crack of thunder made her jump in her invisible bonds. A blast of wind blew into her face, hot and smelling faintly of sulfur.

And a man simply popped into existence inches from her nose. She jolted, swallowing a scream.

"Why, hello there, Erin." He grinned at her, his smile wide and white, his eyes as pale as a wolf's—and just as feral. His hair fell in a gleaming black curtain around his T-shirt–clad shoulders, and black jeans hugged his thighs.

She might have found him attractive if she hadn't seen him kill David.

"Geirolf," Erin spat. "You sick fuck. Still scamming the suckers with the demon act?" God, please let it be a scam. It couldn't be real.

He laughed, a deep, sensual boom. "Darling, it's not an

act." Geirolf turned away from her, strolling up to Champion as he hung in midair, his big body straining as he fought to escape whatever it was that held them.

No. This isn't happening, she told herself desperately. There was no magical forcefield holding them trapped and levitating. Somehow Parker had drugged them without their knowledge, with something that made them both susceptible to suggestion. Then the magician hit them up with a couple of stage tricks while they were too out of it to question what was happening. It was the same scam the shrinks swore he'd pulled on Erin and David a year ago, with such fatal results.

But why? That was the one thing the psychologists had never been able to explain. What was the point? Why not just shoot them and get it over with?

"So, you're one of Merlin's vampires," Geirolf said, looking up at Reece. "He always was a whimsical bastard."

"Vampires?" Erin interrupted. It was the same line of trash Parker had used. She made herself sneer. "Funny—I didn't notice any bat wings."

Parker sneered back. "You really need to wake up and smell the Bloody Marys, sweetheart. Or hadn't you noticed the fang marks in your throat?"

Fang marks? She licked her lips, suddenly aware of the faint ache and pulse in her neck. There was something sticky on her skin, something that felt almost like . . .

No. It was whatever they'd used to make her hallucinate all this. There was no such thing as vampires.

Or demons.

Suddenly she realized Geirolf was watching her with a fixed and ugly gleam. "Oh," he said softly, "this is going to be such fun. I'm going to enjoy blowing all your cool little assumptions all to hell and back."

"Who *are* you?" Champion demanded impatiently. "What's this all about?"

"Geirolf here is a con man and a murderer," Erin told him, glaring at their captors. "He uses drugs to make his victims more susceptible to his parlor tricks, then he gets them to commit his crimes for him. Primarily murder."

"She thinks I'm Charles Manson," Geirolf told Champion, his tone confidential. "I'd be offended if it weren't so damn funny."

"I repeat," Champion said steadily. "What are you?"

"I'd think that would be obvious, vampire. I'm a god."

"Of course you are," Champion said, without a flicker of emotion.

Geirolf sighed and said to Parker, "It's so sad to be forgotten."

"I could kill them now if you want," Parker said, turning a glittering stare on Erin.

She curled a lip at him despite the chilling hunger in his eyes. Damned if she'd show these assholes fear. No matter what they were.

"No, boy, they're perfect." Geirolf started walking around Champion, looking up at him in calculation. "A Latent and the young vampire who could transform her—all magical potential, yet without enough real power yet to be a pain in my ass." He grinned. "The perfect blood sacrifice."

Oh, hell.

Reece stared at the being who stalked around him. Whatever Geirolf and his flunky were, they weren't Magekind. And he had an ugly feeling they weren't mad, either, despite all the babbling about gods and demons.

But they were powerful as hell, and they worked death magic—using the energy released in a murder as a conduit to Mageverse energies.

An act strictly forbidden to Magekind.

"What sort of spell are we talking about here?" Reece asked, trying to sound as if he didn't give a damn.

Geirolf grinned. "You honestly think I'll tell you?"

"Unless I miss my guess, you feed on terror. Death, too, of

course, but definitely terror. So yeah, you'll tell me, if only to scare the hell out of us."

The grin widened. Every tooth in the demon's head was pointed. "You're right."

"So what exactly does this spell do?"

"Kill every last vampire and witch in the Mageverse."

Reece stared, feeling all the blood drain from his face. "That's not possible. Even if you sacrificed us both, the power it would take would be immense."

"Well, yes," the demon said, then spread his hands. "But after all, I'm not your average witch."

"But why?"

The thing bared those razor teeth. "You're in the way."

"Of what?" Reece demanded.

"Of the rebirth of paradise." The demon clasped his hands behind his back and looked up at the stars. "Or hell, I suppose. Depends on your point of view."

"What are you talking about, you lunatic?" Erin snapped.

He glanced at her. "I'm going to bring back the good old days when my people came to this rock. Humans called us names like Set and Baal then, and a hundred others they've forgotten now." His razored smile was chilling. "I'm going to remind them of every single one."

Each time Reece took a step, this mess just got deeper. "You passed yourself off as a god."

Geirolf shrugged. "Or a devil. Depended on my mood. Either way, they gave us sacrifices. Blood, pain, and all the life force we could drink." His expression hardened. "Then Merlin, Nimue, and the rest of their sanctimonious kind arrived to declare war on us all."

Reece smiled coldly as Geirolf's account at last began to make sense. "The Fae were more powerful than you."

The demon snarled. "They drove my people from this world and set up dimensional wards to keep us away. But Merlin particularly hated me because I'd almost managed to wipe them all out. He was afraid to leave me free, afraid I'd find a way to destroy the wards."

"It was never smart to piss off Merlin."

"Merlin?" Erin said. "As in the Round Table?"

The demon ignored her. "He sealed me in a cell on Mageverse Earth. It provided for my every physical need—except freedom. And it was impervious to magic. Without sacrifices, I grew weak. So weak, it took me a millennia and a half just to chip out a chink big enough to send a dream through."

"And yet, you're back."

Geirolf shrugged. "I found Gary Evans, who had just enough talent to see me in his dreams. After I convinced him to sacrifice a dozen or so coeds so I could feed on their deaths, I managed to escape."

"He used drugs and tricks to make Evans believe he was a god," Erin interrupted. Reece craned his neck so he could look back at the bitter fury on her face. "And Gary, the sick fuck, was happy to believe him."

"Until our luscious Erin and her partner blew poor Gary's head off in the middle of a sacrifice," the demon added. "Fortunately that last death gave me just enough power to break free. I've been rebuilding my strength ever since."

Erin jerked at her invisible bonds. "And suckering gullible cultists into committing new crimes."

"I can hardly commit my own," Geirolf said. "Using too much magic would attract Majae attention, and I don't care to have a few thousand pissed-off vampires and witches banging at my door." He smiled. "Not just yet, anyway."

"I can see how that would be inconvenient," Reece said.

"Indeed. So you've all got to go. Luckily, I've got the perfect spell. But to make it work, I need a Magekind couple as a sacrifice."

"But the minute you captured a Maja, she'd send a message to the rest."

"And I'd be back where I started," Geirolf agreed. "But if I had a vampire and one newly turned Maja who didn't quite know how to handle her powers yet . . . Now, *that* would work."

"Good plan. Except, much as it grieves me to point out, you're assuming I'm going to cooperate." Reece bared his teeth savagely. "And I'm not."

The demon smiled. "Well, not willingly, anyway. Then, of course, there's the problem of that magical energy burst when a Maja Turns."

"Oh, take a chance."

"And have the entire Round Table and a coven of witches down around my horns? I don't think so. No, what's needed is a magic-tight cage that would keep the Majae's Court from detecting the girl's Change. Luckily, I've got one."

Reece's heart sank. "The cell Merlin locked you up in."

"Exactly. I did some damage to it, but it should still hold you and your pretty girlfriend." Geirolf shrugged. "Of course, I won't be able to sense when she Turns, so I'll have to check in periodically. But once I have, and once you're dead . . ."

Reece swore silently. With the Magekind eliminated, Geirolf could set himself up as a god, tormenting and killing until he plunged the planet into another Dark Age.

"Oooh, yesss," the demon purred. "You know, it isn't all that easy to scare the hell out of a vampire. And I just have." His laughter rolled, reverberating like thunder. "Fear's got the most delicious taste. Not quite as good as death, but close. Makes a good appetizer."

"Fuck you," Reece growled.

The demon smirked. "No, fuck her. Repeatedly."

Before Reece could flinch back, Geirolf leaned forward and pressed a kiss to his forehead. Reece felt the hot energy of a spell slice into his brain. He cursed.

The demon smiled. "Bye-bye."

Then the world went white.

FOUR

One minute Erin was struggling in the thick, viscous grip of that invisible something Parker had somehow created. The next, light exploded all around her.

And she was falling.

She barely had time to register the plummeting sensation before she hit hard, right on her ass. Rolling, she slapped the floor as she'd been taught in hand-to-hand combat class, turning a fall that might have otherwise ended with broken bones into one that did nothing more than bruise her behind.

For a moment she lay still, catching her breath and getting her bearings as she stared up at the vaulted stone ceiling over her head.

What the hell had happened to the sky?

A minute ago they'd been in Champion's garden, listening to Geirolf spin his fairy tales. But where were they now?

Erin sat up slowly, in honor of both her aching behind and the general dubiousness of the entire situation.

She was sitting in the middle of a huge stone room straight out of The History Channel. The place looked just like a castle chamber, complete with rich tapestries on the walls interspersed with huge Gothic glass windows.

The bed went along with the general medieval motif—a massive dark affair piled with what looked like furs and surrounded on two sides by red velvet hangings embroidered with gold thread. There was a table and a couple of wooden benches, and an anachronism—some kind of small pool, maybe ten feet long and five feet wide, that looked vaguely like a Roman bath.

Over by the opposite wall stood Champion, wearing an expression of deep disgust on his face. In place of the tuxedo trousers he'd been wearing a few minutes before, he was dressed in a pair of loose silk pajama bottoms and a long silk robe, both in pure, unrelieved black.

He looked down at himself and curled his lip. "What am I, Hugh Hefner? Tacky, Geirolf. Very tacky." Looking up, he spotted Erin watching him warily. He lifted a brow, a flash of male interest in his eyes. "I guess we should count ourselves lucky your outfit doesn't have nipple cutouts."

Erin glanced down. And swore.

Her red cocktail dress had somehow become a white satin Merry Widow that cinched her waist and lifted her full breasts until they damn near overflowed the low-cut bodice. Below that, she wore a tiny white lace thong and lace stockings. On her feet were a pair of platform shoes with three-inch soles and six-inch heels. "What's lucky is that I didn't break my neck when I fell," she growled, glowering at the shoes.

Assuming they were even real.

Real or not, though, the shoes were coming off. She wouldn't be able to run in them, much less fight. And the chances were good she'd probably end up doing one or the other before the night was over.

Erin slipped the platforms off, as Champion prowled the

room, running his hands over the stone walls. "Great. Just great," he snarled as she tossed the shoes into a corner.

"What?" she asked warily as she scanned the chamber. Yep, everything was the same as it had been a minute ago— table, Roman bath, canopied bed piled with furs. None of it made a damn bit of sense, but it was all still there.

"There's no door," Champion announced.

"What do you mean, there's no door? There's got to be a door."

But he was right. There were plenty of arched, Gothic-looking windows, but there was no door at all. "How did they get us in here?"

He shot her a look. "Magic, sweetheart."

Her stomach lurched. "Reece, no matter what this looks like, it isn't really magic. They gave us some kind of drugs to make us susceptible to suggestion, and Geirolf threw in some smoke and mirrors. We hallucinated the rest. My guess is we passed out, and they brought us here. Wherever 'here' is."

"Erin . . ." he began.

"Champion, trust me. He did the same thing to me once before. It's how he killed my partner." Frowning, she crossed to the nearest window and tapped on the thick glass. It certainly seemed solid. But though she examined it closely and prodded every inch of it, she couldn't find a latch, and it didn't swing open. "Maybe we could break it."

Reece started to speak, then shrugged. "I doubt it, but it's worth a try." He took several steps back, gathered his big body, and sprinted toward another of the windows.

"Champion, what—?"

He leaped up like Jackie Chan to slam feet-first into the glass. The window bonged, bell-like, as he bounced off and skidded halfway across the room on his back. "Ow."

He rolled to his feet before she reached him. "You okay?" she asked, studying his face in concern.

He rubbed one thigh with a grimace. "Damn near broke my legs. Figured that wasn't going to work, but I had to try. If this place really held Geirolf for sixteen hundred years, we're not going to break out of it with muscle."

She shook her head. "Reece . . ."

"Erin, it's not a hallucination. This is real."

She felt sick, but shook it off with a scornful laugh. "So, you're saying, what? This Geirolf guy really is some kind of immortal demon who's locked us up in a magic cell?"

"That's about the size of it." He moved to the table and looked over the selection of dishes that sat on the linen table-cloth. As he poured something from a pitcher into a pair of jeweled goblets, he eyed her. "Erin, I know this is tough to accept. Particularly for somebody from this century. Everything you've ever been taught tells you there's no such thing as demons. But think about it—does any of this feel like a hallucination to you?"

"No," she admitted. "Everything seems solid. Real. And I don't feel drugged." True, there had been the weird logic and location jumps, first when she was caught in that "spell" of Parker's, next when she was transported here. Yet even that hadn't been precisely dreamlike, either. And—she rubbed her backside absently—the ache in her butt certainly felt real.

Reece strolled over to her, holding the goblet in one big, tanned hand. He took a sip of it, watching her over the rim. He grimaced and extended it to her. "It's a very nice Dom Perignon. You'll like it."

Erin hesitated before accepting the thick pewter cup. "So why did you make a face?" She sniffed the contents cautiously and took a sip. It tasted real.

Champion shrugged. "I was hoping for blood, but I guess that was too much to expect."

Erin choked on her mouthful of champagne. Suddenly she remembered Parker's sneer: *You didn't even recognize a vampire when he had his dick in your twat and his fangs in your throat.* She felt again the ache and burn in her throat. Reaching up with one hand, she explored the injury.

Holes. In her neck.

He'd bitten her.

Champion met her horrified gaze steadily, his green eyes cool. "Yeah, I'm a vampire."

"A vampire." She'd slept with him, and he'd bitten her. Drunk her blood.

He sighed. "I'm not crazy, Erin."

She gave him her best impassive-cop face. "I never said you were."

"This is real, Erin," he told her steadily. "Geirolf really is a demon, and I'm a vampire, and Parker is some kind of necromancer. And you and I really are trapped in a cell in the Mageverse." Champion opened his mouth and peeled his lips back from his teeth. For about half a second, they all looked perfectly white, straight, and human. True, two of them looked a little sharper than normal, but . . .

Then the gums seemed to swell around those sharp canines, and the two teeth visibly lengthened, extending down from his jaw. Becoming fangs.

Erin stepped backward as the universe seemed to reel. "Don't."

"You know this is happening. And you're too much a professional not to deal with it." Tiny fireworks exploded in Champion's eyes, a minuscule explosion of sparks shooting across the green. And he disappeared.

In his place, a huge black timber wolf sat on its haunches looking up at her. Its eyes were the same purely human green as Champion's.

Erin leaped back from the animal with a startled yelp. She glanced wildly around the room, but Champion had vanished. Replaced by the wolf.

She looked down at the big beast and felt herself begin to shake. "You don't understand. You don't know what this means."

Sparks exploded in those green eyes, and it was Champion

again. She almost saw the moment when wolf became man. He stepped closer. "So explain it to me."

For just a moment, she seriously considered hitting him. Then she shook off the impulse. She was a professional. And if she was going to get out of this alive, she had to work with him. Because vampire or not, he seemed to know what was going on. "That *thing* . . . That murdering thing killed my partner! It was all real, no matter what the shrinks said. All of it. Goddamnit." She squeezed her eyes shut. She was damned if she'd cry.

Then she opened them again, squared her shoulders, and told him the story.

July 5, 2003

The silence in the car had the leaden quality of tension and guilt. Erin looked over at David Jennings for the fifth time in the past two minutes. She sighed. He still wore that grim expression, and his fingers gripped the wheel instead of riding it easily with their usually skilled insouciance. "David—"

"You think the profiler's right, and this guy is trying to work some kind of magic spell?" He snorted. "Like the locals need another reason to lose their fuckin' minds over these killings. God help us when the reporters get that little tidbit. They'll start swarming like piranha."

"I don't think piranha actually swarm. David, about last night—"

In the dim blue light from the dashboard, she saw a muscle jump in his jaw. "Yeah. Look, I'm sorry about all that. If you're gonna report me, I don't blame you. I went too far."

"I'm not going to report you," Erin said impatiently. "For God's sake, you'd had a little too much to drink." They'd celebrated the Fourth by taking a twelve-pack back to their motel. While the town put on a fireworks display over the trees, they'd sat on the balcony outside his room and worked their way through several beers.

"That only makes it worse, Erin. One way or another, I was way out of line."

"Actually, you weren't." Erin remembered the heat of his mouth when he'd suddenly pulled her down on his lap for a kiss that had made her toes curl. "Look, the only reason I said no is because I knew you'd react like this in the morning. For God's sake, we've been working together for two years, and we're both single and reasonably young. It's only natural that we start caring about each other."

"It may be natural," David said grimly, "but it's also completely against regulations."

She thought about his hand cupping her breast through the thin fabric of her T-shirt. "You know what? I don't care. We've been ignoring this thing like the elephant in the living room for two years, and I'm getting sick of it."

He shot her a look. For just an instant she saw naked need in his eyes. Then he glanced quickly away. "Maybe, but this isn't the time. We're in the middle of a case. After we catch this guy, we can talk about it."

Yes! To hide the triumph in her eyes, Erin turned to stare out the window at the moonlit fields flashing by the car. She'd finally gotten him to admit it. For a man as relentlessly by the book as David, that was a major hurdle.

Of course, getting him to go any further would take patience, but . . .

A dilapidated barn stood in the moonlight about fifty feet from the road. A strange, faint glow shone from its windows. Firelight. Or candles? Erin felt every hair on her forearms rise. "Stop the car."

"Oh, hell. You getting another one of your premonitions?"

"Yeah." It felt as if she'd been dumped in dry ice. David whipped the car onto the shoulder and reached into his jacket for his cell phone to call the locals. He'd long since learned not to question her hunches. She opened the car door, aware of his deep voice relaying their location to the county dispatcher.

Standard procedure was to wait for backup, but Erin knew

in her gut that somebody would be dead long before help arrived. They had to move *now*.

She jumped the ditch and started across the weedy field in long strides, her gun drawn, her gut twisted in a knot, her mouth dry. David followed at her heels like a brawny shadow, his carrot red hair shining gently in the moonlight.

They both knew this was likely to get sticky. They had no probable cause; if this was the guy, they'd have a hell of a time hanging on to him. But saving a life came first.

Never mind that Erin had no idea how she knew one was even at stake.

The wind shifted, bringing her a whiff of something that made her gag: the sickly smell of rotting meat and blood and human waste. And something else. A sound.

"Well," David muttered, "something's died around here. And it was sure as hell bigger than a barn rat."

"Shhh," Erin whispered, and strained to catch whatever it was she'd just heard.

There it was again. A voice, rising and falling on the wind. "Sounds like chanting."

"Just what I was thinking," she murmured as she tried to make out the words the male voice was reciting. "Could be our boy."

The two agents eased toward the barn together, moving as fast and silently as they dared through the thick weeds. Reaching the rough wooden building, they flattened their backs against the wall beside the door and went still, listening.

David's eyes flashed toward her, and she knew he'd heard the same thing she had.

Under the chanting, a woman's muffled voice sobbed in terror.

Suddenly Erin could make out the man's words. She immediately wished she couldn't. "Dread Geirolf, Lord of Darkness and Death, accept the sacrifice of this unworthy whore that her unclean life might feed and—"

"Do wrap it up, boy. All this foreplay is getting tedious."

Erin glanced sharply at her partner. She could tell by David's startled expression that he'd picked up the voice, too. Yet she hadn't heard it with her ears. Instead it seemed to reverberate in her mind, in her very bones, as though, like the subsonic rumble of a building earthquake, it was too deep for human ears.

She wondered if it gave David the same gut-level sense of sickening horror it did her.

Suppressing her fear, Erin ducked down and edged her neck out until she could look around the doorframe. At first she saw only dark, indistinguishable shapes that might have been farm equipment. She craned farther. There. A dim glow of candlelight.

In the center of the dirt floor, a pentagram was laid out in kindergarten glitter, thick candles burning at each of its points. In the middle of the roughly drawn star, a pair of wooden crates and a board formed a makeshift altar. On top of it lay a young woman, naked and bound, a gag stuffed in her mouth.

A man stood over her, dressed in a cheap blue polyester robe sewn with metallic moons and stars. It looked like something you'd buy at Halloween.

But the foot-long butcher knife he held over the woman's chest was no toy.

Something moved in the darkness, drawing her eye. Erin glanced toward it.

A wavering, glowing *thing* floated in the shadows just beyond the pentagram. All she could make out was an impression of horns and bulk and savage greed in eyes that were not human.

Every instinct she had screamed *Evil!*

A big hand locked into her collar and jerked her back. Erin would have screamed, but luckily terror had frozen her vocal cords just long enough for her to realize she was looking into her partner's face.

David frowned down at her impatiently and mouthed, "How many?"

Erin hesitated, not even sure how to answer that question. Finally she held up two fingers and mouthed, "They've got a hostage." No time to explain more, even if she could think of a way to describe what she'd seen. He nodded and jerked a thumb at the door, then moved around in front of her, taking the point as he always insisted on doing.

Erin gathered herself. All she wanted to do was run as far from the barn and its inexplicable contents as she could, but that girl was about to die. Nothing else mattered—not even the glowing thing she hadn't quite seen.

Together, they charged through the door as David bellowed, "Freeze! FBI!"

The robed man swore viciously and drew the knife back to stab his captive, who shrieked behind her gag.

Erin fired, her gun roaring at the same time as David's.

The would-be killer staggered, blood pouring from two wounds, one in the center of his chest, the other just above his eyebrows. He crumpled.

A triumphant roar filled the room as the glowing thing suddenly became solid. It dropped to the dirt floor with a thump, as though the pull of gravity had abruptly kicked in. *"That wasn't exactly the death I had in mind, but it will do."*

"What the fuck!" David gasped. He aimed his weapon at it. Erin automatically followed suit. She fired twice, the big gun bucking in her hands, gunsmoke filling her mouth and nose.

Light flared. The thing reached out a clawed hand and plucked something from the air. With a jolt, Erin realized it was a bullet. A second projectile hovered nearby, as if the creature had stopped both in flight.

"Well now, that's interesting," the thing said. *"How did you manage to do that?"*

Erin felt her guts turn to water. It had to be seven feet tall at least, its horns almost brushing the wooden roof beams as it walked toward her on its two cloven hooves. Her lips pulled back from her teeth as her finger tightened convulsively on the trigger. The big nine-millimeter roared again and again as she unloaded the rest of the clip.

Every single bullet stopped in the air. The thing, moving toward her, brushed them aside like a beaded curtain. The slugs dropped to the ground and bounced on the hard-packed dirt.

"Erin!" She barely recognized David's voice as it spiraled into a high note of panic she'd never heard before. She dared a quick look at her partner. He stood still, his eyes wide, his gun still pointed at the spot where the thing had been. "What's it doing to me? I can't move!"

"*Of course not,*" the thing said. Her eyes watered at the brimstone in its breath. "*I don't want you to.*" To Erin it added, "*And you shouldn't be able to, either.*"

She shrank back as it leaned toward her and sniffed delicately. "*You smell of magic, girl. One of Merlin's get, I suppose. Not turned yet, luckily—just enough Latent ability to be resistant. And my power is still too reduced to overcome your will.*" It shrugged. "*I'll just have to make the best of it.*"

Erin tried to stiffen her shaking knees and called on every bit of childhood lore she could remember. Hell, it was worth a try. "I order you to leave, Satan, in the name of Jesus Christ the Lord!"

The thing stared at her in astonishment, then threw back its horned head and laughed. "*Oh, I'm not your devil. Though I suppose you can be forgiven for making that mistake, given my current guise.*"

Light flashed. Suddenly the thing was simply a man in an elegant black suit. She would have thought him human if it hadn't been for the red eyes. "I actually prefer this one, but the other is better for impressing mortals," he said, his voice perfectly ordinary now. Shrugging, he turned toward her partner. "David, dear boy, I find myself in a difficult situation. My pawn's death enabled me to enter this universe, but I'm still weak and terribly hungry. I need another couple of sacrifices, and I need one of you to make them. Since your partner is resistant to my influence, it will have to be you. Shoot the naked blonde, would you?"

"Fuck yo—" David began, then broke off with a gasp of horror as he pivoted mechanically to point his Glock at the woman lying bound on the crates. She stared up at him in terror. "Shit. Oh, shit. Stop it!"

"David!" The thing, whatever it was, was doing something to him. Hastily shoving her own gun into her shoulder holster, Erin grabbed for his wrists. She tried to knock his weapon up, but it was like hitting a steel beam. Desperately she fought to pry the Glock from his hands, but his fingers seemed fused to the grip.

"On second thought, why don't you kill your partner first," the demon suggested.

"No!" David yelled, even as he clamped one hand over her shoulder with a grip like a vise and jammed the muzzle of the gun against the center of her chest. Stunned, Erin looked up into his panic-filled eyes as her blood turned to ice. "Erin, Jesus Christ!"

She tried to jerk away, but he was so damn strong. Helplessly she writhed in his grip, staring into his white-rimmed eyes. "David, let me go!" As she fought, every panting breath carried the smell of her partner's Brut aftershave.

And his fear.

"Shoot me!" he gasped. "Erin, you've gotta—"

"Oh," the demon said softly. "All that terror and doomed love! Delicious."

A last-ditch idea hit her. Erin wrapped both hands more tightly around the gun and kicked out. Hooking her foot behind his left ankle, she shoved him over, using the momentum of their falling bodies to finally force the gun upward and clear of her body.

But instead of stiff-arming the weapon above his head, as she'd expected, David bent his arm, shoving it directly under his own chin.

Erin screamed, "No!"

"Pull the trigger," the demon said.

The deep, full throated roar of the Glock seemed to stop the world on its axis.

She dimly heard the demon's voice over the ringing in her ears. "Well, that wasn't at all what I had in mind. And I still need another death." He sighed in disgust. "I suppose I'll just have to find another dupe."

Erin felt his cold presence vanish, but she didn't look around. She was still staring into her partner's empty, fixed gaze as she lay sprawled across him.

In the distance, sirens wailed—their backup finally arriving. Too late.

FIVE

"That pretty well finished my career in the FBI," Erin told Champion as she looked out the window at the moonlit landscape beyond it.

"They thought you were involved." He stood to one side, his eyes fixed on her profile.

"Yeah." There was a knot of tension in her shoulders. She tilted back her head and rubbed absently at it, but it continued to ache. "I damn near got charged with it. They didn't believe me when I told them what happened. Besides, I had gunpowder residue and David's blood on my hands and face."

"They thought you'd killed him in some kind of struggle." He was quick, she'd give him that.

Erin nodded. "Fortunately the hostage confirmed he'd shot

himself, but even then, the brass wondered if the two of us were collaborating for some unknown reason. If we hadn't passed polygraph tests . . ."

"But they still didn't like your story."

"No. They suspended me pending an investigation." She sighed and went on rubbing, but the knotted muscle refused to relax. "Finally some shrink suggested the killer—his name was Gary Evans—had exposed us all to some kind of airborne drug that had made us all hallucinate. David had an adverse reaction to whatever it was and killed himself." Erin shrugged. "That made more sense than the alternative, so I tried to believe it. But even then, I guess I always knew it had all been real."

"But your career was over," Champion said, like a man who knew exactly how the system worked.

"I'd been tainted," she agreed. "They put me on administrative duty while the brass tried to figure out what to do with me. Not that I really cared. I kept seeing David's death in my nightmares. Every night. Every single fucking night." She dug in her fingers and pressed.

Suddenly a hand brushed hers aside. "Let me do that." Reece went to work on the knot with strong fingers.

Erin tensed, wondering if he was going to bite her.

Hell with it. If he did, he'd just put her out of her misery. She relaxed, and the ache began to ease. "Even during the day I thought about what had happened, trying to make sense of it. I kept thinking there had to have been a moment when I could have prevented the whole chain of events. If I could just figure out what it was . . ." She sighed. "It turned into an obsession. Before long, I couldn't even eat, let alone sleep."

"Which probably didn't make your superiors feel any better."

Erin laughed shortly. "No, it's safe to say the concept of an armed and suicidally depressed FBI agent did not fill anybody with enthusiasm." She sighed as his long thumbs found the perfect place to press. "You're not really dead, are you?" she asked suddenly. "Or undead. Like those movie vampires."

"No, I'm most definitely alive."

"That's good." Erin rested her forehead against the cool glass, letting him banish the last of the pain. "Jim Avery came to my rescue," she said finally.

"The man Parker killed?"

"Yeah. Back when I first joined the Bureau ten years ago, we were stationed in the same podunk field office in South Carolina, investigating robberies. Kind of like me and David, except Jim trained me."

"That makes for a special bond," Reece observed after a thoughtful pause. "Must have hurt, seeing him killed."

"Yeah." She sighed, remembering the shocked look on Avery's face when Parker stabbed him. "Another partner I couldn't save." Erin shook her head, rejecting the moment of self-pity. "Anyway, after they suspended me, Jim got wind of what had happened. He was trying to recruit agents for the Outfit at the time." She tapped her bunched fist on the glass. "He was a hell of an agent. When the State Department created the Outfit right after 9-11, they picked him to run it because he was so damn good."

"Sounds like quite a man."

"He was." Having conquered one knot, Reece's hands worked farther up her neck to find another. She let her eyes close. "That feels good. So anyway, one night when I was sitting in my apartment obsessing about David, Avery dropped by. He had a six-pack and a bag of takeout Chinese. Somewhere between three beers and a carton of fried rice, he got the whole ungodly story out of me."

"And offered you a job."

"Which I was about to refuse, until he told me about this Georgia-based Satanic cult he was investigating. The members worshiped somebody they called 'Geirolf.' Which was, of course, what Gary Evans called the demon." She fell silent, remembering that conversation.

"I don't know what the fuck this Geirolf is, but he's real. Maybe he does it all with smoke and mirrors like some kind of fucking David Copperfield clone, but he does exist. And he's using his tricks to get people to kill for him. I'm going to stop his ass."

"He asked me if I was interested," Erin said softly. "God, was I interested. I couldn't turn back the clock and prevent David's death, but I could, by God, bring in the asshole who was responsible."

"You went undercover with the cult, even knowing you might encounter Geirolf?" He tilted his head so he could look into her face. "Big risk, even if he was nothing more than the human con man you thought."

"Yeah, but I didn't care. For the first time in three months, I felt alive. I walked into the Hoover Building the next morning and handed in my resignation. Two weeks later I was working with Avery to shut the cult down."

"But Parker said they already knew who you were."

Erin nodded. "Which explains why I made zero headway. So when Avery told me they'd identified the money man behind the deal, I was willing to do whatever it took." She turned to face him.

Champion stared. "You thought *I* was financing the cult? And you went home with me anyway? *Slept* with me?"

She forced herself to meet his incredulous gaze coolly. "I hoped to build a relationship with you I could use as an entrée into the cult."

"My." He rocked back on his heels, brows lifted. "You don't stop at much, do you?"

"Those cultists are killing people, Reece. There's nothing I won't do to stop that." She eyed him a moment before saying abruptly, "But I was a bit surprised by the strength of my . . . attraction to you."

His gaze cooled. "Are you implying something, Erin?"

She considered the best way to handle the topic, torn by her instinct for diplomacy and her need to know what he was capable of. Magically and otherwise. "Vampires are reputed to have certain . . . powers. Especially over women."

"You mean, did I put some kind of spell on you?"

"Did you?"

His cool gaze heated, but his tone remained level. "No. I can't work that kind of magic. And wouldn't, even if I could."

"You can turn yourself into a wolf."

"That's different. My magic works only inside my body. I can change form, I'm damn strong, and I can heal almost any injury not inflicted by a magical weapon, but I can't cast spells. Sexual or otherwise."

Erin snorted. "Don't underestimate yourself."

She saw the anger drain from that intelligent gaze. "Now you're trying to flatter me."

"Not me." She decided to change the subject. "So what else can you do? Can you turn into a bat?"

"No, too different from my body weight. I can't become a mist either, with all due respect to Bram Stoker—which, come to think of it, isn't much. I do a mean mountain lion, though. Tried to do a tiger once, but I don't have the mass. Ended up looking kind of emaciated."

The image—Champion as a skinny, disgruntled tiger—was so silly she had to laugh. "Okay. So. Crosses, holy water, mirrors, and sunlight."

"I'm not a walking corpse, Erin, so the first three don't bother me. As for sunlight, I get really bad sunburn, but I don't burst into flames. I do have to sleep during the day, but not in a coffin. . . ."

Avalon

Grace du Lac tumbled back on the bed as the vampire pinned her with his greater weight. He bared his fangs, his eyes glittering and hot, as he held a pair of iron manacles before her eyes. "Now, wench," he growled. "Now it's time for you to serve my immortal lust!"

Grace grinned. "God, I hope so."

Lance lost his artistic snarl in a laugh. "Come on, baby, work with me here. I played big, bad speeder for you, didn't I?"

"You *are* a big, bad speeder. I should know—I was the cop who pulled you over. It wasn't a stretch for either of us. But do I really look like a helpless Victorian virgin to you?" She spread her arms.

Lance's gaze dropped as he surveyed the body barely hidden by the fine antique lace of her nightrail. The heat in his eyes increased, and he licked his fangs. "Darling, you look like every fantasy I've ever had. Come on, love. For me?"

She rolled her eyes, took a deep breath, and tried to act. "Oh, no. Please have mercy on . . ."

The vision crashed in on her.

Images hit her mind like a heavyweight boxer's punches, one after the other—*a horned thing with a mouthful of demonic teeth. A blond woman, her face expressionless except for the rage in her eyes. And Reece, roaring in defiance. Then another image: the demonic thing, standing over Reece and the woman, both of them lashed naked to some kind of altar. The demon lifted a knife in either hand. Muscles worked in bullish shoulders as it prepared to plunge the enchanted blades downward. . . .*

"Champion!"

Her husband caught her by the shoulders as she jolted up off the bed. "Hey—hey!" Lancelot said. "What's happening?"

She slumped in his arms, feeling her stomach roll. "Vision. I . . . had a vision. It's Reece. He's in danger."

The fear in her husband's eyes was replaced by relief as he realized Grace was all right. Then his gaze sharpened with concern. "What kind of danger? From whom? That mole he's hunting?"

"No." Grace straightened. "It's something else. Not human, though it's not Sidhe, either. Some kind of Mageverse alien, maybe. It looked like a medieval woodcut of Satan. And it's evil." Her gaze met his. "It's going to sacrifice Reece and a woman I've never seen before in some kind of rite."

"But he's still alive now?"

She remembered the demon's knife. "For the moment."

Lance sat back on the bed. "We need to take this to the High Council."

She nodded grimly. "Now would be good."

The Cell

Reece paced the cell in long strides. Erin sat in the middle of the bed, her legs drawn up under her, her gaze fierce and inward as if she, too, tried to come up with some kind of escape plan.

He hoped she was having better luck than he was. But he doubted it.

As much as he hated to use the phrase, the situation literally sucked. They were trapped together until he Turned her, at which time Geirolf intended to kill both of them in an act of sympathetic magic designed to destroy Magekind.

On the other hand, it could have been worse.

When the demon had pressed that kiss to his forehead, Reece had felt a spell sink into his brain. For a moment, he'd wondered if he'd been placed under a compulsion to rape Erin. They'd dodged that bullet, though he wasn't sure why. It was the logical thing for the demon to do.

Of course, if the spell hadn't been designed to force him to attack Erin, what was it going to do?

Geirolf had to have something in mind. It would take sexual contact to Change Erin; as long as Reece kept his hands off her, there would be no transformation.

Which meant he was keeping his cock firmly inside these silly silk pajamas. As appealing as Erin was, making love to her wasn't worth the death of his people.

Of course, if he did Change her, there was always the chance she'd be able to use her powers to break them out of the cell. That might be beyond even a Maja's powers, of course. But it was possible, particularly if Geirolf had indeed damaged the cell when he'd escaped.

So what should he do? Changing her could free them, or could simply ensure their deaths and the destruction of the Magekind.

Then again, she might just go insane and kill him.

He didn't much care for the odds either way.

It was best to hold off, Reece decided. If he waited, some other alternative might present itself. Maybe he'd get really lucky and some Maja would have a vision. Grace was famous for that kind of thing, and since they were friends, she was even more likely to experience some kind of prophetic dream. On the other hand, if he took action now, the odds were too great he and Erin would end up dead.

In the meantime, he owed it to Erin to explain what her situation was. She needed to know all the possibilities so she could help him make the decision. She deserved a choice.

"Erin?"

She looked up from her steepled fingers. "Yes?"

"We need to talk."

She studied him, her gaze cool with calculation and wariness. "That's obvious, but the topics are literally endless. What have you got in mind?"

"Why do you think Geirolf locked us up together like this?"

Erin frowned. "He plans to make us one of his human sacrifices as part of some kind of plot against your people. Whoever the hell they are." She shook her head. "He talked a lot, but none of it made much sense."

How could he present this in terms she'd believe? Erin might be willing to believe he was a vampire and Geirolf was some kind of otherworldly demon, but she was much less likely to accept the fantastic truth about herself.

"This isn't going to be easy to believe," he began.

"Champion, so far none of this has been easy to believe. Unfortunately, it doesn't look like I've got a choice." Unfolding her long legs, she stood and moved toward him. "I caught something about Merlin." She shook her head. "I thought he was a myth."

"No, Merlin, Arthur, Lancelot—they all exist."

She frowned. "I remember reading that historians believe there was a Celtic warlord named Arthur who lived in the fifth century. But Lancelot is supposed to have been the creation of a French troubadour hundreds of years later. How can he exist?"

"They were wrong." Reece leaned a shoulder against a stone wall and crossed his arms. "The troubadour was actually one of Lance's descendants. He simply put to music the stories he grew up hearing about his ancestor."

"So why did it take so long for Lancelot to appear? Didn't people know about him?"

"People now don't know anything about me, and I've been an agent for the United States government for the past two hundred and twenty-eight years."

She stared at him. "You're kidding. Who the hell recruited you—George Washington?"

"Actually, I was the one who approached him."

"You approached—? Oh, come on!"

"No, really, I'd known George for years. Served with him during the French and Indian wars even before I became a vampire. When the Revolution broke out, I offered him my services." He shrugged. "He took me up on it."

Erin grinned. "I'll bet you've got a collection of war stories to make a historian drool." Then she shook her head. "Too bad I don't have time to hear them if we're going to get out of here. So. The legends about the Round Table are true."

"No, actually, they're about ninety percent bullshit, but the court did exist. But Camelot was more than knights and ladies, and Merlin was a hell of a lot more than the Druid magician of legend. To begin with, he wasn't even human. He and Nimue—"

"Nimue. That was the Lady of the Lake, right?"

"Right. They were—well, I guess you'd call them aliens."

"Aliens." He watched her struggle with her instinct to scoff. "Like ET-phone-home aliens?"

"Not . . . exactly. For one thing, they weren't just from another planet, they were from another universe. This one, the Mageverse."

"Hold on. You're saying we're in another *universe*? Now?" She went to one of the windows. Their cell was surrounded by what appeared to be a garden gone jungle, complete with huge, softly glowing roses nodding in the pearlescent light of the Mageverse moon.

As Reece looked out over her shoulder, a tiny, glowing creature flitted up to land on one of the roses by the window. She—and it was definitely a she, with those delicate breasts— folded butterfly wings and parted the petals until she could reach into the flower's heart. She drew out minuscule fingers covered in glittering pollen.

"Please tell me that's not what it looks like."

"Sorry. It's a fairy."

"Jesus." Erin blinked as the tiny Sidhe began delicately licking the pollen from graceful fingertips. Her hair was as pink as cotton candy. "Hey, you think we could get her attention, ask her to get help?"

"Worth a try." He reached out and tapped on the window. The fairy looked up in alarm and stared into the window. Her big eyes narrowed, and she lifted one tiny fist to extend a finger before flying angrily off.

Erin blinked. "Did she just flip us the bird?"

Reece found himself swallowing a snort of laughter. "Looked like it. I don't think she could really see inside. The Magekind have good relationships with the Sidhe. I can't believe she wouldn't help, if she'd known we were locked up in here."

Heart pounding, Janieda beat her wings as fast as she could. She had to get to the palace and Llyr.

She had to warn her king that something new had been locked up in Geirolf's old cell.

Something dangerous.

She'd seen it the moment she'd stared into the magic-darkened glass: a vision.

The king, his beloved face blank and slack in a sleep that was more than sleep. And a woman—a human, her hands surrounded by a nimbus of magic. It was one of the Majae Llyr had been trying to court.

Janieda's heart contracted at the combination of jealousy and foreboding she felt. Ceasing her frantic wingbeats, she landed on a tree limb and looked back the way she'd come.

No. Telling Llyr there was someone in that cell would be a mistake. Her lover would insist on investigating.

And he could well pay for his curiosity with his life.

Erin frowned, craning her neck to peer outside. "So this is— what? A magical universe that mirrors our own? The landscape out there looks more or less like Earth."

"It is Earth. It's just the part of Earth that extends into the Mageverse. The laws of physics don't work the same way here. Will has a lot more influence than it does back home, for one thing."

She considered the idea thoughtfully. "Actually, that might explain a few things. There's been an experiment or two that suggests thought can influence quantum particles."

Reece nodded in agreement. "Yeah, when you get down to the subatomic level, the barriers between the two universes break down. But otherwise, it's tremendously difficult to get

Mageverse energies to function back home." He gave her a searching look. "Unless you're a Maja."

Erin frowned, trying to put the pieces together. "So Merlin and the Lady of the Lake are from Mageverse Earth."

"No, actually they were from some other Mageverse world altogether. They were travelers—missionaries of a sort."

She rocked back on her heels. "Missionaries? Like saving souls and that kind of thing?"

"Not . . . exactly. For hundreds of years Merlin's people had been visiting other worlds, and they'd noticed a disturbing trend. Intelligent races have a bad tendency to kill themselves off in their adolescence, either through war or by causing ecological disasters."

Cop that she was, Erin didn't find that news particularly surprising. "Huh. Wonder if that explains why we haven't had much luck picking up radio signals from other intelligent races?"

He shrugged. "That, and most of 'em don't use radio. Eventually they discover Mageverse energies work a lot better. Anyway, Merlin's people—we call them the Fae—decided to do something about that. But they couldn't just show up and dump a bunch of technology and philosophy on less advanced people."

"Who'd probably just end up killing themselves even faster."

"Right. So what the Fae did was come up with a kind of bootstrapping concept. They'd visit planets and create a group of guardians to whom they'd entrust the powers of the Mageverse, along with a knowledge of the Fae's advanced technology and philosophy. Then the Fae would leave them to prevent their people from destroying themselves. But only from behind the scenes. The guardians were forbidden to reveal themselves."

"Why all the secrecy? Why not just come out of the closet and say, 'We're here. This is what you need to do.' "

Reece shook his head. "Think about it. Up until the last couple of hundred years, they still burned witches on Earth."

"Good point."

"Besides, the idea isn't just to plop an alien culture down on top of ours. The goal is to enable humans to survive long enough to develop their own advanced culture. The best way to do that is for us to remain as far under cover as possible."

"But you said you work for the government," Erin pointed out. "That doesn't sound like you're hiding to me."

"I haven't told the Feds about the rest of Magekind. As far as my contacts know, I'm just a lone vampire who happens to have a patriotic streak. And even so, there are damn few folks who know about me."

"I'm just amazed some senator hasn't held a press conference and outted your ass."

"Which is precisely why members of Congress have never been in the know. Besides, anybody I decide to tell usually gets a visit from a Maja fairly soon thereafter. One spell later, they acquire a deep inability to discuss me with anybody who isn't already in on the secret."

"Huh." Obviously deep in thought, Erin wandered over to the table to look over the plate of cold meat, bread, and cheeses. "Then how did Parker find out?"

"He's a magic user working with my FBI contact. I suspect he read the information out of the guy's head."

Erin picked up a knife and sliced off a chunk of cheese. "Nice of the Demon Lord to provide munchies, huh?" She eyed the cheese narrowly. "Since he plans to sacrifice us, it's probably not poisoned." She took a healthy bite.

"Might be laced with aphrodisiacs, though."

She choked. "What? Why would he—?"

"I'm getting to that." Watching her eye her food dubiously, he added, "I don't really think he did anything to it. He probably figures we're going to be here a while, so you'll need something to eat."

Erin shrugged and nibbled cautiously. "If you say so."

Walking over, Reece picked up a pitcher and poured them

each a goblet. He was a little too close; when he inhaled, his senses filled with her lush, erotic scent.

Cut that out, he told himself, and moved to a safer distance. "I got off the subject. Where was I?"

"Merlin," she supplied, taking a sip. "Hey, wasn't this Dom a minute ago? Tastes like brandy now."

"Pitcher's enchanted." He took a sip of his own and grimaced. It still wasn't blood. "Anyway, Merlin and Nimue arrived on Earth around 500 A.D. to start setting up Earth's guardians. The first question they had to deal with was, who did they trust with the power?"

"Yeaaaah." She sliced off a chunk of meat and started making a sandwich. "I can think of a lot of people I wouldn't give it to. Parker, for example."

"Right. So they spent the next century testing people all over the planet. In Europe their first converts were Arthur and his half sister, Morgana Le Fay."

Erin plopped a piece of bread on top of the stack she'd made and took a healthy bite. "Did they really commit incest and have a kid?"

"Right, Mordred." A waft of air current carried the scent of her hair to Reece's sensitive nose. His cock twitched behind the silk of his ridiculous pajamas as he tried to remember what they'd been talking about. "They were teenagers, didn't know they were related. That's another story. Didn't end well."

"So where did the vampire thing come in?"

An image flashed through his mind: the raw sensual pleasure of sinking his fangs into the thin skin over her pounding pulse. He cleared his throat. "Fae males and females have a kind of symbiotic relationship. The females absorb and manipulate Mageverse energies; that's basically what they eat. The males can't do that. The only way they can use that energy is after it's been processed in their partner's bodies."

She looked at him around her sandwich. "Okay, you lost me."

"It's like animals and plants. Plants can convert sunlight into what they need to survive. We can't, so we eat the plants. But if you actually eat your females, your race isn't going to survive very long, so the males evolved into . . ."

"Vampires." She took another bite.

"Right. By drinking a small amount of a female's blood, the vampire could obtain the Mageverse energy her body had processed and converted."

Erin sipped her wine thoughtfully. "I'm not sure that makes a hell of a lot of sense."

"Neither does disco. Some things just happen."

"Funny."

"I try. Anyway, when Merlin and Nimue began creating their race of guardians, they used a template they knew worked: their own. So you ended up with vampire Magi who were stronger than hell, and witch Majae who could work spells." As he took a deep breath, her scent teased him. Feeling his cock harden, he buried his nose in his goblet and took a deep breath, trying to drown his senses in the pungent smell of the brandy.

Where the hell was all this lust coming from? He'd been fine at first, but the longer he was with her, the more the Desire gnawed at him.

Oh, hell. His stomach sank. Was this Geirolf's spell, kicking in at last?

And if it was, how was he going to stay away from her? Especially knowing how she tasted, how her smooth, soft skin felt under his hands, how her tight, wet sex gripped him . . .

Spell or no spell, Reece thought, *I've got to stay away from her.*

SIX

Unaware of Reece's growing lust, Erin was still trying to understand the complex relationships between vampires and Majae. "But Merlin could do spells, right?"

He took a deep swallow of brandy and let it burn all the way down. Maybe his preoccupation with Erin was his imagination. But he doubted it. He tried to concentrate on the problem at hand. "Early Fae males once enslaved the females. It was easy, because the males were both stronger and could work spells. So millennia later, when the Fae created us, they made sure our females could defend themselves by limiting our powers. The end result is that we're the muscle and they're the magic."

"Huh." She slid a hip onto the tabletop and absently picked up a strawberry from a tray. "So you're one of the Knights of the Round Table."

Reece blinked, her misinterpretation jolting him from his sensual preoccupation. "Uh, no. That was before my time. Look, you know the Grail legend?"

"Yeah." She bit into the strawberry. He fought to ignore the sensual movement of her lips. "King Arthur sent his knights to search for the cup Christ used at the Last Supper."

"Right, but it wasn't really Christ's cup. That part was tacked on later. The real Grail was Merlin's magical creation. The knights and ladies who proved themselves were allowed to drink from it, and when they did, it transformed them. They became Magi and Majae. From then on, they were able to pass on the potential to become Magekind to their descendants."

"So their children became little witches and vampires. Bet that made for an interesting home life." She angled her head, sending bright blond hair sliding over the globes of the pretty breasts swelling over the neckline of her Merry Widow.

He looked away. "It certainly would have, which is why it doesn't work that way."

"Why not?"

"Well, think about it. Even the best families have kids who don't turn out quite right."

"True." Erin started picking over the tray of fruit again. He focused his attention out the window. "And if one of those Mage kids went bad—"

"—you'd have a royal mess," Reece finished. "So the way Merlin set it up is, you could only become one of the Magekind if they chose to grant you the full power. And you only got the full power through . . . well, sex."

She looked up. "You're kidding me."

"I'm afraid not. Repeated contact with the Majae or Magi's bodily fluids—saliva, sperm, whatever—triggers a gene in the Latent that causes him to transform." *Which,* he told himself sternly, *is what will happen to Erin if you don't keep your hands off*.

She looked dubious. "You mean it's sexually transmitted, like HIV?"

"Basically. You need at least three encounters to trigger it, though. Sometimes more, but never less than three." He'd love to take her like that, over and over again. . . . *Stop that*.

"So that whole thing about being bitten three times to become a vampire—"

"—is complete myth. I became a vampire by having sex with the Maja the Majae's Council sent to convert me."

"They *sent* her?" She was watching him curiously. He wondered if she'd picked up on his unease. "That sounds pretty cold."

He shrugged. "And it was, though I didn't realize it at the time. I fell wildly in love with her, but she dumped me as soon as I made the transformation." Now, that was a thought to cool his burning blood. Maybe if he remembered the way Sebille had laughed at his passionate proposal . . .

"Bitch." Her angry growl made him glance back at her. He instantly regretted it. She'd pursed her lips into a deliciously erotic shape that made him imagine what it would feel like to slide his erection between them. Sweating, Reece focused on the nearest window and tried doing a calculus problem in his head.

Oh, this was not good.

"So what happened?" When he looked over at her blankly, she prompted, "With the Maja who turned you into a vampire. The one who dumped you."

Reece rubbed a thumb against his aching forehead. He was developing a tension headache. "Nothing. That was it. Look, love has nothing to do with Gifting somebody. It's all a very deliberate, very serious business, because you're giving them incredible power. In fact, the Majae have a council whose sole purpose is deciding who gets Merlin's Gift and who doesn't."

"What happens if somebody gets the Gift when they're not supposed to?"

He remembered Lizzie. Now, there was a thought to cool anybody's lust. "The Council hands down an order of execution."

"You mean—they just *kill* the Latent?"

Reece nodded. "Along with whoever turned him or her. The Council doesn't screw around." He took a deep breath, then regretted it when it got him a lungful of her maddening scent. "And that brings me to you."

She stared at him. "Me?"

"You're a Latent, Erin."

Avalon

Lance and Arthur sat at the Round Table in the High Council Hall, a bottle of some Maja's donated blood between them. In contrast to the barbaric splendor of the chamber with its massive wooden timbers and stone floor, both were dressed like the twenty-first century men they'd become.

Lance had changed for the occasion into slacks and a black cable-knit sweater, while Arthur wore a pair of worn jeans and a T-shirt with the slogan, "Once a King, always a King—but once a Knight's enough."

Lance wondered absently what smartass had given him that. It was an odd fashion choice for the Liege of the vampire's Magi's Council, the group that, with the Majae's Council, decided Magekind policy.

He sipped from his goblet, barely conscious of the fiery taste. His attention was focused on the next chamber. Through the massive wooden doors, he could hear the sound of rhythmic female voices. "Hear that?" he said to Arthur. "They're chanting."

His friend frowned. "They shouldn't have to work that hard, not on a simple locator spell. Unless—"

"—something's blocking them," Lance finished the thought. "Something with a lot of power. What are we dealing with here, Arthur?"

The Liege of the Magi's Council combed one hand restlessly

through the short, neat beard he'd recently regrown. "The only thing I know about this situation is that I don't like it. I despise waiting in the dark, not even knowing where the enemy is."

Lance smiled reluctantly. "It's a lot easier when they just point us somewhere and tell us who to kill."

Arthur dropped his hand from his beard to finger Excalibur's hilt. The big blade's enchanted jewels gleamed against the Table's dark wood. "I'll admit, I'd welcome a little action. I don't like knowing one of my men is in danger when there's nothing I can do to help him."

Massive doors creaked open. Both men looked up as Guinevere, Grace, and Morgana sailed through, none of them looking happy. "Somebody's doing a damn good job of blocking us from finding Reece," Grace said, dropping into a chair next to her husband.

Morgana curled a lip, her dark eyes flashing. "They don't know us very well if they think it's that simple to stymie us." She gestured, her long hands moving in a gesture as abrupt as it was graceful.

A massive book appeared on the table before her. Easily a foot thick, the tome's aged leather cover was inset with emeralds, sapphires, and rubies.

"Grim," Morgana said, crossing her arms in the pale cream suit she wore, "we need your help finding a demon." She looked at Grace and said, "Describe your vision for Grim. He should be able to—"

"Uh, Grandmother?" Grace dipped her eyes down at the book, which remained stubbornly closed.

Morgana's brows lowered in concern. "Grim?"

The book didn't respond.

"Merlin's Grimoire!" Arthur thundered.

The book always opened at the sound of Arthur's voice, but today the cover didn't even stir.

A palpable chill settled over the room. "Grim's not—?" Lance began.

Guinevere laid a slender hand on the book's cover, then

looked up at them in relief. "No. It's still alive. I sense its magic. But something has bound it in sleep."

"That thing dared set a spell on Merlin's Grimoire?" Minute flashes of lighting glittered in Morgana's eyes. "He's going to pay for that." She looked up at Grace and Gwen. "I'll call the Majae's Council. We'll break this spell, and then we'll just see what this arrogant bastard thinks he can hide!"

Morgana swept up the Grimoire and stalked out, Gwen and Grace at her heels.

Lance looked at Arthur as the door closed behind him. "This whatever-he-is managed to put a spell on Grim right under the noses of the Majae?" He sat back in his seat and blew out a breath. "Oh, that's just not good."

"No," the former High King said. "It's not."

The Cell

Erin stared at Reece in disbelief as a chill spread over her. "Me? A Latent?" Suddenly the conversation that had been a welcome distraction from their predicament became all too personal. *"A Latent and the young vampire who could transform her—all magical potential, yet without enough real power yet to be a pain in my ass,"* Geirolf had said. *"The perfect blood sacrifice."*

The conversation had made no sense at the time. Now it did, and she wished it didn't. "Oh, shit."

"That's about the size of it."

"There's been a mistake. I don't have any magical powers."

"Yet."

"At all, Reece!" She shook her head. "I'm thirty years old. Don't you think I would have noticed by now if I could wiggle my nose and pull a rabbit out of my butt?"

"Now, that," Reece told her, "is a really revolting image."

"Not as revolting as the idea of me as a witch!"

Champion sighed. "Look, if you think about it, you'll find

it makes sense. Like the time you and David went to that farmhouse that belonged to the killer—"

She frowned. "You mean Gary Evans?"

"Right. You were looking for clues to the kidnapping and killings in town. How did you know that building was connected?"

Erin swallowed, remembering the sudden cold prickle of knowledge that had stolen over her when she'd seen candlelight flickering from the darkened barn. "I don't know. I just had a hunch."

"You get a lot of hunches that pan out like that?"

"Yeah. But so does everybody in law enforcement. Something doesn't quite fit or looks out of place, and when you investigate, you find something's wrong."

"But I'll bet you get more of them than most people."

She hesitated before she admitted, "Okay, there were jokes about it in the Bureau—the way my hunches always seemed to play out. That was why David was so willing to investigate. But a couple of hunches do not constitute evidence that I'm some kind of witch."

"Not yet. But you could be, if we made love often enough."

"No. Forget it. *I* am a descendent of one of the Knights of the Round Table? I don't think so."

"Sorry, babe, judging by the scent, you're one of Bedivere's. Bet you've got a great-grandparent who was born on the wrong side of the blanket."

"You can tell who my great-grandfather was from the way I *smell*?"

"The Magekind are immortal, Erin. We have sex with a lot of people. If you couldn't recognize your own bloodline, you could end up banging your own daughter without knowing it. Or your sister, for that matter. Just ask Arthur."

She raked both hands through her hair and tried to regroup. "So I have at least the potential to gain these . . . powers, right?"

"Yeah." His gaze sharpened and heated. When he spoke again, the words emerged as a sensual growl. "If we make love."

She went still as a thought occurred to her. "Could I break us out of here?"

"Possibly, but there are two problems with that."

"One of which is that Geirolf plans to kill both of us in some kind of sacrifice." Erin grimaced. "So if we do it and I can't get us out, we're screwed. Talk about pressure. What's the other one?"

"You could go insane."

She looked at him a long moment. "Okay, explain that."

"Sometimes new vampires can't control the hunger, though that's comparatively rare. But Majae—when you Change, all the energy of this alien dimension suddenly crashes in on you. Some people can't handle it, and they become dangerous. That's why the Majae's Council vets everybody before they allow them to undergo the Change."

"And executes people who Change without permission as a way to discourage that kind of thing."

"Right."

"Well, that's stupid."

Reece snorted. "Sweetheart, the Majae's Council is the least of our problems. If I do turn you, and you can't get us out of here, it's not just us Geirolf is going to kill. That spell he was talking about is sympathetic magic. It's designed to wipe out every Maja and Magus—all Earth's protectors—in one shot. That would give him free rein to do whatever the hell he wants with humankind. He set himself up as a god before. What's he going to do this time?"

"Nothing good."

"Got that right." Reece stood up and began to pace, his long, muscled legs carrying him from one end of the cell to the other. "Geirolf feeds off death energy. The minute he gets rid of us, the entire human race becomes his personal All-You-Can-Eat buffet. With a side order of Sidhe."

She winced. "That was a truly unspeakable pun."

"Believe me, it's no joke. Because he won't be the only one we'll have to worry about. Other Mageverse aliens will show up looking for the leftovers the minute Merlin's wards are gone."

"Great." She scrubbed both hands over her face. "Just fucking fantastic."

"And that's just the aliens. In the last century the human race has gained the ability to destroy itself hundreds of times over. Magekind has been working our collective ass off behind the scenes, trying to keep the human race from committing mass suicide. But it's always been a fight. Right now we're about one deep breath from a religious World War. We've never had one of those, and believe me, we don't want one. So if the Magekind goes bye-bye—"

"—millions of other people won't be far behind."

His expression was cold and grim when he turned to look at her. "If I don't Change you, Geirolf can still kill us, but he won't be sacrificing a Maja."

"But if you don't Change me, we don't even have a prayer of escaping."

He sighed and fell into the nearest chair. "That's about the size of it."

Erin groaned. "Fan-fucking-tastic."

They spent the next hours pacing and arguing as they tried to arrive at a solution to the problem of escape. Erin banged furiously on the window, trying to attract the attention of one of the magical beings beyond the glass, but nothing responded.

Meanwhile, Reece explored the walls and windows, looking for a weakness he could use to batter an escape route. But the cell was rock solid. All he gained for his trouble were bloodied knuckles and a gnawing, desperate frustration.

And what was worse, every breath he took carried Erin's scent, eroding his self-control another desperate inch.

When he finally gave up, he found her lying curled up on

the floor on a pile of furs. With that unconscious gallantry he'd noticed before, she'd left him the bed.

Her slender arms hugged her own torso as if for comfort as her glorious blond hair tumbled across the dark pelts she lay across. Looking down at her, he felt tenderness tug at him.

He found himself wishing she were a bitch. It would be so much easier to keep his hands off her if he didn't like her so damn much.

Reece bent and started to pick her up so he could carry her to the bed. Then he drew in a lungful of her scent. The wave of lust that crashed over him sent him backing warily away.

Touching her right now was *not* a good idea.

Stymied in his attempts to play gentleman, he stalked over to the bed and flung himself down on it to stare sightlessly at the ceiling.

Unfortunately, he knew there was no way he could sleep. Dawn—and the Daysleep it would force on his vampire body—was still a couple of hours away.

With a sigh of resignation he rolled to his feet and began to pace. If there was only some way he could signal the Magekind . . . But judging by the constellations outside, the cell was on the other side of Mageverse Earth.

He spun on his heel to pace the other way, and his eyes fell on Erin. She lay on her side, the lush curves of her hip and waist in relief against the black fur. One delicate pink nipple had escaped the confinement of her corset, and he could see the gold curls between her legs shimmering through the white lace of her panties. He imagined spreading those sweet thighs, sinking deep, forgetting the impossible situation that confronted them.

Once. He could take her one more time. That would be enough.

Be honest, you horny bastard. Once wouldn't *be enough. Not as long as I'm under this spell.*

His balls literally ached, and the roots of his fangs throbbed. His cock was as hard as a crowbar. Reece jerked his eyes away from the distilled temptation of Erin Grayson's lush little body.

Dammit, he couldn't remember the last time he'd wanted a woman this much. The spell was slowly turning up the heat on the Desire every moment that passed.

Reece wheeled away from her and stripped off his robe in a single violent yank, then dragged his silk trousers off. Naked, he strode to the Roman bath that took up one end of the room.

Stepping up onto the marble lip of the pool, he hoped it was ice cold.

Unfortunately, it wasn't, he realized as he descended the steps into the waist-deep water. *More like blood temperature.* But it was some distraction, anyway.

Reece sat down in the water, letting it close over his head. He concentrated on holding his breath, hoping the eventual need to breathe would take his mind off his clawing desire for Erin.

But as he floated there, he felt the silken slide of the current ghosting over his bare skin like the brush of a woman's fingers. His cock throbbed with the need to sink into Erin's hot, cream-filled sheathe. He shuddered.

Dammit, I will not do this. Spell or no spell, I control my body. My body does not control me.

The water swirled gently against him, caressing his rock-hard shaft and the sensitive skin between his thighs. Erin's hands had felt so soft when she'd touched him there.

Reece stood up, the water sluicing off his aching body. "Dammit." Desperate for some way to distract his clamoring hunger, he looked around the room.

Just in time to see a collection of bottles and jars appear on a tray at one end of the bath. He stared at it. Oh, now that was interesting. What was it Geirolf said: *"The cell provided for my every physical need—except freedom."*

When he stepped dripping from the bath to investigate, a stack of towels appeared on the floor. Reece scooped one up and dried himself off, considering the possibilities.

Testing, he wished for a Stinger Missile and looked around

hopefully. Nothing. He tried wishing for a pitcher of blood next, but when he looked into the ewer on the table, it still held nothing but wine. Damn. Evidently Geirolf had found a way to alter the spell just enough to keep him hungry.

At least when it came to his vampire needs. There was still that intriguing collection of bottles.

When he picked one up and shook it, Reece found it contained some kind of oil. He pulled the elegant cork and sniffed cautiously. It smelled like sandalwood, but there didn't seem any taint of magic to it.

Well, maybe he could take care of at least one hunger. He carried it to the bed.

After pouring a handful of scented oil into his palms, he threw himself down and wrapped his fingers around his cock. He wasn't too proud to jack off, if it made it possible to stay away from Erin.

Reece forced himself to take his time. He needed to spin this out, make it last as long as possible. Maybe it would help him regain control, at least for a while.

Arching his back, he thrust his rigid shaft up into his palm, remembering what it had felt like to slide into her silken cream. She'd gripped him like oiled silk wrapped around his cock, and her nipples had tasted maddeningly of her erotic musk. Inhaling sharply, he found the room full of her scent. Reece closed his eyes with a low groan and drew it more deeply into his lungs as he stroked his shaft, cupping his tight balls with the other hand.

Then, in his mind, he let himself make love to her as he didn't dare do in reality.

The Grand Palace of the Cachamwri Sidhe

Janieda flew into the throne room to find King Llyr Aleyn Galatyn pacing before his throne, his strides long and angry. She stopped to hover in the air, watching him, her wings beating slowly. They'd been lovers since his last wife died, at least a hundred years. Yet even after so long, his royal beauty never failed to take her breath away.

Like all those of the Galatyn bloodline, the king was tall, far taller than Janieda even in her full form. His body was leanly muscled, a fact made wonderfully evident by his dark blue doublet and hose. Intricate embroidery in silver thread glittered against the dark fabric, beaded here and there with emeralds that matched those in the silver coronet he wore. More of the stones gleamed against the soft blue leather of the thigh-high boots that hugged his long legs.

The dark expression on his handsome face made Janieda swallow and hope she wasn't the one who'd aroused his ire. "Llyr?" she asked softly, landing on the gleaming marble floor. With a thought, she grew to her full height and approached him hesitantly. "What has you so angry, my love?"

"They refused me," Llyr growled, still pacing. "Again! Those proud bitches turned their arrogant noses up at every one of my offers."

A shaft of relief cut through her, but Janieda was too experienced a courtier to let it show. "And they always will." He turned toward her, his opalescent eyes flashing. She forced herself to confront his anger. "I'm sorry, My Liege, but you know how the Majae's Council keeps a tight rein on its witches. To allow one of them to become your queen would put her forever beyond their control. They'll not do that."

"Shortsighted fools," he growled and wheeled away, his velvet cape swinging wide from his body. "An alliance would benefit them as much as it would the Cachamwri Sidhe."

Janieda allowed herself a slight sneer. "They care only for this Great Mission of theirs, this plan to save the mortals." She snorted. "A waste of time, if you ask me. They all eventually die anyway."

"Well, if my brother wins this war between us, the Majae may well wish they'd bothered to assist me," Llyr said, dropping into his throne to glower. "I know Ansgar. With me gone, he'd turn his attention to mortal Earth with a conqueror's eye." He tilted his head back and stared grimly at the ceiling. "Unfortunately, I will not be around to gloat."

"Did you . . ." She hesitated a moment, then continued carefully, "Did you tell them about Geirolf?" He had said before he left that he intended to warn the Majae that Merlin's ancient enemy had escaped his cell.

Llyr's handsome mouth tightened. "No." He made an impatient gesture. "Perhaps I should have, but I was so infuriated at their treatment of me that I did not."

Janieda relaxed fractionally. As long as the witches did not discover Geirolf's cell had a new occupant, her secret was safe.

At least for a while.

The Cell

"Erin—" The voice drew her from sleep with its low, male growl of sensual need.

Erin opened her eyes and blinked at the stone ceiling overhead without recognition. She lay on a pile of furs, but the floor below that was hard. Where the hell—

Champion gasped.

She sat up quickly and looked around for him, her heart pounding as the unbelievable events of the last several hours rushed back.

He was sprawled facedown on the bed. For a moment of raw, unadulterated panic, she thought Geirolf had done something to him. Then he moaned, and the rasping hunger in the sound made her take a second, harder look.

He was asleep, his lashes fanned dark against the arrogant angle of his cheek.

Erin sucked in a deep breath and blew it out in relief. He must be in the Daysleep he'd mentioned sometime before she'd dropped off herself. Magi—vampires—needed that deep, almost comatose rest as much as they did blood.

Unlike Merlin's people, they'd been born in a nonmagical

dimension, so the rules were slightly different for them. They took blood and the psychic energy of pleasure from their partners, but it was in sleep that they drew on their connection to the Mageverse to power their abilities.

Champion sighed and moved, his powerful torso flexing. Erin blinked as it hit her he was completely naked.

And beautiful.

When he'd made love to her, his erotic assault on her senses had made it impossible to concentrate on anything but what he was doing. Now her fascinated gaze tracked over the curves and angles of hard-packed muscle, the long, strong legs, the brawny line of his glutes. He had an utterly gorgeous ass. She felt a sudden, wicked impulse to sink her teeth into it.

Grateful for the distraction from a grim reality, Erin sat up and ogled him shamelessly. Even asleep, Reece wore an intense expression on that battered pirate face of his. A tight line cut between dark brows drawn low over his closed eyes, and his mouth was open slightly, revealing the points of his fangs. One arm was bent, hanging off the bed, corded biceps bulging as he held a handful of the fur cover gripped hard in a big fist.

"Erin," he whispered again.

She blinked. Was he dreaming about her?

Then, as she watched, he thrust his hips into the bed beneath him.

Oh.

SEVEN

Erin felt her jaw drop as heat flooded her cheekbones.

Once again, Reece ground slowly, sensuously, into the bed in the unmistakable movements of sex. His chest expanded as he drew in a quick, hard breath. "Silk. Like silk." His mouth looked impossibly carnal as he shaped the words.

She drew in a deep breath of her own. Her nipples tingled and peaked as she remembered what it had been like to make love to him. The feel of his mouth laving her aching breasts, his tongue rolling the little peaks against the edge of his teeth. The way he'd held her so effortlessly still under him as she'd writhed helplessly in his arms.

The memory alone was enough to bring cream welling inside her in a hot, maddening trickle. Impulsively she reached down and slid one hand into the waistband of her lace panties.

Her delving fingers found her lips swollen and dewed with arousal.

He moved again, rolling his beautiful ass as he thrust into the thick fur throw that covered the bed. She remembered the size of his cock, the way it had felt sinking deep, stretching and tormenting her so deliciously. With a soft groan, she thrust one finger deeply into her sex as it grew slicker with every move Reece made. She could almost feel his broad back under her hands as she opened herself wide for his lunging thrusts.

Erin shivered. God, she wanted him again. Wanted to know his fierce hunger one more time.

She also knew she didn't dare. Having sex with Champion meant becoming a Maja—and courting a starring role as a human sacrifice. Not even mind-blowing sex with Champion was worth risking the murder of thousands of people.

Then he rolled over on his back.

"Hot damn." Erin stared. She hadn't gotten a good look at him before. He'd felt huge as he'd slid into her, but even so, she hadn't realized just how thick and powerful his shaft really was.

His cock arched over his lean abdomen from its nest of dark curls, a single drop of pre-cum clinging to its rosy head. Thick veins snaked along its length.

And she remembered how it felt.

She lay sprawled and dazed across Champion's body as his cock shuttled in and out and he gave her what felt like the world's biggest hickey. Somehow the slight, stinging pain made the pleasure that much greater. Her third orgasm of the night rolled over her in a blinding wave. Erin gasped. Champion arched and stiffened, driving to his full length, so deep she had to scream again.

Shuddering in need, Erin added a second finger to the one deep inside her as she pushed down the edge of her corset so she could stroke one hard nipple. Unable to look away from him, barely breathing, she pinched and twisted the swollen peak.

He arched his massive torso and rolled his hips upward as if driving into her. His cock bobbed, as that longing drop of pre-cum caught the light. His balls were drawn tight to the big shaft, as though he was seconds from spilling.

Gasping, Erin thumbed her clit and pumped her fingers, feeling the first pulses of an orgasm. In thirty years of life, she'd never seen anything as erotic as Reece Champion having a wet dream.

Suddenly he stiffened, his big body drawing into a bow of erotic effort. A jet of cum shot across the cobblestone ridges of his abdomen.

"Erin," he sighed.

Oh, God. She threw back her head and closed her eyes, imagining walking over there and cleansing Champion's big body with her tongue until he woke up and did to her whatever it was he was dreaming about.

She clenched her teeth to strangle her own cry as she came, knowing she didn't dare let Champion catch her masturbating. In their current wild mood, that might be more than either of them could resist.

He woke with Erin's scent filling his head and his balls throbbing like a toothache.

Reece lifted his head. The first thing he saw was his own cock, a drop of pre-cum on its tip. More semen covered his belly. He grimaced. Damn, he hadn't had a wet dream like this in centuries.

Glancing over, he saw Erin was awake, standing at the other end of the room with her back to him. Something about the rigid line of her spine—and the rich scent of female musk in the air—told him she'd witnessed his little nocturnal emission.

And it had turned her on. *In fact*— He drew the musk more deeply into his lungs. *It smells as though she*—

Drop it, Champion. He shoved aside the incendiary image of Erin masturbating. Rolling off the bed, he started for his pants, left lying by the pool. As he passed her, the intoxicating smell of her need grew even stronger. The Desire wrapped around the base of his fangs and clamped a burning hold on his balls. It was all he could do not to jerk her into his arms. Instead he snatched up his pants, his hands shaking like a palsied old man's.

Not good. Not good at all.

An image spilled through his mind—Erin, her long legs wrapped around his waist, her head thrown back as her muscles gripped him like a creamy fist.

Reece swallowed, his mouth dry as week-old bread as he tucked in his desperate hard-on and jerked his pants into place around his hips.

"Did he put a spell on you?"

Startled, Reece looked up. She hadn't even looked around. "What?"

"Geirolf. I was thinking just now. About the way you keep looking at me." Erin turned and faced him. "I saw him kiss your forehead before he sent us here. Did he put you under a compulsion to have sex with me?"

Reece sighed. He should have known she'd realize it. "Yeah. I think he did."

Silence spun between them, aching with undercurrents of desperation and lust.

"Guess I'm lucky he didn't just order you to rape me," she said.

He drew in another deep breath, blew it out. "Yeah. I thought for a minute he had, but when we got here . . ." He shrugged.

"I wonder why he didn't."

Champion studied her, trying to decide what to make of her tone. "He likes to play games. Maybe he wanted me aware and fighting it. Or maybe there are preparations he's got to make before he—"

"Sacrifices us."

"Yeah."

"What the hell are we going to do?" Her expression was calm, but he could see the fear deep in her eyes.

"I don't know."

Erin stalked toward the table and picked up the pitcher. Looking into it, she shook her head. "Full. You know, I could have sworn we drank half of it."

He cleared his throat. "The cell's enchanted. It provides for the physical needs of its captives. Or at least some of them. Which means an unending supply of food and drink."

"Well, at least we won't starve." She poured herself a goblet. "I've been thinking."

"Yeah?" He turned and bent until he could splash water on his face from the bath. Wiping off the evidence of his dream with one wet hand, he looked over at her. "If you've got any ideas, I'd love to hear them."

Erin walked toward him in that long, rolling female stride that was damn near enough to give him an erection all by itself. "It sounds as if you're going to end up changing me whether you like it or not. Maybe we need to just go for it."

At those words, such raw lust flashed across Champion's face, Erin felt her knees go weak.

Then he looked away. "No."

"Aren't we fighting the inevitable?"

He whirled on her, his lips pulled back from white fangs. "Yes! If the inevitable is being guest of honor at a human sacrifice and the resulting destruction of my people—by God, I'm going to fight it all the way down."

Erin met his determined stare. Just beneath the rage, she could see his hunger. "But what if I can save us?"

She watched as he paced to the nearest window and braced his arms on the frame. His back looked a mile wide. "And what if you go insane?" he asked in a low voice. "What do you think I'm going to have to do then?"

"What do you mean?"

"I knew a woman once." Reece didn't look around, his attention focused on the Mageverse landscape just beyond the impenetrable glass. "A beautiful woman, an intelligent woman. She sparkled. And she loved my best friend with such intensity, I envied him." He sighed. "But she was a Latent, and he was a Magus, and the Council of Majae refused him permission to turn her. So he Changed her anyway."

"And she went nuts."

He nodded. "Just like that, the woman I knew was gone, replaced by a paranoid psychotic who believed everybody was out to destroy her, including the man she loved. She killed him." He turned restlessly to stare out the window at the moonlit night. "And I killed her."

"You're afraid I'll end up the same way."

"Yes." He raked one hand through his hair in agitation. "Look, the way it works is, the Majae's Council decides who gets the Gift. Maybe somebody's had a vision that particular candidate will play a role in the Great Mission—our task of saving Humanity. Or maybe some Maja or Magus submits the Latent's name for consideration. The Council vets the candidate, casts runes—whatever the hell they do. Then if they decide the Latent can withstand the Change, they send somebody to have sex with her or him."

For something to do with her hands, Erin started slicing off a piece of one loaf of bread. Like the pitcher, it appeared untouched, though she remembered eating from it the night before. "Sounds pretty"—she shrugged—"cold."

"Yeah, well, it's a serious business. Because sometimes even the Majae's Council guesses wrong, and the new Maja becomes a threat. And she's got to be killed."

"You're afraid you'll have to do the same thing to me."

"Assuming you don't get me first."

She turned her attention to a chunk of cheese and sawed off a piece. "Yeah, well, if we don't do anything, I'm dead anyway. Logically, Demon Boy is going to lose patience and put a rape spell on you. Assuming he hasn't already."

"I'm not going to rape you." He gritted the words between clenched teeth.

Erin eyed his back. "Yeah, well, I'd be tempted to walk over there and wrap my fingers around that raging hard-on just to find out. Unfortunately, I've got a feeling it would be like sticking my hand in a tiger cage, and I'm not that brave."

Suddenly he exploded, driving his fist savagely into the window. It bonged like a bell as he hit it again and again. "I'm. Not. Going. To. Rape. You!"

She waited until the reverberations died. "Well, that just fills me with confidence."

He whirled, his mouth contorted in a snarl that sent her jolting back a pace. "Fuck you!"

"Yeah, why don't we? Before you lose what little control you've got."

Reece stared at her, his eyes glittering, a hectic flush on his cheeks. His powerful chest rose and fell with his hard, panting breaths. There was a bulge in his silk trousers that made her want to either look away or touch it. She forced herself to hold his gaze instead.

Finally he spoke, his voice a hoarse whisper. "Erin, don't you understand? I don't want to destroy you."

"Reece, you've been on the job long enough to know— sometimes you just have to take a chance. And we've got to. Our backs are to the wall. If we do nothing, eventually Geirolf's going to come back. And maybe this time he really will give you a compulsion to rape me. Then everybody loses—except that demonic son of a bitch. I don't want to die, but even more than that, I won't be responsible for all those deaths. I'll do anything—anything at all—to avoid that. Including die."

Hoover Building, FBI Headquarters, Washington

Parker looked up from the stack of reports on his desk as Mike Richards walked out of the office with Reece Champion.

Who was not, of course, Reece Champion. Lord Geirolf

had simply assumed the vampire's form in order to quell the assistant director's suspicions that he had a mole among his agents. Which the demon god had evidently done, judging from the unfocused look in Richards's eyes.

The AD led the way to Parker's desk and introduced "Champion." "You two will be working together," Richards said. To Geirolf/Champion, he added, "Why don't you use my office while I grab a bite to eat. I'm starved."

"Sure," the demon god said, smiling Champion's easy white grin. "Come on, Parker, I'll explain where we're going."

Parker rose and followed Geirolf/Champion back to Richards's office as all around them, other agents tried very hard to look very busy. They'd all heard of Champion's formidable reputation, though nobody but Richards knew he was a vampire.

"You don't have to worry about being discovered," Geirolf told him telepathically as they walked. *"Richards now believes you're a good and loyal employee."* He chuckled. *"In fact, you'll probably get a raise."*

"What about the others? Richards wasn't the only one who suspected the FBI has a mole in the ranks."

Geirolf waved a dismissing hand as they stepped into Richards's office and he closed the door behind them. *"I'll take care of them shortly. In the meantime, you'll be assisting 'Champion' with a mission."*

Parker sat down as his master dropped into the thickly padded office chair behind Richards's neat desk. *"You only have to give the word."*

Geirolf smiled with Champion's mouth, but there was something inhuman and smug in his eyes. *"I know. You'll be accompanying me back to the Death's Sabbat compound in Georgia for the ceremonies. I've summoned all the cults together, and I want you to have everything ready when they arrive in a couple of days."*

Parker sat back in his chair. *"A couple of days? Why not just teleport them?"*

"And waste that much magic?" Geirolf snorted. *"I'd rather leave the driving to Greyhound. Besides, I'm spending a great deal of power just keeping the Majae from awakening Merlin's Grimoire. I need to keep them in the dark a little while longer. As long as they're so focused on that book, they can't devote their full forces to finding Champion."*

Since his master seemed to be in a good mood, Parker decided to dare a question. *"Speaking of whom, has he Turned the girl yet?"*

"Oh, no. I designed the compulsion to build slowly, so he can fight it for another day or two." His laugh was unpleasant. *"By the time we're ready, it'll be so strong, he'll pin her against the nearest wall and fuck her like a rabbit."*

Parker frowned. *"What if he decides to Change her deliberately, before the spell can force him? They could escape."*

"Champion?" Geirolf snorted. *"Not likely. He had a very ugly experience with an unsanctioned Maja a couple of centuries ago. He'd never risk Turning her. That's why I chose him rather than one of the other vampires I'd identified. Besides, there's no way a newly Turned Maja would be able to break out of that cell. It held me, after all."*

Parker considered challenging a few of his master's assumptions, but decided that might be pushing it. *"What about the cultists? What's your plan for them, if I might ask?"*

Geirolf shrugged. *"Once the Magekind is dead, I'm afraid we may have trouble with the Sidhe. It's entirely possible Llyr and his brother will decide to put aside their differences and unite against me."* His smile was dark. *"I'm going to have to do something about that—with a little help from the cults."*

Erin was right: Turning her might be the only chance they had, and Reece knew it. Maybe if she'd been any other woman, he would have already yielded to the ruthless, inevitable logic of the situation. If she went mad and he ended up having to kill her, that was still better than being sacrificed in a spell that would kill thousands of people.

But she wasn't any other woman. She was Erin.

That shouldn't make a difference. He had his duty, his sworn oath to do whatever the hell he had to in order to ensure the survival of the human race and its Mageverse guardians.

If only she wasn't so intelligent and honorable and admirable. Not to mention so lush she made his balls ache even when he wasn't under a spell.

But if he Gifted her and it went bad, he'd plunge her into a hell of madness that would end only with one of them killing the other.

The thought made his gut twist. God, he hated killing women. In more than two centuries as America's champion, he'd had to end the lives of only three: Lizzie and two others whose executions the Council had ordered.

There had been women who had probably needed killing—spies, traitors, criminals—but he'd always managed to find other solutions to whatever problem they presented. And he'd never killed a woman he'd slept with.

He certainly didn't want to start with Erin.

Reece grimaced, remembering the visceral jolt in his arm as the sword rammed home in Lizzie's chest. There'd been such gratitude in her gaze. She'd known what Mageverse Fever had done to her, and she'd seen death as a welcome release.

Maybe it was weak. Maybe he was shirking his duty. But he didn't want to have to meet Erin's eyes as he killed her.

"There is one alternative," she said suddenly from the table, picking restlessly at a piece of bread.

Reece looked over at her, trying to ignore the fist of lust that gripped his balls at the sight of her lush body just barely contained in that Merry Widow. She still sat on the table, those long legs crossed. He wanted them wrapped around his waist. "I'd like to hear it," he said, and hoped she didn't notice the rasp of raw hunger in his voice.

"You can kill me now."

He stared at her, feeling like a man who'd taken a hard punch right between the eyes. "What?"

"We can't do nothing, Champion." Her gaze was fierce and direct on his. "Doing nothing is the same as just giving ourselves to that bastard. Sooner or later, he'll make you take me, and we'll be finished."

He should have realized she'd see the situation as clearly as he did. *"I'm not killing you."*

"Stop thinking like a Boy Scout!" Erin exploded, banging the flat of her hand on the table. "You're an American agent. I know you've had to make tough choices before. Make one now. The only no-risk alternative is killing me, and you know it."

Forgetting the danger, he stalked toward her, grabbed her by the shoulders, and hoisted her half off the table until they were nose to nose. "I won't be bluffed into Gifting you, Erin!"

"I'm not bluffing, Champion. Geirolf can't kill me if I'm already dead."

Simmering with frustrated rage, he snarled into her face, "Do you honestly think that hasn't occurred to me?"

"Oh, I know it's occurred to you. You're not stupid."

Reece cursed viciously and let her go before he yielded to his driving need to kiss her. Her bottom hit the table with a thump that rattled crockery.

He was hard as Excalibur, and felt at least that long.

She dared curl that luscious lip at him. "I didn't realize you were this big a Pollyanna."

"Pollyanna, my ass. Do you have any idea how many men I've killed? Not just soldiers and spies, but poor assholes who were simply in the wrong place at the wrong time. I'm nobody's idea of Pollyanna."

"So why are you going chickenshit now?"

He shot her a hot glare, knowing when he was being goaded. "Maybe because for a minute there, I found you likable."

"Hey, if it would make it easier if I do bitch, I can do bitch."

"Would you just back the hell off for a—" He broke off as she picked up a carving knife from the table beside her hip. Chilling calculation filled her eyes.

He watched her, feeling something still and cool slide over him. "You planning to use that on me?" There was a certain logic to that idea. If her death would spike Geirolf's guns, so would his.

Erin looked up and snorted. "Do I look dumb enough to think I could pull that off? I've seen you in action."

"So what are you—?" Calculation became horror as he realized what she was thinking. "No."

"I never understood why David did it." She studied the knife blade, her gaze brooding. "Until now. If your only alternative is to either allow something like Geirolf to destroy you or to take yourself out—"

Reece snatched the knife from her hand. "David wasn't that selfless, Erin. He just couldn't stand the idea of killing you any more than I can." He held the knife up until it caught the light. "But unfortunately, this isn't an enchanted blade, so I don't have the option of suicide." With a flip of his wrist, he threw the knife into the pool. "The only real option I've got is this."

He grabbed a fistful of her blond curls, bent her head back, and took her mouth in the kiss he'd been craving for hours.

Champion's mouth felt like hot, wet silk as he claimed her lips, holding nothing back. She felt one big hand slide under her ass, lifting her up off the table to pull her full length against him. Rolling his muscled torso against her, he let her feel the strength and lust skidding out of control with every flick of his tongue and hungry, biting kiss.

Her head began to spin from the sheer erotic ferocity of his kiss, of his hands pulling her tighter against his hard-on. Her heart thumped with a combination of relief, desire, and fear.

"I thought you didn't want to take the chance," she murmured against his mouth.

He caught her lower lip in his teeth, tugged gently. "I've decided you're worth the risk."

With a soft moan, she wrapped her legs around his waist and hooked her ankles together at the small of his back. Still kissing her, Reece carried her across the cell to the bed. He tossed her lightly onto the mattress, then came down on top of her, pressing her deliciously into the pile of furs.

He lifted his head to look down at her for one wildly carnal moment. His mouth was flushed from the fierce kiss, and his eyes glittered over the white length of his fangs.

Erin stared up at him with a breathless combination of desire and fear. Not the physical fear that he would hurt her—he wasn't capable of that—but the purely feminine fear of being overwhelmed by raw male hunger.

And it didn't get any more raw than Champion's.

She could feel herself creaming, readying for the big cock pressing against her abdomen. He reached up and wrapped his fingers in the bodice of her corset. Jerked downward until her stiff nipples popped free, aching and ready. With a sound somewhere between a growl and a moan, he lowered his head.

Watching him breathlessly, Erin waited for that beautiful mouth to claim her again. Her own heartbeat pounded a jungle beat in her ears.

Then his lips closed fully over the tight pink tip. Erin threw her head back and gasped as he began to suck, flicking skillfully with his tongue. Simultaneously he teased the other nipple with one hand, milking pleasure from it in starburst glitters she could almost see.

Even as the wave of arousal and delight rose, Erin knew they could both be dead within hours. She pushed the thought away. If this moment with Champion was all she'd ever have, she'd damn well make the most of it.

Lifting both hands, she threaded her fingers through the black silk of his hair, enjoying the texture as his skilled mouth teased and caressed her flesh. He groaned in pleasure at her touch. Encouraged, she reached down to stroke the hard muscle of one shoulder, then let her fingers dance over his biceps. His skin felt smooth and supple, the texture seducing her into exploring further.

He lifted his head, gave her a wild look from under dark brows. "Don't do that," he growled. "You're going to send me right over the edge."

She grinned up at him wickedly. "Ooh. That sounds like fun." Reaching around his brawny arm, she ran a testing thumb over his ribs. He jerked away with a gasp. She laughed. "A ticklish vampire. Ah, the possibilities!"

"Minx." He jerked off her in one fluid movement and strode back to the bath.

She sat up, bracing herself on her elbows as he bent to pick up his robe. "Come back! No more tickling, I promise."

"Oh, I know there's not going to be any more tickling." Champion pulled the silk belt from the robe's belt loops, then tossed the robe aside and headed for her again.

"Hey!" She sat up, holding up a hand to fend him off. "No bondage, Double Oh Fang."

"See, now that's the nice thing about being the vampire," he told her, whipping a length of silk around her wrist before capturing the hand she was batting at him. "I get what I want."

After all the anger and tension of the last two days, knowing they were finally going to act on their desire made Erin feel almost giddy. She squirmed and bucked, but she was giggling too hard to put up effective resistance. In seconds, he had both wrists securely trussed.

When she finally subsided, out of breath from laughter, he grinned down at her wickedly. "Voilà. A bound blond buffet—every vampire's dream dinner."

"Pervert." Deciding to get into the spirit of things, Erin gave him a deliberately enticing wiggle.

His grin widened, revealing fangs. "Oh, yesss. The presentation needs work, though."

She gave him a mock-offended sniff. "I beg your pardon?"

"Yeah. You're not naked." He flopped down beside her onto one elbow and reached out his free hand to untie the bow in the white ribbon laces of her corset.

EIGHT

Erin settled back to watch, feeling the heat growing again as his long, clever fingers slowly unlaced the ribbons, pulling and tugging gently. His green gaze flicked from her face to the gap slowly widening between the edges of her corset. Appetite had sharpened his brutal good looks even more. Her own desire coiled in tight, hot spirals in her belly.

Unconsciously she bent her knees and spread her legs. His eyes snapped to her face, so fierce with hunger she licked her lips.

He growled.

Suddenly he sat up, grabbed the edges of her corset in both hands, and jerked. Silk ripped and ribbons snapped. Erin's eyes widened as he dragged the remains of the corset off her body and threw it across the room.

Her fragile thong panties were the next to go, sacrificed to one impatient jerk.

Naked, wearing only her white lace stockings, Erin stared up at him as desire seared her veins in a white-hot wave. The bulge in his silk trousers looked more like a baseball bat than an erection. Slowly, darkly, he smiled. "Naked bound blonde. Now, *that's* the way I like my dinner."

Reece could smell Erin's need. It perfumed the air with a salty, delicious musk he was dying to taste. She lay with her narrow wrists tied in black silk between those luscious breasts, her long legs spread, all that blond hair tumbled around her face. Her blue eyes looked dazed.

Within him, the Desire strained at the leash he'd managed to throw over it. His aching cock twitched. He decided to give her a look at it.

He caught the waistband of his silk trousers in both thumbs and began to tug downward, revealing the thick and straining shaft inch by inch. Erin licked her lips.

He wanted to plunge his cock between them.

Not yet, Reece told the Desire, pushing the pants the rest of the way down his thighs. His shaft bobbed as he kicked free of them.

"So is the horse still crying?" she asked, her voice rough with a mixture of arousal and amusement.

He lifted a brow. "What horse?"

"The one you got that dick from."

Reece laughed. "You're a very bad girl, Erin."

"Yep." Her smile was wicked as he eased down on top of her, catching his breath at the feeling of her warmed velvet curves. "And getting worse every minute. What are you going to do—punish me?"

"Oh, yeah." He eyed the sweet, full mounds of her breasts. Her nipples were flushed pink, hard as cherries. "A tongue lashing is definitely called for."

The feeling of that slim, naked body under his made his head spin. Shuddering in raw need, he closed his mouth over the nearest nipple and began to suck. The taste spun into his head like a Catherine's wheel on the Forth of July, slinging sparks of pleasure with every revolution.

She arched under him, catching at his chest with her small, bound hands. His hold on the Desire slipped another notch. Quickly he caught her wrists and pulled them over her head. If he lost control, it would be over far too fast.

Which was why he'd better speed it up before the thin leash on his need snapped.

With a rumble of hunger, Reece began to nibble his way down her narrow torso, licking and biting gently at the full curves of her breasts. Next came the sweet, pale skin that lay over her delicate abdominal muscles. He paused to swirl his tongue around her navel until she squirmed, then switched his attention to the fragile jut of one hip bone.

"I take back the Boy Scout comparison," she managed. "You've got a sadistic streak."

Reece smiled and buried his nose in the fine golden curls over her pussy. "Who, me?" He gave one labia a gently taunting lick. "I just like my food nice and hot."

Erin threw back her head and gasped. "You make me sound like a Big Mac."

"Oh, no." He pushed his tongue between her nether lips and closed his eyes in delight at the thick cream that filled her. "You're much sweeter than a Big Mac."

She whimpered and spread her thighs in invitation. Smiling, he settled himself more comfortably between them.

The smile became an outright grin as Erin arched into his mouth. Reece gave her another gently sampling lick. "Something more creamy than a Big Mac," he decided, grinning against her cunt as she rolled her hips. "I know. Pudding."

Her laughter held a note of outrage. "Pudding? You're comparing me to pudding?"

"Egg custard?" He closed his mouth over her clit and suckled gently.

"I refuse to be"—she had to stop to pant—"compared to custard. Jesus, Champion, where's the poetry?"

"Crème brûlée." He parted her lips with two fingers and began to lick her with all the skill he'd learned over two centuries. "Sweet and creamy on the tongue."

"Oh, God," she managed. "Well, at least that's French."

It took Champion ninety seconds to rush her to a glorious, shuddering climax.

Lying limp and dazed in the aftermath, she was barely aware he'd sat up between her thighs.

The next thing she knew, he flipped her effortlessly onto her stomach. Her nervous system still jangling from the furious climax, she lifted her head woozily as he pulled her onto her knees, ass in the air. "Champion, what—?"

She had her answer when he drove into her in one hard, stunning thrust. The sensation of being filled so completely, so ruthlessly, damn near blew off the top of her head. She managed a strangled yelp. And then he was riding her, stroking hard in and out of her hot, cream-filled core.

"God!" She pulled herself up and managed to brace onto her elbows. The silk belt tied around her wrists spilled over the fur in front of her as Champion fucked her, jarring her body with his long, steady lunges. Erin shuddered under the onslaught, dazed and overwhelmed by the sensation of so much hard cock stuffing her.

"Oh, yeah," he purred in her ear, bracing his hands beside her head as he lowered himself over her until he covered her completely. "Open yourself up to me. You're so tight. Like a silken fist wrapped around my cock. How does it feel?"

"Big." Her dazed brain couldn't manage any word longer than one syllable. "So hard. Oh, God!"

One hand clamped down on her bound wrists as he braced

himself on the other, pumping deep. She lifted her butt for him, setting her knees farther apart on the mattress. Letting him take her however he wanted.

And he apparently wanted her fast and deep and without mercy, in long, ramming strokes that reached halfway to her heart and sent her building orgasm coiling up her spine. She threw back her head and keened at the tension, at the blinding pleasure just out of reach.

"Give me your throat," he growled in her ear.

Arousal hit her in another hard punch at the rough demand. Obediently Erin tossed her hair back and turned her head, baring her banging pulse to him.

He stopped thrusting and leaned down. She looked up at him from the corner of one eye and saw his open fangs.

The bite made her jolt against him, driving his seated cock another inch deeper. She whimpered in helpless lust.

And then he was feeding, drinking her blood as he began to fuck her again, driving even deeper and harder than before.

Erin quivered at the maddening triple penetration. He was buried to the balls now, taking her in short, ruthless strokes that coiled her rising orgasm tighter and tighter and . . .

She screamed as it exploded in all its ferocious glory, a dark wave of pleasure that dimmed her sight.

Champion drove in one final hard stroke and stiffened with a growl, still drinking from her as he came.

As the aftershocks pulsed through her, Erin collapsed bonelessly. Without breaking his hold on her throat or his penetration of her cunt, he rolled over with her until she sprawled on top of his hard, muscled body.

Spread like an offering as he fed from her throat.

After almost three hundred years, Reece had finally met a woman he could love. And the odds were very good he'd end up destroying her.

The bitterness of that knowledge gnawed at him even now,

as he lay with Erin sprawled on top of his body, limp with sated pleasure, the taste of her blood in his mouth. His cock was still inside her, though he could feel it slipping slowly out as it softened.

She deserved so much better than this.

He thought of the women he'd known and enjoyed over more than two centuries as a vampire. Mortals and Latents and Majae, the beautiful and the brilliant, the courageous and the honorable and the skilled. Erin had it all, wrapped in one luscious package that managed to arouse both his lust and his admiration.

Damn, he didn't want to do this to her.

If the Change went bad, that wonderful mind would crack under the Mageverse's psychic battering, and he'd have to kill her. Even if she proved strong enough to withstand the sudden acquisition of all that power, if she couldn't break them out of the cell, Geirolf would return and kill them both.

Well, no, Reece realized, as his heart sank. He couldn't allow her to be used that way. He'd have to kill her himself.

Their only chance—and it seemed slim—was that Erin could use her power to break them free. And even that was a dicey proposition, because they could easily end up facing a death sentence from the Majae's Council. True, the witches would probably understand, given the seriousness of the situation with Geirolf. But the Majae could be a capricious lot, and he'd learned long ago he couldn't always predict what they'd decide.

All they needed was for someone to have a vision indicating Erin was dangerous, and they'd end up facing a Round Table execution team.

Not that any of that mattered one way or another. Reece was committed to Changing her now, regardless of the outcome. And he'd been in combat often enough to know that if you concentrated on the fact that you were probably going to die, you were virtually guaranteed to do just that.

The thought of his own death didn't really bother him. He should have been dead centuries ago; he could hardly bitch about the hand he'd been dealt now. But Erin was a different story.

If the next couple of hours were all she would ever have, he was damn well going to make them good ones. Starting right now.

Tenderly he unwrapped the silk tie from around her wrists, then gathered her into his arms and rolled from the bed. She stirred and lifted her head as he carried her across the room. "Where are we going?" she asked sleepily as he deposited her on her feet beside the Roman bath.

"I thought you might want to wash," he explained as he went down on one knee to roll those lace stockings down her smooth, endless legs.

She yawned hugely and braced a slim hand on his shoulder as she lifted one foot so he could tug the stocking off. "Actually, I'd kind of like a nap, but I guess we'd better get back on it."

Reece lifted a brow. "Well, if you've got something you'd rather do . . ."

"Mmmm. Definitely not." Erin grinned languorously at the ceiling. Then the humor drained from her face. "But we really do need to get me Changed before Geirolf comes back for his human sacrifice." She frowned as he went to work on the other stocking. "Come to think of it, I wonder why he didn't just hang around to watch us do the deed?"

"Good question." He tossed the wisp of silk aside. "Then again, he's been locked up in this cell since Merlin walked the Earth. Maybe he just couldn't stand the thought of being in here again, even for something like this."

"Makes sense. I'm already sick of this place myself, and we've only been here two days." Naked, Erin turned—giving him an excellent view of her delectable ass—and stepped down into the water. She sighed in pleasure and bent her knees until she could submerge herself to the chin.

Reece moved to the selection of oils and soaps he'd sorted through earlier, lifting them one by one and sniffing until he found a couple that smelled like her: richly, sensuously female. He picked both bottles up and stepped down into the bath with her.

"What's that?" Erin asked, eyeing the bottle with misgivings.

"An aphrodisiac." He grinned at her dubious expression and poured the contents of the bottle into one hand. "Just kidding. I think. No, one of them is shampoo. The other's some kind of massage oil. Courtesy of our amazing enchanted cell. Though why Merlin created it to be so generous to a monster like Geirolf is a very good question."

"Some people are just too civilized for their own good." She tilted back her head as he began working the cream into her long blond hair. "Mmm . . ." Her throaty purr at the sensation made his sated cock twitch in reviving interest. "That feels really nice."

"Yeah," he said hoarsely. "It does." And it did. Her thick hair slid through his fingers like rich, raw silk. The scent alone, lush with femininity and Erin, was enough to make his blood rise hot. Closing his eyes, he let himself sink into pure languorous pleasure, cherishing it—cherishing her—with all the passion of desperation.

Once he'd turned her hair into a pile of lather, he let his soapy hand stroke lower, finding the long, delicate line of her neck, the fragile bone and flesh of her shoulders. His exploring fingers discovered delicate muscle drawn hard and knotted, so he dug in his thumbs there and began, carefully, to massage the tension away.

Erin drew in a deep breath and released it in a long, sensual purr. "God, I needed that." She let her head drop back to rest on his shoulder. Lather slid from her hair to run down his spine in cool, fragrant dollops.

"You're tense," he said, smoothing her soapy hair back with one hand as he continued the massage with the other.

"Yeah," Erin admitted. "I'm scared of messing up. Scared

of not being able to hack the transformation." Her tone hardened. "But not scared enough to back out. Not with everything that's riding on it."

He studied her, hearing the sincerity in her heartbeat. "You really were willing to use that knife, weren't you?"

She hesitated, then sighed. "Yeah, I was. You've got to admit, there's a certain logic in it."

He went back to work on her slender, knotted muscles. "Where did all this come from?"

She groaned. "Damn, you're good. All what?"

"All that toughness and dedication."

"I'm not that damn heroic, Champion." She didn't even open her eyes as he massaged her neck. "I'm just trying to do the job."

He lifted a brow. "Somehow I don't think fighting demons is in the FBI oath."

"I'm not FBI anymore. I'm not even Outfit."

"Very true. Yet here you are, ready to risk your life and your sanity to stop Geirolf. Why is it so damn important to you?"

She opened one eye and turned her head to look at him. "What, preventing the destruction of mankind isn't a good enough reason?"

"Well, yes, but it's such an overwhelming task, most people would have trouble taking it seriously. And I think it's more personal to you than that."

He felt her narrow shoulders tighten even more under his hands. "I've told you about David."

"But why were you in the FBI to begin with? You've got to admit, it's not the typical career."

She hesitated, then shrugged. "I come from a long line of soldiers, that's all. I grew up listening to the propaganda. You know, Semper Fi and all that stuff."

"Oh?" He started massaging the length of her back, rubbing circles around each fragile vertebra.

"Mmmm. Yeah. My dad was a Marine. He died in the last

fighting in Vietnam when I was just a baby. Never got to know him at all."

"Tough break."

"A lot of people in my generation caught that particular break, though. And my granddad worked really hard to provide that paternal . . . whatever. Oh, down some—yeah, that's it." Her sensual purr had his body tightening, but he ignored it, hungry to hear more of her story.

He wanted to know her, know more about her. He told himself it was because he needed to understand his ally in this unlikely mission. "So your father was a hero."

Erin nodded. "Though there was a time I didn't see it that way. I was maybe fourteen or so, and we were studying the war in U.S. History class. I ended up railing about it to my granddaddy. Something about old politicians sacrificing young men."

He made an encouraging noise in his throat as he explored her slim muscles looking for another knot.

"My little anti-war speech didn't sit too well with Granddad." She shrugged. "Not surprising. I'd known he'd been in the Army during World War II, but what I hadn't known was that he was one of the GIs who'd liberated the Jews in the death camp at Dachau. He'd never talked about it before."

"The ones who've seen the worst side of humanity don't," Reece said softly, remembering some of his own past battlefields. "Talking about it means reliving it."

"Yeah. And this was evidently pretty damn bad. The whole story just *exploded* out of him in this wave of horror and rage. He talked about the emaciated corpses piled up like discarded garbage, about the crematoriums, about the horror and the stench and the pity. About how stopping the Nazis had been the right thing to do, no matter how many good men we'd had to spend to do it." She took a deep breath and blew it out. "And then I said something really stupid. 'But that was a *good* war.' And he said, 'Erin, there is no good war when you're fighting it. There's only necessary wars.'"

He nodded. "Smart man."

She was silent a long moment. "My brother ended up enlisting in the Marines, too. Fought in the first Gulf War. He came back talking about Saddam and starving Khurds." Erin shrugged. "Sounded a lot like Granddad."

Reece nodded thoughtfully. "Quite a legacy."

"Yeah. I considered going into the service myself, but while I was still in college, my roommate's little sister got molested by a neighbor. I watched what the family went through—my friend and her mother and the little girl. That was when it hit me that I didn't need to go overseas to find evil." She shrugged under his hands. "So I decided to use my degree and try to get on with the Bureau. I succeeded, and here I am."

"No wonder you've got that self-sacrificial streak," he said aloud. "It's practically written into your family's genetic code."

"No, actually, I have no desire to sacrifice myself." Her voice firmed with determination. "Like Granddad said, the idea is not to die for your country, but to make the other son of a bitch die for his. And I'm not going to die. I'm going to make this work, Champion. I'm not going to fail."

"I know that." And he knew he had to believe it. Any doubt on his part could infect her, and that alone could doom them.

Erin pulled away and threw a quick look at him over her shoulder. "Didn't you say earlier that there was a good chance I'd go nuts?"

He hesitated, weighing how to answer. "You're a strong woman, Erin." Unfortunately, he would have said the same of Lizzie. Apparently, there was more to it than strength, though nobody was sure what. Sometimes even the Majae's Council made mistakes.

She grunted. "Let's just hope I'm strong enough." Bending her knees, Erin plunged her head under and shook her hair, sending streamers of soap and gold swirling around her lush body.

When she stood again, turning toward him, lust hit him in a

hard, low blow in the belly. The soaking blond strands had plastered themselves over the delicious curves of her pale breasts. Water streamed down her body. She tossed her head and peeled the sopping mass back from her face. The unconscious arch of her body as she moved made his cock rise to full, aching erection.

Opening her eyes, Erin caught sight of his face and grinned a bit wickedly. The raging lust he felt must be written all over his face. She glanced down at his groin. "Whoa," she said, taking a half step back. "You don't need much recovery time, do you?"

Reece swallowed, trying to get some moisture back into his dry mouth. "We don't, as a rule."

Erin gave him a sidelong look that held more than a little flirtation. "You as in vampires?"

"Yes, we as in—" He broke off with a gasp as she reached out a long, slim hand and cupped him. "You're good at that."

"I know. So are you all hung, or are you just blessed?"

He let his head fall back as those slender fingers circled his shaft. "Right now I'm feeling exceptionally blessed."

She laughed softly, still caressing him. "Based on the evidence, I think I'm the blessed one."

NINE

The water swirled around Reece and Erin as she caressed him until he was just short of squirming. His gasps bounced off the stone walls as she gently cupped the tight pouch of his balls and stroked the aching length of his cock.

Tempting as it was to let her do as she pleased, Reece reminded himself the idea was to give her pleasure, not to simply take it. He stepped back, tearing himself reluctantly from her clever fingers. "That's enough."

She gave him the smile Eve must have given Adam right before she fed him the apple. "Not even close, Champion."

He shook his head. "No, you don't get it. This time is for you. Your pleasure, not mine." Then he gave her his best wolfish smile. "Though I'm sure I'll get my turn sometime."

* * *

Champion moved around behind her as if taking himself out of the path of temptation.

Then he proceeded to turn the tables. His big, warm hands came to rest on her shoulders, a sensual masculine weight that made her knees buckle before she caught herself. "Not feeling weak, are you?" he asked in her ear, his voice low.

She shivered at his breath on her ear. "Maybe a little."

He swore softly. "I shouldn't have drunk from you so soon the last time."

Oh, he thought her weakness came from feeding his hunger. "It's not that kind of weak, Champion."

He stilled behind her, then began stroking his hands over her shoulders, rubbing and caressing just as he had earlier. "You sure about that?"

"Believe me, a girl knows." Then she had to catch her breath as those skilled hands once again sought out the knots in her muscles and began to rub them away.

"I'm glad," he said as his soapy hands trailed down her arms to encircle her ribs. Slowly, teasingly, they moved upward to capture and weigh her breasts. "I want you to be able to appreciate this."

Erin caught her breath as his slick fingers teased her nipples, stroking and tugging until she shuddered in pleasure. "Oh, that's definitely not a problem."

"Good," Reece breathed into her ear. "Because I want your undivided attention."

He had it as skillful hands tweaked and pulled both hard, rosy peaks for long glittering moments. As he caressed the taut globes of her breasts, Erin let her head fall back on his brawny shoulder. With a whimper of surrender, she gave herself up to the slow, seductive tightening of arousal he won from her with every stroke.

Finally he let one hand drift down her sensitive belly to the soft, fine hair of her sex. He parted her, slipped one finger between her folds to tease her clit and the creaming opening of her cunt. Pleasure unfurled within her in a slow, lazy bloom. "God, that feels so good," she moaned.

"Yeah," he agreed in a rough growl. "It does. But it's about to get better." He turned her around and caught her under the backside, then lifted her off her feet before striding with her to the edge of the bath. She groaned in pleasure at his easy strength, wildly aroused, and wrapped her legs around his waist. But before she could get down to the serious business of grinding against him, he deposited her on the edge of the pool and tipped her onto her back. Then he draped both her legs over his shoulders and lowered his head between her thighs.

The first time he'd pleasured her with his mouth, it had barely taken him five minutes to drag her to a ruthless climax. Now he took his time, tonguing her clit in slow circles and wicked little flicks, licking and teasing. Simultaneously his fingers were busy in her depths, first one and then two, teasing glowing curls of pleasure from her jangling nerves. With the other hand, he returned to her nipples, pinching and rolling them. Pleasure stormed her body from so many different directions, she could only moan.

And so he gently seduced her into orgasm after orgasm until she writhed helplessly on the marble, half maddened from the pleasure he gave her.

At last, when she was limp and stunned, he lifted his head and surveyed her boneless body with a hot, possessive smile. Then he scooped her off the floor again. Water swirled around her legs as he pulled her back into the pool—and right onto his rock-hard cock.

Erin yelped as she found herself suddenly impaled on him. Blinking, she met his carnal gaze. "How's that?" he asked with a wicked, lazy smile.

"It's, uh—" She squirmed, feeling him touching her in places that had never been touched before. "A lot."

"You have that effect on me. Hold on, sweetheart."

Wrapping her arms around his broad shoulders, she

obeyed as he began, lazily, to thrust. Which was a good thing, because she still felt a little tender from the rough, dominating ride he'd given her last time. Not that she'd objected.

Yet there was something just as arousing in being cradled in those powerful arms, feeling him use his cock like a wizard's wand to lay a spell of pleasure over her shivering body.

He probably knows I'd be sore from prior experience, she thought muzzily.

Centuries of prior experience.

And he seemed to be making good use of every year of it now as he patiently rolled his hips, stroking the sensitive depths of her body with breathtaking tenderness. As her arousal spiraled with the lazy rise of her latest climax, she found herself wanting to grind against him, take him deeper.

And as if sensing that rising hunger, he began to thrust harder by carefully controlled increments, his green eyes watching her face. She returned his gaze and found herself blinking at its intensity. No man, even David, had ever looked at her like that—as if she was the center of his universe.

The orgasm burst within her in a shower of iridescent bubbles. She threw back her head and moaned at the gently extravagant pleasure.

As Erin went limp in his arms, Reece lowered his dark head toward the arch of her throat. She tensed, remembering the delicious sting of his fangs sinking into her throat.

But at the last moment he closed his mouth and turned his head. Before she could wonder why he'd denied himself, his powerful body bowed with the force of his orgasm, pistoning his cock to the balls. He came, shuddering against her.

For a moment, she was aware only of his width and length pressing so deep inside her.

And then something happened. It seemed a white-hot light rolled across her vision, leaving only Champion in its center. For a single, blazing instant, she felt the universe shift around her, as if it was about to crack open and spill.

Erin caught her breath in a combination of anticipation and terror. *Three times. He'd said it would take three times. It's only been two!*

Or had it been three? That time at his house, after the party—no, he'd worn a condom, then. It only counted if he came in her . . .

And then everything settled again, the normal rules clicking into place like a sliding glass door jarring back into its track.

Sucking in a deep breath, Erin wrapped her arms around Champion and held on to the only stable thing in her world.

As if sensing her fear, he tightened his own hold. The arms that normally felt so powerful abruptly seemed like an insufficient barrier against . . . whatever it was. *So that's the Mageverse.* Suddenly Erin understood a little too well why women went insane when they became Majae.

It was an insight she could have done without.

Champion drew back a little and looked down at her, a concerned frown on his mobile mouth. "What's wrong?"

Erin licked lips that suddenly felt dry and chapped. "I felt it," she said, working to keep her voice steady. "The Mageverse. Just for a moment—let me go." She needed space.

Something in her voice had him lifting her off the cock that still hadn't softened. The minute her feet touched the floor of the pool, Erin turned to the edge and hoisted herself up. Dripping, she stood and waited for her pounding heart to slow.

"Erin—"

"Stay back a minute, would you?" Propping her hands on her hips, she stared down at the floor battling her fear as water dripped around her. "Just give me a damn minute."

"You felt it, didn't you?" He climbed the steps out of the pool, then hesitated when he saw her stiffen. "I'm not going to hurt you."

"No, of course not." She lifted her head and made herself meet his eyes. "It was just a little overwhelming."

Reece looked at her, both dark brows lifting. "Well, that has the distinct ring of understatement." He turned to stride for the stack of towels, collecting one for himself and pitching her another. She caught it and wrapped it around her shoulders, grateful for his sensitivity in keeping his distance.

"I'm not sure I can hack it, Reece," she admitted, driven to express the fear that had hit her when she'd felt the universe crack. "It's a hell of a lot stronger than I thought it would be."

Champion looked at her, wrapped in her towel. Despite the scent of fear in the air, her back was straight as a soldier's. And that gave him hope. Surely that kind of strength meant she'd make it. "From what I gather from talking to other Majae, everybody feels that way the first time they touch the 'Verse, Erin."

With brisk, no-nonsense movements, she began toweling off. "You're right, of course. This doesn't change anything. I know what I have to do."

He hesitated. "You know, there is a chance that someone from the Mageverse will notice I'm missing. They may even have launched a search party."

She shot him a hard look. "Must be a damn slim chance, or you'd have mentioned it before now."

Reece shrugged, uncomfortable. "Depends on too many *ifs. If* somebody noticed that I haven't been back to Avalon—"

"Avalon?"

"The High Court. It's kind of our base of operations. Anyway, *if* they got worried enough to start looking, and *if* they realize I'm not back on Earth—"

"—and *if* they send out a search party that somehow manages to stumble across us in this magic-shielded cell." Erin shook her head. "You're right, Reece. Too damn many *ifs*." Her gaze hardened. "We need to stick with the original plan."

"Which terrifies you."

"No, it doesn't terrify me," she denied, as if by knee-jerk reaction. Then she added reluctantly, "It may frighten me, but it doesn't terrify me. This really is the only shot we've got to stop him." She clenched her fists. "I've got to make it work."

Despite her brave words, Erin could almost sense the Mageverse out there, waiting for her, as malevolent in its way as the demon was.

And no matter what she'd told Reece, it scared the hell out of her more than anything ever had.

Except looking into David's eyes as he'd shoved his gun against his own chin and pulled the trigger. He'd sacrificed himself for her. He'd died to stop the demon. She owed him more than cowardice. Somehow she was going to have to overcome the Mageverse and defeat it.

Swallowing, Erin looked up. Her gaze collided with Champion's emerald gaze. She saw the sympathy in his.

And the doubt.

He doesn't believe I can do it, either, Erin realized. *He's afraid he's going to have to kill me.* Which was oddly comforting, in a way. If she did lose it, Champion wouldn't let her suffer long.

But what will happen to you in the meantime? a chilly voice whispered in her ear. What did it feel like to go insane? To feel your mind peeling away like an onion?

She didn't mind dying. She'd been on the job long enough that the idea of death no longer held the same sting of the unknown.

But madness was another story. She'd dealt with crazy people, had looked into their eyes and wondered in fear and pity what monsters inhabited their thoughts.

Apparently she was about to find out first hand.

Stop it, Erin told herself savagely. *Just stop it. This isn't helping. Have a little fucking guts, why don't you?*

Something touched her shoulder. She jerked around to look into Champion's concerned green gaze. "It's all right to be afraid, Erin. There's no shame in it."

"I know that. The only shame is in letting fear stop you." She remembered walking into the Death's Sabbat temple for the first time and looking around at the hundreds of people looking back at her.

In retrospect, it was miraculous they hadn't cut her throat, given that they'd made her. If Geirolf hadn't had other plans for her, they probably would have. But she'd faced them and her fear anyway, and she'd survived.

She squared her shoulders. "I've never let it stop me before."

He smiled and reached for her. "I know. You're a hell of a woman, Erin Grayson."

Her first instinct was to shy away from him, as though even such innocent contact could bring madness.

But Graysons did not run from anything. Not Nazis, not Vietcong, not Iraqis. Not even vampires who could crack the entire universe just by making love to you.

She stepped into his arms.

He felt warm and strong as he cuddled her against him, stroking her chilled flesh comfortingly. A bubble of disbelieving laughter broke free of her throat.

"What's so funny?" he asked softly, settling her a little more securely against his body.

"It just hit me that I'm cuddling with a vampire. Maybe I'm already nuts."

He shook his head, the stubble on his cheeks scraping her face. "You're not crazy."

"Aren't I? Vampires, soul-sucking demons that live off human sacrifices, a universe of magic where fairies fly past the windows of cells that have no doors." She wrapped her own arms tighter around him. "Maybe I'm already in the loony bin and just don't know it."

"You're the least crazy person I've ever met, Erin."

"Coming from a possible delusion, that's not really all that comforting." She laughed shortly. "What does it say about a situation when you'd rather be nuts than accept it as real?"

"Well, it's probably a good indication that it sucks." His arms tightened around her in a hug that was more comradely than romantic.

She relaxed into him. There was something so comforting in his strength. "Yeah," Erin agreed, and tried out a faint grin. "Sucks like a porn star."

For several minutes they simply stood like that, wrapped around each other. Finally she asked, "Was becoming a vampire anything like this?"

"Considering that I didn't have to worry about becoming a human sacrifice—no." He rested his chin on top of her head. "And I had a professional seducer, which looking back on it today seems like a blessing. Though I certainly didn't realize it at the time."

Erin pulled back enough to eye him. "A *professional* seducer? What, there's somebody who does this kind of thing for a living?"

He shrugged and caught her by the hand, towing her toward the bed. As he collapsed on the mattress in an elegant, boneless sprawl, Erin sat down facing him and pulled her legs beneath her, tailor fashion. "I told you the Majae's Council approves which Latent gets Merlin's Gift. Well, then somebody has to have sex with the Latent the required number of times. Sometimes the decision is based on the recommendation from a Maja or Magus, who then does the honors him or herself. But the rest of the time the Council sends one of the Court Seducers who specialize in romancing Latents."

Erin looked at him. "Oh, now that's perverse. Couldn't you just take turns or something?"

"Well, no. It's easier to botch than you might think. First, you've got to tell the Latent what he or she has the potential of becoming—"

"And then you've got to convince them you're not a lunatic," she tossed in.

"Right. Though I'm told turning into a wolf for them usually works."

"Certainly convinced me."

"Then you've got to tell them the risks, yet get them to take the chance anyway."

"Now, there's where I have a problem with this concept." Erin unfolded her legs and slipped off the bed to go to the table and pour herself a goblet. When she lifted the pitcher toward Reece, he nodded, so she poured him one as well. "I'd have real trouble convincing somebody to do something that could drive them crazy and result in their possible execution." She carried both goblets back to the bed and handed him one. "That's just cold."

Reece shrugged and took a sip as she sat down on the bed beside him. "It's actually fairly rare that the Majae's Council makes a mistake about Gifting somebody. They've been doing this a hell of a long time, and they're good at spotting the ones who can make it through the transition." He grimaced. "Of course, sometimes they make mistakes."

"Like I said, I wouldn't want to take the chance." Remembering the glimpse of the Mageverse she'd gotten, she grimaced. "Especially after getting a free preview."

"True, but there is the whole immortality thing," Reece told her. "The idea of living forever is a pretty powerful lure."

Erin rocked back from him, struck by the implications. "So in the unlikely event I actually manage to survive this—"

"You won't be dying for a very long time. Assuming we don't screw up and let humankind destroy itself."

She thought about it. Witnessing the passage of centuries as Reece had, the technological advances. One day she might step foot on another planet.

And watch her brother die, along with his children, and their children. Losing every mortal friend she had or would ever make, one by one. The thought chilled her.

Glancing up, Erin saw Reece, sprawled in splendid nudity against the headboard. *On the other hand, there might be compensations.*

Then she remembered the feeling of the universe cracking and sliding slowly sideways under her mind. "Still, it's a big risk."

He shrugged. "Only game in town, Erin."

"True." She sighed. "I guess we should probably just go ahead and—you know. Get it over with."

Reece shot her a look. "I've had more romantic proposals."

"Well, excuse the hell out of me," she snapped back, suddenly irritated. "I'm just not feeling particularly romantic."

He looked downward pointedly. "Neither am I."

"Oh." Erin blinked at his cock. Though still impressive, it lay curled over his muscular belly, obviously not up to the task. "That wasn't a problem before."

"Believe me," he said, "it's *never* been a problem."

Irrationally she felt a little twinge of hurt. "Oh."

"Don't look so damn wounded. I don't like the idea of doing this to you."

"Especially since if it doesn't work, you're going to have to kill me." Erin met his gaze steadily. "And I'm not just talking about if I go crazy. If we can deprive him of one of his sacrifices . . ."

He shook his head. "I've been thinking about it, and I don't believe that's good enough. Even if I kill you, all he has to do is kidnap another Latent, and then we're in the exact same mess all over again. At least if I die, too, he's going to have to find and kidnap a Magus."

She frowned at him, studying his grim face. "Are you talking about a suicide pact?"

Reece sighed. "Yeah, I know. Tough to do if you're not in the heat of a really ugly depression. You'll have to enchant a blade for me, though."

Knowing perfectly well she was stalling, Erin asked, "Wouldn't I need one, too?"

"No. Majae can use magic, but they aren't physically magic. Our connection with the Mageverse is much closer, so to kill us, you need a magical weapon."

"So what's that like—being magic?"

"Well, it's not really all that different. Other than the drinking blood and avoiding long exposure to direct sunlight. And no, I don't burst into flames, but the sunburn is a bitch."

Silence fell. They stared at each other.

"I have a massive case of performance anxiety," Erin said.

He snorted. "Tell me about it."

"There's so damn much riding on this. What if I go crazy? What if I don't go crazy, but I can't break through the cell? *How* am I supposed to break through the cell? I mean, I don't know any spells. Are there chants, or what?"

"Not usually. Oh, there's more preparation with big, elaborate spells, but most of the time Majae just do it, and it happens. I think they picture the outcome they want, and somehow manipulate the energies of the Mageverse to get it."

She stared at him. "Oh, that's a big help, Champion."

"I live to serve."

"Smartass."

"Hey, I'm not a Maja. I don't know how to do this stuff, either."

"Well, we're going to have to figure it out before the god of assholes comes back."

He smiled reluctantly. "God of assholes. I like that."

She felt her own lips twitch. "We could make it an acronym. G.O.A."

"We're stalling."

"I don't think I've ever felt less like sex in my entire life."

He regarded his stubbornly limp cock. "Me either."

Erin looked at the softened shaft. "Oh, I'm going to have to do something about that."

Reece settled back and arched a brow. "Whatever do you have in mind?" His cock twitched.

"Does it have to be penetration? I mean, would a blow job work?"

At that, he began to harden. "I assume so, since I Turned during oral sex." Then he gave her a wicked grin. "I certainly wouldn't mind trying."

Despite the grim situation, she laughed. "Somehow I didn't think you would."

"I also wouldn't mind returning the favor," he said. "In fact, I'd prefer it."

Erin considered the idea. It was extremely tempting. But—"Not this time," she decided. "I'd like to be in control." Grimacing, she added, "Of *something,* anyway."

She looked up to see warm sympathy in his eyes. "Yeah. I can understand that."

Rolling onto her hands and knees, Erin crawled over to him as he sat against the headboard. For a moment she paused, looking down at his powerful body, taking in the ridges and curves of muscle under his tanned skin. Curiously she reached out to touch him. "Why do you have a tan if you never go out in the sun?"

Reece shrugged. "I had a tan when I Turned. It never faded."

She stroked the pad of her thumb over one small male nipple. It came to a tiny brown peak.

Erin considered it. Maybe if she concentrated on him, just stopped worrying about what would happen at the end of this, they could both get through it.

And maybe she should damned well make the best of it anyway. She'd never had a lover like Reece before, and the odds were very good she'd never have one again. At all. Might as well thoroughly enjoy the opportunity while she had it. Anyway, it was much more pleasant concentrating on him than on the grim future they both faced.

She bent her head and flicked her tongue over that small male nipple. He caught his breath.

Oh, yeah. Much better.

Erin sat up and threw one leg over his hips so she could sit astride his thighs. He looked up at her and lifted a dark brow. For a moment she did nothing, just enjoying the sensation of his hard, strong thighs under her bottom.

His cock lengthened and grew even harder.

She grinned down at it. "Can't keep a good man down."

He gave her a wolf smile. "You can if he's underneath a good woman."

"Or better yet, a bad woman." Erin lowered her head and kissed him, sampling the soft, damp velvet of his lips. "And you're making me feel like a very bad woman."

TEN

They kissed slowly, a delicate mutual sampling of lips and teeth and tongue. Somewhere in the middle of it, Reece cupped her breast, savoring the soft, satin weight, thumbing and stroking one nipple. Sighing, she threaded her hands through his hair and nibbled her way along one cheek. Her soft mouth made him shiver as he imagined what it would feel like when she finally worked her way down his body.

She stopped at his ear for a sampling bite, then swirled her tongue around his earlobe until he moaned. Hungry to discover if she was as aroused as he was, he slid his free hand under her from behind. He was delighted to discover that thick, rich cream as he quested between her lips, dipped into her opening, and began to stroke.

"Mmmm," she purred in his ear. "Not that I'm complaining, but you do realize the idea is for me to give you a blow job, not for you to get me all hot and bothered?"

"Yeah, but unfortunately"—he turned his head to give her ear a little nip of his own—"I find myself pathologically unable to leave your magnificent body alone."

"Magnificent." She licked one of the thick cords of his neck. "I like that. You're not bad yourself, Slick."

"Glad you"—he caught his breath as she nibbled her way lower—"approve."

"Oh, I definitely approve." She discovered one of his pecs and paused to sample it with her tongue before working her way down to his nipple. He gasped.

"Like that?" she purred.

"A little too much." He was in danger of coming outside her if she kept it up.

But she gave him no mercy as she continued down his body, planting alternating licks and tiny bites down the ridges of his ribs and abdomen. Reece felt his balls tighten as his driving arousal increased. The heat rose until all he could think about was grabbing her hair and shoving his cock into her mouth.

But when she reached the thick stalk, she continued past it along his abdomen in a series of tiny, taunting nips. At the same time she slid her body slowly, sinuously down his thighs.

"Has anybody ever told you you're an evil woman?" Reece gasped. He'd stopped stroking her in favor of digging the fingers of both hands into the mattress as he clung to his self-control.

She lifted her head to give him a wicked smile. "Who, me?"

"Yes, you." He groaned, flexing his hips until his straining cock bobbed pleadingly.

"Li'l ole me?" Erin ran her tongue over the tight flesh of his groin, missing his balls by a millimeter.

"Sadistic goddess you, yes."

She gave him another tiny lick and looked up. "Do you want me to stop?"

"Do you want me to hold you down and bang you like a screen door?"

She closed her fingers around his cock, turning his growl into a choked gasp. "Don't threaten the sadistic goddess, Reece."

"Wouldn't dream of it."

Erin grinned. "Good." And she engulfed the flushed head of his cock with a single, mind-blowing swoop.

Engulfed in sweet, wet heat, Reece groaned helplessly at the sensation of her velvet lips sliding over his shaft. When she rolled her tongue across its sensitive head, he had dig both hands into the mattress, fingers curled into claws.

He'd had more than his share of blow jobs over the years, but Erin turned it into an art. She explored him with her mouth, her lips, her teeth, her hot little tongue, slowly, as if worshiping his cock like a supplicant at an altar. Despite his jaded sensibilities, despite the ugly situation, he found himself utterly focused on her, on every tongue flick and suckling pull. He could feel the hot pressure of his climax building in his balls. Reece knew he was seconds from spilling into that hot, luscious mouth.

And he didn't want to do it.

Because when he came, her Gift would trigger. He wanted her to feel his arms wrapped around her, holding her when the Mageverse slammed into her mind for the first time.

With a groan of effort, Reece reached down, grabbed her by the shoulders, and dragged her luscious mouth off his straining cock.

"Reece, what are you—!" she protested as he pulled her up over his body to straddle his hips. He caught her waist in one hand, lifted her, and aimed his aching erection at her core with the other.

And drove himself to the hilt in one frantic thrust.

Erin gasped as Reece began shafting her in long, driving strokes that shook her body, both big hands gripping her bottom. The gentle arousal that had bloomed while she suckled him suddenly burst into roaring blaze. Each jolt of his body into hers stoked it hotter.

Finally he rolled over with her, covering her with himself in a gesture that seemed more protective than possessive.

Then, as he rammed in a particularly hard thrust, a starburst exploded behind her eyes. At first she thought it was the first onslaught of the orgasm she could feel building, almost within reach.

But the next entry brought another flash, even more blinding than the first. Then two exploded as he drove into her again, spangling her vision with purple afterimages.

She came with a strangled cry as he convulsed over her with a bellow of tortured pleasure. "Erin!"

And the universe went insane, like a thousand flashbulbs going off around her all at once. Her next scream held a note of horror and inevitability as she realized her transformation had begun.

The energy slammed through her in a wave of molten heat—directly into Reece's body. He bellowed in mingled astonishment, pain, and pleasure as his face began to glow like heating metal. The light was so blinding she had to look away.

Then the force came rolling back out of him again. And slammed back into her.

Erin screamed.

Reece had never Gifted a Maja—that was a job for Court Seducers like Sebille and Lancelot. His own vampire transformation had been a far different process.

Like all Magi, Reece was Mageverse energy in human form. That first, signaling pulse from Erin triggered an explosion in his as the Mageverse poured from him into her, forcibly transforming them both into pure energy. For a fiery instant they fused into a single consciousness.

The first thing she felt was the sheer, blunt-force weight of centuries of experience blazing into her mind. Faces flashed through her memory, thousands of them, some famous, some not. She felt the jolt of a sword blade driving into a man's heart, the erotic slide of fangs sinking into a woman's throat. She felt his hunger and his intelligence and the loneliness he could never quite shake. She knew his grief for lovers lost and his satisfaction at battles won. And beneath it all, she felt his bedrock belief in his Great Mission, in the utter necessity of what he was doing.

And she felt his fear that he'd have to look into her eyes as he killed her.

She was so damn young. That was the first thing that struck him—how short her life had been next to the length of his own. Yet even so, there was a fire in her, a burning thirst for justice planted when she'd watched David sacrifice himself. Nothing would satisfy her but Geirolf's destruction. Even her fear of madness was no match for that relentless drive.

But there was more to her than a need for revenge.

When he'd touched Sebille's mind, Reece had found dedication, intelligence—and a profound refusal to let any man get close, even him. He'd known then that he could never make her love him.

Erin was just as intelligent, just as dedicated to her cause, but with those qualities burned both a fierce passion for life and an awareness of how quickly and easily death could wipe it all away.

He wanted her. Something in him recognized her, responded to her as if she was some missing part of his soul he'd always sought. She must have felt the same; he felt her flowing around him, welcoming him, blending with him in some sweet alchemy he'd never known before.

But even as they reached for each other, an opposing force dragged at them, hauling them apart. They fought to hold on, but it was too late.

The connection snapped. It felt as if something had torn her out by the roots. He yelled a protest. . . .

* * *

Their simultaneous cries of anguish ringing in her ears, Erin opened her eyes.

Champion looked down at her, his green eyes dazed and vulnerable as he lay over her, his weight braced on his arms, his cock still seated deep inside her.

"Oh," she said softly, a note of wonder in her voice as she remembered the touch of his mind.

"Yeah," he said. As if his trembling arms could no longer hold him, he rolled off her and lay on his side, breathing like a marathon runner in deep, shaking gasps.

For a long moment they simply lay still, gazing at each other, remembering the stunning moment when they'd fused.

"I touched your mind," Erin told him. After a pause, she said, "It was . . . you are . . ." She stuttered to a halt. No words she could think of did him justice.

His green eyes looked impossibly deep. "So are you."

"Have you ever—?"

"Linked with somebody like that?"

"Yeah."

"When I turned. But it wasn't the same. She wasn't anything like you." A lock of sable hair tumbled over his brow. Erin focused on it, entranced by its silken gleam. Within each strand, infinitesimal patterns of energy swirled around larger clumps of energy, each tiny system jostling against the next. Dimly she heard him continue, "You're so . . ."

"I can see the atoms in your hair," Erin interrupted dreamily. "All the little electrons and neutrons, and whatever the hell those other things are. Little glowing things."

Reece began to lose the look of dazed wonder. His eyes narrowed and his mouth tightened. "How do you feel?"

"High." She blinked. "Somebody slipped me some acid once when I was in college. Like that. I didn't like it." She shivered. It seemed the room was growing colder by the second. "I don't like this."

Helplessness flashed across his face. He reached for her. "Come here. I'll hold you."

Shivering harder, she went gratefully into his warm arms. It felt as though the temperature in the room had dropped ten degrees in as many seconds. Her teeth began to chatter. "Cold. I'm so cold."

Suddenly a blazing fire leaped up in a stone fireplace in the wall beside the bed, spilling heat across the room. Both of them jumped at the sudden crackling roar.

Erin stared uneasily at the leaping flames. "Was that fireplace there before?"

"No," Reece said grimly. "And did you create a flue?"

"A flue?" Smoke began billowing into the room. "Oh, a flue. No. How do I do that?"

"I have no idea," Reece said tightly, letting her go and easing back from her.

The fireplace vanished. "I'm not sure how I did *that*, either," she told him, dropping back to the mattresss, "but it was probably a good idea."

"Maybe you should try getting us out of here next."

"Right." That was the next logical step. "How?"

"You need to create a gate to Avalon." He rolled off the bed and onto his feet. As he moved, he left a glowing trail of swirling energy behind him.

"Damn, that's pretty."

He looked down at her, those fine lines tightening around his mouth again. The muscles in his sculpted abdomen rippled as he braced his hands on his hips.

"You know, you're naked," she told him. "Maybe I should try to do clothes before I try this gate thing."

"That probably would be best."

An image flashed through her mind, and in the next blink he was wearing the tuxedo he'd had on when she'd met him. He looked down at himself. "Not the best choice for running like hell."

Erin frowned at it. "Good point." An image flashed through

her mind, something she'd seen once in a movie.

A fur loincloth rode his hips, along with calf-high leather boots and jeweled bracers. A sheathed great sword hung from a baldrick between his shoulder blades. He laughed, a surprised male boom that made her own lips twitch. "You've got to be kidding me."

"Yeah, I guess Bond the Barbarian is not your best look." Another image flashed into her thoughts, and he was wearing a black T-shirt, black jeans, and black running shoes.

"That's good," Champion told her hastily. "Stop right there. I don't want to end up looking like one of the Village People."

Erin giggled and thought of her favorite worn jeans and cross trainers. For vanity's sake, she imagined a little white crop top that showed off the flat belly she'd been honing with countless trips to the gym.

As she scrambled off the bed, she saw male approval in Champion's eyes as he caught sight of her outfit. Then he frowned. "I thought Geirolf said this cell was magic tight. How are you able to make this stuff?"

She shrugged. "Hell if I know." Something zipped across the room, trailing sparks. Erin jumped and stared after it nervously. "Maybe he meant you just can't send magic out. There's sure as hell plenty of it in here." She jerked a thumb in the direction the mini-comet went. "I don't suppose you saw that?"

"Saw what?"

Erin sighed. "I didn't think so."

Now that she was beginning to think again, she could feel energy swirling around her like a hot soup, ready to become whatever she wanted to make of it. A fireplace, clothing, anything. All she had to do was think, and her wish became reality.

It was a seductive concept.

"This is easier than I thought it would be," she told Reece, as some of the fear drained out of her. "Damn, I wish I'd had this kind of power a year ago. Could have saved David and killed Geirolf and avoided this entire mess."

"Speaking of whom, we need to get out of here as soon as

possible," Reece said, looking worriedly toward one of the windows. "We don't know when that bastard will come back."

"Let him come," Erin said with a reckless baring of her teeth. "He's not going to find me easy pickings this time!" She envisioned a broadsword—something big and impressive, like she imagined Excalibur must be.

She almost dropped the massive weapon as it instantly appeared in her hand. Tightening her grip on it, she examined its gleaming length in satisfaction. "Oh, yeah. Devil Boy's in for a nasty surprise."

When she looked up, she found Reece staring at the blade in her hand. He paled and stepped back a pace.

Frowning, Erin looked into his eyes—and saw a series of flashing images. Lizzie, the sword in her slender hands. Westlake, dying with a froth of scarlet blood on his lips, the sword buried in his belly. Lizzie's scream of fury as she'd turned on Reece.

And the horrible, gut-searing jolt as Champion had driven the sword into her chest and watched the life drain from her eyes.

A cold chill rolled over Erin as she tore her gaze from his, knowing he was wondering if he'd have to kill her the same way.

He was afraid she was going mad.

And in a moment of raw, black terror, Erin found herself fearing the same thing.

No. She couldn't allow this. She had to hold on, retain control of the power she'd been handed. Her life hung in the balance. And so did everyone else's.

Erin remembered that brief, painfully intense moment when she'd touched Reece's mind, seen the courage and intelligence and strength in him. She hadn't been able to save David, but she could, by God, save him. Assuming she could get them both out of here before Geirolf came back.

Despite the feeling of invincibility her new powers had

given her, logically she was no match for an other-dimensional alien who'd once been worshiped as a god.

Erin made the sword disappear. "What do I do? How do I get us out of here?"

He relaxed slightly at the evidence she was beginning to take this seriously. "You need to open a gateway into Avalon."

Erin licked her lips, feeling a trickle of sweat work its way down her spine. Something was shimmering over in one corner, but she was damned if she'd look at it. "What's Avalon again?"

"The home of the High Court. Come here, I'll show you." He moved toward her and took her hand in his. His fingers felt so warm, she knew her own must be ice cold. "Look into my mind," he said softly.

Looking up, she met his green gaze—and saw fantastic buildings jumbled against a shimmering skyline of alien stars. Then there was a single room with a long bar surrounded by clusters of tables, all in dark wood with accents of gleaming brass. Massive leather chairs sat around the tables, and on the walls were paintings in thick, intricate frames. Some depicted battles ranging from the medieval period to the second Gulf War, while others showed women, often nude, in various erotic posses.

In a place of honor near the bar stood a huge tome of a book, lying open on a stand.

"You want me to take you to a bar?" Erin asked, amused.

"Actually, it's the Lord's Club." He shrugged. "I need to talk to Merlin's Grimoire. It would know about Geirolf if anyone does."

She frowned. He must be talking about the thick book. "Isn't a grimoire a book of spells? How do you talk to . . ." She trailed off as she saw the answer in his mind. Merlin's Grimoire was, in fact, sentient. "Wow. A talking book."

"Sometimes you can't get it to shut up," Champion agreed. "With luck, it'll be able to tell us how to defeat the demon. While we're at it, I'll request an appearance before the High

Council. We'll need to explain ourselves before somebody puts out an order of execution on us."

Erin winced, seeing his various memories of what had happened to others who'd Turned a Latent without permission. "Yeah, we definitely need to make that a priority." She swallowed and released his hand to rub her damp palms on the legs of her jeans. "So I gather I'm supposed to just *will* us there?"

"Well, yeah, but I'm not sure it's going to be that easy. Not if this cell was built to hold Geirolf, who was presumably pretty damn powerful when Merlin put him into it."

And if she couldn't do it, Reece was going to have to kill her. Or she was going to have to kill herself, though she wasn't even remotely sure she could pull it off. *Where's a good suicidal depression when you need one, huh?* She drew in a breath and blew it out as her stomach knotted around itself. She fumbled for his hand, grabbed it in a death grip. *Can't forget him.* "Okay, concentrate on your bar."

And he did. She could see it there in his mind, could almost smell the leather, hear the rumble of masculine laughter and the taste of the bottled blood the Majae donated. *Okay, there was a detail I didn't need,* Erin thought, swallowing hastily as her stomach lurched.

Then she *reached* out for it in some way she didn't even understand herself, squeezing her eyes shut as she focused ferociously on their need to stand in that bar, safe, among all Champion's vampire friends. *Now!*

She opened her eyes to see Reece looking down at her patiently. They still stood in the cell. "Fuck." She shut her eyes again. *Do it, dammit,* she told herself grimly. *Do it or you're dead.*

She *reached* again.

This time she felt it. Felt the universe stir under her like some huge animal waking. Felt it *lift* . . .

SLAM!!!

Something picked her up, jerked her hand from Reece's, and

slapped her all the way across the room. Her back hit the stone wall hard enough to knock the breath out of her. She saw stars as her head smacked into the wall. The world spun, and then she felt another bruising impact as she hit the floor on her belly.

"Erin!" She heard Champion's shout only distantly through the ringing in her ears.

A tender hand explored her back. "Are you all right?"

She realized she couldn't breathe. Panicked for an instant before her chest finally started working with huge, desperate gulps. "Oh, Jesus," she gasped.

"Lie still! Did you break anything?" His long fingers gently worked through her hair, evidently searching for bumps. They paused, probed. "You've got quite a knot there."

"Not surprised." Dazed, Erin pushed herself onto one elbow and took stock. Everything ached viciously, but all the relevant parts seemed intact. " 'M okay," she slurred, wishing for an aspirin.

A bottle instantly appeared on the floor.

"It would be quicker to magic the pain away," he told her.

"Good point." She closed her eyes and managed to concentrate despite the throbbing in her skull. Assorted aches and pains—including the one from the knot on her head—instantly disappeared. "Damn," she said, and got to her feet easily. "If I could bottle that, I could put the entire pharmaceutical industry out of business."

"Which is why we're not allowed to do it," Reece said. "What happened?"

Erin snorted. "The cell did not like me trying to leave."

She looked up to meet his gaze. She didn't even need to read his mind to know what he was thinking. "No," she gritted. "I'm not done yet. I'm not going to just give up and die."

He frowned heavily. "If you keep this up, you won't have to. The cell's going to kill you first."

"So we try something else." Erin turned and stalked toward the nearest window. Kneeling, she started examining it. "Demon Boy got out of here, so it has to be possible."

"Yeah, if you've got somebody willing to make human sacrifices on your behalf."

"But didn't he say he'd done something to the cell?" She touched the glass and concentrated, willed herself to see the molecular structure of the glass.

And just like that, she could. The glass dissolved into a tight latticework of particles and energy that, unfortunately, was all too sturdy. She growled a soft curse and went on to the next. "Maybe he didn't try to create a gate directly out of here," she explained to Reece. "Maybe he tunneled through the wall, and then made his gate. And if I was going to try to break through—"

"—the windows are the logical place to do it." Reece shook his head. "But I tried that, and it didn't work."

"You tried brute force." Erin was moving more quickly now, touching each of the windows in turn. "I'm going to try—Ah!" She stopped. There, in the second-to-the-last window, was a tiny gap in the molecular structure. "This was the one he broke," Erin said, smoothing her hands over the glass.

Suddenly she could feel it—the spell slamming into the glass, stinking of death and despair and evil.

Erin jerked back, shivering. "Yeah, this was it, all right. Jesus, does death power every spell that bastard casts?"

Reece moved up behind her. "Probably. Remember how Parker killed Avery before he called Geirolf?"

"Yeah. And somebody's going to pay for that." Cautiously she rested her fingertips on the glass again, ready to jerk away in case of another ugly jolt. "Geirolf repaired the glass before he locked us up, but there's still a weakness in the structure. If I can pour enough power into it, maybe I can break it."

"Okay." Champion stepped up behind her and wrapped his brawny arms around her in a warm, secure hold. "Try it. I've got you."

Assuming she could actually concentrate with all that delicious masculinity plastered against her.

Well, might as well make the best of it. Erin settled herself against him, braced her feet, and flattened her palm against the cool pane.

No, she thought suddenly. *What I want is something like a laser. Something tight and focused.* She took her hand away and pressed one fingertip there instead.

Then she hesitated. *What am I doing? This shit is impossible. There's no such thing as vampires and demons. Maybe I've already gone nuts. Maybe I'm actually locked up in some psych ward somewhere.*

"You're not crazy," Reece murmured in her ear.

She took a deep breath and blew it out. "You started reading my mind, Champion?"

"Reading, hell. You were broadcasting so hard, I'm surprised they didn't pick you up in Avalon."

"Don't I wish. Then maybe they'd come rescue us."

"'Fraid we're going to have to get out of this one all by ourselves, darlin'."

"Yeah." Erin closed her eyes, gritted her teeth, and focused her full attention on the fingertip touching the cool, hard surface of the glass. She imagined a beam of force shooting out to bore into the smooth, hard crystal, eating it away layer by magical layer.

She felt it first as pressure on the inside of her skull, like the beginning of a vicious headache. The tip of her finger began to heat. The sensation spread slowly up the finger, into her hand, then up her forearm and biceps and shoulder, spreading and intensifying as it went until it felt as if her entire body was blazing with pain. She heard Reece gasp softly in her ear, and knew he felt it, too.

But she didn't stop.

Time unreeled slowly, in white-hot increments. She was distantly aware of the sensation of sweat rolling down her face until it dripped from her chin. Still she refused to stop.

They had to get out of here. That was all that mattered. Not the pain. Not the heat. Nothing but escape.

Staying meant death.

ELEVEN

"Maybe you should take a break." Erin heard Reece's voice through red-hot waves of agony, like heat radiating from molten steel.

"No." She had to push the word out through teeth tightly clenched against the need to scream.

"How much more of this do you think you can take?"

He was right. The structure of the glass was weakening, but not as fast as the flow of her power.

She was running out of energy.

No. She couldn't fail. She couldn't fail David. And she wouldn't fail Reece.

Gathering everything she had left—every last erg of will, magic, spirit, whatever the hell it was she had—Erin flung it from out of her body with a raw, hoarse shriek of effort. She felt it slam into the window the instant before her legs went out from under her.

But she didn't fall. Reece's warm, strong arms held steady around her. She felt him lower her limp body to the floor. Saw his lips moving, though she couldn't hear the words. He wore an expression of fear and desperation. She tried to reassure him, but she couldn't manage to shape words. Her entire body felt boiled, as if one wrong move would make the skin drop away like meat from the carcass of a chicken that had cooked too long.

Slowly, with infinite effort, she turned her head.

The window still stood in its frame, without so much as a single crack.

Reece looked from Erin's drawn, exhaustion-dulled eyes to the window—and hissed in a breath of pain. "Ah, hell." She'd poured so much power into it, he'd suspected she'd given it part of her very soul.

And still it stood.

Goddammit, it wasn't fair. He'd never seen anything or anyone as heroic as Erin Grayson fighting to break that window, her lovely face contorted with suffering, her blue eyes burning with raw will.

She'd awed him.

"Do it now." Her voice was so faint, even Reece's vampire hearing barely picked it up.

He looked down at her and felt his heart clutch. She was staring at the window, a lone tear wending down the curve of her cheek. Her face was blasted with desolation, the skin drawn tight over the bones, as if she'd suffered weeks of starvation in a matter of minutes.

Reece recoiled, knowing what she was asking for. "No. Forget it. Just wait. Rest. You'll feel better in a few hours."

Then he winced, realizing he was suggesting she go through this all over again.

He wasn't sure she'd survive.

Her dry, cracked lips moved again. "Nothing left. Used it all."

His heart sank as he realized she was right. The live-wire feeling he'd had in her presence just a half hour before was gone. In fact, he'd never encountered a Maja with so little power. She almost felt like a mortal.

"Burnt myself out." Her eyes closed and she drew in a breath. "Like a lightbulb."

Reece pressed two fingers against the pulse beating in her throat. It felt much too faint. "You'll be okay," he told her, and hoped he was right.

"Kill me."

"No!" Reece shot to his feet. "Forget that. It's not happening." Not after watching the way she'd fought for them. He'd rather rip out his own heart. It would hurt less.

"You can't let him sacrifice us." She opened her eyes and looked at him. Weak as she was, he could feel the power of her will. "Don't let this be for nothing."

"I'm not killing you," he said fiercely. "If it comes down to it, I'll commit suicide."

"Don't be melodramatic." She let her lids close again. "You don't have a magic blade. I got rid of it."

Goddamn it, he should have made her hand it over instead. Now what the hell was he going to do?

Frustration and fear roiling in him, Reece looked away from her ravaged face. His gaze fell on the window.

Before he knew what he was doing, he flung himself at it, driving his shoulder into the glass. It rang like a bell, almost throwing him back, but he dug in his feet and rammed it again. And again, and again, each impact jarring his body.

"Reece!" Erin actually managed to lift her voice enough to be heard over the reverberations. "Stop it!"

"No!" Savagely he drew back a fist and slammed it into the window with every last bit of his boiling rage and frustration.

Glass exploded out into the night in a rain of glittering shards.

Reece froze, staring at the fist-sized hole he'd put in the glass. "Damn," he breathed. "Erin, you did it!"

"What?" Hope made her voice a little stronger. "What did you—? You broke it!"

"You bet your ass!" He reared back on one foot and pistoned the other into the remaining glass, intent on enlarging the hole enough for their escape. More glass flew. "Oh, yeah! Here we go!" He kicked again, furiously. The hole widened. Another vicious kick and one last punch, and he had an opening large enough to fit his body through.

Which was when he suddenly became aware of a crawling sensation along the base of his neck. "Oh, shit!" Whirling, he bent and picked Erin up, then, careful of the jagged shards, bent to maneuver her out the window. "Can you stand?" he asked, putting her onto her feet.

"No, but I can sit," she said, and hissed as her legs gave under her, collapsing her slowly to the ground. As Reece crawled out after her, she looked up at him, her brows furrowed in worry. Her face was far too pale, and her lips were blue. "Something's coming." She had to stop to pant. "Something big. Powerful."

"Yeah, I sense it, too," he said, wincing as a jagged shard raked a furrow across his shoulder. "The window was warded." The minute he had both feet on the ground, he bent, picked her up, and eased her across his shoulder into a fireman's carry. There was no way she could walk, let alone run. "Geirolf must have set a spell to warn him if we escaped. Hold on, baby. We're going to have to run like hell."

As he wrapped his arms more securely around her and took off in a ground-eating lope, neither of them noticed the small, glowing figure watching from the concealment of a rose.

It was a good thing she'd kept watch on the cell, Janieda thought grimly. She'd had a feeling the woman inside would find a way to escape, and she'd been right.

Of course, she hadn't expected there to be a vampire in there as well, but that hardly mattered. The two still stunk of Geirolf's death magic, which meant they were either in league with him or part of one of his spells. Either way, they had to be stopped.

She was going to have to tell Llyr about this. He wasn't going to be happy about it, but once she told him about the vision she'd had, he'd know what had to be done.

Concentrating, Janieda aimed a spell at the fleeing couple. The vampire didn't even look around when it hit, too busy trying to escape to notice. She nodded in satisfaction, knowing she and Llyr would be able to find the pair now, no matter where they went.

With a flick of her wings and a shower of sparks, she lifted off the rose and flew off toward the palace.

The Cell

Steven Parker concentrated on standing very still, hoping to escape his raging master's notice.

"I'll rip them apart!" Geirolf snarled, pacing across the cell, his cloven hooves clicking on the stone, his black, curving horns almost brushing the ceiling. He'd taken a form suited to his fury. "I'll spill their guts and burn them in front of their living eyes as they shriek for mercy!" He stopped in the center of the room and threw back his head to howl.

Instinctively Parker hunched his shoulders and lowered his head as the sound made his rib cage reverberate. He relaxed only slightly when the demon god began pacing again.

"Dammit, couldn't the horny bastard wait until I'd finished gathering my army?" Geirolf spat. "The spell I put on him was just enough to dull his appetite." He stomped one cloven foot in frustration. "I was certain he'd stay away from her after what happened with that first Maja bitch. He must have wanted Grayson more than I expected."

More likely, Champion had simply yielded to the logic of the situation and realized he had to take a chance. Geirolf had underestimated both of them badly. Not that Parker was stupid enough to point that out.

Restlessly Geirolf stalked to the shattered window and stuck his horned head out. "And she used the same window I did. But I repaired the glass myself. It should have held against anything a Maja could do to it." He snapped off a shard of glass and glowered at it. It was, Parker saw, tipped in blood. "She must have a great deal more power than I anticipated."

The demon god flicked out his forked tongue and took a sampling lick. He blinked at the taste, and a speculative expression grew in his eyes. He licked it again.

A terrifying grin spread across the monstrous face. "And she used every bit of it up." He threw the shard against the nearest wall, where it shattered spectacularly. Geirolf pivoted on a cloven hoof and aimed that bloodcurdling smile at Parker, who managed not to cower. "She's burned herself out. She's got nothing left. Find her for me. Find them both, and quickly."

"Me?" The agent swallowed and looked at the dark, alien landscape beyond the window. "Out there?" It was one thing to take on the vampire in the flush of power from a murder, but quite another to track him through some accursed magical universe at night.

Geirolf shook his horned head. "I can't stay here. I put out too much power—the witches will sense my presence and come to investigate. It's all I can do to hide from them even in Realspace. If I stay here much longer, they'll sense me." He looked around the cell with a mixture of loathing and appreciation. "Luckily even broken, these walls provide some shielding. Which no doubt accounts for the fact that they'd forgotten I was here."

"But once I step outside, won't they sense me? Not to mention the vampire and the witch?" If Geirolf feared the Majae so much, Parker was damn sure he wanted nothing to do with them.

Geirolf shrugged his massive shoulders. "There are so many magical beings out there, the three of you will be lost against the general background hum. Track them down. Call me. I'll take care of them." He glanced outside at the moon. "In the meantime, I've got to make sure the Majae don't break the spell on Merlin's Grimoire before it's too late to do them any good." His red eyes flashed toward Parker's face, and his voice dropped to a menacing hiss. "Which means I'd better have my sacrifices back by then. I will, won't I?"

Parker swallowed. "Yes, my Dread Lord."

Geirolf smiled, showing a mouthful of razored teeth that would have put a Rottweiler's to shame. "That's what I like to hear."

The Forest

Reece leaped over a bush and skidded to a halt. Erin's limp arms swung against his back with the motion. She'd blacked out during their run, but he hadn't dared stop. Now they were finally far enough out into the wilds of the Mageverse to have a few moments' breathing space.

Tenderly he lowered her into a patch of softly glowing bracken. "Erin? Erin, baby, wake up." He caught her cold little hand. Her skin was tinged with gray.

Reece felt his own heart stop, until he heard the faint thump of hers. She was still alive. Barely. But how long would she stay that way?

He lifted his head and scanned the surrounding forest. Massive trees that had never known an ax towered against the alien starfield overhead, and magical wildlife rustled and called in the darkness. Here and there, he thought he saw a flash of red eyes or the sparks of a magic trail. He had no idea where they were.

Yet it was painfully obvious he didn't dare carry her another foot. She was too weak to take any more jarring.

Dammit, he'd never heard of a Maja using her own life force to power a spell. He hadn't even known it was possible. Yet he wasn't surprised Erin had found a way to do it. She'd been utterly determined to free them no matter what it took.

The question was, how was he supposed to save her?

A Truebond, maybe? Reece reached down and smoothed her tangled blond hair away from her face. He winced at the chill of her cheek.

If he could just link their minds, he could lend her his strength. He could save her. Of course, once made, the Truebond could never be broken. They'd be united mentally for all time. She'd be able to reach into his thoughts anytime she wanted. As he'd be able to reach into hers.

Secretly, Reece had never liked the idea of a Truebond. Never liked the thought of giving a woman—or anybody else, really—that much power over him. He'd been astonished that Lancelot had been willing to Truebond with Grace, even given how much they loved each other. Of course, at the time Grace had been dying, and the bond had been the only way to save her, but still . . .

Now looking down into Erin's pale, drawn face, Reece understood why Lance had done it: The rest of his life would have been a wasteland without her.

Reece remembered the way Erin's blue eyes went dark and mysterious when he touched her. The cool drift of her silken hands on his skin. Her laughter, deep and throaty. That wicked wit and razored intelligence.

And the hot, dogged determination on her face as she poured everything she had—literally—into breaking that window. She'd destroyed herself to free them so Geirolf could be stopped.

He remembered her explanation of why she'd slept with him, even believing he was working with the death cults:

"Those cultists are killing people, Reece. There's nothing I won't do to stop that."

And there was nothing Reece wouldn't do to keep her alive. *Merlin's Gift,* he thought, *I'm in love with her.*

The thought carried a sweet pleasure. And an equal terror. He was so damn close to losing her.

So, yes, he'd Truebond with her. Hell, he wanted nothing more than to be able to reach out and just . . . touch her. Wherever she was. Wherever he was.

But did she love him? Would she thank him for chaining her to him in a bond neither of them could ever break?

Not that he had a choice. Regardless of her feelings for him, being Truebonded was better than dying, and he had no intention of letting her die. If he had to live with her resentment, so be it.

"Erin." He took her face in both hands. "Erin, wake up." If he could get her conscious, he could use the remnants of the psychic link that had formed when she'd Changed to build the Truebond. But he couldn't form it alone. She had to open the way for him. "Erin, baby, you've got to wake up now. I don't want to lose you. Please, Erin. Please."

She didn't move. He felt her heartbeat weakening.

"Erin!"

The Cell

Parker flinched from the sonic boom and the stench of brimstone as his master returned to Realspace. The bang of collapsing air couldn't be avoided, but he knew the brimstone was purely for effect, a silent warning he'd better not fail.

As if he needed one.

Bloody hell, how was he supposed to track one vampire and a depowered witch across Mageverse Earth? "Talk about needle in a haystack," he grumbled.

He was about to turn around and start pacing in agitation

when he sensed something he hadn't been able to feel in Geirolf's overwhelming presence: a lingering energy in the air, a delicious miasma of female agony that made his dick harden.

The girl.

His master was right. She'd fried her idiot self escaping. And it had hurt. A lot.

Eyes narrowing thoughtfully, he considered the afterimage of her pain. It wasn't a death, but he could use it. All he needed was a little something more of hers to complete the spell.

He moved to the window, looking for the spot where Geirolf had found the shard of glass with her blood. Sure enough, snaking, red trails marked two of the chunks. He put out a finger and touched each of them. Evidently the vampire had cut himself, too; one was from Champion, judging by the faint, psychic signature.

Perfect.

Carefully Parker broke off fragments of glass smeared with blood from each of the escaped captives, then carried the pieces to the center of the cell. He reached into a pocket and pulled out a piece of red chalk, then knelt and began drawing an inverted pentagram on the floor. The design wasn't really necessary to the spell, but he'd found making it helped focus his concentration.

After putting the shards in the center of the star, he sat back on his heels and concentrated on the swirls of residual magic floating in the room. As Geirolf had taught him all those months ago when he'd made his first sacrifice, he mentally captured one of the skeins of energy and drew it in. The taste of agony lingering in it made him shudder in pleasure.

One by one, he absorbed each of the skeins. His cock throbbed at the pain in them.

Not as good as killing her, Parker thought, *but she's so close to death, it doesn't matter.* Then, when the power pulsed, he shot a stream of it at the bloody glass fragments on the floor. The blood steamed and hissed as it boiled instantly away.

Concentrating with his inner vision, Parker watched a tendril of white smoke rise from the glass and waft toward the shattered window. He rose to his feet and followed in long strides.

He knew he'd better hurry if he wanted to find the little bitch before she died.

The Forest

"Erin!" Reece's demanding shout rang out. All around him, the creatures of the Mageverse went still at the agony in his voice.

Only Erin herself failed to respond.

Too late. He was too late. She was too far gone. If only he'd thought of this when she'd still been conscious. . . . But he'd been too focused on escape.

What the fuck was he supposed to do now? She was so damn pale, her lips bloodless, bruised shadows lying under her eyes. Worse yet, he could hear her heart laboring in that ugly way he knew from watching too many people die.

And he had no idea what to do for her.

Of course, a Maja could probably cure her with a finger-snap. The problem was, Avalon was thousands of miles away.

As if the situation wasn't dangerous enough as it was, daybreak was all too close. He'd used so much of his own magical reserves freeing them, he knew he'd be unable to fight his vampire compulsion to sleep.

Reece was terrified he'd wake to find her dead.

Something made a questioning sound out in the brush, and he looked up warily. Glowing yellow eyes looked at him before their owner vanished with a rustle.

A flicker of hope ignited in his chest.

That was it.

Mageverse Earth was full of magical beings who could help. A unicorn, a fairy, a kindly dragon—any of them would be able to save her. He just needed to find one of them. And he needed to do it fast. If he changed to wolf form, he'd be able to quarter the area at full speed.

Still, he didn't like leaving her alone. Geirolf and Parker were looking for them by now, and if they found her . . .

But if he did nothing, she was going to die anyway.

Hell.

He had no choice. Finding help was the only option he had.

Mentally cursing Geirolf, Reece took one last look at Erin's too-pale face, concentrated, and slid into wolf form. Wheeling, he took off at a lope.

And prayed Erin would still be alive when he got back.

The Grand Palace of the Cachamwri Sidhe

King Llyr Aleyn Galatyn stared at Janieda in narrow-eyed disbelief. "You knew someone was being held captive in Geirolf's cell, and you did not tell me? *Why?*"

She jumped as he rose from his throne. Even though she'd returned to her full height, the top of her head barely came to his heart. She twisted her hands together in agitation. "I told you, I had a vision. Given the chance, she'll be your destruction."

"So you took it upon yourself to protect me," he said in a low, silken voice. "How fortunate I am."

"Llyr, I love you!" Janieda burst out. "I could not simply stand by—"

"But you did stand by," Llyr snapped in the cold tone that meant his temper was seriously tried. "You kept me in ignorance. Had I known there was someone in Geirolf's cell, I could have taken action to thwart whatever scheme that creature has at work. Now it seems this Maja is dying, and I may have lost the opportunity."

"But Llyr—"

"Silence!" he roared.

"I placed a tracking spell on them," Janieda dared in a tiny voice. "I can find them for you."

Llyr's anger eased. "Well. Perhaps it will be possible to salvage this after all." He lifted his chin. "Show me where she is.

The Forest

Nose to the leaf-covered forest floor, Reece quested along, breathing deep of the scents that lay in snaking patterns on the ground. He caught a trace of direbeast here, there a hint of something acrid that was probably some kind of troll, but no dragon, no fairy, no unicorn. And certainly no Maja.

He lifted his furry head and looked around, frustrated. He had to find someone who could help. And fast, or Erin would be dead before they even made it back.

She deserved better. She'd fought so hard, given their escape literally everything she had. He had to save her.

Reece had known many amazing women over the centuries—Avalon was full of them—but Erin was something special even among that rarefied company.

He remembered the feel of her long body rising against his, silken and strong. Remembered the taste of her mouth as she'd kissed him back with starved intensity. Remembered the fire in her eyes as she'd committed herself to defeating Geirolf.

And he remembered her dogged determination to free them, even at the cost of her own life.

He began to run, all his senses open for the scent of fairy on the wind, for the phantom brush of magic against his mind.

As he flung himself through the night, he found himself remembering the last time he'd loved a woman.

He hadn't been able to save her, either.

Rebecca Champion had died in childbirth before Reece had become a vampire. He'd been just seventeen when they'd married. Rebecca had been sixteen, a rawboned farmer's daughter with a razor wit and a wicked laugh. He'd loved her with all the ferocity of the boy he'd been.

And all these centuries later, he could still remember the anguish of listening to her scream as she'd struggled to give birth to their only son, Caleb.

Unable to stand it any longer, Reece had rushed into the

room and stood over her, helpless, despite the midwife's outraged demands that he leave.

He'd been unable to do anything for her but hold her hand as she died. He'd been all of nineteen, but the anguish of that moment had branded his mind so deeply he still felt its echo.

Unable to face bringing another woman to Rebecca's home, Reece had never married again, though it had meant raising Caleb alone.

His son had been nineteen, a man grown and gone, when Sebille had seduced and Changed Reece. Even then, however, he had never stopped loving his son, never stopped worrying about him. He'd used his new skills to start the shipping firm that would eventually become Champion International, largely because he'd wanted to make sure Caleb and his children and his children's children would always be cared for.

Thanks to CI, Rebecca's descendants had never known want. It was all he could do for her.

Yet now he realized that as much as he'd loved her, he loved Erin even more. It made no sense. He'd met the girl only two days before. How could her loss scar him worse than the death of the wife he'd loved for two years?

What was it about Erin that had sunk into his soul so deeply? Was it the link that had formed between them when she Changed? Or was it something about Erin herself—the intelligence and courage and humor he found so appealing?

Oh, hell, did it really matter why he felt this way? All that mattered was finding someone to heal her.

He was damned if he'd let Erin Grayson die.

Erin was floating.

She felt oddly like a balloon, tethered to her body by a fraying ribbon. Any second now, the knot would slip and she'd go bobbing slowly away.

The only reason she hadn't let go already was that she'd heard Reece calling for her, his voice shaking with need and helplessness. For a moment, she thought she'd felt the touch of his mind again. She'd tried to get back to him, but the effort seemed beyond her.

Now she floated in cool darkness and wondered how long it would take her to die.

It was too bad. She'd really wanted to kill Geirolf. For David, of course, but also for Reece, so grimly determined to save the world. And for herself, snatched away from a perfectly good life. All Geirolf's fault.

He really did deserve to die.

Though dying wasn't as bad as she'd expected, all things considered. It didn't hurt. She wasn't even scared, really; didn't have the energy for it.

Maybe she should just let go now and float. . . .

"Come back."

The deep male voice rang through the fog. Reece?

"You're needed."

No, that wasn't Reece. It wasn't Geirolf, either. She'd never heard that voice before. *"Who's there?"*

"Ahhhhh, there you are." Just like that, something snagged her, like a fist closing around a balloon's string. She felt a jerk.

And her eyes popped open.

There was an angel leaning over her.

Hmmm. Evidently she'd already died and just hadn't noticed. "'M 'n heaven?" she asked. That was good, if she'd gone to heaven. She hadn't been at all sure they'd take her.

The angel smiled, a flash of perfect white teeth. "No, I'm afraid you're still earthbound. More or less."

She regarded him dubiously, taking in the exquisite lines of his face. It didn't seem possible that something that beautiful could be so thoroughly male. "Not an angel?"

"An angel? Me?" He threw back his head and boomed out a laugh. A curling lock of his long blond hair teased her nose. She found herself studying it woozily, fascinated by the iridescent gold highlights dancing along the fine strands.

"He is His Highness King Llyr Aleyn Galatyn, you ignorant Maja wench," a female voice spat impatiently. "Lord of the Cachamwri Sidhe."

With an effort, Erin looked for the source of all that anger. Her blurring eyes slid in and out of focus before they locked on a tiny figure hovering just above her head. A woman, barely the height of her hand, with elegant butterfly wings that shed sparks of energy with each slow beat, and hair as pink as cotton candy.

Erin's failing brain suddenly produced a meaning for the tiny woman's sentence. She returned her attention to the angel. "So you're—?" But her vocal cords couldn't seem to manage the rest.

He smiled. "King of the fairies. Yes, I'm afraid so."

TWELVE

Erin blinked up at the fairy king. As she watched, his face seemed to recede. She felt so weak, everything seemed more like a dream than reality. And the idea of a fairy king was pretty dreamlike as it was.

She licked her dry lips. "Liked you better . . . as an angel." Her eyes drifted closed.

"Are you that ready for your heaven?"

The snap in his voice made her lids flutter up. Anger, perversely, made him even more breathtaking as it sharpened his arrogant male beauty. Erin gazed up at him in wordless admiration. The universe seemed to revolve around her once, with his handsome face as the pivot.

"I said, are you that ready to die?" He gritted the words through his teeth.

"My Liege, you can't mean to save her!" The tiny fairy

woman zipped back and forth over Erin's chest. The sparks from her wings turned bright red as she flew. "I told you what I saw in my vision. We'll all be better off if she dies!"

The king's gold brows lowered, but he didn't even glance at the hostile little fairy. *Do you want to live?*

Did she? It would be so much easier to simply float away on this pleasant wave of numbness. No more hopeless battle with a demon, no more worry about possibly homicidal witches.

But Reece would be left alone. Erin remembered the expression on his face when he'd flung himself at the window—the angry desperation that had been more than the need to stop Geirolf. He'd wanted so badly to save her.

She could almost feel the warm strength of his big body moving against hers, the heated silk of his lips on her mouth. To touch him again, kiss him again—that was a reason to live.

She opened her dry mouth and forced out the words. "Help me . . . live."

Triumph flashed over the Sidhe king's face. Strong arms closed around her, lifting her from the bracken as his face swooped down. Instinctively she tried to turn her head, but his mouth had already closed over hers. His lips felt hot against her chilled skin.

And then they got even hotter. Erin sucked in a breath, and it was like inhaling fire. Something rushed from his mouth into hers in a flaming wave, pulsing down her throat and into her lungs. She screamed weakly into his mouth, but he didn't stop kissing her as he forced the blazing energy deep.

It swelled inside her like a fireball, driving her failing heart into a frantic pounding, sending hot blood surging through her veins until it seemed every cell in her body lit up like a Christmas tree.

A burning Christmas tree.

She screamed again as her body convulsed in his arms, writhing against him.

Then, between one gasping breath and the next, the fire changed, metamorphosing from burning pain to blazing pleasure. Erin felt her nipples harden against his chest. And she felt Llyr hardening too, a thick, demanding ridge growing against her belly.

Somewhere inside her, something cried out in wordless protest. No matter how handsome he was, no matter how powerful he was, he wasn't Reece.

Instinctively she began to struggle, but she couldn't break Llyr's grip.

The scent of Sidhe hung on the ground. Nose down, Reece followed it in wolf form as fast as he dared. He wanted to break into a lope, but he was afraid of overshooting the trail.

The only question was, would they save her? The Sidhe were an unpredictable lot at best, touchy and proud. And given that Lance had told him the Majae's Council had recently insulted King Llyr yet again, they might be even less inclined to help.

But he'd damn well talk them into it. Somehow. He wasn't going to let her die.

The scent trail intensified, riding the wind. They were close now. Reece wanted to bay like the wolf he'd become as he lifted his head and broke into a full run, following the shimmering, woodsy scent.

Even as he raced over the leaves, he realized his surroundings looked familiar. He was too desperate to care as he bounded over a tangle of brush and into the clearing where he'd left her lying helpless and unconscious.

A tall, blond man knelt in the leaves with Erin in his arms, kissing her with a hunger that brought Reece skidding to a stop in shock. The stranger, whoever he was, wore a blue doublet and hose, a velvet cape draped over one shoulder, a jeweled sword at his hip.

As he held Erin plastered against his body, power flowed around them so intensely even Reece could see it—sheets of energy, tinted with that glittering iridescence that was uniquely Sidhe. Reece throttled his first impulse to leap at the intruder and take revenge for that devouring kiss. He didn't dare interrupt.

The Sidhe was bringing her back to life.

As Reece watched, Erin began to struggle, trying to turn her face away from the Sidhe's kiss. A ripping growl tore from Reece's throat, but he couldn't interfere until he knew the spell was complete.

Then the magic faded and the Sidhe male lifted his head, masculine satisfaction in his smile. Erin glared hotly up at him, yet Reece could smell a trace of her arousal in the air. He told himself it was nothing more than her body's response to the stranger's life-saving magic.

"Let. Go." The chill rage in her words had Reece tensing. Savior or not, he'd rip out the bastard's throat if he tried to take this further.

The blond lifted a brow. "Is this my thanks for saving your life?"

"Thank you. Let go." Her tone had not warmed one iota.

Reece reinforced her demand with a rippling snarl, stalking forward on four stiff legs.

The man threw him a look and laughed, rising easily to his feet even as he pulled Erin to hers. "Peace! There, free and alive."

She stepped quickly back from him and tugged the hem of her crop top into place. "Well, that certainly cleared up the question of whether you're an angel."

"No man is an angel where a beautiful woman is concerned." He was watching Reece stalk closer, silent warning in every line of his lupine body. "Isn't that right, vampire?"

Reece shifted to human form at Erin's slender back. "It certainly is in my case." He gave the other man a smile every bit as threatening as the snarl he'd worn as a wolf. "Particularly when it comes to Erin."

"See how little gratitude they show you, my Liege?" a tinkling voice demanded. Reece turned to see a tiny fairy glaring at him from inches away, her wings holding her at a hover. "I told you to let her die."

"But it would have been such a waste." The blond's expression was watchful despite his amused smile.

Abruptly Reece recognized their opportunistic savior. "You must be King Llyr Galatyn." A man they did not need as an enemy, with daybreak barely a half hour away and a demon on their trail. Never mind that Reece would rather punch the Sidhe's teeth in for that kiss—this was the kind of king that could order them killed if they pissed him off. Hell, with his power, he could do it himself.

Falling back on the elaborate courtesy he'd learned at Arthur's court, Reece gave the man a sweeping bow and introduced himself and Erin. Laying a subtly possessive hand on her shoulder, he met the king's eyes. "I'm honored, Your Majesty. And very grateful for your swift action in saving Erin. I owe you a great debt."

Llyr smiled coolly. "Yes. As a matter of fact, you do."

Erin watched in admiration as Reece turned into a polished courtier before her eyes. Somehow he managed to acknowledge Llyr's power without seeming like a sycophant. At the same time he used gentle touches to her shoulder or arm to subtly communicate that the two of them were very much involved. The gestures were just as possessive as his blatant fang-baring had been earlier.

Had it been any other man but Reece, Erin would probably have been irritated. But it was Reece, and she found that there was something warming about watching him warn off a king on her behalf.

Besides, Llyr was up to something. She'd sensed that much when he'd touched her mind during the healing spell.

He was at his core a decent man, but he was completely dedicated to the survival of his people, and utterly ruthless in pursuit of their well-being. He'd saved her only because it served some purpose of his.

The real question was, of course, what that purpose was, and when he'd get around to revealing it to her.

"Our lovely friend tells me you've encountered a little trouble with Geirolf," Llyr drawled at last, apparently judging that protocol had been served.

"When did I tell you that?" Erin asked, tugging a dried leaf out of her hair. She was all too aware of Reece's speculative gaze. She had the sinking feeling he knew she'd been turned on by the king's kiss, whether she'd welcomed it or not.

"I read it in your thoughts," Llyr told her. His lids dipped over those opal irises. "Among other things."

Evidently the link had gone both ways.

"You know about Geirolf?" Reece asked.

"I should," the king said with a shrug of those elegant shoulders. "I helped your Fae capture him and drive his kind from Earth, even before Merlin sought out Arthur." His mouth twisted. "My father gave his life in that cause."

Erin frowned, puzzled. "So how are the Sidhe and Merlin related? Did he create you, or what?" When Reece winced, she realized she'd committed a blunder.

Llyr gave her a frosty glower. "Of course not. We evolved on Mageverse Earth, just as you did on your own. Our races are mirror images of each other, as our Earths are."

She nodded. "So you're basically magical humans."

"Or *you* are powerless Sidhe."

Erin smiled slightly. "Touchè." She shrugged. "Merlin's people are called the Fae, which is another name for Sidhe, so I assumed . . ."

His frosty expression warmed. "A natural assumption. Your people have confused two concepts that are unrelated. Not unusual, with mortals."

Stung, she muttered, "Land on the moon lately?"

"As a matter of fact, yes. But that's a story for another time."
Llyr glanced toward the horizon. "The sun is very close. May I
offer you the hospitality of my palace for the Daysleep?"

Reece's gaze flicked from the king's face to the brighten-
ing sky, then toward Erin. She got the strong impression he
was wondering what she and Llyr would do while he was
helplessly unconscious. He gave a coolly infuriating little bow
of the head. "I would be grateful. I used a great deal of
strength escaping from that cell, and I need to replenish it."

"Then come, and I will open a gate for us." The king made
a gesture with one elegant hand. A shimmering dot appeared
in the air to swell outward into a glowing window. Erin felt the
magic of it dance over her skin, and something within her
woke and responded.

"I've heard a great deal about Sidhe hospitality and the
beauty of your palace," Reece said as they prepared to step
through it. "I look forward to enjoying both first-hand."

As the king and Reece stepped through, Erin stepped to
follow them—only to have the way blocked by a tiny glowing
figure.

Janieda's eyes were hot and angry. "Whatever schemes you
harbor, creature," she hissed, "my Liege will see through
them. And if he does not, I will!"

Okay, she'd had more than enough of this. "Listen up, Tin-
kerbell," Erin growled. "The only scheme I'm harboring is a
deep and burning desire to mount Geirolf's head on a pike.
Unless you've got a problem with that, we've got no problem.
So lose the attitude."

"I saw you, whore," Janieda hissed. "I saw what you'll do!"

Thoroughly fed up, Erin stepped through the gate, too irritated to hesitate even in the face of such unfamiliar magic.
Even so, her knees buckled as alien forces washed over her.

A big hand wrapped around her arm, supporting her. She
looked up into Reece's concerned eyes. She forced a smile
and jerked her head at Janieda as the fairy flew through the
gate. "You wouldn't happen to have a flyswatter on you?"

He grinned. "Not even a rolled-up newspaper." His eyes tracked to Llyr and his voice dropped to a mutter. "Though I sympathize with the thought."

"Where's a bug zapper when you really—" She broke off in amazement as their surroundings suddenly penetrated her consciousness. "Damn."

They stood in a towering foyer built of shimmering white marble, polished to a mirror gleam. The twenty-foot ceiling overhead was supported by arches that appeared to be solid gold. The white marble floor underfoot was set with smaller jeweled tiles—sapphire, ruby, emerald. And everywhere, magic swirled and eddied in sparkling trails that made Erin's eyes ache. She shivered, feeling the power stir under her skin. "It's . . . beautiful."

The king smiled at her awed tone, then nodded to Reece. "Come. I'll lead you to your quarters. You can tell me of Geirolf's schemes on the way."

She watched as the two men started down the glittering foyer, comet trails of magic swirling in their wake. Her head began to throb as she followed. Somehow during her brush with death, she'd forgotten the way the energy of the Mageverse pressed against her mind.

She'd been able to manage those forces before when she had a clear-cut purpose—escaping the cell. But now Erin could feel them whipping around her like a nest of snakes she had to somehow capture and control.

It was a terrifying thought.

"What a weakling you are," Janieda sneered.

Erin turned to glare at the little fairy just in time to see her grow in a blink to a full-sized woman, impossibly slim and delicate, her face a sweet, big-eyed triangle beneath a waving cluster of pink curls. To her irritation, Erin instantly felt like a cow.

The fairy lifted her delicate chin and sniffed. "Why my Liege should feel any interest at all in a creature who cannot even manage her own magic, I do not understand."

Erin bared her teeth in an expression that was not even remotely a smile. "Oddly," she said, "I find your lack of understanding does not surprise me."

Janieda huffed, turned on one bare heel, and flounced off after Llyr, her short, diaphanous skirts twitching around her long legs.

A trail of sparks hung in the air in her wake, glittering seductively. Erin gritted her teeth and followed.

Reece could feel the need for the Daysleep pressing harder on his body as he struggled to explain the situation to the Sidhe king.

He was relieved when Llyr's expression grew grim. "This spell of Geirolf's would destroy the Magekind?"

"Down to the last vampire and Maja," Reece told him. "So you can see why the High Court needs to be informed immediately. If you could get a message . . ."

Llyr's opalescent gaze narrowed with calculation. "Not just yet."

"Your Majesty . . ."

"Geirolf can't work his spell without a sacrifice, which means he's blocked for the time being. The High Council can continue as they are for a few hours more."

Reece put a tight grip on his temper. "Unless he decides to kidnap another vampire and Latent."

"Which would take a great deal more time and effort to arrange than simply recapturing you and Erin. He'll try for that first. Again, the situation can wait until you awake. You can report to your High Council yourself."

"But the sooner they learn of this, the more time they have to find a spell to defeat him."

Llyr shrugged. "I'm sure such capable people are more than up to the task of handling Geirolf."

He was too damn tired for diplomacy. "The High Council has always considered you an ally. Were we wrong?"

"Any alliance works both ways, Lord Reece," the king said coolly. "My people, too, face threats, yet yours have been less than willing to assist me in vanquishing them."

Damn, Reece had known the Majae's Council's arrogance would come back to bite them one day. But he'd had no idea his own anatomy would be the target for the teeth. "Your assistance now could change that," Reece pointed out carefully.

Llyr made a dismissive gesture, his eyes drifting to Erin's elegant profile. "Be that as it may, your High Council will simply have to wait."

Reece's heart sank at the interest in the king's gaze. He needed to find a bed, but watching Llyr watch Erin, he'd never dreaded sleep more. It didn't take a tactician to realize the Sidhe was mentally spinning plans around her.

Was Llyr considering romancing her? Reece could see why he might be tempted, even aside from Erin's considerable attractions. The Majae's Court had refused him over and over again, but Erin had no ties to the court. Hell, they might even execute her. From the Sidhe king's point of view, she was ripe for the plucking.

On the other hand, since she had no Court connections, wedding Erin would not gain Llyr the close alliance with Avalon he needed. So what exactly were his intentions?

Either way, she seemed unaware of Llyr's interest. Reece would have found that encouraging, if she hadn't been paying such wild-eyed attention to things that weren't there.

"She is still adjusting to her powers," Llyr said softly, watching Erin as the four of them walked down the hall. Her wary gaze was fixed on something that seemed to be pacing her, about six inches from her eyes.

"It's a profound adjustment, Your Majesty," Reece said, forgetting his unease at the other man's intentions in his concern for Erin. "She's done well with her new abilities, all things considered, but it's going to take her a little while longer to get used to them."

The king's lids veiled his opalescent gaze. "Assuming the

Majae's Council doesn't kill you both first. They've been looking for you, you know. A locator spell."

Reece felt his muscles tense. A group of Majae could arrive at any time to check on him. And they wouldn't be pleased to discover he'd turned Erin without permission.

"Don't worry—I blocked it as soon as I discovered you," the Sidhe told him bluntly. "They're casting about on the wrong side of the planet now, following a false trail."

Reece blinked, not sure whether to be relieved or outraged. "Why?"

The king's full attention was focused on Erin, who had stopped dead in the hallway, staring intently at some invisible something. "I don't want them killing her."

"Contrary to your evident belief, they're not totally inflexible. When I explain the threat Geirolf poses and the risk Erin took to free us—"

"—they may spare you," Llyr finished. He shrugged. "Or not. Were I you, I would be disinclined to take the chance." His gaze returned to Erin. "She deserves better."

"Of course she does," Reece snapped back.

The king shot him a cool, calculating look. "Then perhaps when you return to Avalon, you should leave her here until you have convinced your Majae's Court you were right to Change her."

He stiffened. "I don't think that would be wise."

"I am more than capable of protecting her."

"They'll need to examine her to determine she's sane."

"They can send an emissary here."

"What's your interest in Erin?" The Sidhe king stiffened, his face taking on a mask of arrogant offense at the question. Reece shrugged. "With all due respect, you just met her."

"That is no business of yours."

"Actually," Erin said suddenly, "it's a good question." Her eyes met the king's in challenge as she moved to join them. "I wouldn't mind knowing the answer to it myself."

Llyr's expression softened. "When I saved you, I touched

your mind." He reached up and brushed a lock of hair from her face. Reece felt raw jealousy stab him at the tenderness of the gesture. "I liked what I found."

Erin's lips parted. Before she could speak, the king turned to gesture at a nearby doorway. "These will be your quarters for the Daysleep. When you awake, I will transport you to Avalon."

Reece opened his mouth to ask to be sent to the High Court immediately. But he could feel the sun pressing against the horizon, and knew it was doubtful he could remain conscious long enough to explain the complex situation. And what would the Majae do to Erin before he awoke? She'd be safer here until he was awake to defend her.

Dammit, he should have thought of this earlier. Probably would have, if he hadn't been so distracted by his uncharacteristic jealousy. Still, he had to make sure the court was warned about the demon's plans. "Please, Your Highness—send a message to the Court. Warn them Geirolf has escaped."

The king hesitated. "I will consider it."

He knew he didn't have time to argue further. Reece turned on leaden feet and pushed the door aside as he felt the sun shove its leading edge into the sky. He staggered.

Suddenly Erin was beside him, one slim hand gripping his biceps as the other arm circled his waist. "Can the sunlight reach him in here?" she demanded over her shoulder.

"No, I've polarized the glass."

She threw him a questioning look. "Will that be enough to protect you?"

"Yeah," he managed as he forced his legs to carry him toward a shape he recognized as a bed. "I wouldn't . . . really turn to dust, you know."

"I know." She shrugged. "But I just wanted to make sure."

"Watch out for the king," Reece gritted. "He wants something from you."

"Yeah, I figured that out," Erin said. "Sleep now."

"Persuade him to warn Avalon," he managed as they struggled the last couple of feet. He tumbled onto something soft the instant before the Daysleep fell on him like a velvet hammer.

Erin watched Reece's handsome face go lax as sleep claimed his big body. She found herself feeling a little abandoned.

Vampire or not, he'd become her refuge in a world gone thoroughly alien. In that moment she wanted nothing more than to crawl into the bed next to him and wrap herself around his warm strength.

"Come," Llyr said from the doorway. "I would like to show you the rest of my palace."

Erin looked down at Reece's still profile. His dark eyelashes lay on his high cheekbones like feathers. "I'm not sure I'm up for a tour, Your Highness. It's been a rough night."

"Ungrateful creature," Janieda said.

Erin stiffened and turned. The fairy eyed her maliciously from behind the Sidhe king's shoulder. Llyr watched her coolly, as if wondering whether Janieda was right.

It occurred to Erin that if she wasn't careful, the fairy would poison the Sidhe king against them before they woke. And God knew what situation they'd face then.

Besides, Reece was right. Avalon needed to be warned about Geirolf, and Llyr was the logical one to do it. She shoved away her exhaustion. "I am deeply grateful for my rescue. And I would love to see your palace."

No expression stirred behind Llyr's watchful eyes. He nodded and extended a hand. "Then come, and I will show it to you."

Putting aside her longing, Erin walked away from Reece's big, powerful body and took the Sidhe king's hand.

The palace was indeed impressive, as much artwork as architecture, filled with dazzling colors and fabrics.

Not to mention the Sidhe themselves. They were the most

uniformly beautiful people Erin had ever seen in her life. There was none of the imperfection one would see among any group of humans she knew: no overweight bodies, bad teeth, big noses, receding hairlines. The men were lean and tall and broad-chested, with long, angular faces and gently pointed ears. The women were small, slim, lovely enough to make Erin's teeth ache. Yet she would have mistaken them for human, had it not been for the whimsical color of hair, eyes, and skin: blues, screaming reds, iridescent purples, and metallic golds.

She found herself just enjoying the view.

For their part, they all seemed fanatically devoted to Llyr. Everywhere they went, beautiful, elegant people paid homage to the Sidhe king. And they weren't just currying favor with a powerful man; Erin sensed they genuinely admired the king and viewed him as a hero.

The longer she spoke with him, the easier it was to see why. He might be a ruthless opportunist with ulterior motives, but he was also intelligent, witty, and genuinely concerned about his people.

Add that to astonishing good looks, extreme wealth, and a kingdom full of adoring fairies, and you had a devastating package all the way around.

Yet even as she watched Llyr charm both her and his court, she found her thoughts drifting to Reece. When would he wake—and what would he do then? He'd have to return to Avalon to warn the High Court about Geirolf's plans. It was his duty; he had no choice, and she knew it.

But what kind of reception would he get? For that matter, what kind of reception would *she* get when they discovered Reece had changed her? True, he'd had excellent reasons, but the High Court sounded like a ruthless bunch. What if they viewed her as a threat?

Damn, she wished they didn't have to go to Avalon. It would be so much better if they could sidestep the whole problem.

"You've grown quiet," Llyr observed, his glowing gaze searching her face as they walked together in the palace's sprawling gardens.

"I'm concerned about Reece," Erin admitted, watching a fairy in winged form standing on the petals of an exotic flower, busily doing something to it. "I'm worried about how the High Court will react when they learn he's Gifted me."

"You have reason to be concerned," Llyr said. "The Magekind can be extraordinarily ruthless where their Great Mission is concerned."

Erin lifted a brow. "Great Mission?"

He shrugged his shoulders and took her by the hand, leading her farther into the garden. "To save humankind from itself. They have no objection to spilling blood when it comes to accomplishing that goal. And I would hate to see yours among the blood they spill."

"So would I," Erin said dryly. She hesitated, then took a chance. "Could I prevail upon you to send a message to the Magekind explaining the situation? It would make things much safer for us if we didn't have to go to Avalon."

"Unfortunately, Reece doesn't have the luxury of staying away," Llyr pointed out. "He has to go back, or he'll be suspected of treason." Reading the expression on her face, he shrugged. "I know I wouldn't take it well if one of my soldiers defected to a foreign court rather than face my justice."

"But there was nothing Reece could do except Change me! If we hadn't escaped from that cell, all of Magekind would have been destroyed."

"They have seers of their own, Erin," Llyr pointed out. "It's entirely possible they would have foreseen Geirolf's intentions."

"Or perhaps they wouldn't have. We had to warn them. We still do."

"Champion does, perhaps," the king said. "But you don't."

Erin shook her head. "Your Highness, I can't just stand by and let Geirolf destroy Magekind. And I can't leave Reece to face the High Court alone."

"Both Champion and the Magekind are more than capable of taking care of themselves," Llyr said. "You're not."

Something zipped by, shedding sparks. She automatically pivoted to watch it go, then returned her attention to the king. "That may be, but I can't hide from the High Court forever. They'd find me."

Suddenly long, warm fingers closed over her hand. "Not if you stayed here in my palace," Llyr said. "With me."

Erin turned to look up at him, shocked. And saw his head lower. Before she could step back, he was kissing her, his mouth moving in hot demand over hers.

THIRTEEN

Llyr was a tall man, with the rangy, sculpted build of a long-distance runner and a talented mouth. Yet though it was pleasant being kissed by him, held by him, Erin's body didn't leap in response as it had when he'd brought her back to life. Instead, as he thrust his tongue deep between her startled lips, she felt only anger.

Who the hell did he think he was? He wasn't Reece.

She turned her head away from his kiss and tried to step back, but once again, he wouldn't release her. "Let me go!" she growled as he raked his teeth over the tensed cords of her throat.

He jerked his head up. For just an instant, as he studied her, angry frustration blazed in his eyes. Then his face went blank, as if he'd smothered his anger like a man pinching out a candle. "So, you do love him."

Erin blinked, startled out of her outrage. "What? No—" She broke off, realizing the idea felt far more right than it had any business being. Straightening her shoulders, she rejected it firmly. "I've only known him a couple of days. Nobody falls in love that fast."

"It certainly isn't rational," the king agreed.

"But no more so than asking a perfect stranger to live with you," Erin pointed out. "I don't believe in love at first sight, Your Majesty."

"Actually, my proposal is entirely rational," Llyr said, moving to drop into a carved marble bench. "And as much as it pains me to say so, this has nothing to do with love." He paused. "At least, not yet."

She studied him warily. He was, after all, a king; it wouldn't do to anger him. Yet his bald-faced proposition was insulting. "So, Your Highness, what entirely rational reason do you have for wanting me to move in with you?"

"Ah." Understanding flooded his eyes. "You think I want you to be my consort. I'd wondered why you were insulted. No, that's not what I have in mind at all." He settled back into an elegant sprawl, extending both arms along the back of the bench. Only a blind woman would have failed to see his staggering beauty. "I want you to be my queen."

"Oh." Erin blinked and rocked back on her heels. Something glittering shot past her, but this time she was too stunned to notice. "Why?"

He shrugged, a lift of a brawny shoulder in his doublet. "You'd be good at it."

He had to be playing her, but she was damned if she could see why he'd bother. "What leads you to that conclusion?"

"I touched your mind, Erin. I've never met a female with more steel, more strength. When you decide on a purpose, you are utterly focused on it." He smiled slightly. "I have some familiarity with that trait. It's a good one in a ruler."

Erin lifted a brow. "I'm flattered, Your Majesty, but you've got an entire kingdom full of fairies here. Surely one or two of them is as stubborn as I am." And every last one of them was certainly more beautiful.

He shrugged. "But they're Sidhe. And there's a problem with the Sidhe; we're not a very fertile lot. Normally, that's more blessing than curse, since we're also immortal. If we were as prolific as humans, we'd quickly overrun the planet."

Erin studied him cautiously. Her first instinct was to give him a flat refusal, but she had a feeling that would be a very bad idea. Besides, there was something going on here, something she'd do well to understand. "So why do you need a royal broodmare? I assume that's what we're talking about."

He looked up at her, warning heat stirring in his eyes. No, this was not a man she wanted to piss off. "I'm not sure whether I find your bluntness refreshing or irritating. People are usually more diplomatic when dealing with me."

"I'm an American cop, Your Majesty." She spread her hands. "We don't even have royalty, and diplomacy has never been my strong suit anyway."

"Indeed?" he drawled, "I would not have guessed."

She smiled slightly, acknowledging the sarcasm. "All of which makes me an unlikely candidate for queen. Which begs the question: Why do you need children badly enough to offer *me* a crown?"

Llyr sighed. For a moment he looked almost vulnerable. "The Sidhe are not really immortal. We may not age, but we can die in battle—or from an assassin's knife."

"And like leaders everywhere, Sidhe kings make particularly attractive targets," Erin guessed. "Who's gunning for you, Your Highness?"

Llyr pulled a hand through his waist-length hair. "My brother, I'm afraid. Sixteen hundred years ago, shortly before he died in battle helping Merlin defeat the Dark Gods, my father divided his kingdom between the two of us. For centuries, Ansgar has dreamed of reuniting it."

"By killing you."

He nodded. "Yes. By killing me."

"Forgive the observation, Your Highness, but your brother sounds like a bastard."

"He is," Llyr said bluntly. "And I don't want him ruling my people. He'd abuse them the way he abuses his own."

"What happened to your other children? Surely you've had some in sixteen hundred years. Not to mention a queen or two."

"Oh, yes." His eyes turned inward and brooding. "Unfortunately, those around me don't seem to have as much luck dodging assassins as I. I lost my fifth queen a century ago. My last son died two years past. He was little more than a boy—only one hundred and ten—when one of Ansgar's magical assassins struck him down as he hunted a Dark Beast."

Erin shook her head. "All right, I see why you need a palace full of heirs, though none of this fills me with enthusiasm for giving them to you. But why me? Realspace Earth has a population of six billion, half of them women, a good chunk of those highly fertile and unmarried. Any of them would leap into your arms with hosannas of thanksgiving."

"I don't need a human wife. I need an immortal with powers of her own, yet all the fertility of a mortal."

"So you proposed to the first Maja who came along?" Something shifted behind his opalescent eyes, and she knew. "Oh. There've been others."

He shrugged. "A Maja's first loyalty is to the Great Mission."

She rocked back on her heels and studied his otherworldly beauty. "It must be, if they turned *you* down."

"Actually, the Majae's Council wouldn't even let me approach any of them." His wide mouth twisted in frustration. "The Council has a tight grip on its witches, and no intention at all of relaxing it."

"And then I came along." Erin folded her arms. "An outlaw Maja facing the possibility of execution, with no commitment to this mission of theirs and in desperate need of protection."

Llyr looked up at her sharply. "I meant what I said. I want you for my queen because of your strength and courage as much as any practical consideration. And you have the strongest natural talent for magic I've ever seen in someone not a member of my direct family. All you need is instruction in its use, and it would be extremely difficult for anyone to touch you, even my brother's assassins." His eyes sharpened. "Or the Knights of the Round Table."

All right, how the hell was she supposed to get out of this without pissing him off? She could think of only one argument this hardheaded, strong-willed man would have to accept. "That's fine, Your Highness, but what about my children? What kind of mother would knowingly bring a child into a world where he's a target the minute he's born?"

"Ansgar's assassins never managed to touch my offspring in childhood. I surrounded them with bodyguards and wards to keep them safe. It was only as they became adults and chafed under my protection that they became vulnerable." He caught her hand in his. "And by then, they were seventy or eighty years old. How long would your children live, Erin?"

"Still—"

His long fingers tightened on hers, warm and strong. "Give me a chance, Erin. My people need you. I need you."

Looking into those beautiful, demanding eyes, it was hard to tell him no. "Your Highness—" She sighed. "If we were in love, it might be different."

Llyr's opalescent gaze hardened, though his tone was light. "Well, milady, if it's love you want . . ." Sudden heat flashed from his fingers into hers. Erin actually felt it roll up her arm in a shimmering wave that made her gasp even as her nipples drew to tight buds behind the thin fabric of her T-shirt. Low in her belly, lust roared to sudden life. She stared at Llyr helplessly, her eyes tracking from his sensual, perfect mouth to the broad expanse of his shoulders, and down to the bulge growing swiftly behind his codpiece. Deep, intimate muscles clenched as she felt herself run like hot butter with the need to feel him within her, driving hard and deep.

Even as her body leaped in helpless response, hot temper

stirred. "Stop," she gritted, trying to jerk her hand free. For a moment she seriously considered slugging him, king or no. "Dammit, cut that out!"

His brows lifted as he read the anger boiling beneath her need. A second spell rolled from his fingers, this one cooling and soothing the vicious ache he'd created. He released her, and she stumbled back, fists clenched as she fought the need to hit him. "I meant only to make a point," he told her, his voice low and strained. "I could have lied to you to get what I wanted. I could have bewitched you into feeling something that's not real. But I wanted there to be honesty between us, even if that honesty did not serve my cause."

"I don't care if you are a king, *Your Majesty*," she growled, "I won't be forced!"

Llyr sighed. "Perhaps it wasn't such a wise thing to do at that." He hesitated. "You should know that anyone with my level of power could have done the same thing. However, there are ways to shield yourself. Techniques that will also allow you to control your powers more effectively so you don't find the energies of the Mageverse so distracting." He met her gaze levelly. "I can show you, if you're willing to permit it. I swear I won't violate your trust again."

Erin hesitated, studying his breathtaking face. Despite his little demonstration, she'd learned when he'd healed her that he had a deep core of ruthless honor. If he gave his word, he wouldn't violate it. Slowly she nodded. "If you can teach me how to shield myself, I'd like to learn."

Erin pushed open the chamber door and walked inside, a vicious headache pounding behind her eyes. A shaft of light fell across Reece's handsome face as he lay, sprawled in handsome exhaustion. She closed the door and crossed the room to him, feeling helplessly drawn to the shelter that big body offered.

She had worked with Llyr for the past three hours learning

how to shield her mind from magical probes. By the time they finished, her face had run with sweat, but the last time he'd tried to reach into her mind, she'd been able to block him out.

Not that it was easy. Llyr was so damn powerful, keeping him out of her thoughts was like trying to arm wrestle Arnold Schwarzenegger. But she'd done it.

Now her hands shook with exhaustion as she peeled the T-shirt over her head and sat down on the edge of the bed to pull off her running shoes. She watched the first one thunk to the floor, remembering her conversation with the king just before he'd left her.

"It's a big palace, Erin," Llyr had said, as they stopped outside the door. "I could assign you another bedroom."

"I know," she replied softly. "But I'd rather be with him." Never mind that she couldn't say exactly why. "I'll sleep better." It was as good a reason as any.

The king's restless gaze turned toward the door as if he could see through the massive oak. "He's a good man," he said abruptly, then shrugged. "Or a good vampire, or magus, or whatever he chooses to call himself. He is honorable, certainly. Perhaps too honorable." He looked at her, and she was struck again by the raw beauty of those eyes. "Don't let that honor fool you into believing you're safe with him. He won't betray the Great Mission for love of you. Even if it meant spending the rest of his immortal life mourning your memory."

Erin had winced at the sting of his words—a sting all the more intense, she knew, because they were so true. "I know. But you know, Your Highness," she added gently, "you're an honorable man, too."

He looked at her for a long moment, then gave her a small, dark smile. "And you wonder why I'd offer you a crown." Giving her a small half-bow, he turned on his heel. But before he strode off, he looked back at her. "Join us for the evening meal when you wake." His gaze hardened. "I'll anticipate your answer to my proposal then."

She'd nodded tightly. "I'll . . . consider it."

The thing was, if not for Reece, she'd be seriously tempted to tell him yes. High-handed and arrogant and dangerous as he was, there was something about him that appealed to her. And it wasn't just his astounding male beauty, though that definitely had its appeal. She respected him—his intelligence, his power, his determination to protect his people. He'd do damn near anything to see them safe.

Which made him a very bad man to push. In that sense, he and Reece were a great deal alike.

Now she looked down at her lover as he lay in his deep vampire sleep. "It took me nearly thirty years to find a man I could love, and Geirolf promptly killed him," Erin said aloud. "And now I've met two more of you in the space of a week. Does that suck or what?" With a sigh she stood up to shuck out of her jeans, then, dressed only in her panties, climbed in the bed next to him.

His big body radiated warmth, and Erin spooned herself against him, letting herself luxuriate in his heat. Confident she couldn't wake him even if she tried, she twined one arm around his waist and let herself fully relax for the first time in hours.

She lay for a long time simply listening to him breathe, feeling his broad chest rise and fall in the curve of her arm. A sense of peace stole over her. It was as though she was finally exactly where she was supposed to be.

Odd, she thought sleepily. *He's a vampire, yet nobody has ever made me feel this safe.* Not David. Not even Llyr, powerful though he was.

Llyr's right, she realized suddenly. *I'm in love with Reece.*

Oh, this was bad, she thought, with a rising sense of panic. Losing David had wrecked her. Losing Reece would be even worse. He was so damn much more that David had been—more intelligent, more capable.

And more driven. The king was right when he said Reece's sense of honor would make him choose duty over her. Even if it destroyed him.

No. She'd been there, done that, and had no intention of sticking her head in the lion's mouth again.

Yet she couldn't bear the thought of turning her back on Reece. She'd lost one man she'd loved. She wasn't going to let another one fall without a fight.

There had to be something she could do.

Llyr.

Her eyes narrowed thoughtfully. Now, that had potential. The king had a hell of a lot of power, magically and politically. If she could harness it, she could use it to protect Reece from his Council.

And the only way to do that was to marry the king.

Under normal circumstances, she'd never consider it. But Llyr intended to use her, too—her, and the children she could give him.

She didn't much like the idea of bringing children into the danger swirling around the Sidhe court. So she wouldn't. She'd tell Llyr they had to find a way to take care of this brother of his before she'd agree to give him children.

Suddenly Champion stirred against her, muscle flexing all along his powerful back. He murmured something in his sleep, his voice deep and rumbling. She lifted her head so she could see his face. He looked like a boy in sleep, his eyelashes long and dark as they lay against his cheekbone. Something in her heart clenched hard at the sight of him.

Erin sighed and dropped her head, snuggling her face against his back and breathing deeply of his scent.

Deep in her chest, her heart ached from the weight of a love she knew had no hope at all—and the choice it was forcing her to make.

She fell asleep trying to decide on the best way to save him.

Reece woke to the mingled scent of Erin and another man.

Frowning, he lifted his head and looked over his shoulder. She lay spooned against him, her delicate body limp in sleep.

He inhaled again, sampling the air, and recognized the Sidhe king's scent.

Along with the far more familiar scent of Erin's arousal.

Reece glowered. The bastard had been romancing her again. And what was worse, she'd responded. He could smell it on her scent.

No, they hadn't actually made love, despite her arousal. Or if they had, Llyr hadn't come within her sex—though that left no shortage of alternatives.

And then she'd come to Reece's room and crawled in next to him wearing nothing more than her panties. Now she lay there, sprawled in innocent slumber, her pretty bare breasts mounded together as she lay on her side. Her nipples were flushed and pink, soft and sleeping, as though waiting for a male mouth to awaken them.

He wondered if Llyr had tasted those luscious little peaks.

Jealousy coiled through him like a snake until he wanted to turn into a wolf and howl. And rip out the Sidhe king's throat.

The strength of his own anger surprised him. He'd never been a jealous man; among the Magekind, you couldn't be. It wasn't uncommon to make love to a Maja, only to find she'd gone on to make love to one of your good friends the next day.

That had never bothered him. Magi needed the blood of Majae to survive, and Majae needed to donate it; unless they did, their health could be at risk. It wasn't personal.

This, though—this was very, very personal.

He rolled out of bed and began to pace, trying to burn off some of his anger. His deep, vicious jealousy was irrational, and he knew it. He and Erin had known each other barely three days, and she'd made no vows to him. No vows meant no betrayal.

That, however, was the voice of rationality, and he was feeling anything but rational at the moment.

Reece pivoted to pace in the other direction, and his gaze fell on her face. Her lips were parted as though for a kiss. He stopped in his tracks as pain stabbed him. He drew in a breath.

You're being an ass, he told himself, impatient with his own roiling emotions. He'd always despised insanely jealous men. Erin was not his possession; she was her own person, and she had a perfect right to want the Sidhe king. And why shouldn't she? Just look at the gorgeous palace he'd built, not to mention his beautiful Sidhe subjects. He was richer than hell, and so damn handsome he made Reece's back teeth ache.

And what did Reece have, after all? True, there was Champion International, but the company belonged more to his descendants than to him. Even if she'd wanted him, he was always being called off to some war zone or other on behalf of either the United States or Magekind.

His body was decent enough, but he'd always thought his face looked like ten miles of bad road, particularly compared to Llyr's inhuman beauty.

Why shouldn't she prefer the Sidhe to him?

But I Gifted her, a voice insisted in the back of his mind. *I fought for her.*

But Llyr had been the one to actually save her life. Without his kiss, she would have died.

Reece, on the other hand, had repeatedly talked about killing her.

Ass.

His shoulders slumped as his anger tumbled into a confused depression. Wearily he turned to pace the other way.

"Good morning," Erin said sleepily from her mound of sheets. She smiled at him, her face lighting up with it. "Though 'Good evening' would probably be more apt." She stretched sinuously, her full, bare breasts arching. His mouth went dry. She yawned delicately. "Sleep well?"

"Well enough," he said gruffly, thinking of everything he wanted to ask her. *Did you sleep with Llyr?* He winced, imagining her reaction to that question.

She rolled out of bed and reached for her jeans, then wrinkled her nose at the dirt and leaves that covered them. He eyed them, trying not to wonder if she'd been rolling on the ground with the king.

"Man, these are nasty. I wonder if they've got a washing machine around here somewhere?"

"Why don't you just magic them clean?" The suggestion emerged with more of a snap than he intended, and he winced.

But Erin didn't seem to notice his tone. "Good idea." She gave her jeans a brisk snap, and sparks danced over them. Holding them up in front of her, she gave them a once-over and nodded in satisfaction. "Much better."

Reece looked away as she started wiggling into them, her breasts bouncing. He could feel his cock hardening behind the zipper of the jeans he'd worn to bed.

"Need yours clean, too?" She asked.

At his tight nod, she flicked her fingers at him. He felt the dance of Mageverse energy over his skin and looked down to see his clothes looking freshly laundered. "You seem to be more comfortable with the magic," he observed carefully.

"Yep." Erin looked at her hand. A brush appeared in it, and she started vigorously brushing out her hair. "Llyr showed me a couple of tricks."

Reece barely bit back the words *I'll bet he did.* "That was nice of him," he managed.

She nodded. "He taught me how to create a mental shield so I can control my contact with the Mageverse. I'll also be able to block anybody who wants to touch my mind without my permission."

Remembering the times various Majae had used spells to manipulate him, Reece nodded. "That's a skill I wouldn't mind having myself."

"Yeah." She bent over and flipped her hair over so she could brush it out upside down. The sway of her breasts drew Reece's gaze like magnets pulling in iron shavings. "I think he was feeling guilty."

"What about?" Her legs looked a mile long the way she had them spread. He wanted to run his hands along her thighs.

"He put some kind of arousal spell on me." She straightened up and shook her hair back.

Reece stiffened. "What?" The rage he'd almost managed to subdue roared back to hot life. "He used magic to seduce you?" He swore viciously and turned toward the door. "King or not, I'll kill the son of a bitch!"

"Hey!" Wide eyed, Erin caught his arm. "No, he wasn't trying to seduce me—he took the spell off the minute he cast it. He was trying to make a point."

"I'll bet he was!"

She shook her head. "No, Reece, his intentions really were honorable. He asked me to marry him."

"What?"

Reece listened in disbelief as Erin described Llyr's proposal and the reasoning behind it. He felt as if he'd taken a hard blow to the face he wasn't expecting. "You're actually considering this."

"He makes a good argument." Then she frowned. "Though I'm not that comfortable with the idea of bringing children into this war with his brother. We're going to have to do something about that." She shrugged. "But he's right. We don't know what kind of welcome I'm going to get from your Magekind. Besides, I'm not sure I'm comfortable belonging to any group that would execute us just because you didn't get all the proper paperwork filled out."

It was as though something precious was slipping through his fingers, and he had no idea how to stop it. He said the first thing that came into his head. "Are you in love with him?"

Erin stared at him. "Oh, please. I just met the man yesterday. I don't even know him."

Reece himself had met her only three days ago, yet she'd managed to slide barbed hooks into his soul anyway. "He evidently knows you well enough to propose."

"It's a business deal, Reece, not a romance."

"What about your job?"

She stretched her long legs out in front of her and studied the toes of her bare feet, brooding. "Considering my boss was just murdered, I don't think I've got a job. And even if I did, how could I do it with your Council sending hit teams after me?"

"Which brings up the question of Geirolf." Blessedly, anger was beginning to crowd through his panic. Was she just going to abandon him, now that she'd gotten an offer from a royal protector?

She looked up at him and frowned, probably sensing his growing temper. "Actually, I've been thinking about that. The Sidhe are pretty damn powerful, right?"

"Not as powerful as we are," Reece growled.

"Okay, but do you think Llyr and his people could take out Geirolf?"

He frowned. "Possibly, but Llyr has never been particularly interested in Magekind concerns."

"Yeah, I sensed that. But what if I made it part of the deal—help us kill Geirolf, and I'll marry him? That would help you get out of dutch with the Council." She sounded as though she were thinking aloud. "And if I'm queen of the Sidhe, maybe they'll be less inclined to offend me. I could make a big deal about how you saved both of us from the demon during our escape, and how grateful Llyr and I are. Given that, and the good reasons you had to Turn me, plus our killing Geirolf, the Council should leave you alone."

Dammit, she had the whole thing worked out. He felt his frustration come to a boil. "Don't worry about the damn Council. I'll take care of the Council. I've been Champion of the United States since it was thirteen impoverished colonies, and I've pulled the Great Mission out of the fire more than once. I'll convince them to back off even if they decide to be difficult about this."

Erin stared at him. "But I thought you said you couldn't predict how they'd react."

"Generally I can't, but I won't let them kill you." He stalked across the room and knelt in front of her to bring himself to her eye level. Reaching out, he caught her hands in his. "Look, you can't marry Llyr. You're a Maja. You belong with your own kind."

"Come on, Reece, I didn't even know there was such a thing as Majae until three days ago. I've never even been to Avalon. Why should I—?"

Before he knew what he was doing, he was on his feet, and he'd pulled her off the bed and into his arms. Fiercely he stared down into her mutinous, lovely face. "You're a Maja, Erin. What you need, no fairy can give you. But I can."

Then he was kissing her with all the desperation, anger, and hunger in his soul.

FOURTEEN

What Llyr had done with a spell, Reece did with a kiss. His tongue slid into her mouth in long, mating strokes as he drew on her lips hungrily. Erin gasped against his mouth as heat raced through her body to gather in her nipples and between her thighs. He dragged her close, then closer still, as if craving the contact. His arms felt hot as they circled her. One big hand cupped her butt and lifted until her soft belly pressed against his thick hard-on. She caught his shoulders out of sheer instinct, clinging to the one solid thing in a world that had suddenly gone molten around her.

He was biting at her lips now, his teeth just short of stinging. She threw her head back, fighting to suck in a breath through the sudden, staggering arousal whipping through her body. He went right on kissing her, stringing tiny licks and bites over her chin and across the angle of her jaw. When he reached her ear, he breathed, "I don't need a spell to make your body burn, Erin. You're Maja now. And I'm going to show you just what that means."

"You can't . . ." She had to stop to gasp. ". . . can't change my mind with sex, Reece."

"Don't bet on it."

For a dizzy instant she felt herself falling with him. She landed on the yielding softness of the bed behind her, Reece's big body pressing down on hers. He lifted his head, and his jungle-green gaze burned, wild with hunger—and something else she didn't dare name. Then his hands were on her, cupping and stroking her bare breasts until she arched into his hold with a low moan. "Yes," he purred. "That's right." He moved down her body and lowered his head just over her jutting nipples. Watching him, she held her breath in anticipation.

But instead of licking or sucking her as she'd expected, he inhaled deeply, breathing in her scent. "God, you were delicious before, but now you smell like distilled sex."

Automatically she drew in a breath and realized what he meant. She'd never been so aware of the eroticism in a man's scent. His was clean, but with a trace of some dark musk she couldn't identify.

Vampire?

Then he bent his head lower, and she went still in anticipation. His first lick across the peak of one breast made her suck in a breath. That tiny, hot contact felt so much more electric than before. He looked up at her, and a small, satisfied, very male smile curled his lips. "Maja to my Magus, Erin. We're two halves of a whole."

Then, his gaze still locked with hers, he closed his mouth over her nipple and began to suck. Each pull of his mouth sent streamers of pleasure curling through her body to coil in a burning ball low in her belly.

By the time he lifted his head again, she was trying not to writhe on the slick, cool sheets. "Feels good, doesn't it? Even better than it ever has before," he said, in a low, knowing voice.

"Yeah," she admitted on a gasp, unable to lie in the face of such searing pleasure.

He gave her another lick, and her spine arched. She caught that satisfied smile again before he sat up and reached for the button of her jeans. "You're not just a woman anymore, Erin." She heard the zipper hiss, then felt his big hands catch her waistband. "You're a Maja, and a Maja is more than magic." She watched, feeling dazed with need as he stripped her, dragging the jeans off her legs.

Then he simply wrapped his fist in her panties and jerked. She caught her breath as he reached between her legs to find her hot, buttery core. The entry of one of his long fingers dragged a whimper from her lips. Possessively he watched her face as he stroked deep. "You're as wet as I am hard. You want me as much as I do you." His voice hardened. "The way you'll never want that fucking fairy."

Erin blinked at the sudden ferocity in his voice even as she recognized the truth in his words. "He's a good man. Ruthless, maybe, but he loves his people. I could see myself falling in love with him—"

"No," he growled, his hands leaving her body as he rose from the bed with an easy, muscular flex. His hands went to his zipper, but his hot eyes were locked on her face as he stripped off his jeans. "Oh, yeah, I'm sure you'd come to feel some pale affection. But it'll never be what it could be with me."

She licked her dry lips as his cock sprang free, thick and hungry, a drop of pre-cum on its tip. "Getting a little arrogant there, Champion."

"I have a lot to be arrogant about."

Well, she thought, looking up at that broad, powerful body with dazed admiration, *it's hard to argue with that.*

Naked, he slid a knee onto the mattress and reached down, jerking her up and into his arms. She caught her breath as her body collided with the hard muscle of his. "The Gift made you a vampire's perfect mate." His breath was hot on her lips. The hunger in his eyes was suddenly more than a man's need. More consuming, more predatory. "You crave me now, as much as I crave you."

As Erin looked into his blazing green eyes, a delicious kind of fear stole over her she'd never felt before. A woman's fear of losing herself in a man's hunger—and her own. She denied it anyway. "I don't make a habit of giving into my cravings."

"Maybe not, but you'll find this one a lot harder to fight." Sitting back on his heels on the mattress, he spun her around to face away from him, then pulled her back between his spread knees. She felt his breath on her pulse as he lowered his head to her throat. "Because you'll know how it feels when I feed from you, when my fangs slide into your skin. When I drink of your blood."

She shivered at the velvet threat in his low whisper. "I already"—she had to stop to lick her dry lips—"already know."

He licked one of the tense cords of her throat as he cupped one breast in long fingers. "But it's never been like this. It's different when you're a Maja. Hotter. More intense. Spread your legs."

Erin blinked at the rough command, but found herself obeying, easing her knees apart.

"Wider," he growled.

She swallowed and did as he demanded. Then she felt his long fingers tangle in her hair, pushing her head down. She bent and braced her palms on the mattress.

"Yeah," he said, his tone dark with anticipation. "Like that." Erin fisted her hands in the sheets as he stroked one calloused hand over her backside as he kept the other wrapped in her hair. Not pulling, but sending a silent message that he was firmly in control.

She knew she should protest the blatant dominance in the gesture, in the way he touched her as though establishing a claim. But she couldn't seem to manage the words.

It felt too damn good.

"God, I love your ass," he said, caressing her with those deliciously rough fingers. "Just enough muscle, with a perfect peach curve." He found the cleft of her bottom and slid his index finger down it as she gasped. "I love to watch you walk across a room. Makes me want to bend you over every time."

"Aren't you being a little . . . Ah! . . . politically incorrect?" she managed, then moaned as he worked that wickedly skilled finger into her tight sex.

"Definitely," he agreed, a dark male chuckle in his voice. "But I just don't seem to care." A second finger joined the first, stretching her deliciously. "And I don't think you do either."

She closed her eyes as he began giving her slow, arousing strokes. "I should kick your butt for this," she managed.

He laughed. "And you probably would if I were anybody else." A third finger joined the other two, and she jolted. "But I'm not, and you like it."

The bed shifted as he moved off the mattress. Almost shaking with arousal, Erin gripped her fistful of silk sheets and waited to see what he'd do next.

She didn't wait long. Suddenly she felt his face against her backside as he angled his head to slide his tongue through the seam between her sex lips. Erin caught her breath.

"You always taste so damn good," he rumbled. "I could bathe in you."

And if he kept that up, he'd be able to, she thought, dazed, as he went to work with tongue and fingers, lips and teeth. Stroking and teasing until she braced herself on her elbows and let herself float in exquisite sensation. Her aching nipples brushed the cool silk each time he angled his head to torment some new and ever more sensitive part of her sex.

It didn't take her long to feel the first hot coils of her orgasm tightening around her spine. Normally she would have gone over in minutes, but this time . . . This time she felt the need for something more.

She wanted to feel him take her—and not just with that powerful cock. She wanted to feel the erotic sting of his fangs sinking into her throat, his mouth working on her skin as he drank from her. *Okay,* she thought. *Getting kinky.*

She didn't care.

"Reece . . ." Erin moaned.

She felt him lift his head. "Need something more?" His voice was dark and knowing.

Her first instinct was to deny it, but she couldn't. "Yeah. Please . . ."

He straightened. When she felt the broad, rounded head of his cock touch her damp curls, she moaned in relief.

Then he started entering her.

It seemed to take forever, an endless slick glide of shaft stretching her creaming channel, working deep and deeper. Slowly. She felt her knees shake.

"Ah," he purred. "That's nice. So wet. So tight." He flexed his hips against her ass, sliding the last fraction home. "How does it feel?"

Stuffed. She was completely stuffed. "I don't seem to remember you being quite this"—she had to stop to breathe—"big."

He laughed softly. "You have that effect on me."

Then, as she bent before him, her hands braced on the bed, he fucked her in slow, deep thrusts, working that thick cock in and out as he stood beside the bed. Each thrust slid pleasure through her, burned and teased her closer to the orgasm she could feel building just beyond the next deep thrust.

She found herself bending her arms and lowering her head to the mattress, letting him in deeper and deeper.

It wasn't enough. Even as full as he was filling her, she needed something more.

She needed his bite.

"Reece," Erin panted.

He pulled out of her. "There something you need?"

The rich amusement stung. "Dammit, you know what I want."

"Oh, I know." He picked her up and tossed her farther onto

the bed, then pounced after her. Caging her in his brawny arms, he drove into her in one hard, deep thrust. "Because it's exactly what I want," he said in her ear.

"Yeah!" She angled her head, offering her throat.

But he ignored it as he instead began to lunge against her in jarring strokes that made her gasp at the ruthless delight. "God," he growled as his hips slapped her butt. "You make me so damn hot and hungry, all I want is to empty my balls and sink my fangs in that long swan throat."

"Now would be good," she agreed.

Reece laughed in a triumphant masculine rumble. "You want my fangs, Erin? Is that what you need?"

"Yes!" The admission exploded from her, forced out by desperation.

He chuckled, pressing lower, his weight urging her to relax her braced arms and legs until she was spread on her belly, her ass lifted into his thrusts. Propped on his elbows, he gathered her into his arms, still spearing her. "Your wish is my command." A big hand closed over her chin, cocked her head at the angle he wanted. From the corner of one eye, she saw him bend toward her pulse.

Just before his lips touched her mouth, he rumbled, "No goddamn fairy can give you this, Erin."

The sting of fangs sinking deep jolted her with a lushly erotic pain that was somehow shocking. It hadn't felt like this the last time he'd taken her.

He drove in a particularly deep thrust just as he took that first deep swallow.

Heat and fire roared out of nowhere. "Reece!" she screamed as the orgasm engulfed her in a crashing wave of pleasure.

She tasted like straight white lightning as he drank her blood in searing, erotic mouthfuls. He could hear her heart pound-

g. She writhed helplessly in his arms, overwhelmed by a
aja's pleasure in feeding a vampire for the first time.

He knew just how she felt. Deliciously erotic as it had al-
ys been, the experience of taking a Maja had never been so
ense. Maybe that was because the Maja he'd known had
en too wary to surrender themselves, too conscious of their
wer to welcome any attempt to dominate them.

But he knew this was more than just a simple sex game, a
t of delicious kink.

This was Erin.

His beautiful, courageous, intelligent Erin, whom he'd
me so close to losing. Erin, magnificent enough to attract a
ng's attention.

Llyr was right, Reece thought as he drank from her. She
uld make a magnificent queen.

Should he step aside, stop fighting, let it happen? She was
ght; the High Court would be unable to touch her once she
as Queen of the Sidhe.

No.

As he felt her silken depths caress the length of his cock,
s entire being rebelled at the thought of giving her up. He'd
otect her, even if he had to take on the entire Round Table to
it. She was his, and he wasn't giving her up, not to Llyr.
ot to anyone.

He loved her.

As that realization rolled over him, he stiffened, feeling the
at detonate in his tight, aching balls. Releasing her throat,
eece threw back his head in a bellow of raw need and deter-
ination. "Erin!"

And he knew as he emptied himself in her depths that he'd
ver let her go.

hen Llyr walked out into the palace gardens, he wasn't sur-
ised to find Janieda perched on the petals of a rose. But for

once, she showed no interest in harvesting nectar, normally her favorite treat. Instead she sat with her tiny legs drawn up to her chin, an expression of deep melancholy on her little face. She looked up at his step and stood, stepping off the petal and growing to full size in a blink.

She met his gaze with her own rainbow stare. "Did you propose?"

He wasn't surprised she knew his plans. Janieda was far more intelligent and perceptive than anyone else realized. She'd told him once she chose to play the fool because it made others underestimate her. She'd have made a good queen if she wasn't so hot tempered and impulsive.

Llyr sighed, knowing he was probably in for a display of those less attractive qualities now. "Yes, I did."

Janieda studied him with that too-perceptive gaze. He'd long suspected she could read his mind right through his shields. "And she's considering it." She grunted in disgust, an odd sound in that high, musical voice. "Of course she is."

Llyr shrugged. "I caught her at a vulnerable moment."

"I should have let her die," Janieda growled as she turned to pace. "I knew from the moment I saw her in my vision that she'd destroy you. Then, when she escaped, I thought I had best warn you anyway." Bitterly she added, "What a fool am I."

Llyr sighed. "She won't destroy me, Janieda."

"Doom hangs around her, My Liege." She turned to him, imploring. "Send her back to the Magekind where she belongs."

He moved to take her small shoulders in his hands. "You know as well as I do there's no evil in her, Janieda."

The fairy waved a dismissive hand and pulled from his light grasp. "Perhaps not, but she'll be your destruction anyway. Or at the very least, mine. She'll accept your proposal, and then you'll never touch me again." Her mouth pulled into a bitter line. "You'll not risk dishonoring your wretched queen."

"Janieda, you knew I would wed sooner or later."

"Yes!" She spun toward him, glaring at him. "But all I

wanted was another century or so. Can't you give me that much time? She's immortal—she can wait."

Llyr sighed and raked his hands through his long hair. Janieda's passionate nature was one of the things he loved most about her, but it could also make his life extremely difficult. "One of the primary attractions of my offer is that it would keep the Majae's Council from ordering her death."

"Oh, let them kill her. It would solve a multitude of problems."

He shot his lover a chiding look. "Janieda."

"She's a threat, Llyr!" his lover exploded. "Can't you feel it?" Suddenly she froze. Her face went blank, eyes wide in an expression that made the hair rise on the back of his neck. "I see thee lying in thy castle, thy magic gone, drained away to her. And the great demon laughing at the terror of your people."

Llyr took a step back, feeling the chill spread over his skin. "No."

Janieda blinked, life flooding back into her face. She frowned, reading his expression. "I had another vision, didn't I? I don't . . . I don't remember this one. What did I say?" Sometimes when the future spoke through her most strongly, it left her with no memory of what she'd seen.

In this case, that was a very bad sign.

"Geirolf is going to be a problem." Llyr straightened his shoulders. He'd diverted Janieda's predictions before, and he'd do it again. He'd built a life from wrestling his fate in the direction he chose, and he wouldn't let her frighten him from his course now. "But I'll deal with it. As to Erin"—he focused on her face, willing her to listen, to yield to his will, to stop fighting him—"I need her as my queen, Janieda. I need her strength and her sense of duty, and I need the children she'll give me. And I mean to have them."

The fire bled out of Janieda's rainbow eyes, and her wings drooped. "Even if it costs us our love?"

Despite his determination, Llyr felt a shaft of pity. She really did love him with all the considerable passion in her small body. And in his way, he returned it, though he'd never felt the same blazing emotion he'd sensed in her.

He stepped close to her and lifted her chin. "I have my duty, love. No matter how I may feel about it."

She gave him the small, rebellious pout he'd always found irresistible, even when his better judgment advised otherwise. "I would have made as good a queen as she."

"No, darling," Llyr said gently. "You wouldn't have. Your heart has always been stronger than your head. And perhaps that's why I love you." He leaned down and brushed his lips across hers in a tender kiss.

Something told him it would be the last they'd ever share.

When he drew back, a single tear rolled down her fragile cheek. "The thing I hate about you," she said in a low, intense voice, "is your refusal to give me the comfort of a lie."

In a blink she was no bigger than his index finger. With an angry beat of her wings, she soared off.

As she flew past, he thought he heard a tiny sob.

Parker crouched in one of the clumps of thick foliage that surrounded the palace, stewing with frustration. He dared not go a step further for fear of running into the wards he could sense mere feet away.

The trail of his spell had led here, only to veer suddenly and wildly away. He strongly suspected it had been diverted by someone's magic. And now Champion and the little bitch were safely ensconced among a collection of magic users of some kind. They had a different feel to them than Erin had— some other species, perhaps, but he wasn't sure what. In any case, Parker knew they'd chew him up and spit him out if he were stupid enough to test those wards.

On the other hand, that was nothing compared to what Geirolf would do when he learned his sacrifices had slipped beyond his reach. Parker swore.

Just then, something glowing zipped past the wards. He ducked instinctively.

The tiny figure stopped in midair and screamed in pure rage. "That bitch! That thrice-cursed bitch is going to ruin it all!" She took a sobbing breath and called, "Ahern! Are you here? Come out!" She darted off.

Parker eyed her glittering path in speculation. "Well now. That's interesting."

He rose from his nest of bushes and slipped off in pursuit of the tiny glowing figure.

Erin lay still in the cage of Reece's arms, listening to his heart pound in concert with hers. He covered her, a hot, lightly sweating blanket of masculinity. Though he braced his body on his elbows, she was acutely aware of his weight and strength.

She had never had a man take her like this, not even him. When they'd made love before, he'd always played the laughing, tender lover. But tonight he'd been a ruthless seducer determined to stake a claim to her, to possess her. To take her in every sense of the word.

And he'd done it.

He'd branded her senses and her body with himself so thoroughly her body seemed to resonate with his.

And God, it felt so good.

She found herself imagining what it would be like to stay with him just like this. To give herself up to him, to his stunning, dizzying passion. To become part of him forever.

He was right, she realized, with a bitter sense of desolation. She'd never know anything like this with Llyr, no matter how many centuries they lived together. She'd crave Reece for the rest of her life.

Love him for the rest of her life.

And that was why she had no choice. Ironically, the sweet,

erotic interlude he'd just given her had driven that home. She'd lost one man. She had no intention of losing another.

"That was incredible," she said hoarsely, honestly.

She felt Reece smile against the curve of her cheek. "It was my pleasure." He nuzzled her neck, breathing deeply of her scent. The feeling of his lips against her throat made Erin close her eyes as her body instantly responded to his need.

"But," Erin said softly, "it didn't change anything."

Reece stiffened against her. "What?"

"You're right," she told him. "I love you. I need you. And I'm going to miss you for the rest of my life."

She was unable to keep her eyes off him as he rose from the bed, naked and glorious. Anger and frustration heated his eyes as he realized what she was driving at. "It's a good thing you can have me, then."

Erin sighed. "No. I can't." She rolled off the bed, aware that he was watching her with a hot-eyed concentration. "The king has asked us to join him for the evening meal," she said. She hesitated, then added steadily, "After that, he's going to expect my answer."

Reece clenched his fists. "Tell me you're going to say no."

"I can't."

"Goddamn it, Erin!"

"Reece, all the reasons I gave you earlier still apply! The fact that I love you, that I need you, doesn't do one damn thing to change the situation we're in."

"*We* can change the situation we're in! Yeah, if you'd gone insane, I might be in trouble with the Majae's Council now. Even then, I could argue that I'd had no choice except to take a chance. They're not completely rigid, Erin. That's why there's an appeals process."

"And what if you lose, Reece?"

"I won't!"

"But you could. If I marry Llyr, I won't lose. I'll have the power to protect you and kill Geirolf."

"At the cost of everything else we have! Since when did you become too big a coward to take a chance?"

"Since I got sick of watching the men I love die."

"Dammit, Erin, I might as well be dead, because I'll never be able to touch you again." Angrily he whirled away and stood rigid, his big fists bunched. "This is such bullshit."

"Losing David ended my career and broke my heart," she told him softly. "Losing you would rip out a chunk of my soul. And no, I'm not willing to risk that."

He looked over his shoulder at her, his eyes narrow. "Fuck that. You're rationalizing. This isn't a gallant act of self-sacrifice. You're just afraid to let go and open yourself up to me. You don't want to be hurt again. You'd rather live a millennium in a bloodless union with that damn fairy than risk letting yourself love me."

There was just enough sting in those words to make her wonder if he was right. She pushed the doubt away. "Reece, I want nothing more than to spend the rest of eternity making wild jungle love with you, but that isn't an option. The Council—"

"—is not made up of complete bitches who won't listen to reason. But that's not the issue. Not really. If it was, you'd be willing to take a chance."

"It's not just the Council. Geirolf? Remember him? Demonic alien who wants to sacrifice us? Does any of this ring a bell?"

"Oh, it rings a bell, all right. But it's beside the point." Slowly he pivoted and began to stalk her. She resisted the impulse to back away. Barely. "The point is, I'm not just Reece Champion, I'm the American Champion. I'm always getting sent out on somebody's dirty little mission—the High Council's or the U.S. government's. Either way, people try to kill me on a regular basis."

She glared at him. "I wonder why?"

Glaring back, he growled, "You don't want to take the

chance that I'm going to die out from under you like David did. But if you marry the Sidhe, you don't have to worry. You know you're not going to fall in love with him, so if he buys the fairy farm, what difference does it make?"

Erin clenched her fists. "Think what you like. I know what I've got to do. And I'm going to do it."

FIFTEEN

The fairy was talking to a unicorn.

Amused despite the effort of maintaining a shield spell to hide himself, Parker lay still on his belly. The whole situation reminded him of boyhood hunting trips in the Georgia mountains years ago, when his father had taken him bow hunting for deer. He'd learned to move silently and stay downwind of his prey on pain of his father's fist and his own hunger. Venison had been a welcome relief from the endless hamburger and macaroni that was all the family could afford. He'd taken his first buck at the age of ten.

Odd, he thought, how the thrill of killing never dimmed. Particularly now that he was hunting men.

Or a reasonable substitute, anyway.

"What am I going to do, Ahern?" the fairy moaned. She'd grown to full size, and now she was draped across the unicorn's bare back. The thin, filmy gown she wore draped deliciously over her ass, baring legs that were surprisingly long, though he doubted she'd have made five feet in heels. "He's going to marry that little bitch, and there's nothing I can do about it."

There was a lot of power in those two. Parker could almost feel it, despite the shield that kept them from sensing him. If he could kill them . . .

"'Tis just as well," the unicorn said, in a deep, sonorous voice, like James Earl Jones playing Mr. Ed. "Thou hast no business coming between thy Liege and his duty. And taking a Maja to wife would smooth his path to an alliance with Avalon. An alliance he doth need."

Parker snapped to full alert, silently cursing the time it had taken to work his way close without being overheard. It sounded as though they were talking about Grayson.

But that was impossible. She'd barely been at the palace a day. How could she have wormed a proposal out of some fairy king that damn fast?

The fairy lifted her glowing pink head. "But she's tied up with Geirolf, Ahern! There's doom hanging over her. I can feel it!"

"Doom for thy Liege—or thy hopes?" the unicorn asked. "They are not the same, much as thee may wish t'were different."

Hell, they were talking about Erin! Parker ground his teeth against a vicious curse. This was all they needed. If that little bitch got herself a powerful fairy ally, there was no way Lord Geirolf could touch her. And to make matters worse, she and Reece had probably already alerted the Magekind, which meant the whole plan had just slid right down the tubes.

Fear slid over him as he imagined his master's reaction to that bit of news. Would it be possible to slip away before Geirolf found out?

"But Llyr loves me, Ahern!" the fairy said, interrupting

Parker's frantic thoughts as she sat up on the unicorn's back. "And he doesn't care at all for that bloodless little human."

The unicorn heaved a deep sigh. "Thou wert always the most stubborn of my pupils. Have I not told thee that a king must follow his duty and not his heart?"

Hmmm. It sounded as though this Llyr had a thing for the little fairy. Now, that was an interesting piece of news.

Interesting enough, in fact, to save his ass.

Thoughtfully Parker reached for the gun that hung in his shoulder holster. With the absent skill of long practice, he pulled back the slide and extracted the bullet from the automatic's chamber.

He thought he might have just enough magic left for one last spell.

Erin was going to accept Llyr's proposal.

Reece felt oddly numb as he watched the king lift her knuckles to his mouth and press a kiss there. He hoped a little viciously Llyr could smell his scent on her skin.

How could she do this to him? She'd responded to him as sweetly as any woman ever had. Yet ten minutes later she'd risen from the bed where he'd had the best sex of his life and cut his heart out without batting an eye.

Well. It seemed she'd become a Maja in every sense—all power-hungry ambition, just like all the other witches, with a heart locked behind a wall of ice.

He wanted to hit something. Preferably Llyr's perfect fairy nose. Bastard.

As Reece felt his muscles knot with the need to strike out, a ray of self-awareness pierced his jealous anger. Look at him. He'd always felt such contempt for men who couldn't accept a woman's rejection. Yet here he was, acting just as much the asshole as all the other needy bastards he'd ever looked down on. He had to get this under control.

Much as it hurt, Erin had a perfect right to choose whomever she wanted. He'd taken his best shot at changing her mind, but it hadn't worked. Now he was just going to have to suck it up and get on with business.

Reece heard the low murmur of her voice and looked around to see her blond head bend toward the king's. Pain stabbed into his chest. Somehow he managed to bite back the grunt, like a man taking a hard blow to the balls.

He'd lost every woman he'd ever wanted, ever needed, from his wife to Sebille. He'd thought Erin would be different.

It seemed he'd thought wrong.

Janieda pressed her face to Ahern's silken hide and watched a tear roll down her nose to fall to the ground a long way down. The unicorn was old and wise, and he'd been her confidant since her childhood, when he'd taken on the task of tutoring her in the finer points of magic she'd had no patience for. For centuries there'd been no pain she'd felt that his calming presence couldn't soothe.

Until now. Now, when she felt a chilling, unfamiliar presence she'd rarely experienced in her long immortal life.

A presence she suspected was death.

But whose? Hers? The king's? Or merely, as Ahern believed, the death of her childish dreams of having Llyr for her own?

"I can't believe you don't feel it," she said into his warm mane. Unlike a mortal horse's, it felt like silk beneath her cheek.

Ahern's great barrel chest rose and fell between her legs. "I have never had thy gift of sight." Then he hesitated.

Something in his silence made her lift her head. "But you feel it anyway. Don't you?"

"There is something," the unicorn admitted. He gave his horned head a toss. "Mayhap 'tis only that thy unease has spread to my spirit."

"You know better than—" Janieda broke off, sensing the sudden presence of something evil, like a death stench on the wind. Ahern sidled in fear under her. She jerked herself upright on the unicorn's back, glancing around wildly.

A man rose to his full height from the shelter of a tangle of brush. He grinned at her.

Recognizing his species, Janieda relaxed, though Ahern's haunches bunched under her as he prepared to leap away. "Oh, it's only a human. It doesn't even have any magic."

"Now, there," the human said, lifting something and pointing it toward her, "is where you're wrong."

The thing lurched in his hand before it belched fire and smoke with a dragon's roar. Ahern threw up his head with a sharp whinnying squeal, one of the few times in his long life he'd ever sounded equine.

Then they went down. Sheer instinct had her shrinking to winged form and flying clear. Janieda looked down, frantic, to see the unicorn lying in a tangle of long legs. "Ahern!"

To her horror, she saw a long, glittering rope of energy winding from him toward the human. The creature was stealing Ahern's life force as he died! But she could stop it, she could heal him. . . .

Even as she started to throw a healing spell over him, Janieda saw the human gesture. A wall of light appeared before her eyes. Her spell splashed off it.

Wings beating frantically, she spun to see herself surrounded by a globe of force—swirling Mageverse energies. She flung herself at the curving shell, only to tumble back in agony as it repelled her. "No!" Janieda screamed. "Let me save him!"

The human strolled over to scoop her energy cage up in one hand. "I'm afraid I've got other plans for your magic than wasting it on a four-legged hat rack." He examined her through the field with such gloating satisfaction she folded her wings and sank into a cringing ball. "Lord Geirolf is going to be real pleased to see you."

Geirolf? Her eyes widened as the full horror of her situation rolled over her. Gods, had she brought on the very destruction she'd tried to avoid—just as she'd doomed Ahern?

Fear chilling her, she looked down at her old friend's cooling carcass and let the tears flow for him.

And herself.

In her misery, she barely noticed when the human used his stolen magic to transport them. Numbly Janeida watched through the shimmering walls of her cage as the Mageverse melted away, replaced by cold, dark stone. The magic here was so thin, she suspected he'd transported them to mortal Earth.

At first glance she thought he'd taken them to one of the human cathedrals, given the towering granite walls and stained-glass windows. Then she realized there was nothing holy about this place.

The windows depicted images of sex, torture, and death, while the walls were decorated with profaned Christian symbols cut into the black stone—pentagrams, inverted crosses, the swirling glyphs of magical wards designed to keep anything good away. Every few feet, goat's heads hung on the walls like torches, thick red candles driven onto their horns.

"What?" The roar of rage brought her jerking around in her cage, her wings beating in agitation. A demonic creature that could only be Geirolf rose from a black marble throne to tower over the cringing Parker. "Llyr means to wed the bitch? And you *allowed* it?" He lifted a clawed fist for a blow Janeida knew would tear off the human's head.

Parker threw up a hand to protect himself. "But you can turn this to your advantage, My Lord! I have a plan!"

The demon stayed his fist. "Speak quickly, then."

Through a fog of despair, Janeida listened as the human told Geirolf how he proposed to make use of her. Her tears became tearing sobs.

But this time she cried for Llyr, the man she loved. And whose doom she'd sealed.

* * *

"This . . . has possibilities."

Parker relaxed, knowing himself safe as the towering demon form shrank down to that of a man. Thoughtfully Geirolf turned back to his throne and dropped onto it, bracing an elbow on the marble armrest. Looking closer, Parker saw human shapes carved into the stone, writhing in either agony or fornication.

Geirolf must be feeling more confident in his power if he'd taken the time to create this temple to himself, though the Satanist symbols were probably intended strictly to impress the mortals. Parker wondered how many women he'd had to sacrifice to both work the creation spell and shield the results from the Mageverse. He wished he'd been there to watch. He'd always enjoyed a good sacrifice.

And Geirolf had a real flair for the theater of murder.

"Yes, I do think this could work." His master gestured, and the fairy's cage floated to his hand. Parker watched as Janieda's colorful wings fluttered in agitation. "You do seem to have found a prize. I suppose you've won the right to keep your life after all."

Parker didn't dare even flick an eyelid in reaction, though he wanted to remind the demon lord that none of it had been his fault. He knew that was completely irrelevant.

It was, however, a good thing he still had plenty of magic left over from killing the unicorn. He had a feeling he might need it, if only to defend himself from his master's uncertain temper.

With a thought, Geirolf sent Janieda's cage spinning in the air as he contemplated it. The little Sidhe hunkered down, spreading her wings for balance as she watched him like a canary eyeing a cat. "Logically, Llyr will have already notified Magekind about my plans, which is a problem. But if your suggestion works and I can get my hands on the vampire and his bitch, I can work the spell and destroy the lot of them anyway."

"Avalon won't take that lying down," Parker dared to point out. "They'll try to launch a counterattack before you can finish."

He shrugged. "I hope they'll hold off a little longer. They're still working on breaking the spell on the Grimoire, which is a good sign. And my forces are almost ready. Once I finish transforming them all, they'll be able to battle the vampires on equal terms." Geirolf rose to his feet. "Or almost. They won't be a match for both the Majae and the vamps, but all they have to do is delay them long enough for me to complete the spell."

Parker trailed after him as he moved to fling open a set of double doors and led the way out onto a balcony overlooking a courtyard. Below, men and women waited in ten long, snaking lines to reach one of Geirolf's priests. At the head of each line, an acolyte knelt before the priest and was offered an obsidian cup.

As Parker watched, a woman drank the draft the priest held to her lips. She took one swallow and choked, then fell back in convulsions. Writhing on the ground like an epileptic, she kicked and shrieked as all the color leeched from her skin. Inside her screaming mouth, her canine teeth lengthened to fangs.

At last she rose, her skin as waxy as a corpse. The hungry look she turned on the mortals in line made them flinch before the priest drove her away with a crack of magical energy. She retreated, snapping her fangs at him like a dog.

"I got the idea from Merlin," Geirolf said idly, "Though I don't believe the original ceremony with the Knights of the Round Table was quite this dramatic."

Parker looked around to see that his lord held a cup that matched the ones the priests held down below. "Now," Geirolf said. "It's your turn." He smiled slowly. "My loyal lieutenant should partake as well, don't you think?"

The agent licked his lips as fear stole through his guts on a wave of ice. For a wild moment, he thought of transporting himself back to Washington and forgetting the whole thing.

Then he took the cup.

Erin sat at Llyr's right hand and took another mechanical bite of whatever exotic dish the Sidhe had laid before her now. They might have saved themselves the effort; she tasted none of it.

Her eyes were focused on Reece as he sat across the table from her, his handsome face as cold and impassive as if he'd turned to ice. She'd used her magic to dress him in the courtier's clothes the other Sidhe wore. She wasn't surprised the stark black velvet doublet with its silver embroidery only enhanced his rough beauty.

"It isn't easy to serve duty when the one you love does not understand," Llyr said in a voice pitched for her ears alone.

She blinked and looked around at him. "I beg your pardon?"

He smiled a little bitterly and took another sip of his wine. Glancing down at his plate, she saw he'd eaten as little as she had. "I know too well how you feel. Janieda flew out of here in a rage when I told her you were considering my proposal."

Erin stared at him. Now, there was a twist she hadn't expected. "You're in love with Janieda?"

Llyr shrugged. "We've been lovers for the past century. Unfortunately, however, she would not make a good queen." His lips quirked again in that bitter smile. "Too passionate." Lifting his cup toward Reece, he added, "Like your own lover there."

"Reece understands duty perfectly well," Erin said tightly. "He's been Champion of the United States for more than two hundred years."

"So long?" Llyr's eyes twinkled at her over the rim of his cup, and she found herself wondering if she was being gently mocked. Quite probably, considering how long the Sidhe lived. "But there is a deal of difference between obeying the common dictates of obligation and doing that duty when your heart cries for mercy."

"I am well familiar with ignoring the demands of my heart," Reece said suddenly. His challenging gaze met theirs.

"Your pardon, Lord Reece," Llyr said, then murmured softly to Erin. "One gathers vampire hearing is even more acute than that of the Sidhe."

Reece smiled in a cold stretch of the lips. "I'm a spy, Your Highness. I eavesdrop for a living."

The king's gaze hardened. "And evidently you do it well." To Erin he added, "As do others, I'm reminded. Walk with me. I find myself in need of privacy."

Erin felt her heart give a convulsive thump. He was going to ask her for her answer now. She managed a nod and rose to her feet.

At least she'd dressed for the occasion. Her own court gown was a brilliant red, embroidered with gold and glittering with gems, chosen to set off her blond hair and pale skin. She'd tinkered with the design for half an hour, trying to get it just right. Erin knew she would never be a match for any of the Sidhe in looks, but at least she could make the best of what she had.

The rest of the table rose with the king, Sidhe lords and ladies fixing them with polite attention. Llyr waved a royal hand at them. "Finish your meal. I wish to have a word with my lovely guest."

As he turned and strode from the table, Erin followed at his heels. Her mind spun in frantic circles like a dog chasing its tail. Should she do this?

An image flashed through her mind—the pain on Reece's face when she'd told him she planned to marry Llyr.

If she told Llyr yes, she would never again know the dizzying fire of the vampire's touch, the hot pleasure of running her hands over his strong body. She'd never again taste Reece's mouth or feel the erotic sting of his fangs. Or the heavy thrust of his cock.

Everything in her rebelled at the thought of giving all that up.

Yet if she said no to Llyr and stayed with Reece, they could still end up dying at the hands of the Round Table. To say nothing of Geirolf's.

And even if they met those challenges, what about the ones that would follow? If she loved Reece this much after three days, what would it be like after three centuries?

With a little spurt of shame, she remembered his taunt that her plan to marry Llyr had more to do with fear than a need to protect them both. Maybe he had a point. Was she playing a fool's game? Was she courting misery in agreeing to marry Llyr when they both loved someone else?

Then the Sidhe king turned to face her, breathtakingly handsome in his court garb. When he reached out both big hands, she placed her own in them.

What the hell was she going to do?

"What is your answer, Erin?"

She opened her mouth. And realized she had no idea what she was about to say.

But before she could speak, light flashed in the corner of her vision. Erin spun and stepped back, automatically reaching for the gun she no longer carried even as Llyr stepped in front of her.

A tiny glowing cloud appeared in midair a few feet away. As they watched, it dissolved, revealing Geirolf's deceptively human-looking face. He smirked at them from the projection. "Oh, dear. I hope I'm not interrupting anything."

"As a matter of fact," Llyr said as he created a spell shield around himself and Erin with a snap his wrist, "you are."

"Yes, I know." The demon's grin revealed a mouthful of razor-sharp teeth that would have put a Rottweiler's to shame. To Erin he added, "You have been a busy girl, haven't you?

Fucking your way into the Gift with a vampire, then worming a proposal out of the King of the Sidhe. Your work ethic is impressive even by my standards."

"What do you want, Geirolf?" Llyr growled.

"Actually, it's what *you* want. I've acquired something of yours, and I suspect you'll want it back."

The king lifted a brow, his expression silently communicating skepticism that Geirolf could possibly have gotten his hands on anything important. "Oh?" His tone was as bored as his face, yet as she stood next to him, Erin could feel his gathering tension.

"Yes, though Erin may be just as happy to have her gone." Geirolf's face dissolved into an image of Janieda, curled into a miserable ball inside a globe of yellow light. She straightened convulsively, an expression of desperate hope on her face, as though she could see them looking at her. Her lips shaped Llyr's name. "After all," Geirolf continued in that suggestively oily tone, "it could be awkward sharing the palace with the mistress."

"If you're about to propose I trade Erin and Champion for Janieda, I suggest you reconsider," Llyr drawled, though Erin felt him stiffen. "A queen for a consort seems a poor bargain."

"Only to a man far more shortsighted than any Sidhe king could ever be," Geirolf said, his image replacing Janieda's. "Consider, if you will, the question of who will be the power in the Mageverse with Avalon gone. You—and your brother. And with my help, soon only you."

"You propose an alliance?"

Geirolf inclined his head. "It could be advantageous to us both."

"Then again, perhaps not," Llyr said coolly. "My people have a saying: He who allies himself with a dragon may well find himself eaten."

The demon waved his hand in a dismissive gesture. "I have no interest in conquering your kingdom. My taste runs toward richer and less complicated pickings. Bluntly, mortal Earth would be far easier prey. Since you have no interest in those quarters, perhaps we can arrange a treaty: Mageverse Earth and its Sidhe for you, the mortals for me."

Llyr looked at him a long moment. "It could be an advantageous arrangement."

Erin threw him a shocked glance. The king prided himself on his ruthless pragmatism, but would he really sacrifice Reece and her if he thought it would benefit his people?

Oh, sweet Jesus, he just might.

Geirolf's gaze was fixed hungrily on her. "But before any treaty can be made, I must have the vampire and the witch. They are the key."

"I will think on it." He lifted his hand.

"Llyr!" Erin burst out.

"One hour," Geirolf said quickly. "You have that long to agree, or your lovely Sidhe consort will find herself the centerpiece of a ceremony she won't enjoy at all."

Then he winked out.

"You aren't seriously considering allying yourself with that monster?" she demanded furiously.

"Shh!" the king snapped, his hands describing a complicated pattern in the air.

Belatedly remembering her own powers, Erin quickly reached out with a spell. The next instant Reece stood beside her as she erected a magical shield around them both.

"What's going on?" he asked, tensing.

"Geirolf captured Janieda and has threatened to kill her unless the king turns us over to him," Erin replied tightly. "And he's offered to help him defeat his brother."

Reece looked at Llyr. "And you're considering this?"

The king shot them a cold look through the glowing barrier she'd created. "Now you're being insulting. Do I look fool enough to enter into any bargain with Geirolf? I'm only strengthening the palace wards against any attempts to eavesdrop."

Erin glowered at him suspiciously.

Llyr sighed and opened his arms. "Here. Read my intentions, then."

Cautiously she reached out to him through her shields. He let her no deeper than the surface of his thoughts, yet still she could clearly read that he wanted nothing to do with any offer of the demon's. With a sigh of relief she dropped her shields. "It's all right," she told Reece.

"As if I'd deal with any creature who'd kidnap and threaten Janieda," Llyr growled.

"Would someone please bring me up to speed," Reece demanded impatiently.

"Erin can explain it to you," Llyr told him. "I must put my guards on alert and find out how he got his hands on my consort." He swept from the room.

"Janieda's his consort?" Reece snorted. "No wonder she was so hostile."

"Hostile or not, she doesn't deserve Geirolf." Erin outlined the situation for him.

He swore. "Are you sure he isn't tempted? That deal would solve an awful lot of his problems."

"And leave me with one far worse," Llyr told them, stepping back into the room with a parade of Sidhe courtiers in tow. "As soon as he'd eliminated Avalon and my brother, he'd turn his sights on me. I have no desire to see my people enslaved by such a creature. Assuming he allowed me to even live that long."

"The nasty thing about Geirolf is, he probably would," Erin said. "He'd want to enjoy your suffering."

"But if you will not deal with him, what of Janieda?" asked one of the advisers, a delicate brunette woman in an elaborate iridescent court gown. She looked about forty, which given Sidhe aging rates would make her very old indeed. "You dare not let him sacrifice her. You do not know what spell he would work."

"I wouldn't do that in any case," Llyr said. "The question is, how to rescue her?"

"The obvious thing is to set a trap," Reece pointed out.

Erin nodded as she met the king's eyes grimly. "And we all know what the bait must be."

SIXTEEN

"Out of the question," Llyr snapped.

"If you appear to comply in turning us over," Erin pointed out, "you can stage a rescue."

The king shot her a dark look. "And risk getting you killed in the process? I think not."

"Be not so hasty," the brunette woman said. The surrounding advisers gave her a scandalized look at her contradiction of the king, but Llyr's expression was tolerant. "Perhaps we could put a spell on them which would kill this creature without placing them in danger."

Reece nodded slowly, interested. "Like a booby trap."

The woman shrugged. "Perhaps. I am not familiar with the term."

Llyr frowned. "Do you have a particular spell in mind, Grandmother?"

"Not at the moment," she admitted. "But perhaps if we had more knowledge of this creature and its weaknesses, I could think of one. I remember the battle we fought with Geirolf and his kind, of course, but that was sixteen hundred years ago." Her mouth drew into a grimace. "My memory is not what it once was."

"I suspect we'd find the answers we need in Merlin's Grimoire," Reece said. "Grim would know about Geirolf's people and where they came from. Hell, if they have any weaknesses, he can probably list them alphabetically."

Llyr lifted a brow. "But to gain access to this book of yours, you would need to return to Avalon."

Erin stiffened.

Reece shrugged. "I need to do that anyway. I still have to alert the High Council to the threat. Actually, I should have done that when I woke, but I was distracted." He threw her a dark look.

"But what if—?" She stopped. What if they turned on him? What if they killed him? The idea filled her with pure terror.

"I've got my duty, Erin," he told her.

The Sidhe king studied him, then nodded slowly. "So you do. Very well, then. I'll transport you."

"And me," Erin said firmly.

"Absolutely not," Reece said in a rough chorus with Llyr's flat "No."

She glowered at both of them stubbornly. "If you have to cast a spell on both of us, I'll need to be there."

Reece glowered back. "And what if the Majae's Court decides the simplest solution to the problem is to kill you?"

"Triggering Janieda's murder? I don't think so. Besides, if it comes down to that, I can make my own gate to Avalon."

Llyr bared his teeth. "Geirolf isn't the only one who can create a spell of containment, Erin."

"Enough!" his grandmother snapped. "The child has a point about being needed for the spell, and you know it. Take her with you."

The king turned a regal frown on the old Sidhe. She glowered back at him as Erin tensed. Finally he gave a bad-tempered grunt. "I suppose I can protect her, if it comes to that."

"It won't," Reece said coolly. "I can give her whatever protection she needs. But don't you think you need to divert Geirolf first? The deadline he gave you is almost up."

Erin frowned. "What *are* you going to tell him? He doesn't exactly strike me as trusting."

Llyr smiled, a chilling stretch of the lips. "The thing about dealing with a creature who specializes in betrayal is that he always expects to be betrayed. All you have to do is suggest you're betraying someone else, and he'll happily swallow the lie whole."

Erin looked at him for an admiring beat. "Oh, you're good."

Maybe a little too good, a wary voice whispered in the back of her mind.

Janieda lay at the bottom of her cage, her mind working frantically as she tried to come up with a way to escape the trap she'd sprung around herself. As she plotted, she held her drooping wings close around her body, trying to present the picture of a thoroughly beaten victim. Everyone always wanted to believe her less than she was. This time she was going to make their poor opinion work to her advantage.

Behind the fragile barrier of her wings, she listened closely as the demon spoke to his mortal henchman.

"The last of the acolytes have drunk from the potion," the human said. He had developed a faint lisp along with the new fangs that would have been amusing, if not for the hungry way he looked at Janieda. She found herself grateful for her cage. "They're ready to move whenever you give the word." He licked his bloodless lips. "In fact, they're eager for it."

Geirolf grinned. "Oh, I'll wager they are. But if they demonstrate a little patience, soon they'll bathe in Maja blood."

"But now that the Majae have freed the Grimoire . . ."

The demon made a dismissive gesture. "Don't trouble yourself. It's far too late to do them any good."

Beneath her wings, Janieda shivered. Horrific creatures. How was she to escape from this place without ending up a meal for one of them? She didn't even know where she was.

Suddenly she heard a familiar, beloved voice. "I have considered your offer . . ."

Llyr! Instinctively she opened her wings and leaped up.

". . . and I agree to your bargain," the king announced.

Janieda gaped at him in a combination of hope and fear—hope that she might escape after all, and fear for her lover and her people. *Oh, don't trust this creature,* she thought desperately.

Geirolf made a humming sound of anticipation that made her blood chill. "Then send them on, and I'll transport your consort to you."

"It's not that simple," Llyr said. "The Maja is surprisingly powerful. I doubt even I could send her anywhere she doesn't want to go. I'll have to strip her of her powers first."

Geirolf gave him a hungry smile. "Let me into your palace. I'll take care of her."

Llyr lifted a haughty brow. "I think not. No, there's a better way. She and the vampire have volunteered to set a trap for you. I have told her I'll cast a spell on her that will strip you of your power when you trigger it."

"But in reality she's the one who'll lose her powers," Geirolf said. "Clever." He laughed, the sound rolling over Janieda like a wave of maggots. "Very clever."

"Of course. I will, however, need time to work the spell."

The demon sighed. "These things are always time consuming. How long?"

"Let's say five hours or so."

Geirolf nodded crisply. "Done."

Oh, Llyr, Janieda thought in despair as her lover's image disappeared, *what are you doing?*

Erin and Reece looked up as Llyr stepped back into the room.

"Did he buy it?" she asked.

The king smiled darkly. "Of course." Rubbing his hands together briskly, he turned toward Reece. "Now. Where will we find this Grimoire of yours?"

"Wherever it's needed, actually," Reece said. "It literally has a will of its own."

"Very well. Think of the substance of it, and I'll use that as an anchor."

Reece had worked with enough Majae to understand how the process worked, so he obediently began building an image in his mind. For a moment he felt the touch of the Sidhe's thoughts.

The next instant they stood in the ruins of the cell as Grace, Lance, and Arthur gaped at them. Morgana, holding the Grimoire in both hands, glanced up in surprise.

"Reece!" Lance began. "Where the hell have you—?" He broke off, his gaze narrowing as he saw Erin standing by Reece's side.

"King Llyr." Arthur gave a small, civil half-bow, which the Sidhe returned. "I see you've found our prodigal."

"Indeed," Morgana drawled, looking at Erin in a way that made the hair raise on the back of Reece's neck. "Apparently more than one of them. I don't believe I know you, child. And I should."

Hoping to forestall any unpleasantness, Reece launched into introductions. No sooner had he gotten Erin's name out of his mouth than Grace interrupted. "This is the woman I saw in my vision, Grandmother," she said.

Llyr glowered at Reece. "Is there anyone who hasn't had a vision involving you?"

Erin frowned. "That's right, Janieda said something about some kind of vision, too, didn't she?"

"That's not a good sign," Arthur said, leaning against the wall as he studied them.

Correctly interpreting Erin's questioning look, Grace explained, "When a lot of seers start having independent visions about the same situation, we're in trouble."

"More so than usual, anyway," Reece put in.

Erin studied her. "So what exactly did you see in this vision, anyway?"

The blond grimaced. "You and Reece, naked and bound on some kind of altar. A big, demonic-looking horned creature was about to plunge a pair of knives into you."

Erin winced. "You're right—that's not good at all."

"Do you know who this creature is?" Morgana demanded.

"His name's Geirolf," Erin said, rubbing absently at a knot of tension gathering in the base of her neck. "He's some kind of demon or alien or something. You know all those Death Cults springing up in the U.S. over the past few months? His work."

Morgana nodded as she moved to put the massive Grimoire down on the table. "We suspected as much. We knew whoever it was has a great deal of power, but was definitely not Magekind or Sidhe. The creature from Grace's vision seemed a logical suspect."

Merlin's Grimoire spoke up in a sonorous rumble. "It sounded like Geirolf, based on her description. But for once, I would not have minded being wrong. Of all the Dark Kind, Geirolf was the worst." Muttering to itself, it added, "And if Merlin had listened to me and killed him sixteen hundred years ago, we wouldn't be in this situation now."

"I assume," Morgan said, her eyes narrowing as she looked at Reece, "this Geirolf has something to do with why you made this girl a Maja without the Council's permission."

Reece knew damn well he'd better make this good. "I was trying to avoid being used in Geirolf's death spell, the one Grace saw in her vision. He plans to sacrifice Erin and me as

part of some kind of ritual designed to wipe out the Magekind."
Quickly he explained.

When he finished, there was an appalled silence for several
minutes as everyone tried to digest the sequence of events.
"You should have come to us at once, Lord Reece," Morgana
growled at last.

Grace snorted. "Really, Grandma, are you that surprised he
didn't? The Council isn't exactly known for its tolerance of il-
legal transformations."

"Cases like this are why we wait to hear from the couple
before passing judgment," Arthur said. "Sometimes there are
good reasons for making a Maja without permission." He met
Reece's eyes. "This was one of them."

Reece relaxed fractionally. If Arthur gave them his stamp
of approval, no one else would quibble. Beside him, he could
feel the tension drain from Erin as she, too, realized they were
safe. "So what do we do now?"

"Now we get the information to work that spell," Llyr said,
then looked at the Grimoire. "What can you tell us about the
demon?"

"First, he's not a demon," the book said, projecting an image of a floating planet over its pages. The world's thick red
cloud cover appeared to seethe, putting Reece in mind of
Jupiter. "He and his kind are from another planet in the
Mageverse around a star hundreds of light-years away. They
are empathic parasites, feeding on violent emotion as well as
the very force of life itself."

"Which is why they like to kill people," Erin said.

"Preferably in the most violent manner possible," the Grimoire agreed. "They first arrived on mortal Earth thousands
of years ago, when humankind was ripe for the kind of tricks
the Dark Kind love to play." The planet faded away, replaced
by the image of an altar and what looked like an Egyptian
priest, his hands lifted in a gesture of prayer. "Some of
them were worshiped as gods, while others were feared as
demons. Love or terror—it didn't matter which—as long as

the humans felt something. That was enough to feed the Dark Kind."

"Until Merlin came along and stuck a stick in their spokes," Erin said.

"Oh, it wasn't Merlin alone," the Grimoire said. "No, not even he had that much power. Many Fae came with him to rid Earth of its dark gods. Given the infestation, they knew it would take them all."

"My people played a role as well," Llyr told them. "My own father died in that battle."

"And a good thing they did. It took Fae and Sidhe both to defeat Geirolf and the Dark Kind," Grim agreed.

"Normally we stayed out of human affairs, but my father told me this time we had to intervene," Llyr said, his expression brooding. "The Dark Kind would have eventually turned their attention to us. But it was only when Merlin and the Fae arrived that we were able to rid ourselves of them."

"Even so, it was not an easy fight," the Grimoire said. The image shifted, revealing ghostly, glowing figures locked in battle over the planet as lightning flashes danced around them. "Eventually, the allies drove the Dark Kind away from Earth and into the Mageverse. Only one managed to hang on, too powerful and stubborn to be banished: Geirolf. It was all Merlin could do to lock him in this cell."

"Why didn't he just kill him?" Erin asked. "It would have simplified things considerably."

"That's not how Merlin operated," Morgana said. "He didn't believe in killing." Judging from her tone of voice, she didn't agree with that particular stance any more than Erin did.

"I wonder how Geirolf got out?" Arthur said.

Grace shrugged. "He'd had sixteen hundred years to dig at the walls. It would have been surprising if he hadn't created a chink or two."

"Enough of one to reach into the dreams of a mortal serial killer, anyway," Erin said. "Once the killer had murdered a few sacrifices for him—"

"Necromancers." Morgana curled her lip in disgust. "Filthy creatures."

"The question is, what do we do about this particular filthy creature?" Llyr asked the Grimoire. "Do you know of a spell that would do the job?"

"Naturally," the book said. "But it's not without its dangers."

"When are these things *not* dangerous?" Morgana said dryly.

"Just so," the Grimoire agreed. "This spell, however, is going to need a great deal of power. And that's likely to be quite . . ."

A female voice gasped, a raw, deep sound of pain. At the same instant Lance gasped, "Grace?" Reece whirled to see his friend catch his wife as her knees buckled. "Grace, what is it?"

The Maja was staring at Erin, her eyes chillingly blank. "The price you'll pay to save us all will be high," she said in a dreamy voice.

"She's having a vision," Morgana said, then added to Grace, "What price, Grace?"

Grace stared at Erin without blinking. "Her sanity."

Dread clutched at Erin's heart. "Wait a minute. Is she saying I'll go insane if I do this?"

"No, forget it," Reece said. "We'll have to—"

"Silence!" Morgana snapped. To Grace she said, "Can the madness be averted?"

But the Maja slumped as if all the strength had run from her body. "Damn," she moaned as the dreamlike blankness was replaced by a grimace. "I hate that."

"What did you see?" Reece demanded.

Grace reeled to a chair and sat down in it. "Not a lot. Myself, King Llyr, and Morgana, pouring magic into Erin." She frowned. "I think Llyr and I were the donors, with Grandma working the spell. It was a hell of a lot of power, anyway. For a minute there, I felt what Erin was feeling." The Maja made a gesture with her hands, like something bowing under the strain. "I could feel her beginning to give. But somebody was there, strengthening her." She looked at Reece. "You. You're going to have to Truebond with her, Reece, or she's not going to have a prayer."

"Truebond?" Erin said. "What's a Truebond?"

Reece was frowning. "It's a kind of deep psychic link, a sharing of minds."

"It's marriage without the possibility of divorce, is what it is," Lance said, his expression doubtful. "How well do you two know each other?"

"Marriage?" Erin turned to stare at Reece in shock.

He gave her a sardonic smile that held a tinge of pain. "Hey, you were ready to marry the king a couple of hours ago. One marriage of convenience is as good as another."

"There's nothing 'convenient' about a Truebond, Reece," Arthur said. "Assuming you can forge the link, which you may not even be able to do."

"Arthur has a point," Lance said. "If you don't have a strong bond now, it's not going to work." And the skepticism on his face seemed to suggest he doubted they did.

Reece shrugged. "Grace's vision suggests otherwise."

Erin turned to the two Majae. "The question is, will the *spell* work? Will it allow us to kill Geirolf?"

"I didn't see that far," Grace said. "But it was a hell of a lot of power. As booby traps go, it would make a good one."

Arthur folded his arms and stared down at his feet, a deep frown on his face. "If you can only find out where he is and break his wards, the rest of us could attack in force. However much power he has, he's not a match for all of us."

"He's close," Llyr said. "He's very, very close. When I spoke to him, I could feel his power." He grimaced. "His followers have been gorging him with murders."

Erin looked at him. "If he's so powerful he's a match for both kingdoms, how are the three of us supposed to kill him?"

"It's not going to be a direct attack," Morgana explained. "You're right—if he's as strong as Llyr claims, that won't work. What you're going to do is reflect his own death spell back on him."

Erin scratched a spot between her brows. "I don't think I like the sound of this. If Grace and Llyr pump that much power into me, what's it going to do to them?"

"It will leave us vulnerable," Llyr told her. "That must have been what Janieda had her vision about. She said she saw me lying unconscious with my power drained away to Erin as Geirolf laughed."

"It'll do more than leave us vulnerable," Grace said. "If he manages to kill her while we're all linked, you and I will die as well."

"Now, wait just one bloody minute," Lance began. "If you seriously think I'm going to let you . . ."

His wife shot him a look. "If we don't do it, he could eventually get his hands on a Magekind couple, and we all die anyway. I'd rather go down fighting."

"But it doesn't have to be you!"

"Yes, it does," Morgana told him bluntly. "Remember the vision I had that convinced me you had to Gift Grace? I saw a man's face, laughing, and I felt a sense of . . . evil. It was all very vague, but I had the sense she was going to be absolutely vital in destroying a threat against Magekind."

"All right, dammit," Lance growled, frustrated. Reece knew exactly how he felt. "I just wish to hell somebody'd had a vision that she'd come through this thing all right."

Llyr gave him a small, regal bow of the head. "Thank you, Lord Lancelot," he said. "I will not forget this. Without your wife's help, Janieda has no chance at all." He aimed a cool, direct look at Erin and Reece. "What about you?"

"If she does," Reece said in a deep, low rumble, "Erin won't be your queen."

"I'm aware of that." His attention shifted to Erin with a trace of male regret. "And it is a pity. But I won't turn my back on Janieda."

Erin straightened her shoulders. Her mouth felt like cotton, and she felt that particular blend of excitement and terror she always felt before a mission. "Yeah. I'll get her back for you, Your Highness."

Llyr's face softened. "I do not doubt it." He lifted his hands. A glowing doorway appeared. "In the meantime, I must make preparations and tell my people our plans."

"Well," Morgana said, lifting a brow. "It seems we're going through with this after all." She turned to the Grimoire and leaned against the table. "So. The spell. I believe I know the rough outlines, but help with some of the finer points would be welcome."

The book's pages began to flip by themselves. "It's a complicated ritual with a large number of steps. It's going to take several hours to prepare. First we must—"

"In the meantime," Grace said, moving to Erin's side, "let's talk, shall we?" With a gesture, she opened a doorway in the middle of the cell.

Erin eyed it dubiously. "But don't we need to start work on the Truebond?" she asked as the other woman urged her toward it.

"That'll only take a few seconds—if you're ready for it," Grace said. "Right now I don't think you are. Maybe I can help with that." Correctly reading her glance back at Morgana and the Grimoire, she added, "Believe me, when she wants you, she can find you."

They stepped through the doorway. Again, Erin shuddered as she felt the race of magic over her skin.

Looking around, she found they stood in a wide central square surrounded by beautiful buildings in a jumble of architectural styles. It should have looked like a mishmash as gothic cathedrals stood next to Greek temples and French chateaus, but somehow the air of magic about it all seemed to unify everything.

As Erin gaped around at the soaring buildings, she was vaguely aware of Arthur and Lance urging Reece through Grace's gate after them. Reece threw her a quick look over his shoulder as the three walked away across the square.

"All this was a little easier for me," Grace said, guiding her toward a garden planted in the center of the square. "Becoming a Maja, I mean."

Erin had been straining to hear what the retreating vampires were saying. At the other woman's words, she looked at her. Grace appeared no older than her late twenties, but knowing the Magekind, she could be a thousand years told. "So how long have you—?"

Grace smiled slightly. "About six months."

Erin blinked as they walked down a paved path surrounded by huge white roses that seemed to shimmer in the moonlight, as though imbued with a magic of their own. "You're kidding. And you've got that much power?"

The Maja shrugged. "Genetics. Morgana is my grandmother."

"Yeah, that would do it."

"Which is one reason it was easier for me to accept all this. I grew up in Avalon. I knew court politics, I understood the complex relationship between the Magi and Majae." She shot Erin an understanding glance. "And I knew what a Truebond was, which made it much easier to enter into one with Lance. I get the distinct impression you're a little less comfortable with the idea."

Erin grimaced. "You're not wrong there."

"You want to talk?"

Oddly, she did, though she didn't even know this woman. "This Truebond. It will be permanent?"

Grace shrugged. "If it really is a Truebond. There are lesser bonds, which is why we call it a Truebond. It's very . . . profound."

Erin studied the other woman as they walked. She could hear a fountain tinkling nearby, the sound musical and soothing. "What's it like?"

"Most of the time you're just aware of your partner. A presence, even when he's not physically with you. You can reach out to him and feel his thoughts, though he can block you if he chooses. Lance usually doesn't shield from me." She seemed to gaze into the distance. "Right now Reece is telling them—" She stopped.

"What?" Erin finally asked, when she didn't speak for several minutes.

Grace shook her head. "Normally I wouldn't say this, but if you Truebond with him, you're going to find it out anyway. You hurt him, Erin. Badly." The look she turned on Erin was cool. "Making love to him, and then going off to accept Llyr's proposal. That was cold."

Erin felt a stab of shamed guilt. "Okay, maybe I shouldn't have done it, but I thought it was the best way to save us both." She shook her head. "Besides, he shook me. I'm not used to being vulnerable to a man. Plus he was doing this whole dominant male thing, and that just ticked me off."

Grace's expression warmed into wicked understanding. "Ohhhh, yeah. That's a universal personality trait among Magi. Seems to go with the whole vampire/predator thing."

"Yeah, well, I'm an FBI agent. Or was. I don't do submissive."

"Really? Cool. I was a Tayanita County sheriff's deputy. I'm not submissive, either, but it can be a really fun game to play in the bedroom." Her eyes glinted. "When I'm not being Mistress Grace."

Erin eyed her lusty smile. "Oh?"

"Oh, yeah. Sometimes we play speeder and bad, bad deputy. I just love pulling Lance over and frisking him."

Erin dissolved into giggles, picturing slim Grace handcuffing her big, brawny vampire. "Not to mention reading him his rights."

"Mmm. You haven't lived until you've seen that ass bent over a patrol car." Grace gave a mock shiver.

Erin snickered. "Too much information."

"Oh, come on! Tell me you wouldn't love busting Reece. God, those shoulders—" Grace stopped and laughed. "Yes,

Lance, I know you heard that!" She wrinkled her nose. "He gets so jealous."

Erin laughed even as she felt a twinge of envy. To have that kind of relationship . . .

With Reece.

"I'm scared, Grace," she said suddenly. "I'll be so damn vulnerable to him."

The laughter drained from the Maja's eyes, leaving warm understanding behind. "And that's a good sign."

"Why?"

Grace studied her a long moment before she spoke. "I strongly suspect you're the kind of person that focuses on the mission," she said at last. "If you didn't care about him, the Truebond wouldn't worry you. You'd be more focused on killing Geirolf and saving the rest of us. If you love him, it'll make the Truebond that much stronger."

Erin hesitated. "Okay, yeah, I love him. But . . . my track record's not that damn good."

"Oh?"

"I've been in love before." Remembered pain made her look away from the Maja's perceptive gaze. "Another agent. Geirolf killed him. Or rather, he killed himself rather than obey Geirolf's compulsion to kill me."

Grace winced. "That's rough. On a whole bunch of levels." The Maja studied her thoughtfully. Erin tried not to shift under her penetrating stare. "You scared history's going to repeat itself?"

"Yeah. Yeah, I am. And I'm not sure I'd survive it a second time." She grimaced. "Assuming I even get that option."

They rounded a bend in the path to find Reece waiting for them. His gaze locked on hers, hot and intent. "Let's go."

She hesitated only a moment, aware of Grace's sympathetic eyes.

Then she reached out and took his hand.

SEVENTEEN

As they walked away from Grace, Reece looked down into Erin's lovely face and felt his heart ache. There was a good chance that he'd lose her to death tonight. A good chance he'd end up dead himself. "I want to make love to you," he said in a low voice. "I want to touch you."

He was prepared to argue and desperate enough to lie if she'd refused him: *It's necessary for the Truebond.* But instead Erin said softly, "I'd like that." She hesitated. "Where should we go?"

Reece smiled slightly. "My place." He felt the brush of her thoughts as she picked up the picture from his thoughts, then the flash of light and cool air as she transported them.

They stood in his bedroom of his Avalon home. It was a simple place next to those of most Magi and Majae—hell, even next to the homes he owned back on Earth. Instead of hiring some Maja to create it, he'd built it himself with the techniques he'd learned as a boy. The walls were rough plaster, the floor polished heart of pine. A magical fire burned in the fireplace, and candles stood around the room, casting a golden glow over the simple wooden furniture: the oak armoire, the sturdy chest and chair, the canopied bed with its velvet hangings. He watched Erin look around in surprise.

"It's beautiful," she murmured. "Like being transported back in time."

"It's a replica of a house I owned when I first became a vampire. I come here to think, to get back to myself." He hesitated a moment. "I've never brought a woman here before."

Erin turned to look at him, her eyes mysterious in the candlelight. "I'm honored." She reached out to lay a palm on his chest. "Especially after the way I hurt you. You were right, Reece. My willingness to marry Llyr had more to do with cowardice than anything else."

"Cowardice?" He took her hand in his own, caressed the long, cool fingers. "You're the least cowardly woman I've ever known."

Candlelight slid over the shimmering silk of her hair as she shook her head. "No. Oh, I don't mind risking my life. I wouldn't be in my line of work if I did. But when it comes to the emotional stuff, that's different."

"The emotional stuff can be a lot more frightening."

"Especially when you haven't had much luck with it. I knew David, my partner, for two years before I admitted I was falling in love with him. And I might have put it off even longer if he hadn't been so damn safe." Sadness shadowed those lovely cobalt eyes. "He was even more skittish than I was, all tied up in rules and regulations. We could have danced around each other for years before we actually did anything about it." As if unable to hold his gaze, she looked toward the fire. "But we didn't have years. What does it say about him that he found it easier to sacrifice his life for me than take me to bed?"

That he was an idiot, Reece thought. He managed to keep his mouth shut.

"We both were." She turned to give him a small, sad little smile. "But then you came along. You had no interest in taking it slow and sweet. You just roared over me like a tidal wave, all fearlessness and sex. And so damn much more. Falling in love doesn't seem to worry you."

Reece hesitated, brushing his thumb over the silken skin on the back of her wrist. "The thing about being immortal is, you have the experience to realize how rare something special is when it comes along," he said at last. "You know if you don't grab it now, you may never have the chance to taste anything quite that sweet and strong again."

"On the other hand, imminent death also does a pretty good job of focusing the attention," Erin said dryly. "It was only when I thought everything was going to be all right that I got stupid again. I knew Llyr and I would have a nice, comfortable, bloodless relationship." She grimaced. "Almost professional. I know how to do that. I don't know how to do love."

Reece could feel his heart pounding, but he kept his smile easy. He didn't want to scare her off again. "It's not that hard to pick up."

Her blue eyes looked endlessly deep. "Certainly not where you're concerned." She rose on her toes and kissed him, her mouth moving over his hungrily, hot and wet and wickedly skilled. Reece's body instantly leaped in response. With a deep-throated groan, he pulled her against him and thrust his tongue deep, greedy for every bit of her she was willing to let him have.

By the time he pulled free, his heart was pounding. Breathing hard, Reece rested his forehead against hers, looking deep into her eyes. For an endless moment they stood like that, body to body, feeling the warmth and strength of each other, feeling the contrasts between them, male and female, hard and soft. Just listening to each other breathe.

In an hour, perhaps two, they'd plunge back into the war again. It was possible one or both of them would die. But for now they existed in a precious bubble of peace. And only a fool would fail to make the best of it.

Without a word, Reece bent and slid a hand behind her knees, scooping her easily into his arms. She looped hers around his neck, gazing into his eyes as he carried her to bed. As he laid her down on the thick quilt, she made their clothing fade away.

Naked, he eased down over her. Erin took his weight with a soft murmur of pleasure, spreading herself into a cradle for him. His cock lay hard along the length of her velvet belly as she rested her hands on his chest.

The green of his eyes, normally so catlike and fierce, looked soft in the candlelight. His lids came down as he lowered his head to kiss her again. His lips felt like sun-warmed silk as they moved across hers, his tongue easing into her mouth. She opened wider for him and slid her arms around the tight flesh of his waist.

He brushed his fingertips along the line of her jaw, stroking gently as he kissed her. She found the hollow of his spine and traced it with her nails until he laughed against her mouth in a deep purr of male pleasure, twisting his broad shoulders in mock protest. "Wench," he whispered.

"God, I love a ticklish vampire," she murmured back.

"Oh, now, you don't want to go there." He raked his fingertips across her ribs until she writhed and giggled. He nuzzled under her chin, nibbling gently at the line of her jaw as his hand found one full breast, cupped, squeezed. A thumb stroked over her peaked nipple. She caught her breath and sighed.

"Have I ever mentioned," Erin murmured, slipping her hand down to his muscular backside and tracing a teasing pattern, "how much I love your ass? It's just so . . . biteable."

"You're pretty biteable yourself." He gave the curve of her throat a promising lick.

She laughed softly. "I should have known better than to make a crack like that to a vampire."

"Never hesitate to flatter me, love." He kneaded the peak of her breast between thumb and forefinger until swee streamers of pleasure curled through her and settled between her thighs. "Though you do make my . . . head swell."

She rolled her hips against the thick erection pressing into her belly. "Your head isn't the only thing that's swelling."

He laughed softly, still teasing her nipple with slow, gentle pinches. "Darlin', where you're concerned, that's a perpetual state of being."

"My pleasure." She caught her breath.

"Like that?"

"Oh, yes."

"More?"

"More."

He moved down her body, stopping briefly to explore the curve of her collarbone with his tongue, then pressing tiny bites along the upper curves of her breast. She threaded her fingers through his hair and let her head fall back on the pillow.

Reece reached the aching peak and gave it a long, slow lick. Erin made a purring sound of approval. He looked up at her, his smile lusty and male. "Like I said. Biteable."

"No . . . *ah!* . . . teeth, Double Oh Fang."

"Oh, come on—just a little tooth." He caught her nipple in a gentle not-quite-bite.

She caught her breath. "Well, maybe a little."

Reece rumbled something approving and began to suck, his mouth moving in long pulls that did wonderful things to every nerve ending she had. Especially the ones between her legs.

Meanwhile, one of those clever hands went exploring down her body. Delving between her thighs, he slid inside. Erin bit her lip at the feeling of that big finger working its way deep. "God, you're"—she had to stop to swallow the saliva pooling in her mouth—"good at that."

His green eyes lifted to her face, and he lifted his head, giving her nipple a last contemplative lick. "Oh, darlin', I'm just getting started."

He pushed onto all fours and looked down her body. She

grabbed a handful of his hair. "Why don't you let me return the favor this time?"

Reece grinned, his teeth flashing white and wicked. "Well, that's an offer I'm not going to turn down."

"Good to hear it. Let me get on top." She scooted out of the way. He flung himself down on the mattress, watching hungrily as she started to straddle him. Their eyes met, and they both stopped to look at each other for a long, suspended moment.

Erin had never seen such love in a man's eyes. His gaze seemed to physically warm her, even as it created a wild, swooping sensation in the pit of her stomach. Impulsively she bent and kissed him, sinking back into the wet hot silk of his mouth. His fingers threaded through her hair and held her there as they licked and suckled one another.

She was panting when she pulled away. "I love you."

"I've lived almost three centuries, but I've never known a woman like you." Reece smoothed her hair back from her face, his hand shaking just slightly. "And I've never loved a woman like I love you."

Erin blinked at the sweet sting in her eyes. "Keep that up, and you'll make me say something stupid." She tried out a watery grin. "Maybe I'd better just suck your cock now."

His chest shook with silent laughter. "Well, nothing says 'I love you' quite like a blow job."

She shot him a look of mock disgust. "Sometimes you're such a *man*."

"God, I hope so. Now, turn around and let me have that ass."

"You romantic, you." Even as he chuckled, she obeyed, straddling his torso as she caught his thick cock and aimed it upward. Her first sampling lick won a purr of approval from him, as well as a wet velvet stroke of his tongue. She whimpered as he spread her cheeks so he could gain access to her sex. His clever tongue laved between her lips and made her gasp around his cock.

With a soft moan, she went to work, sucking and licking the broad plum head, stroking the thick length of his shaft with one hand as she caressed his furry balls with the other. He tasted of salt and masculinity and felt like hot silk sliding over her tongue.

It was wildly exciting, taking him like this. He filled her mouth thoroughly, rolling his hips in short little thrusts as if he couldn't quite help himself. Each tight lunge goaded her, made her want to take him even deeper. She doubted she'd ever experienced anything hotter than feeling Reece Champion skid out of control.

Adding to the pleasure, for every lick she gave him, he retaliated with one just as wet and lingering. Her orgasm gathered like a warm tsunami, deceptively lazy as it built.

Until he clamped his mouth fiercely over her clit. The climax slammed into her with a force that stole her breath and arched her spine. She groaned helplessly around his cock. He stiffened under her. For a moment, she thought he was going to come.

Then she was flat on her back so fast she hadn't even seen him move. Reece loomed over her, both her knees in his big hands. He met her gaze with glittering, hungry eyes and spread her wide.

Erin caught her breath as he aimed himself for her slick little slit. Slowly he pressed his way deep, forcing her clinging flesh to spread around his width. Even after she thought herself full of him, he came on and on in a slow, creamy impalement that made her shudder in animal delight. It was only when she felt his balls brush her ass that she knew she had all of him. "How's that?" he breathed in her ear.

"Oooh," she groaned. "Good. It's so good."

"Think I can make it better?" He began to ease out.

Erin bit her lip. "I'm not sure I'd survive better."

"Let's find out."

In. Stretching her wide, pulling deliciously across sensitive nerve endings. Out, in a long, erotic rake of flesh on wet flesh.

She twisted under him, wrapping her legs tight around his ass, pulling him close with her calves. His muscled butt worked between her thighs. Green eyes stared into hers, fierce with pleasure.

She licked her lips, staring up at his hungry, handsome face as he possessed her. Lowering his head, he kissed her slowly, sliding his tongue in and out in concert with his cock. He slid one arm under her shoulders and the other beneath her hip and picked up the pace, lengthening his strokes, jarring her clit deliciously.

The climax poured hot up from her core like a burning spring. She keened, throwing her head back on the pillow, arching into him. "Reeeeece!"

"Yes! Oh, God, Erin, I love you!" He began to pound her, driving hard. Her climax strengthened into long rolling waves.

Reece stiffened, roaring in pleasure as he came, driven to the balls.

Minutes passed before she could move again.

Dazed, shivering with the aftershocks of the erotic storm, Erin looked up at him. He panted, braced above her on trembling arms. Despite the shattering orgasm they'd just shared, there was hunger in his eyes.

He lowered his head. Knowing what he wanted, she tilted her chin and arched her throat. His lips felt like hot silk as they touched her skin. His fangs sank deep with that startling, feral pleasure that tore a strangled scream from her throat.

"Reach for me," the words came clearly through the ghost of the light mental bond they'd formed when she'd changed. Instinctively she obeyed.

He must have been holding back before. This time he opened himself, gave himself, surrendered to the thrust of her power the same way she'd just surrendered to the bite of his fangs. They flowed together.

And she could taste her own blood in her mouth, feel the

clamp of her sex around . . . something that had never been there before.

His cock.

She could feel his cock wrapped inside the slick fist of her cunt. She could feel how her body felt against his, so small and soft and female.

And she felt *him*. His mind. His spirit. The age and strength and vampire nature that was simultaneously so alien and so familiar. Fear rose in her, bringing with it an instinct to break the connection.

"*No*," he said in her mind. "*Stay with me. Be part of me. Let me be part of you.*"

It took an effort not to throw herself out of the link, but she fought down the instinct and instead wrapped herself around him. At the same time he drew her closer, letting her feel all the love she'd seen in his eyes.

Trust me, he said in a velvet mental demand. *I'd cut off my own arm before I'd ever hurt you.*

And he meant every word. He loved her, just as she loved him. They belonged together.

With a silent click the Truebond snapped home.

For a long time after that, they lay still, neither wanting to move as they listened to the double thump of their mutual heartbeat. Their new mental connection glittered psychically between them, a bond neither had any desire to break.

Finally Erin spoke. "This is amazing."

And odd. She could hear her own voice with Reece's ears. Because his hearing was so much more sensitive than hers, the sound carried a resonance it never had for her.

"Damn," he said dreamily, staring at the ceiling. "Look at the sparks. So that's what you see when you stare at nothing."

Erin knew he was referring to the Mageverse energies she'd slowly ceased to notice. She laughed. "Welcome to my acid trip."

"Do something."

He wanted to feel what it was like to work magic. She smiled and concentrated. An ostrich feather appeared in her hand, and she danced it across his ribs. And giggled at the sensation she felt through the link.

Reece grabbed her wrist. They both stopped dead, feeling her feel his grip. "Oh," Erin said, "this is going to take getting used to."

"Yeah." Reece's tone turned grim. "Too bad we don't have the time to do it." He'd heard footsteps out in the hall.

A moment later knuckles hit the closed door in a sharp rap. "Hey, Reece," Lance called. "You finished in there? Morgana and Grace said to tell you the spell's ready."

"Would it have killed them to give us a little more time?" Erin grumbled. With an impatient gesture she dressed them both in the jeans, T-shirts, and running shoes they'd worn before.

But when they went to open the door, they found Lance dressed in glowing plate armor that had been heavily engraved with runes of protection. A scabbarded long sword hung at his hip.

"Damn." She eyed him up and down. "Haven't you people ever heard of Smith & Wesson?"

Lance's grim expression lightened into a grim smile. "You don't kill something like Geirolf with a gun. And by now he's probably turned his human flunkies into something just as tough."

"Has somebody had another vision?"

Lance's smile flashed. "Arthur watched CNN. The top story is that the Death Cult compounds have all mysteriously emptied out. Thousands of people disappeared overnight."

"Which means—" Reece began grimly.

"—Geirolf has either killed them all or transformed them into a magical army. Morgana said he's sure as hell shielding something. Either way, it's not good."

"Should I—" Erin broke off. "Never mind. Human sacrifices don't wear armor, do they?"

"Judging from Grace's vision," Reece drawled, "we're not even going to get to wear clothes."

"Have I mentioned this sucks?"

He laughed and caught her hand. "Actually, I've noticed that myself."

"That's pretty well the universal conclusion." Lance wiggled two fingers in a come-along gesture. "And we're not making it any better standing around here. Come along, children."

As they followed his armored back down the hall, Erin asked, "I don't suppose anybody actually had a vision that this is going to work and we're all going to live happily ever after?"

He looked over his shoulder. " 'Fraid not."

She sighed. "Didn't think so."

To save Erin the power expenditure of creating a gate, they walked to the central square she'd seen when they arrived. But now the streets were full of grim-faced people dressed in the same intricate armor Lance wore. Moonlight glinted off gleaming silver and gem-encrusted weapons. It seemed every breath Erin took was choked with magic, and Reece's senses were swamped with the enchanted blood-scent of vampire, Majae, and Sidhe.

Yet big as the crowd was, it was almost eerily silent, with none of the rumble of conversation one would normally hear in a group of such size.

As nervous sweat began to snake down her spine, Erin reached out and grabbed Reece's hand. He squeezed her fingers comfortingly as they worked their way through the press of magical humanity. It was easier than it should have been; when people turned and saw them, they nodded respectfully and stepped aside.

"Damn," Reece said to Lance, "it looks as if all Magekind is here."

"They are," Lance told him, "along with most of the Cachamwri Sidhe. Arthur and Llyr decided we need every sword we can muster."

Erin licked her dry lips and tightened her sweating grip on Reece's hand. He smiled at her, his green eyes glittering brighter than the gems in Lance's sword. *"We'll be fine,"* he told her through the Truebond.

Seasoned warrior that he was, he'd fallen into the deep, deadly stillness he always felt before a battle. For Erin's part, she almost vibrated with the same blend of adrenalin and tension she remembered from the days she'd kicked down doors with the FBI. *"My stomach's knotted like macramé,"* she told him.

"Wait until the fight starts. You'll steady down then."

They stepped into the central square and instantly became the focus for thousands of eyes. The crowd stood in a great ring around them, leaving the center free.

Morgana stood there with Grace, Llyr, Arthur, and a blond woman Reece recognized as Guinevere, Arthur's Truebonded wife. Like everyone else, they wore armor. Erin focused on the massive jeweled sword at Arthur's hip, wondering if it was the legendary Excalibur.

"Yes," Reece murmured in her ear.

She threw him a glance. "I'm going to have to get used to the mind-reading thing." But come to think of it, it could come in handy in a fight . . .

He grinned. "It could, at that."

"Show off."

Arthur stepped to the center of the square and lifted his mailed hands. The crowd, already silent, instantly focused its attention on him. Erin could see why. He wasn't a tall man, but something about him, some aura of power and authority, instantly riveted the attention.

"Tonight the Magekind faces the greatest threat we've seen

in millennia," Arthur said, his deep voice rolling over the square, amplified by his wife's magic so that every person could hear him as clearly as if he stood next to them. "In this hour of peril we of the High Council are deeply grateful to King Llyr Aleyn Galatyn and the Cachamwri Sidhe for standing shoulder to shoulder with us."

Llyr inclined his head in a royal bow, one king to another. The face within his open visor was as stern and handsome as a Renaissance warrior angel.

"And we also owe our thanks to Reece, our American Champion, and Erin Grayson, newly Truebonded, who have agreed to serve as bait in our trap." The former High King extended a hand toward them. Reece bowed. Erin followed suit, stiff, uncomfortable, and miserably aware of her jeans and T-shirt in the face of this magnificently armored assembly.

"They will take a great risk for us today," Arthur continued, "putting themselves into the hands of the alien Geirolf with neither armor nor helm to protect them. The threat will be no less real for King Llyr and Grace du Lac, who will lend their strength to this spell, and who risk losing their lives should it fail." He lifted his beautiful voice until it rang. "We must be ready to take advantage of the opening their courage will give us. We must strike hard, without hesitation or mercy, to destroy this threat against us, against the Sidhe, against all Humankind. Or we will all surely fall."

Arthur paused, letting the seriousness of the situation sink home. Then he smiled. "Yet I have no doubt, my friends, that we will prove ourselves worthy of this challenge, as we have met so many others. For Avalon!" He pumped his mailed fist upward.

"For Avalon!" the crowd roared back.

"For Cachamwri!"

Erin added her bellow to Llyr's as the crowd howled the name.

"And for Earth!"

This time the mass shout was echoed by a thousand glitter-

ing explosions overhead as the Majae in the crowd detonated
magical bursts in the sky.

When the echoes finally faded, Morgana stepped to the top
point of the intricate triangular glyph inscribed in the stones
of the square. Llyr and Grace moved to the other points of the
triangle as she looked at Reece and Erin. "Come."

Erin's heart began to pound hard as Reece led her forward.
Her fingers gripped his so hard, her knuckles turned white.
His hand was cool and steady in hers as they stepped between
the three sorcerers into the center of the glyph.

The silence was so complete it seemed to ring. No one
coughed, no one scraped a foot on the pavement.

Then the three began to chant, Llyr's deep voice twining
with the lighter, higher ones of the two Majae. Erin braced her
shaking knees and faced Morgana as the witch's eyes went
black, magical explosions bursting in their depths.

Suddenly three shimmering curtains of energy appeared
around Erin and Reece, springing into being between the sorcerers along the lines of the glyph. As she watched, the energy
triangle began to shrink inward toward them, glowing brighter,
Mageverse forces writhing more violently with every millimeter it contracted.

Erin caught her breath, feeling the pressure growing
against her mind. Despite her battle to remain calm, pure terror rolled through her veins.

She tightened her grip on Reece's hand as the walls of
force grew closer. The instant before they touched her, she
shouted into the link, "Reece! I love you!"

"I love you, Erin!" he roared back.

With a crackle, the walls of force converged.

EIGHTEEN

It felt as if her skull was being crushed in a red-hot vise. Instinctively Erin threw her will against the mystical energy, trying to hold it at bay with the skills Llyr had taught her.

"You're fighting us, child!" Morgana cried. She heard the witch's voice only dimly through the roar of power. "Let it in!"

"Let go, Erin," Reece said in her mind. *"I've got you."*

Swearing silently she dropped her instinctive resistance. Simultaneously she saw Llyr and Grace fall to the ground, rendered unconscious as their power surged into her.

A bolt of energy seared into her side, and she screamed, her voice blending with Reece's bellow. Another snapped into her left eye as a third crackled along her skin.

Then there were too many to count, dancing electrical

crackles burning in waves across her body. The pressure grew inside her head, howling like some demonic blizzard.

"Reece!" she screamed, terrified.

"I'm here. Baby, I'm here." She felt his warm presence trying to absorb the pain. *"You're not alone."*

The crackling discharge ended as the spell vanished completely within her. Erin dropped to her knees like a marionette with cut strings, panting, sweating.

For a moment she was aware of thousands of faces watching her as the crowd stared in frozen, wide-eyed silence. A strong male hand caught her shoulder. She looked up to see Reece standing over her, his face pale. She tried, tremulously, to smile, opening her mouth to reassure him.

The fire leaped in her mind, roaring up like an atomic firestorm.

Erin bent double with a startled shriek of agony. Suddenly it felt as though the magic was ripping her body apart, running amok between her very cells.

In that first terrified instant she realized if she didn't get control, it would utterly destroy her. Instinctively she snapped upright, flung both arms at the sky, and let the magic pour. The sky detonated in brilliant colors over her head, not as simple fireworks, but with the deafening rolling booms of howitzer blasts. The ground shook under her knees. Screams rang out around her as the crowd dived for the ground. She wished fleetingly she could soothe their terror, but she had to wrestle the power under control first.

Blast after blast tore across the sky, comets of energy shooting from horizon to horizon. The explosions were deafening.

"Jesu!" The thought rang clearly in Morgana's mind, as easy for Erin to read as a newspaper headline. *"We've created a monster. She'll destroy us all!"*

And the witch wasn't the only one who was afraid. Erin could feel the same thought taking root in other minds, a wave of fear spreading through the crowd that could too easily turn it into a mob.

Maddened by the searing pain burning inside her, she snarled. *I did this for them, and now they dare turn on me!*

She could wipe them all out with a thought. All she had to do was redirect the energy she was aiming skyward, and . . .

"Erin." A voice cut through the searing heat, cool, deep, and soothing.

"Reece?"

"It's overwhelming you, love. You can't let it. Fight it. Control it. Let me help."

He's right, she realized suddenly. *I'm losing it. I've got to . . .*

But even as she fought for calm, she heard Morgana reaching out to Guinevere for the power to kill her, knowing it would take both elder Majae to do the job.

Bitch, Erin thought, furious.

"Morgana, no!" Over the babble of mental voices, over the rolling reverberations of magical explosions, Lancelot's voice rose in a desperate bellow. The knight crouched beside his unconscious wife, cradling her in his arms as he glared at the witch. "Killing Erin will kill Grace and Llyr—and we'll have no chance at all against Geirolf!" Erin wasn't surprised he'd sensed Morgana's intentions. He knew her well.

"If we don't act now," Morgana shouted back over the blasts, "Geirolf will be the least of our worries!"

"Remember Grace's vision—Reece will help her regain control. Give them a minute! Reece, dammit!"

"Listen to him," her lover said, his thoughts a soothing counterpoint to the burning madness in her mind. *"Let me help. You can't do it alone, Erin."*

But she'd always done it alone. Always.

"Not this time. Trust me."

The energy seemed to blaze just below the surface of her skin. Shaking, burning, she felt as if she were about to split open and spill fire everywhere.

Reece could help her.

She needed him. Needed that cool, immortal steadiness. Frantically she threw herself open and reached for him along the Truebond.

He came surging in like a bracing rain pouring over a forest fire. Erin gasped in relief as he wrapped her in his strength, in the power that came from centuries of life.

He knew exactly who he was, who she was. Looking into the mirror of his soul, she remembered herself, remembered the strength she had.

Overhead, the explosions stopped.

Erin opened eyes she didn't even remember closing. Her face felt hot, tracked by cold tears. She took a deep, shuddering breath and looked around.

Pale faces stared at her. It seemed everyone in the square was hugging the pavement for dear life.

Reece got stiffly to his feet. "It's all right," he called, though his voice cracked. "She's all right. We've got it."

"Jesus, man," Lance said, drawing his wife protectively close, "it took you long enough!"

The close call cost them another half hour as everyone recovered. Reece attached himself firmly to Erin's side, sensing the crowd's wary mood. He couldn't really blame them.

He knew he'd never forget the sight of his lover on her knees, her entire body blazing like a star, her hair streaming away from her face as if a violent wind poured from her head, blasting power into the sky. Reece had seen aboveground atomic tests that hadn't been that violent. It was a testament to her amazing control that she hadn't killed anyone.

Now Erin looked almost bloodless, she was so pale. Standing hunched, she refused to look at anyone, her shame so acute he could almost taste it in his own mouth.

It was only when Arthur approached them that she lifted her head. Reece could feel the effort it cost her to meet the former High King's gaze. "I'm sorry," she said. "It almost got away from me."

Arthur gave her a long, searching look. "Have you got control now?" When she nodded, he lifted a dark brow at Reece.

"She just needed to adjust," Reece said honestly. "That enchantment packed a hell of a lot of power. Anybody would have had trouble with it."

"But can you work the spell on Geirolf?" Morgana demanded as she stalked toward them. Her mouth was pulled into a tight line. Reece could almost smell the doubt in her. "If you can't, tell us now."

Erin met the witch's gaze head-on, tilting up her chin. Reece knew she was still angry over the Maja's narrowly diverted plan to kill her. "I can do it," she gritted.

"You'd better," Lancelot said, stopping beside them. The team of healers walked on toward the castle, the comatose Llyr and Grace floating between them. Reece knew Lance and several other Magekind and Sidhe would remain behind to protect the two during the coming battle.

"If you can't," the knight continued, his gaze cold with warning, "the woman I love is dead. And if that happens, you'd better pray Geirolf gets to you before I do."

"I'll protect her, Lance," Reece said. "You have my word on it. You'll get her back."

Lance nodded shortly and strode off after his wife.

"Now," Arthur said, turning to Guinevere, "I need to look like Llyr."

Erin was barely aware of the final preparations the others were making. All her concentration was focused on her own task.

For this to work, she had to appear powerless and defeated, despite the Mageverse energies roiling inside her. She had to tamp it all down, control it. Hide it. If Geirolf caught the slightest whiff of those forces, the trap would fail, and she, Reece, and all of Magekind would pay the price.

Erin was damned if that would happen. She had no intention of screwing this up, particularly after coming so close to blowing it all.

She'd been so sure she could handle it. She'd always prided herself on being the strong one, the one in control. The one who'd never hesitated to go through any door, no matter what waited on the other side.

Erin had even learned to deal with her own Mageverse energies easily enough, once Llyr had shown her the trick of it. That had made her arrogant, despite Grace's warning of the insanity she courted.

And look what had happened. If it hadn't been for Reece, she'd have destroyed them all.

Idiot.

"*You're not an idiot, Erin,*" he said in her mind. "*Anybody would have had trouble with that much power, even Morgana herself. Not that she'd admit it.*"

"*Yeah, well, if I'm not careful, Demon Boy will take one look and see me lit up like a Christmas tree, and then we're screwed.*" She hesitated, then blew out a deep breath. "*I need to hide it. Can you help me?*"

Erin could feel the warmth of his smile in her mind. "*Always.*"

The vampire was staring at Janieda from just beyond the walls of the energy cage, his eyes wide and fixed, pupils shrunk to pinpricks. His face had a yellow, waxy pallor, with deep shadows scored under eyes and hollow cheeks. His once-gleaming blond hair had gone lank and unkempt. Every few minutes he licked his fangs hungrily with a pointed, pale pink tongue.

If Parker had ever been human, he wasn't anymore.

Janieda watched him from behind her wings and tried not to move. Moving seemed to excite him.

What was worse, the room was full of monsters just like him. A restless mob of them, snarling and snapping at each other like wolves. She suspected they'd have been fighting among themselves if they hadn't been so afraid of Geirolf's ugly temper.

"Silence!" the demon roared from his throne a few feet away. He'd abandoned his human disguise in favor of the devil form he wore when he wanted to terrify. Janieda wondered what he really looked like, assuming he had any physical form at all. "The Sidhe king wishes to speak!"

Every vampire in the room fell into a reptilian stillness. Janieda bit back a moan. What was Llyr thinking of, to deal with these creatures?

A glowing orb appeared in the air, flared bright, and faded to reveal Llyr's familiar face. "I have them," he said. "I've stripped the witch of her powers. They're ready for you. Where's Janieda?"

"Llyr!" Janieda cried, then cringed as Parker bared his fangs at her with a warning hiss.

"I will transport her to you after I have them." Geirolf smiled, all terrifying teeth. "With all due respect, Your Majesty—I find I do not trust you."

"And I should trust you?"

"You have no choice," the demon said coolly. "I can always find another Magekind couple, but there's only one Janieda."

Llyr snarled. "Very well, damn you. I'll send them to you. But I expect you to keep your word!"

Janieda stared at his image, going still. That didn't sound like her lover. Oh, the voice and face were right, but there was something subtly off about him. Was he under some kind of spell? Uneasily she remembered her vision of him lying helpless while Geirolf laughed.

What was going on?

"Send them now, then, if you expect to see your lover again," the alien commanded, his voice sharp with contempt.

"And where, may I ask, am I supposed to send them?" the king demanded. "You've shielded so well, I have no idea where you are."

Janieda scarcely dared to breathe. Had they set a trap for the demon?

Geirolf did not seem worried about the possibility. He made a bored gesture. "There. Send them."

A gate opened before him as he lounged on his throne. Reece and the girl stumbled through it, shoved by rough hands. Both were bound in shimmering lines of magical force. Erin seemed shrunken, her power stripped away, her face pale as milk, her eyes rimmed white with terror. Janieda felt a twinge of pity.

The crowd of vampires surged closer with a rumbling mass growl of hunger. Even Parker forgot his fascination with Janieda in favor of larger prey.

The young Maja cringed back against her vampire lover, who bared his fangs at them like a wolf.

"Patience, children!" Geirolf purred, rising endlessly to his cloven hooves. "You'll get all the blood you want in a moment." He flashed gleaming saber teeth. "My spell will strip the Magekind of their powers and kill them so slowly you'll have plenty of time to feed."

The vampires arrested their half charge, grumbling.

Janieda had seen enough. She lifted her voice in a shout. "You have your sacrifices! Now return me to my Liege."

Geirolf threw her a dismissive look. "I think not. I've got another spell in mind for you, one that will come as a very ugly surprise to your lover." Bitterly unsurprised, Janieda watched as he gestured, replacing his throne with a broad stone altar big enough for two. "Now."

Light flared. When it faded, Reece and Erin were stretched out across the altar, naked, still bound in magic.

And there was a snaking dagger in each of Geirolf's clawed hands.

* * *

Erin lay still on the cold stone of the altar, concentrating every bit of acting skill she'd ever learned undercover on projecting an air of terrified defeat.

Inside, she burned.

Hiding the power of the death spell meant bottling it up, letting it sear her mind. Without Reece's strength of will reinforcing her own, she could never have held it. Even with him, she had to battle her instinct to send it boiling out.

But she didn't dare. Morgana had warned her she had to wait until Geirolf launched his own spell, or the effect would be blunted and he would survive.

"Just a little longer," Reece said in her mind, his mental voice warm and soothing. *"Hold on, baby."*

Somehow she managed to keep the pain off her face as the demon stepped to the head of the altar and smirked down at them. "And you thought you could beat me," he said with a nasty smirk. "All that effort, and you still ended up just where I intended. Helpless, naked, and shortly, dead."

"Fuck you!" Erin gritted, fighting the urge to smash the death spell right into that ugly face, too soon or not.

Reece, playing his part to the hilt, writhed in his magical bonds and cursed viciously.

The demon's's laughter reverberated between the temple's black stone walls. "Poor Erin! So much for your revenge." He tilted his horned head. "I wonder if your death will taste as delicious as sweet David's." Licking his black lips, he smiled. "Let's find out."

Geirolf lifted the knives in either hand, threw back his head, and began the chant, the words rolling in incomprehensible alien syllables. The magic began to dance over Erin's skin in tiny hot pricks, like the legs of burning spiders.

"Wait," Reece breathed in her mind.

Inside her, Morgana's death spell boiled hotter, reacting to the demon's ritual. She clamped down on it fiercely. The moment had to be just right.

"*Waaaiit*," Reece said.

The pressure built behind her eyes, throbbed in her skull. The magic of Geirolf's spell pricked harder, red-hot needles digging into her flesh.

"Auo rithc t'ch iaw g'evc ouir," the demon chanted, and the needles became gouging dagger points. The vampires moaned with excitement, sensing her pain.

"*Almost,*" her lover said.

"K'ari auo t'ch cari tova." Geirolf's voice was growing louder, his eyes bright with anticipation for the deaths he would cause.

A stillness slid over her, a deadly, waiting silence. The pain drained away. She saw David's eyes staring up at hers as he forced his service weapon beneath his chin.

"Ruret ai b'nar!" Geirolf roared, his massive shoulders flexing as he started to plunge both knives downward.

"*Now!*"

Erin sent the power blasting upward, snapping the bonds Morgana had created and driving the spell right toward the demon's crimson eyes. She felt the energy wave bite into his death spell and twist it back on its owner. Geirolf cried out, black lips peeling away from his teeth as he realized what was happening. He threw his will against hers, trying to wrest the spell away from her. She felt the death force writhing, trying to break free. She knew it would kill her if it did, taking Llyr, Grace, and even Reece with her.

Gathering everything she had, Erin rammed the spell home into the demon's skull. She felt his scream of agony in her soul.

He plunged his knives toward their hearts in one last attempt at the sacrifice that could save him. Erin had an instant to realize she was about to die. . . .

Reece's hands flashed upward, catching Geirolf's wrists and stopping the blades an inch above their chests. He jackknifed, smashing both bare feet through the demon's skull. As the alien fell, Reece somersaulted onto the floor, jerking the knives from Geirolf's lifeless hands. He landed in a combat crouch, a blade in either hand and a snarl on his face.

"No!" Parker roared. "Master!"

"Erin!" Reece shouted as the vampires surged toward the altar with a mass howl. Sweating, she flipped around on the altar and sent the last of her power toward the cathedral walls, blowing apart the wards that would have kept out the Magekind.

There was a thunderous double boom as the doors rammed open before the wave of Magi, Majae, and Sidhe that boiled through with howling battle cries. Geirolf's vampires wheeled and ran to meet them.

But the acolytes nearest the altar kept coming, maddened by Geirolf's death. "Kill the bitch!" roared the one in the lead, leaping on the stage and swinging his sword straight for Reece's head.

Reece ducked, stepped inside the vampire's guard, and drove the narrow blade of the knife through his opponent's faceplate with one hand. With the other he grabbed the dying vampire's great sword and spun away, planting himself in front of Erin as she lay dazed on the altar. His naked body gleamed with sweat and blood as he parried a savage blow to his head.

"I don't suppose"—he drove the left-hand dagger he still held between his attacker's ribs—"you could get me some armor?"

Erin focused on him and tried to work the spell. But despite the boom of magical explosions around her, she couldn't see any of the familiar glitter of Mageverse energy. She swore and strained, but Reece remained stubbornly naked. *"Jesus, Reece, it's gone!"*

"All right, don't worry about it." A swing of his sword sent somebody's head flying. *"Get up. We've got to get you out of here."*

Erin rolled off the altar, but her legs would no longer hold her weight. She fell to one knee and crouched there, panting as she tried to gather her strength. *Well,* she thought grimly, *at least losing my powers didn't kill me this time. Yet, anyway.* Glancing up, she saw Janieda zip by overhead, freed of her cage.

Scanning the cathedral, Erin saw a thousand battles raging as Geirolf's vampires battled Majae, Magi, and Sidhe. "How the hell are we going to get out of here?" she shouted at Reece. "The entire cast of *Lord of the Rings* is between us and the door!"

"You're not, you little bitch. You're going to die."

Erin looked around wildly to see Parker rise from Geirolf's body. She hadn't even seen him approach it.

The demon's corpse shimmered and disappeared into a glittering mist that poured into Parker's body. He seemed to grow as she stared at him in disbelief, his armor going black and massive, his eyes burning red in his white face. Even as magic-blind as she was, she could see the power boiling off him. "What'd you do, you cannibal—eat your master?"

He bared his fangs. "And you're next." He started for Reece, who was fending off the clumsy attacks of three sword-welding acolytes. "After I gut your boyfriend."

He drew back his sword, aiming right for her lover's broad back.

Erin realized Reece wouldn't be able to break free of his opponents in time to parry. "Reece!" she screamed.

Glowing armor shimmered into being around him the instant before the sword struck. The blade glanced off the gleaming metal with the ring of steel.

Parker cursed as Reece spun free of his opponents and lunged for him.

Startled, Erin looked around to see Janieda standing in front of the altar in full plate armor, a glowing sword held in a two-handed grip. She must have created Reece's armor. "Oh, God, Janieda! Thank you!"

"You carry the scent of Llyr's magic!" Janieda shouted over her shoulder as Reece's erstwhile vampire opponents charged her. "What did you do?"

"Morgana linked us in a spell."

The Sidhe swore and blocked a stroke at her head. "Then why are you on the ground, you fool? If you die, so does my Liege! Get up! I'll transport us out of here!" A spark began to glow in the air as she started to open a gate.

"No, you won't," Parker snarled, throwing them a furious look as he and Reece surged against one another like bulls. The spark winked out.

Janieda cursed and braced herself to defend Erin as the three vampires closed on them.

Breathing hard, Reece circled with Parker. Between the hell-spell that had made him a vampire and the life force he'd absorbed from his dying master, the bastard had turned into Superman. It was all Reece could do to block the rain of savage sword strokes the turncoat rained on him.

From the corner of his eye, Reece saw the Majae and Magi engaging Geirolf's vampire forces with ferocious swordwork and explosions of magic. Arthur battled in the middle of the pack, swinging Excalibur with single-minded savagery as he fought to get closer to the altar.

Unfortunately, their own magical armor helped protect the enemy from the full brunt of the Magekind attacks. Reece had hoped they'd break and run after Geirolf's death, but all they seemed to care about was getting the Majae down and feeding on them.

And then there was Erin.

He could feel her, weakened from the power blast that had killed Geirolf. Janieda was defending her, but how long could one little Sidhe hold off three vampires?

He had to take Parker down.

Gritting his teeth, Reece drove at his enemy with hacking right-handed sword attacks while sending his dagger flicking in search of an opening.

But what Parker didn't parry, his armor deflected. And his return attacks rattled Reece's teeth.

"After I hack off your head," Parker shouted over the screams of the dying, "I'm going to fuck your little girlfriend to death before I rip out her throat!"

"You're not going to do anything except die!" Reece dropped his sword to parry a wild blow toward his thighs.

But the enemy's sword wasn't there. *It's a feint!*

Too late. Something bit into his shoulder. Steel gave way, and a blade struck flesh.

Reece looked down to see Parker's sword in his shoulder. Instinctively he spun free, biting back his cry of pain.

Parker grinned at him and charged.

Janieda deflected a sword blow aimed for her ribs, fear and frustration a sick knot in her stomach. Behind her, the Human had made it to her feet, but she was so weak and drained, it was all she could do to back away.

I won't lose, the Sidhe chanted to herself. *If I lose, he dies. I won't lose. I won't. Lose.*

She deflected a double attack with one sweep of her sword and kicked one of her opponents back with a snarl. She was about to drive her blade into the other when a savage blow snaked from nowhere, hitting so hard it tore the helm from her head. She thrust out blindly with all her strength and felt her sword sink home, driving through the enchanted steel of a chestplate. A death scream rang in her ears.

Something jarred her side. Janieda parried another sword-stroke, but a sensation of spreading cold and weight made her look down.

A blade was buried to the hilt in her side.

Janieda blinked down at it stupidly. *How did that get there?*

A blur, a howl, and she hit the ground on her back. A helmeted head loomed over hers. Instinctively she swung a fist but the vampire didn't even seem to notice as he slapped up his visor and dived for her unprotected neck. She screamed.

The last thing she heard before fangs sank in her neck was Erin's furious shout. "Get the fuck away from me, you blood-sucking leech!"

I've lost, Janieda thought in dazed despair, catching her breath in a hiss of pain as she bucked in the vampire's vise-tight grip. *I've lost, and Llyr's going to die with the Human.*

Erin dragged herself backward as the third vampire stalked her. Smirking, he pulled off his helmet and threw it aside, baring yellowed fangs. His bloodshot eyes scanned her naked body, lingering on her breasts before fastening on her pulse. He pulled off his gauntlets and flexed his hands.

Panting, she backed away, knowing there was no way she could fight the son of a bitch off.

"*Erin!*" Reece's mental voice rang in her mind. "*I can lend you enough strength to fight him.*"

She jolted in terror, knowing that if he diverted anything at all to her, Parker would rip out his throat. And he was in pain. Had he been hit? "*No! Dammit, you need it to kill Parker!*"

"*Erin!*" A third voice rang in her mind.

Janieda.

Automatically Erin glanced toward the little Sidhe and stared in horror. Janieda writhed in the grip of the second vampire, who had her down and was feeding on her. "*Open to me,*" the dying Sidhe demanded. "*Let me save my Liege!*"

Beyond her, Reece was hacking savagely at Parker, ignoring his own wound as he tried to take him down before the vampire got his hands on Erin. Erin opened her mouth to tell the fairy yes.

Before the word was out, her vampire stalker struck.

It was like being hit by a train as three hundred pounds of armored monster hit her, smashing her to her back on the ground.

Superhuman fingers closed around her bare breast in an agonizing grip. The vampire loomed over her, jerking her head back with the other hand. Rolling her eyes, Erin managed to meet Janieda's gaze and drop the last of her mental shields. A link snapped into place between them.

"Save my king!" Janieda demanded, and poured her fading life force through it.

Erin convulsed as the power surged through her, hot and strengthening, jolting her own magical abilities back to life. Her vampire captor tightened his grip, trying to hold on to her as she convulsed.

Her gaze met his. She saw his eyes widen as he realized she was no longer helpless.

With a snarl, she shot a wave of energy directly into his eyes, searing him to ash. His empty armor rolled away as she surged to her feet, her own armor shimmering into being around her, a sword in her hands.

As she looked around at Reece, she saw him lift his great sword in both hands to hack down on Parker. Blood snaked from his armored shoulder.

The turncoat lifted his weapon for another parry.

With a thought Erin transformed Reece's sword into a massive battle-ax. The blade chopped right through Parker's lighter sword and buried itself into his chest, smashing the traitor to the floor.

"That's better," Erin said as the sword fell from Parker's lax hand. Spotting the vampire rising from Janieda's body, she whirled to hack off the thing's head. As the vampire fell, she stalked toward Reece and Parker.

Her lover grinned at her. "Nice," he said. "Very nice."

"Don't gloat . . . yet," Parker hissed from the floor.

Erin saw his eyes begin to glow through his visor. Instinctively she raised her sword, only to feel the power wave roll over the room before she could strike.

Voices cursed, metal clanged and rattled. Erin looked

around to see the Sidhe and Magekind staring at one another in bewilderment.

Their vampire opponents were gone.

A bubbling laugh drew Erin's attention down to Parker. "Good luck . . . finding them all," he choked out. "Wonder . . . how many they'll kill?"

Reece took the sword from Erin's hand and beheaded him with one blow.

NINETEEN

"*A bloody plague* of vampires," Arthur growled, pacing the High Council chamber. "God knows how long it's going to take us to find and kill them all. That bastard Parker shielded them somehow."

Llyr sat at the Round Table, watching the other man pace off his anger. He himself felt blasted, empty. It was so hard to believe that Janieda was dead.

Through some trick of the spell that had linked him to Erin, he'd woken with her last words ringing in his. *"Save my king!"*

She could have escaped, even if it had meant shrinking even further and flying out some chink in the wall. Instead she'd donned armor and gone to battle for him.

Why in the name of all the old gods had she loved him when he'd never done a damn thing but hurt her?

Except now, he was the one in pain.

"We discovered Geirolf had escaped long ago," Llyr said dully. "If I'd told you, perhaps all this could have been avoided. She'd still be—" He broke off, unwilling to expose such a naked wound to another monarch.

Arthur flung himself into a chair with a weary sigh. "Perhaps. But we'd been slighting you for years. I'm not sure I would have done any differently if I'd been in your boots." He braced an elbow on the tabletop and rested his head on his fist. "I told the Majae's Council you don't treat a monarch like that, but I'm afraid our women have an arrogant streak. I'm only Liege of the Maji's Council now, not High King. They listen only when it suits them."

A shaft of pain tore through Llyr. "I'd comment, but I'm afraid kings are not immune to stupid arrogance, either."

The Old Gods knew he hadn't been.

"No, but I think it's past time we get a little smarter." Arthur straightened, his gaze direct, honest, reminding Llyr why he'd always liked the Magus. "You were right. An alliance is in the best interest of both our peoples. You proved that today."

Odd. Here was the offer Llyr had waited centuries to hear, yet now he felt nothing.

But that didn't mean he had to be stupid about it. "I will agree to such an alliance if, and only if, it means not only that I'll help you in your vampire hunt, but that you'll help me bring my brother to heel."

Arthur inclined his head. "Of course. In retrospect, it was stupid of us to attempt to remain neutral in that fight anyway. Geirolf has taught me just how much damage a sorcerer can do when he chooses. And judging by what I've heard of Ansgar Galatyn, your brother could well give the demon a run for his money when it comes to sheer destruction."

Llyr rubbed a hand over his jaw, bitterly remembering the children and wives he'd lost to his brother's assassins. "That's an understatement."

"I will, of course, have to work out the details with my

High Council," Arthur told him, rising to his feet. "Though I strongly suspect this time, they won't give me much of a fight. After that, you and I can arrive at a strategy on the best way to pluck the thorns from our mutual flesh."

He extended his hand. Llyr looked at it a long moment, thinking bitterly of everything he'd lost in pursuit of that gesture.

"A handshake is an old custom among my people in sealing a gentleman's agreement," Arthur explained.

"I'm . . . familiar with the concept." He rose and took the other man's hand, careful to make his grip firm and sure. It wouldn't do to show weakness, even to an ally. He met Arthur's gaze. "Though you'll pardon me if I also want it in writing."

The other man barked out a laugh and clapped him on the shoulder. "Any liege worth his crown would. In the meantime, perhaps you'll join us for dinner."

"I believe I will." As the two men started for the door, Llyr said softly, "It's ironic, really. This was what I wanted all these years when I tried to persuade your Majae's Council to let me take a Maja to wife. And it's the one reason I never married Janieda." Compelled for reasons he didn't even understand, he met Arthur's dark, sympathetic gaze. "The last thing I said to her was that she wouldn't make a good queen." He squared his shoulders and willed away the sting in his eyes. "She was always proving me wrong."

Erin took a sip of her wine and listened as Reece and Lance argued over the best way to track down the escaped vampires. She tilted her head toward Grace, who was cutting into her steak with a tolerant expression. "Do they ever quit?"

Grace forked up a bite, chewed thoughtfully, swallowed, and said, "No."

Erin laughed. "I didn't think so." She bit into some strange Mageverse vegetable and looked around the sprawling banquet room. Tables were packed with Majae, Magi, and Sidhe all chatting companionably as they grabbed a little dinner before what would undoubtably be a grueling hunt. "Not that we can really afford to quit, with that lot out there doing God knows what to God knows whom."

Grace grimaced. "Please, I don't even want to think about it. I feel like I'm still a quart low, even after Morgana broke the link spell between the three of us."

"Me, too," Erin admitted. "By the way, thank you. If you and Llyr hadn't lent me your power . . ." She shook her head. "We'd have an even bigger problem than a bunch of psychotic vampires on the loose."

"Yeah, but you're the one that actually went face to face with Geirolf. Nice work, by the way."

Erin snorted. "Hardly. I damn near lost control of the power and got us all killed."

"But you didn't," Grace reminded her. "You got it back together and you handled it."

"Thanks to Reece." She looked around at him as he and Lance leaned back to argue. Concentrating, she felt the warmth of the link shimmering between them.

Sensing her touch, he turned to her and smiled.

"He's so damn strong," Erin said softly. "I never expected to feel like this about anyone."

"Yeah," Grace gave her husband a fond smile. "There's a lot of bullshit to living in the Court. But . . . some people make it worthwhile."

Feeling the need for some fresh air, Erin stepped out through towering double doors onto the castle balcony. She stopped dead in wordless admiration at the sight of Avalon spread out beneath her, all towering spires and elegant architecture glowing in the cool light of the Mageverse moon. An impossibly beautiful sky spread overhead, awash in shimmering nebula colors of pink and blue, more brilliant than she'd ever seen on Earth. Half-hypnotized, she stepped toward the railing.

She didn't hear the doors open behind her, but she sensed the psychic warmth of Reece's presence. "It's gorgeous," she said as he stepped up behind her.

"It's not the only thing," he said, and pressed a kiss on the shoulder her gown left bare.

Smiling, Erin leaned back against his strength and warmth. The fine linen of his black tuxedo felt gently rough against her spine as his big hands slipped around her waist. "We made it, babe," she said softly. "We beat him. I didn't think we would."

"I never doubted you for a minute," Reece told her, nuzzling her hair.

"Liar. You thought we were screwed."

"Like a Swiss Army knife into a champagne cork."

Erin laughed, suddenly feeling giddy. "I got him for you, David," she called to the sky.

"Now if only we can get all his little vampire friends." Reece caught the tender lobe of her ear between his fangs in a gentle nibble. "That's going to be a bitch. If dawn wasn't so close, we'd all be out there looking now."

"We'll get 'em," Erin said, as a reckless confidence filled her. "We can do anything. Man, I feel like I could fly." She grinned wickedly as a sudden thought struck her. "And come to think of it"—her feet floated free of the ground—"I can."

"Hey!" Reece caught her hips to keep her from rising further. "You're not going anywhere."

"Oh, come on, vampire!" She spun weightlessly in his arms and wrapped her long legs around his waist. "Haven't you ever wanted to fly?"

"Not without benefit of wings, rotors, and a good solid cockpit." Feeling his feet leave the ground, he grabbed for her. "Cut it out!"

"What are you, chicken?" she demanded as they rose slowly higher.

"Chicken?" He eyed the receding ground warily. "I just slew a demon, lady."

"That would sound a lot more convincing if you didn't have a death grip on my waist. Don't you trust me?"

"With my heart, my life, and my sacred honor. Dammit, don't drop me!"

"You're immortal, you big pansy. It wouldn't kill you."

"But it would hurt!" He tore his gaze from the Magekind's shrinking castle to gave her an evil glare. "And as for that last crack, just wait until I get you on the ground. We'll see who's a pansy."

Erin heaved a put-upon sigh. "Would you feel better if you had a visible means of support?"

Suddenly there was thick, knotted wool under his Gucci loafers. Reece looked down at it with a lifted brow. "An Aubusson flying carpet?"

"You're the one who likes brand names, Gucci Boy."

"That's Gucci *Man* to you, babe. And Aubusson is hardly a 'brand name.' "

"Well, if you don't like it . . ." She lifted her hands.

"Like it?" Reece toppled with her, landing in the center of the carpet to the sound of her startled yelp. He grinned evilly. "I plan to give you a serious case of rug burn."

His hot mouth cut off her delighted giggle. She tore her mouth free to tease him. "You sure you want to distract me when we're three hundred feet in the air?"

Reece lifted his head and gave her a wild look.

Erin laughed. "I'm kidding. This thing will go right on flying without any further effort on my part. Except maybe when I want us to land."

A slow grin spread over his face. "Well, in that case, it's time I work a little magic of my very own."

She moaned as Reece kissed her hungrily, his big body pressing hers into the thick, soft wool of the carpet. One big hand tangled in her hair, turning her head this way and that as he angled it to his satisfaction for each nibble and lick.

When he finally let her come up for air, she smiled at him dreamily. "You know the real reason I made the carpet?"

Reece nuzzled her chin, breathed. "Why?"

"To block the view from the ground when I do this." Their clothes melted away like mist.

"Mmm," he purred, drawing back to study her pale, naked body with hot male approval. "That's what I love about you, sweetheart. You're so efficient."

She smiled. "There's a long, long list of things I love about you." As Reece lowered his head to lick one of her hard nipples, she let her head loll on the carpet. "And that tongue is definitely near the top."

"This tongue?" He flicked it over the tight peak, sending sweet little jolts along her nervous system.

"That tongue."

Reece paused to suckle until she moaned. "So where on the list is it?"

She groaned as he bit delicately. She gasped, "Where's what?"

"My tongue. On the list."

"You expect me to *count*?"

"Too much for you?" He gave the other peak a thought-ful flick of his tongue, then settled in for a long, drawing suck.

"Definitely too much," Erin sighed. "More, please."

Reece lifted his head and scanned her slim, naked body possessively. "Maybe you need more data."

She wriggled on the carpet and hooked one bare heel over his butt. "Data?"

"To determine where my tongue is on your Favorite Reece Body Parts list." He licked delicately down the length of her sternum.

"Data. Oh, yeeaaaaah. I just love research. . . ."

He swirled his tongue around her belly button, then planted a string of tiny bites down her abdomen. Erin moaned, staring dizzily at the Mageverse sky sliding past overhead.

His big hands parted her knees, and his hair brushed the in side of her thighs. And that wonderful tongue danced over the lips of her sex before dipping between them.

The sensation had her arching with a drawn-out moan of pleasure.

"Figured it out yet?" He circled her clit.

"Need more samples." Erin cupped the back of his head, drawing him closer.

As his tongue swirled over her most sensitive flesh, one finger found her core and slipped inside. He rumbled in pleasure against her sex. "Like butter."

She moaned at the moon. "You have that effect on me."

"Well, that's encouraging news." He rotated his wrist, pumping his hand slowly as he licked and swirled and strummed between the slick folds. Erin draped her calves over his broad shoulders, floating on sweet waves of delight.

Her legs felt delightfully warm across his back as cool night air whispered along his spine. She tasted of salt and sex, richly intoxicating. Reece knew he'd never get enough of her.

The Truebond shimmered between them, throwing him a delicious echo of her pleasure as he played with her. The sensation of female anatomy he didn't have responding to his own tongue made his head spin. Happily seduced, he experimented, trying to find the perfect combination to send her right out of her brilliant mind.

Reaching up her torso, he found one full breast and palmed it. Another glittering alien sensation spun through his nervous system. He squeezed and rolled her nipple. *"I think I like this Truebond thing,"* he murmured in her mind.

"You do seem to be having a good time. Ooh! Oh, yeah. Right there."

Knowing exactly what she liked about "right there," he started doing more of it until her spine arched and his own cock pressed, rock hard, against the flying carpet.

Her orgasm rolled over them in long, delicious ripples that brought him shuddering to his own peak.

When it finally passed, he rested his cheek, dazed, against

the inside of her thigh. "Man. It's true what they say. Women just go on forever."

Erin lifted her head and gave him an impish grin. "My turn."

"Your turn? At *what*?"

"I want a blow job." She sat up and pounced on him.

"Well, far be it from me to argue," Reece said as she tumbled him onto his back. "Don't fall off the carpet."

"Big carpet," she ordered it. "Big, big carpet." It obediently expanded.

Erin took his sticky, softening cock in her hand and engulfed it in her mouth. Her first, hard suck had them both groaning.

Her long, cool fingers rolled and caressed his balls as her tongue danced. Now it was his turn to enjoy her experimentation as she drew back to nibble the tiny folds on the underside of his cock, just behind the head. She tongued his length as he hardened in a hot, sweet rush, then tried to take him as deep as possible down her throat.

Reece threaded his hands through the long gold silk of her hair and held on. Overhead, the Mageverse Milky Way snaked through the darkness, an iridescent ribbon of stars.

Finally he'd had as much of it as he could take. He tore himself free with a hot groan. "That's enough. I've got another hot, wet place in mind now."

"Mmm," she purred, and went to her hands and knees as he positioned himself behind her. "I do like the way you think."

"Good thing, too. You're stuck with me." He found her core, aimed himself. Slid endlessly inside. "Or stuck on me."

She laughed, the sound half groan. "Definitely. Ooooh, definitely."

Erin braced her palms on the carpet and her knees apart as Reece stroked inside her. The double pleasure braiding along the True-bond was damn near enough to make her come all by itself.

Dreamily she stared at the moon-washed forest sliding by

beneath the carpet. The trees looked like props from a toy train set, while the river snaking between them shimmered like a ribbon of light.

Reece drew out and pumped back in, long and lazy. She shivered at his thickness.

As he took his time in sweetly endless strokes, spinning them both gently toward another climax, Erin sighed. "I'm ridiculously in love with you."

"Mmm. It's mutual." Suddenly his arms wrapped around her, and he sat back, pulling her with him as he impaled her to the balls.

She gasped. In that position he felt about as big around as a baseball bat.

He leaned down to her ear. "Now who's a pansy?"

"Ah! Jesus, nobody I know!"

Reece laughed. "That's what I thought." As he ground up into her, he sank his fangs into her pulse.

Erin convulsed as her mind swamped with multiple layers of hot pleasure—the feel of his fangs, the heat of that thick, meaty cock banging into her, his fingers kneading and tugging both her nipples.

She felt as if she was about to explode.

Flinging out both arms, she let the magic fly. Great globes of red, green, and violet burst soundlessly around the carpet as Reece rolled his hips and fed. Each short thrust jolted them both another increment toward orgasm.

Until they exploded in a furious climax, writhing together as Mageverse energies popped around them like the Fourth of July.

By the time he drew his fangs from her throat, she was limp. Cuddling her, still seated deep, he murmured. "It's going to be a big wedding."

That woke her up. "Oh, is it?"

"Oh, yeah. We'll have to catch all those vampires first, which will be a pain in the ass. But a wedding will make a nice victory celebration once we do."

"You really think it's going to be that easy to catch them?"

"Probably not, but I don't want to spoil the mood."

"Good point. Got a guest list in mind?"

"Well, I've got a really big family, and they're all going to want to come." He toyed lazily with her nipples. "And then there's all the Champion business partners. And my FBI and CIA buddies. And that's not even mentioning the Magekind. . . ."

"Didn't we skip a step?" she demanded.

He chuckled, knowing exactly what she meant. "Which one?"

"The one where you go down on bended knee and *ask*, Double Oh Fang."

"I am on bended knee."

"And buried in my—!"

"Picky, picky, picky." He lifted her off his lap with that effortless vampire strength and turned her in his arms.

"That's better." She curled her legs around his waist and her arms around his neck and settled down again.

"Now, where was I? Oh, yeah." The moonlight blazed into his face as he looked down at her, his eyes green and glowing. "Will you marry me, Erin Grayson, and be my wife, and keep my heart, and have my children?"

She smiled up at him and let her love pour through the Truebond. "I will marry you, Reece Champion, and be your wife, and keep your heart. And have your children."

The kiss was long and hot and silken, illuminated by another dancing fusillade of magic. Neither of them bothered to look around.

They both knew there was plenty more where that came from.

Turn the page for a special preview of
Angela Knight's next novel

Master of the Moon

Coming soon from Berkley Sensation!

The Grand Palace of the Cachamwri Sidhe

He opened his eyes to see her standing over him in slim and glorious nudity, her body gleaming silver in the moonlight. As is the way in dreams, he didn't question who she was or what she was doing in his chamber. He only gazed at her and felt his need rise.

She was all lithe muscle, like a young cat, with small, sweet breasts, rose nipples flushed and swollen. But though his male libido automatically registered the curves of her body and the length of her strong legs, it was her eyes that drew him. They looked almost too big for her triangular face, with its broad cheekbones and pointed little chin. They were pale, those eyes, though he couldn't make out the color in the dim light. Pale and wild and shimmering under the darkness of her short-cropped black hair.

"I'm in need," she said in a low, whiskey voice that seemed to cup his sex. She had the most erotic mouth he'd ever seen: full, sweetly curved, naked of paint. "Will you make love to me?"

"Yes. Oh, yes." He watched hungrily as she slid onto his bed, oddly weightless in motion, as though she were far stronger than she should be. "We're going to be together," he told her, knowing this was more vision than dream. "We'll meet each other soon."

"Not soon enough," she said, her eyes going even paler until they glowed like molten silver. "I burn tonight."

"Come to my arms then," he said, reaching for her. "And I'll make you burn even brighter."

She slid against him, rubbing herself across the length of his body. Her skin felt so hot and smooth he gasped in pleasure. "You're beautiful," she murmured, tracing her long, slender fingers over the curve of his chest. "Are you real?"

"As real as you, my dream," he said, and cupped one sleek breast. She sighed and let her head fall back. He sat up and drew her astride him, groaning at the sensual delight of her silken backside settling over his thighs.

Then her gaze captured him again, silver with magic and feral femininity. Her lids lowered, veiling her eyes with long lashes as she bent to kiss him, her mouth wet and burning. He gasped and hardened in one long, hot, sweet rush. As she moaned against his lips, he set himself to pleasure her, swirling his tongue between her teeth. Her corner teeth felt oddly sharp, but he didn't care.

He caught the back of her head in one hand. Her hair felt as soft as a cat's fur against his fingers, and he stroked her, loving the sensation. Discovering the sensitive whorls of one delicate ear, he stopped to explore. Unlike his own, it wasn't pointed. "You're human," he murmured.

"Not really," she whispered, and pulled back to look at him with those burning silver eyes.

It was then that he knew. "Oh," he said, "that's going to be a problem."

King Llyr Aleyn Galatyn of the Cachamwri Sidhe sat up in his bed to find himself naked and alone, his cock hard as a broadsword. He looked around wildly, but his magical lover was gone, as if she'd never been there at all.

Which of course, she hadn't been.

He fell back against his silken pillows with a huff of frustration and eyed his rampant prick. It seemed to eye him back. "Yes, I know, I woke too soon," he told it, smiling in reluctant amusement.

Then, with a sigh, he took his cock in one royal hand and attended to the problem himself.

Diana London jerked awake, wet and aching. Automatically she glanced around, but the beautiful blond man was gone.

She rolled out of bed to stand in the moonlight, naked and sweating, her every nerve burning with erotic frustration. She remembered the way he'd looked sprawled across those dark silk sheets of his, his hair a fan of gold beneath his broad, muscular shoulders. His eyes had gleamed up at her like opals, filled with magical sparks of color. When they'd kissed, his wide, firm mouth had moved against hers with such delicious skill that she ached even more just thinking of it.

And his cock . . .

Better not think about his cock. Not when she was alone with no man in sight, and the Burning Moon blazing in her blood.

She'd never had a dream so intense, so real. So erotic. She had to do something or she'd explode.

Diana glanced speculatively at her nightstand where she kept the vibrator that had become her nightly companion since her Burning Moon began. Unfortunately, the dream had ignited a need that couldn't be soothed with cold plastic.

She needed to run.

Recklessly, Diana strode naked to the window and jerked
up the sash so hard the glass reverberated with an echoing,
booming rattle. A cooling breeze blew in, chilling the hot
sweat on her body as she stared out at the night.

The moon rode full over the shadowed trees behind her
house. A whippoorwill called, its voice high and mournful in
the darkness, sounding as lonely as she felt.

The wooden privacy fences on either side of the yard were
higher than a man's head. No one could see her.

Stepping back, she closed her eyes, concentrated, and
turned herself into a wolf.

Then she leaped out through the window and began to run,
trying to escape her own clawing need for the dream man's
touch.

The Verdaville City Council was locked in political mortal
combat over window treatments for City Hall. They'd been
debating the merits of dusky rose over navy blue for the past
forty-five minutes, and Diana wanted to bite somebody. She
was still feeling the combined effects of both the Burning
Moon and last night's dream, and her patience was not what it
should be.

I'm a professional city manager, Diana told herself sternly.
*I am polite and in control. Professional city managers do not
turn into wolves, leap over the council table, and bite the
Mayor on the ass. It's a bad career move.*

"Look at that frou-frou material," Mayor Bill Thompson
said, pointing a gnarled finger at a fabric swatch draped across
the table. Cabbage roses the size of Diana's hand bloomed
against a pattern of swirling leaves. His bony features drew
into a sneer. "What kind of message is that gonna send potential businesses looking to move to Verdaville?"

"A message of taste and refinement," snapped Carly Jeffries. She was a matronly woman with the round, warm face

of somebody's grandmother and the cold eyes of a Borgia pope. "Which is just what we need to bring new jobs to this town."

"Looks expensive," Roland Andrews said, giving the fabric a jowly grimace. "Seems to me we should just stick with the blinds. They've always been good enough before."

"Those dingy things?" Jeffries shot him a dismissive look. "We've lost three textile companies in five years. We've got to spruce things up if we want to attract businesses."

The other four members of the council either nodded wisely or looked cowed, depending on their respective personalities.

Diana resisted the impulse to sigh. The population of Verdaville barely topped five thousand, and its budget only edged up to two million when the fire department bought an aerial truck. That did not, however, prevent the city council from practicing old-style Southern politics: a thin layer of good-'ol-boy over a seething core of backstabbing ambition.

Jeffries and Thompson in particular had been political rivals for a quarter century, including years when one or the other had been voted off the council. Diana knew neither really cared one way or another about the window treatments. The argument was just another round in their running feud.

But as far as Diana was concerned, they could have picked a better time of year to squabble. *I can handle this,* she told herself, drumming her fingertips on the table in front of her. *I've done it before.*

Looking down, she realized her nails had just grown beyond the limits of her champagne polish. She fisted her hand. *I am calm,* she chanted desperately in her head. *I am professional.*

Diana had been city manager for Verdaville for the past three years, having managed an even smaller town for two years prior to that. She'd dealt with the Burning Moon all five years without giving herself away, and she could do it again.

As the argument droned on, she jotted down notes and

fought to concentrate. Despite her best efforts, her thoughts began to wander.

The man's powerful torso gleamed gently in the moonlight, muscle flexing in long ripples. A big hand swept a curtain of silken gold hair back from an arrogantly handsome face. Opalescent eyes gleamed as he watched her come to him. "We're going to be together," he told her. "We'll meet each other soon."

Just remembering the deep male purr of his voice made Diana's nipples draw into peaks under her silk blouse. It was a good thing she was wearing a linen jacket. When she crossed her legs in the matching charcoal slacks, she could smell her own heat.

Glancing around the room, she saw a man in the audience staring at her, his eyes hot and glazed. Diana swore silently. Men weren't consciously aware of her scent, but they still reacted to the pheromones her body produced during the Burning Moon.

"What do you think, Diana?" the Mayor asked.

Her eyes flicked back to the council table to see all seven of them staring at her. Smoothly, she said, "That decision is up to the council. I'll do whatever you direct." After a delicate hesitation, she suggested, "Perhaps this is a good time to bring the question to a vote."

An hour later, the last council member was gone and it was fully dark. Diana stepped outside and locked the front doors of City Hall. Looking up, she scanned the red brick front of the narrow building, automatically making sure none of the flood lights had burned out. Doric columns rose to either side of the double doors, looking a little silly on a structure roughly the width of a double-wide mobile home. Once upon a time the building had been the main office for a textile plant; Dian suspected its resemblance to a Southern plantation had been intended as a subliminal message from company management

"Hey, Diana!"

She turned to see a Verdaville police car pulling up to the curb behind her. She waved. "Hey, Jer! What can I do for you?"

The officer hooked one arm out his open window. "Chief needs you at a crime scene. Want to follow me?" Jerry Morgan was a short, stocky ex-Marine whose usual expression was a sly grin. Tonight he looked pale and tense in the back spill from the floodlights.

Diana frowned. Jerry was a Desert Storm vet; he liked to say his tour of the Highway of Death had left him with a cast iron stomach. Anything bad enough to make him blanch had to be pretty damn bad. "I'll get my car," she told him, and strode to the spot where she'd parked her ten-year-old Honda.

The trip did not take long—no drive within the Verdaville city limits did. Two minutes after leaving City Hall, they pulled into one of the mill villages that formed the core of the town.

The little clusters of homes had been built by the town's textile plants as employee housing. Most of the four-room houses dated from the 1920s, when employees rented from the mills, picked up their mail in the mill office, and shopped in the company store. That lifestyle had slowly disappeared as Verdaville had grown. Even so, the town had been left with a gaping economic wound when the plants closed, one that still hadn't healed three years later.

Plant closures or not, though, the villages were tight-knit little communities where everybody knew everybody. Diana wasn't surprised to see the crowd gathered outside the yellow tape strung around one particular bungalow. Anywhere else, this kind of group would have worn avid expressions of morbid curiosity. Here, they visibly grieved for somebody they'd probably known all their lives.

She knew there would be relatives in the crowd, too, notified by neighbors the minute the cops pulled up. All of them ready to pounce on the first authority figure to show his or her face. Sighing in resignation, Diana reached into her glove compartment for her badge and gun.

After she and Chief Gist had reached their understanding, she'd obtained a commission as a reserve officer, training for six weeks in everything from how to shoot a gun to issuing traffic tickets. Such volunteer cops were invaluable to small town departments that couldn't afford much manpower, and Verdaville's ten-man police force was no exception.

Of course, Diana's commission put her and the chief in a somewhat murky relationship, since she was nominally his boss except when she was wearing a badge. But their relationship was so spectacularly weird anyway that the issue of who gave whom orders rarely came up.

The point was, the badge gave Diana a legal right to come onto crime scenes. Without it, any defense attorney worth his salt would have asked uncomfortable questions about her presence.

Besides, her reserve commission also gave her an excuse to drive around Verdaville late at night, keeping an eye on her town. There was nothing like terrifying a would-be convenience store robber to help a girl sleep.

This, however, wasn't going to be anywhere near that much fun.

Knowing what was coming, Diana felt her gut tie itself into a knot as she got out of the car. She barely managed to clip her badge onto her belt and slip on her shoulder holster before somebody in the crowd called her name.

Oh, well. She really hadn't thought she could get through this mob without being recognized anyway. She made the front page of the local weekly too often.

The entire bunch surged as one in her direction, voices lifted in anger, fear or distress. "Miss London, do they know . . ."

"Have they caught . . ."

"*. . . need to see my brother!*" That last was a howl from a sobbing young woman whose face was swollen with tears. She tore herself from the restraining hands of a young man and lunged to grab Diana's wrist. "You've gotta tell me what happened! Is he dead? They said he's dead. Please, please tell me what's going on!"

Diana froze, battling half a dozen conflicting instincts. She'd never liked being grabbed, but this was a particularly bad time of year for a stranger to lay hands on her. Especially a woman. It took her a moment to squelch her more lethal impulses enough for speech. "I probably know less than you do right now. If you'll let me by, I'll send the chief out to talk to you." Her voice emerged at a rumbling register that didn't sound quite human. *Oh, hell.*

The woman jerked away from her as if scalded. Fear blazed up on a score of faces as the entire crowd shrank back. "You . . . you do that," she managed finally, obviously trying to convince herself she'd imagined whatever she'd seen in the city manager's face.

"I'll send the chief out in a minute." Diana nodded shortly, put her head down to hide her burning eyes, and strode toward the front door of the house. The crowd melted from her path. Humankind might be at the top of the food chain now, but they still knew a predator when they saw one.

Whether they could admit it or not.

Dammit, Diana thought. *I've got to watch that.* In old movies, pulling crap like that was what got the torch-wielding mob after the monster.

"Sorry I wasn't here sooner," Jerry panted from behind her. "Had to park up the street. By the time I got back, they were all over you." She looked around to see him wearing an apologetic smile. He'd evidently missed her near-transformation. "Maybe you should start keeping your uniform at City Hall so you can change. Public's not as obnoxious when you're in blues."

She grinned, remembering some of her own more recent adventures. "Unless they're drunk. Then they're worse."

He grinned back. "There is that."

Jerry led the way up the irregular cement steps and pushed

open the screen door. As Diana crossed the narrow front porch behind him, she automatically sized up her surroundings. The vinyl siding was relatively new, though she'd bet the house itself was pushing ninety. The shutters and wooden door were the same dark shade as the steps, though in the dark, it was hard to tell the color. Even so, she could make out the wooden swing hanging at one end of the porch. A couple of lawn chairs stood across from it, looking out over a postage-stamp yard that had been recently cut. There was no trash or beer bottles in the yard. The owner might not have much money, but he'd cared about appearances.

Poor bastard.

Jerry paused in the act of reaching for the door to meet her eyes. At five-eleven, she was actually an inch taller than he was, a fact that had never stopped him from trying to protect her like the Southern gentleman he was. Diana would never dream of telling him just how little she needed his protection. "It's pretty bad," he warned her.

"I figured that out. Please tell me it's not a kid."

His white smile flashed in the dim light. "Grown man."

"Good." She grimaced. "I hate it when it's kids."

"Everybody hates it when it's kids. But I gotta tell you, what the killer did—well, it's sickening."

He opened the door. Death spilled out with the ripe stench of blood and human waste. Even in human form, Diana's sense of smell was so acute, she had to swallow hard. "What'd they do, gut him?"

"Pretty close." Jerry lifted a brow at her as he led the way inside. "You could tell that from the smell?"

"I've got a good nose."

"That ain't exactly a blessing in here." He jerked a thumb at a closed door to the right. "Chief's in the bedroom. Unless you need me, I'll be in the kitchen."

"No, that's fine."

Jerry gave her an absent wave and headed across the little den for the even smaller kitchen, where male voices rumbled in conversation. The sheriff's office must have sent men to help out, since the Verdaville PD couldn't muster enough men for a crowd on its own.

Somebody laughed, but the sound held the strained note of a man trying very hard not to think about whatever he'd just seen.

Oh, yeah. This was going to be bad.

ABOUT THE AUTHOR

As a reporter in South Carolina, **Angela Knight** covered murders, car crashes, fatal fires, and school board meetings (which often had more in common with the first three than you might expect). She once spent one sunny winter morning watching her husband, a police sergeant, look for pipe bombs. It's an experience she devoutly hopes never to repeat.

She finally left all that to write romances in which there are murders, car crashes, and fatal fires, but very few school board meetings. That's just as well. There's only so much reality a girl can take.

Jane's Warlord

by Angela Knight

The sexy debut novel from
the author of
Master of the Knight

The next target of a time travelling killer,
crime reporter Jane Colby finds herself in the
hands of a warlord from the future sent to
protect her—and in his hands is just where
she wants to be.

"CHILLS, THRILLS...[A] SEXY TALE."

—EMMA HOLLY

0-425-19684-4

**Available wherever books are sold or at
www.penguin.com**

BERKLEY SENSATION
COMING IN NOVEMBER 2004

Miss Fortune
by Julia London

The third book in the Lear sisters trilogy, in which the last of the sisters must get her head out of the clouds and her feet on the ground to find love in order to fulfill her father's last dying wish.

0-425-19917-7

The Demon's Daughter
by Emma Holly

Inspector Adrian Philips' job is to keep the peace between humans and demons, and he's hated by both sides. But when he meets Roxanne, a fellow outcast, he will risk everything for a dangerous love.

0-425-19918-5

Arouse Suspicion
by Maureen McKade

Ex-cop Danni Hawkins must come to terms with her father's murder and, along with the help of an ex-Army Ranger, she must track the path to a brutal murderer.

0-425-19919-3

The Prince
by Elizabeth Minogue

Prince Florian wants only to reclaim his throne. But when he is forced to help Rose of Valinor, he finds the last thing he ever expected—love.

0-425-19920-7